# SKELMERSDALE

## FICTION RESERVE STOCK
LL.60

| AUTHOR | CLASS |
|--------|-------|
| AYRES, D. | F G |

| TITLE | Other girls | 11 |
|-------|-------------|-----|

D0280999

## Praise for Diane Ayres and
## *OTHER GIRLS*

"I was struck time and time again by Ayres' intelligent humor, witty
dialogue and the puns that sparkle throughout the book."
—*The Lambda Book Report*

"The book—at turns wry, dark and racy—deals with many levels of
the intimate relationships women have with each other."
—*Philadelphia Weekly*

"This debut novel is a frothy good time, packed with sex, seduction,
betrayal, revenge and a healthy addiction to midnight poker. We've
heard this girls' school high jinks tale before, but it's rarely been
this much good plain fun."
—*Out*

"The skill with which Ayres captures campus life of the 70s will keep
you reading."
—*The Patroit-News*

"Interesting and believable."
—*The Philadelphia Inquirer*

"A romantic, erotic, hilarious, and at times, heartbreaking story
about love among women. *Other Girls* is a dazzling debut."
—*Philadelphia Gay News*

"In this day and age where nothing is as predictable as it used to be,
*Other Girls* mixes all of the requisite ingredients and takes a not-so-
predictable path to the finish."
—*Woman's Monthly*

"A serious coming of age story."
—*Philadelphia Daily News*

"An impressive debut. Take this one to the beach."
—*New York Jewish Week*

# OTHER GIRLS

# DIANE AYRES

KENSINGTON BOOKS
http://www.kensingtonbooks.com

KENSINGTON BOOKS are published by

Kensington Publishing Corp.
850 Third Avenue
New York, NY 10022

Copyright © 2002 by Diane Ayres

All Kensington titles, imprints and distributed lines are available at special quantity discounts for bulk purchases for sales promotion, premiums, fund-raising, educational or institutional use.

Special book excerpts or customized printings can also be created to fit specific needs. For details, write or phone the office of the Kensington Special Sales Manager: Kensington Publishing Corp., 850 Third Avenue, New York, NY 10022, Attn. Special Sales Department. Phone: 1-800-221-2647.

Kensington and the K logo Reg. U.S. Pat. & TM Off.

ISBN 0-7582-0112-5

First Hardcover Printing: May 2002
First Trade Paperback Printing: December 2003
10  9  8  7  6  5  4  3  2  1

Printed in the United States of America

To My True Heart, Stephen Fried

# PROLOGUE
## The Dingus

The handbook that was presented to each incoming freshwoman came right out with it: WILLARD COLLEGE FOR WOMEN—it said—WHERE A WOMAN CHOOSES HER OWN DESTINATION . . .

The ellipsis was included, presumably, to imply that anything could happen.

The handbook was embossed in post-psychedelic typeface, bold condensed, on glossy bond paper in the school colors: white and off-white.

"Yes, well," as one professor put it with the same big sigh every September, "Welcome to WCW."

Six hundred women between the ages of seventeen and twenty-three would assemble during the coming week at this, one of the oldest, fully accredited, four year liberal arts colleges for women in the nation. The school was situated in the residential bosom (or cleavage rather, considering the rolling topography), of a neighborhood called Upper Alban Hill, in what was surely America's Most Romantic City: Weston, Pennsylvania.

The class of '78 and parents were milling around the parlors of Willard House, their stately student union for the traditional Bloody Mary Brunch, where they met those members of the faculty most inclined to tout the school when cocktails were provided. For this assurance of Good Will and True Wit in the WCW spirit, the public relations office counted invariably on the English Department.

Dr. Beatrice Ellis Brock, herself an "alum," class of '65, was especially good with the "frosh" and their parents when she was "schnockered," as she said, which seemed more like a word in

Middle English to describe some movement of her spindly knees. Dr. Brock charmed easily on the school's behalf, having perfected the old "pleased to be a dingbat teacher, yes indeedy," routine, confounding everybody with words. Archaic and spurious words. Her digits fluttered through the tissue sheets of the O.E.D. even when it wasn't really there.

"Let's see, ah . . ." scattering the ash of her queen-sized cigarette, "I'm thinking of a device. What is it?—Ah yes!" Brightening. "A dingus."

Those moms and dads and daughters she was holding captivated at the Bloody Mary Brunch all shifted nervously or tittered, "Oh dear," assuming that Dr. Brock was talking about a dildo—a device too often associated with exclusively female institutions by men with limited imaginations.

But "No, actually," Dr. Brock explained, "I meant 'dingus' not in the sense of some 'unmentionable thing,' but in the sense of a 'contrivance.' Literally."

The ice cubes in her third Bloody Mary chuckled maniacally. She stood in some etymological reverie that no one dared to disturb. She was talking about the necessary artifice of small colleges. But few of her listeners grasped that, and least of all owned up to what they could not grasp, being more determined to maintain some upper middle class pretense than to seek comprehension. Essentially then, this was a little test. Their first quiz.

Dr. Brock's ability to bowl over their parents by saying things like dingus right in their faces and getting away with it made her instantly popular with the students. Although they soon found out that being in the apostolate of Dr. Brock had a price. At the tutorial boards of her "favorites," for instance, Dr. Brock had a tradition of serving her own homemade mead. "Lemon juice," she would explain to her tutees, smacking deliciously, "over eggshells sitting in the cellar for weeks," as if they didn't have enough trouble trying to get the stuff down, hoping to God she wouldn't force-feed them her favorite recipe for blood pudding.

"Please excuse me," said Dr. Brock, suddenly bowing out of the group whose minds she had been boggling. Her distraction coincided with the entrance of a fellow with a neatly grizzled beard who looked exactly his age, which was forty. Dr. Geoffrey Maddocks, Chair of the English Department.

"Yoo-hoo! Geoffrey!"

Dr. Maddocks spewed smoke as he groaned and pivoted. Dr.

Brock reminded him of a schnauzer in a tabard sometimes, especially when she was wearing one of those woolly numbers she had pulled from her enchanted spinning wheel, inspired, no doubt, by her exploits in the Society for Creative Anachronism. Her pageboy looked to be permanently matted from the hood of chainmail she had worn over the weekend at some creatively anachronistic massacre.

"Yoo-hoo!"

Dr. Maddocks tried to dodge Dr. Brock around the buffet table, but he found himself trapped instead between a monstrous sideboard and her pointy extremities.

"Geoffrey."

"Beatrice."

"How are you?"

"Tolerably well, thank you. And you?"

"Pissed," she replied, meaning "drunk" to an American stricken with Anglophilia.

Dr. Maddocks actually harrumphed.

"Free booze and caviar before noon? Why not?"

"It's not caviar. It's lumpfish. Albeit, top-shelf lumpfish." Dr. Maddocks was forever grumbling about the bourgeois nonsense of private schools, even though he had attended, taught at and sent his own children to them.

"How was your summer, Geoffrey?"

"Splendid," he lied, considering his wife had left him for another man in June, sued him for divorce in July, and tried to turn their two grown children against him in August. He was not in the mood for Dr. Brock's leathery puss and play daft commentary, and as she was also sloshing her Bloody Mary in close proximity to his khaki chinos, Dr. Maddocks put her off by firing up a cigarette in her face.

"Oh," she brightened responsively, like the little girl that she had never really been, "may I 'bum' one of those?" affecting whatever lingo of her students.

And Dr. Maddocks rolled his eyes even as he said "certainly," because Dr. Brock was forever bumming cigarettes, an affront to his frugal nature.

All right, that wasn't it entirely. There was also the matter of Dr. Brock being on the tenure track and Dr. Maddocks wanting to derail her.

"Do you intend to oppose me, Geoffrey?"

She was referring to his position as head of the Faculty Promotions and Tenure Committee.

"Bea, for pity's sake. This is neither the time nor the place."

She was looking directly into his face, and there was nothing eccentric about her then. They were both remembering the time they had found themselves afloat in a sea of dry sherry at a faculty shindig. He had offered her a ride home—actually, he had insisted because she was even further beyond the legal limit than he was. Evidently, she mistook his stern concern for "passion's slave." He pulled up (very very slowly) to the curb in front of her apartment building and put his car into park, assuming she would bid him anon and simply exit, stage right. But it turned out Dr. Brock mistook that momentary idling of the engine as a sure sign Dr. Maddocks was just pausing long enough to pop in a refreshing breath mint, and would be revving up his own engine immediately. Dr. Brock was on him faster than Mistress Quickly. In her defense, she had not been with a man since the invention of the printing press.

"Oh, Geoffrey," she had burbled—if that was a word.

"Oh Lord," he had replied, remembering the rules of civil defense he ducked and covered. He considered himself fortunate, indeed, that no damage had been done, except, of course, for his eternal mortification. But he had long since been resigned to suffer that fate having been weaned on the Protestant Ethic.

"You're looking gaunt, Geoffrey. Have you been on a hunger strike?" He had a reputation for getting involved with liberal causes. "By the way, I meant to ask you: What do you know about a frosh named Elizabeth Breedlove?"

"Breedlove? Why do you ask?"

"She was signed up for my Brontë seminar and I just found out that she was bumped. What do you know about this?"

"Quite a bit, as a matter of fact, Beatrice. Your seminar was overbooked, so Miss Breedlove was placed in Dr. Crews's seminar."

"Why wasn't I consulted about this?" She regarded him with a courtly suspicion: "Don't tell me Dr. Crews is behind this?"

"I sent you a memo. And—oh, say—here's Dr. Crews now. Hello, friend!" he bellowed affably in another direction, "How the hell are you?"

The statuesque professor to whom Dr. Maddocks so eagerly offered his hail-fellow hand—and not just to get away from Dr. Brock either but because he really felt a great affection—was Dr. Josephine "Jojo" Crews, Chair of the Psychology Department. Dr. Crews and Dr. Maddocks had been tennis playing, beer drinking and politicking buddies for years.

The warmth with which he addressed his colleague only served to rub more lemon juice into Dr. Brock's eggshell wounds, because she had some aversion to Dr. Crews, the exact nature of which she would never divulge. They had been classmates at WCW, though they were never friends. Now, she resented the chummy relationship that Dr. Maddocks and Dr. Crews enjoyed on the basis of certain liberal, democratic, and feminist principles, which offended Dr. Brock, who was "something of a Tory" herself. Whereas Dr. Crews had just returned from Paris, her last stop after spending the summer break traveling through Third World countries with an international women's group active in the politics of birth control.

Dr. Crews was a woman accustomed to being observed, revered and sometimes feared. As she mingled with colleagues and students, she was able to pick up or transmit even the most subtle glancing admiration or hostility, with extraordinary deftness and discretion. There was something brilliantly sly about her as she swayed back and forth, lean and gracefully draped in an embroidered dashiki she had picked up in Ghana. At certain turns the garment would offer a slice of her lovely gams. When Dr. Maddocks said something amusing, this riveting, wide-eyed lady with the razorback nose and the highest cheekbones in the room, arched and laughed.

"Excuse me, Josephine," Dr. Brock cut in, "What do you know about an incoming frosh named Elizabeth Breedlove?"

" 'Incoming,' Bea? You make it sound like air traffic control. Ms. Breedlove is in my seminar."

"Ms.?!" Dr. Brock exclaimed. "You're not serious about using that loathsome 'Ms.' are you? Must you 'radical feminists' take the innocence and charm out of everything? *Ms.* It sounds so smarmy. But that's beside the point. Elizabeth Breedlove was in *my* seminar."

Dr. Crews exchanged a sidelong glance with Dr. Maddocks to indicate they were restraining some amusement. "As I understand it, Bea, you had one too many."

"*Miss* Breedlove is an English major. She should be in my Brontë seminar, or at least in Geoffrey's, er, multimedia thing."

And here Dr. Maddocks was compelled to protest: "I would hardly call my Classicism seminar a 'multimedia thing . . .' "

While Dr. Maddocks blustered, Dr. Crews was saying, "According to her entrance application, Bea—and Geoff will back me up on this—Ms. Breedlove is an undeclared major."

"A mere technicality."

Dr. Crews shrugged, "Nonetheless, she didn't commit. So she was up for grabs . . ."

"And you certainly *grabbed* her, didn't you, Josephine?"

"Now, Beatrice," Dr. Maddocks attempted to mollify, regretting that the politics of higher learning could come down to this: quibbling over a freshwoman's future potential as a tutorial candidate for one's own department. But Dr. Brock was bucking for tenure, and every outstanding student she could recruit to the study of literature proved her worth to the department. There was also a little cash bonus for each tutee, as students were required to do a tutorial senior year in order to graduate.

"What's the matter, Beatrice?" Dr. Crews asked, "Are you afraid that a psychologist, such as I, might not be literate enough to advise your first semester English majors?" She had said "psychologist," but meant something else, and they all knew it.

"Tut! Perish the thought," Dr. Brock protested. "We are, all of us, astounded by the interdisciplinary range of your multiple degrees," including a master's in English Literature. "I was referring to something else entirely."

"Oh?"

"Yes, I'm just a tad curious as to whether or not you *grabbed* Miss Breedlove from my seminar before or after you got your copy of *Mugs & Plugs?*"

*Mugs & Plugs* was what they called the pamphlet published each year by the college, which featured the high school photographs of incoming frosh laid out among advertisements from local establishments welcoming the new class of "Willard women." It was given exclusively to students and faculty members as a valuable reference guide for assigning names to faces most expeditiously. But in the collegiate underground, *Mugs & Plugs* was available on the black market for local college boys who were willing to pay, particularly the ones from the brother school, Benedict and Arnold, whose students the WCW sisters referred to ever so fondly as *The Dicks*—or just plain *Dicks*, for short.

Dr. Maddocks could not believe the effrontery of Dr. Brock: "Beatrice, what on earth are you trying to insinuate? Surely, you don't mean to say that Dr. Crews deliberately . . . ?"

But Dr. Crews cut him off: "Geoff, I appreciate your loyalty but Beatrice did ask me a question, and I would like to reply if I may."

"By all means, Jo, forgive me."

"Well, I must say, Beatrice, after all these years, you finally caught me in the act of trolling for brainy, buxom babes to lead astray with my *ee-vil* radical, feminist, *lesbian* separatist ways. "

Blinkity-blink-blink went their eyes on each other.

"I spent most of my summer vacation in Third World mills of human misery, among women and girls who have real problems—Beatrice. And life is too short for this rarefied bullshit."

"Good point, friend!" Dr. Maddocks agreed. "So let's plunge ahead, shall we?"

"God's bodykin!" said Dr. Brock, preparing to deliver an attack of too much politeness. It was her belief that the most effective way of insulting someone is to be overly polite to them (vicious!) and today she saw fit to punish her colleagues, Maddocks and Crews, roundly by dissolving into the crowd with a perfectly gracious "Anon!" that was certain to devastate them.

The moment they found themselves free to speak privately, Dr. Crews turned empathetically to her friend. "Geoff, I'm so sorry to hear about you and . . ."

"Oh, for heaven's sake, I'm fine. Really. The worst is over. Surely."

"Hm . . ."

"Lord knows I've been here before."

This would be his third divorce.

"Yes, well . . ."

He seemed forever to be looking for some minor distraction from his own ongoing emotion. Removing his horn-rimmed glasses to wipe the lenses with a handkerchief, he looked naked somehow.

All clear. Vision restored. Dr. Maddocks asked Dr. Crews if she was free for the evening. Hearing that she was, he proposed that they reserve a court for later in the day, and then have dinner and hang out.

"I don't know about you, friend, but I'm in the mood for a thick bloody steak, obligatory baked potato and all that jazz . . ."

This could mean only one thing to Dr. Crews: "Happy Frank's," she beamed, referring to one of Weston's oldest and most esteemed jazz clubs, which was their favorite haunt. After being abroad for a couple of months there was no place like home and Happy Frank's.

"We'll get *pissed.*"

"Absolutely . . ."

"And shout strange academic things between sets."

They were both palpably gleeful in a *tête-à-tête* making plans. It wasn't until they were about to part that Dr. Maddocks asked her, in his peremptory way:

"So?"

"*So* what?"

"As I recall, Jo, you did seem rather—shall we say—*anxious* to get 'Ms.' Breedlove bumped into your seminar."

"Did I? Hm. I'm afraid it's not quite the Elizabethan court intrigue or conspiracy insinuated by Her Majesty, Queen Bea."

"Nothing ever is."

# CHAPTER 1
## Big Sister

When Elizabeth Breedlove received her room assignment, she was told she was lucky.

"So *you're* the one who got Fey Five," said a junior named Hays, pointing at Elizabeth from behind a utility table. She handed over a quaint set of keys, which looked more like tokens from a game of Clue.

"Don't tell me," said Elizabeth, who didn't sound anything like she looked, "Corporal Ketchup . . . in the root cellar . . . with the keys to the chastity belt of Miss Mulch?" She registered the appreciative titters before asking, "Why me?"

Hays offered no explanation as to why a lowly frosh would be assigned a choice single in an upperclasswomen's dorm, but some scandal was clearly insinuated.

"There's one in Fey House every year."

"One what?"

Why she felt singled out, not by random, but set apart from the rest of her classmates by some force behind the scenes—false walls, maybe, in this Gothic mansion—Elizabeth could not say. But she felt like an ingénue all of a sudden, backlit by a klieg light.

Or else she was getting her period.

The gregarious Hays was saying, "Since you're moving into Fey Five, we had to reassign you a Big Sister."

"A Big Sister?"

"A Big Sister is a sophomore who lives in your dorm and helps you find your way . . ."

Elizabeth begged her pardon, but, "What do you mean 'find my way'? Where? Like, to the bathroom or something?"

And she really did not mean to be flip, it was just that she didn't need anybody to show her the way. "I'm not that kind of a girl," she said, referring to the kind who actually looked forward to participating in silly sister stuff.

Hays remained ladylike in the face of Elizabeth's rebelliousness, being a Willard girl through and through, as she continued, "Big Sisters have to be in the same dorm as their little sisters. And Big Sisters are supposed to be sophomores, and the only sophomore in Fey House this year is Dusie Hertz, so Dusie's going to be your Big Sister."

"But I . . ."

"It's a Willard tradition. Right, Dusie?"

"That's right!" came a bubbly voice over Elizabeth's shoulder. Elizabeth turned to meet her designated Big Sister, wondering how long she had been standing there behind her beaming, palpably pleased as Fruit of the Loom punch in a T-shirt, vest, and blue jeans frayed at the knees like she was looking to be this year's spokesmodel for flagrant androgyny.

"Hi!" she giggled, and then, "Wow! You're even cuter than your picture, Elizabeth!"

It was Dusie "as in Uzi," and she informed Elizabeth that she had been named after her father's favorite car, "a 1930 something or other . . . Duesenberg. I dunno." She could never remember the year.

Still, Elizabeth wanted to know, "What picture?"

"*Mugs & Plugs*," Dusie said, producing a copy of that very pamphlet from a stack on the sign-in table, adjusting her visored newsboy cap lower on her forehead, so it looked less jaunty and more like a prop in a soft porn pictorial. She stood by pertly, bouncing on the heels of her cowboy boots as Elizabeth flipped through the booklet.

"So," she said, "you already know our mugs, eh?"

"You bet! I'm really glad I got you too, Elizabeth. I took one look at you and I knew you were, like, cool?"

Elizabeth would not have known how to respond to such a comment even if she had been given a chance. "Here," babbled Dusie, pressing the pamphlet into Elizabeth's hand, "You can have this. Everybody gets one."

It was the sophomore's responsibility to show the frosh to her room, where her belongings had already been delivered by members of the maintenance crew. So Dusie led her little sister across a winding lane to Fey House. As they walked up the main staircase, Dusie explained that she was a "communications major."

"Communications? Like you watch a lot of television or something?"

Dusie puzzled over this question, "Sorta . . ." She also mentioned that she did some modeling for the finer department stores downtown.

"This is a great room," Dusie said, as they arrived at the top of the stairs and walked to the first door in the corridor. "I should know. I had it last year. Yep," she added, twisting at the waist and tossing her dark, curly hair back over her shoulders in order to look into Elizabeth's face, anticipating her double take. "The same thing happened to me last year. Isn't it amazing?"

She stopped at the threshold slipping her palms into the back pockets of jeans so tight it seemed impossible.

"Some senior dropped out at the last minute and I lucked into this room. Just like you. You're gonna love it here."

"How do you know?"

"I just know these things. I'm, like, what's that word? Like *sensitive*, but not *pathetic?*"

"Empathetic?"

"Yeah, that's it."

The charm of the room distracted Elizabeth from further questioning any weirdness she sensed, either in the coincidence or the tour guide. She stepped through a dusty sunbeam that fell across the middle of the floor, admiring the slanted ceiling. The room had been built into a gable. It had a large dormer window that opened out through ivy high above the garden terrace behind the house.

"See," said Dusie in a childish whisper, "this is the best part about this place. We have our own little stairway to the stars . . ." She was gesturing to a fire escape outside the window that led to the roof. Fey Beach, they called it. Ultra private. Even in the daylight. Great for tanning naked. Of course those "helicopter horn-dogs from the Channel 6 News are always flying over, but fuck 'em, you know? If they wanna risk their lives just to see our boobs, er, 'breasts,' that's their problem. And they say men are smarter than women? Ha! How smart is that? They're the 'boobs'—if you ask me."

Dusie could tell that Elizabeth was wondering about the "we" part of it and explained, "Me and my roommate, Pip Collier. She's a senior. Her real name is Penelope, but don't tell anybody I told you that, OK? We're right below you."

Elizabeth noticed that the fire escape also descended to the story below before it stopped, folded up and was inaccessible to the ground for obvious security reasons.

"This place is haunted," said Dusie matter-of-factly, "and our room used to belong to Fey Ray, herself."

"Fay Wray? You mean like in *King Kong?*"

"Nope. Fey Ray like in some dead old lady who used to own this place. Ray Fey was her name, but everybody calls her 'Fey Ray' for some reason I dunno—but she still haunts us, you know? She, like, lives in our closet."

"Your closet?"

"Yep. It's great. A walk-in. Best closet on campus. It's so big you wouldn't believe. I can fit two rolling racks of clothes!—But anyways, Fey Ray was a Willard woman. I mean, like, one of *the* Willards, you know? From up there?" She gestured vaguely beyond the window to a rooftop barely visible above a distant clump of trees. "I got set up with one of those Willard guys on a blind date last year. Randolph is his name. Ugh! He had the best dope, but what a jerk!" giggling as she scolded herself, "Whoops!—shouldn't be talking about dope around my little sister," as if that were actually some rule she had learned in Big Sister training.

Dusie seemed not to notice that Elizabeth was staring at her incredulously, and not because of any reference to the existence of a ghost, a real Willard, or dope. She was imagining two rolling racks of clothes.

"Poor Fey Ray," said Dusie with a sad sort of sigh, "they say she died in the closet. Our closet! Isn't that exciting?"

"Yeah. Sure. Real exciting, ah . . . What did she die of? An overdose of accessories?"

Dusie giggled.

"A clash of plaids? Too many pinks and greens?"

"You're funny, Elizabeth. I mean, like, in a good way?"

Shrugging diffidently, "Thanks . . . I guess."

In a moment, Dusie left Elizabeth to her unpacking. "If there's anything you need, just let me know. I'm right downstairs. I mean, I'm, like, your Big Sister, you know, that's what I'm here for." And Elizabeth could have sworn that she winked.

*    *    *

Elizabeth spent the rest of the afternoon getting her room into order, thinking "priorities." From a cardboard box she removed the World's Largest Ashtray and put it in the center of the floor so that she could flick her cigarette into it at an equal distance from any place in the room. She set up her stereo components and fumbled with the dial on the receiver until she found the most obscure, "progressive" rock station in town, WAFA–FM, broadcast from the nearby campus of the Weston Academy of Fine Arts, which included a prestigious drama school and was a quarter of a mile down the hill, housed in buildings designed by Frank Lloyd Wright.

Elizabeth retrieved a handful of photographs of her family and friends, mostly boyfriends, and stuck her favorites in the mirror frame above her dresser. She pushed the little dorm bed over to the window because it fit perfectly lengthwise into that space and would serve very nicely as a makeshift window seat where she could lounge on pillows propped up against the wall with an overview of the back yard. Having put everything in its place, she lay back on her bed just to muse for a half hour or so, relishing the sensation of being alone. Preferring solitude on a day chock-full of activities meant to help freshwomen become acquainted with each other and their surroundings was aberrant behavior. All over the campus cliques were forming while Elizabeth remained singular and thoughtful. She was enjoying the late summer breeze, flicking an ash from her cigarette in an arc to meet the ashtray halfway across the floor, feeling like the odd freshwoman out, though not undesirably so. She was actually looking forward to what she could learn rather than who she could come to know.

Yes, well.

For all of her airs, Elizabeth Breedlove was too green yet to realize that such motives were not necessarily opposed.

On her way downstairs sometime later, she had to pass what had once been the master bedroom on the second floor. The door was ajar. She recognized her Big Sister's voice coming from within. Dusie sounded upset.

"I just wanted to surprise you," she whined, "I thought you would be happy about this."

Elizabeth could move fairly close to the door without being noticed, and glimpsed Dusie perched on a window seat like a jumpy bird, nibbling on her cuticles compulsively. From Elizabeth's perspective, Dusie appeared to be talking to her closet.

Was it that ghost? Elizabeth wondered, Old Whatshername? Fey Ray?

"Are you even listening to me?"

From that place where the former mistress of the house was said to have died mysteriously, came a sigh, then a voice, *sotto voce.* "There's a difference between surprise and manipulation, Baby D."

Baby D? A strapping woman, with thick blond hair in a radically short coif, came out of the closet carrying a foil—for fencing. Her unique entrance gave Elizabeth a start but had no such effect on Dusie, who wasn't afraid of trying the patience of a woman who was armed.

Elizabeth had never seen anyone like her. She was a disconcertingly plain looker. Her outfit matched Dusie's, more or less, from the satin-backed tailored vest in charcoal over a white T-shirt, to the frayed seat in her ancient Levi's. But the garb seemed more authentic on her somehow, more natural to her angular proportions and aura, giving any observer the immediate impression that she was an original while Dusie was, well, a model.

The woman flicked the blade a couple of times and then positioned herself before a full-length Victorian mirror whose gilt frame was flaking draconically. With her back to Elizabeth, she executed an elegant fencer's salute to herself.

That was when she spotted Elizabeth, reflected in the mirror.

Surprise or manipulation?

Elizabeth was certain that her own appearance qualified as a surprise, at least judging by the look in the woman's eyes, which were rather sultry. She lowered her foil before turning to face Elizabeth. Haughty, but then, Elizabeth had been spying.

"Hello."

"Hello," Elizabeth replied, smiling cutely, hoping that her Big Sister would come to the rescue, which Dusie did just as soon as she could shake off her palpable snit, remembering her Willard duty in the face of disaster.

"Hey, 'little sister!' " she said, straining for cheerfulness, "Come on in! So, howz it going? This is my roommate, Pip Collier. Pip, this is my 'little sister,' Elizabeth Breedlove."

Pip's curt nod and accompanying silence caused Elizabeth to revert to her nervous habit of flippancy: "So, Pip"—she said it like 'cheerio,' considering the grotesquely time-stopping feel of the place—"Where's Miss Havisham?"

To which Dusie said, "Huh?" not knowing her Dickens, while Pip sort of smiled or smirked or scowled. It was hard to tell. Probably all three.

As Dusie took to yammering and Elizabeth stood by listening politely, Pip went about the business of unpacking her belongings, not ignoring the other women exactly, but seeming rather supremely preoccupied . . . *oh those moody world-weary seniors* . . . as she filled a creaky old dresser with fastidiously folded clothes.

Glancing around the large master bedroom, Elizabeth noticed that the only furniture that was not part of Fey Ray's original suite were two regulation dorm beds, and that they had been pushed together. She looked away a little too quickly.

Dusie caught her eye and smiled, while Pip just stared at her, stone-faced as a tintype in the antique mirror.

# CHAPTER 2
## Bloody Mary Brunch

Downstairs, the incoming class was shifting uncomfortably about the parlors of Fey House, nibbling caviar (lumpfish) and an international array of cheeses and flatbread rather irritably because nobody felt independent enough, as yet, to mortify her mother by lighting up a cigarette.

"Put that away young lady," said Mrs. McNaught as she caught her daughter, Mary Constance, removing her Lady Buxton cigarette case from her shoulder bag. "Do you want them to think you're a common tramp?"

"A common tramp, as opposed to, say, an extraordinary one, Mother?" would have been the young woman's reply had she been foolish enough to smart-mouth at that moment. She remembered that the last time she smart-mouthed her mother, she got smacked in the kisser, so she withheld her remark. Besides, Mrs. McNaught would be gone soon enough, back to their home down in The Valley. Not *The* Valley as most Willard women would know it, the bucolic countryside east of Weston where the deer and the privileged roamed, but rather, the floundering working-class neighborhood on the other side of Weston where the steel mills were. To Mary Constance, her valley was a hellhole, and she could not wait to rewrite her own history from the vantage point of Upper Alban Hill. When anyone asked her where she was from, she would say "The Valley", and they would just assume she meant the place with the estates. She had the inborn advantage of looking the part, however, and made the most of it: being a tall young woman on the pretty side of plump, with curly rose-blond hair, a high forehead and eyebrows that she overplucked, which gave her the arch cherubic look of Henry VIII, her favorite tyrant.

"I'll be going now," said Mrs. McNaught with the terminally ener- vated sigh of a woman who had borne and raised eight children and waited slavishly on her husband, while holding down various other menial jobs outside the home. Mary Constance blamed her mother's exhaustion on her father, who represented what was rapidly becom- ing a classic Weston tale of woe, being a steelworker when the best of times became the worst. Over the past five years he had been laid off or on strike much more than he had worked.

Mrs. McNaught had been invited, along with the other parents to President Barbara—"call me Buffy"—Buford's house on the campus for a champagne reception, followed by a formal buffet dinner in the WCW dining hall. But Mrs. McNaught declined simply because she knew she would not feel comfortable mingling a moment longer with the presumably educated and overly polite people who could actually afford to send their daughters to WCW. And it was just as well since Mary Constance would have found it unbearable to know her mother's discomfort and watch her behave in a servile manner around these people when she was, in this specific context, a peer. The reason Mrs. McNaught felt unworthy was because she had worked at the college as a "kitchen lady" when Mary Constance was growing up. That's when she had filled her daughter's head with stories of the glories of Willard girls.

It was by virtue of Mary Constance's own academic accomplish- ment that she had received a full scholarship making at least one of her mother's dreams come true. And so she had arrived at this place with a determination to succeed with a vengeance, assuming that the reason her own poor family suffered so much was because the afflu- ent families of Willard girls did not.

Mrs. McNaught started to cry as she was saying goodbye.

"Aw, Mom . . ." Mary Constance commiserated affectionately, pull- ing her mother aside, "It's a ninety-cent bus ride, for cryin' out loud. Mother? Are you even listening to me? Listen. There's only one trans- fer. It's not so far away. Aw jeez . . ." She gave her mother one last squeeze, affecting great perturbation in an effort to staunch her own weepiness, hoping that none of her classmates were watching.

"Your father doesn't know about this," said Mrs. McNaught, furtively pushing a wad of cash, along with a soggy tissue into her daughter's hand—as if a man dissociated from the world like her husband would have spies.

"Thanks, Mother."

"Buy yourself a nice outfit. A box pleat skirt and matching sweater would be nice. Gimbels has the best sales."

Mary Constance rolled her eyes.

"You can't wear blue jeans every day, my dear. It's not ladylike."

After her mother had gone, Mary Constance counted the cash and used the tissue to dry her own eyes before returning to the parlor, resolved to keeping her family background to herself. When anyone asked, she made up something and changed the subject deftly, assuming correctly that most Willard girls equated such evasiveness with modesty and good breeding.

# CHAPTER 3
## Ante Up, Suckers!

The show put on for the freshwomen and their parents, what few diehards remained, did not end at the champagne reception given by President Buffy. They gathered once more for their daughters' first dinner in the WCW cafeteria.

A four-foot-square ice cube had been sculpted into a swan that was Avon-worthy. It was glistening in one big glorious drip at the center of the buffet table, roosting in a nest of fresh flowers beside a white and off-white layer cake decorated with the school emblem and motto: FILLAE NOSTRAE SICUT ANTARII LAPIES, from Tremellius, who took it from Psalms, ". . . that our daughters may be as cornerstones, polished after the similitude of a palace."

An elderly gentleman named Hans, who had an accent that could only be described in the context of postwar Hollywood Germany, was poised at the finish line of the buffet table, dressed in crisp chef's whites, serving a side of roast beef. And while the international flavor, however peculiar, impressed them immeasurably, assuming it confirmed some long-lost barony, the way the old man's hands trembled as he sliced the beef made everyone laugh a bit nervously, anticipating a blitzkrieg. Eventually, it took every bit of their good breeding to keep from grabbing the carving knife from his tremulous hands and shouting at him through clenched teeth, "Please, Your Excellency! Allow me!"

Little did they know that this hoary old fellow had been adopted from a community halfway house—between the harsh world and a mental hospital—where he had told everyone he was Kaiser Wilhelm. His palsy was a side effect of his medication. Hans was here

because of Dr. Jojo Crews, who had guilted the college into providing employment and housing to a few perfectly pleasant former
mental patients. So they had given Hans a white chef's hat and put a
carving knife in his hands on these special occasions calling for
Baron of Beef.

It was because of the buffet bottleneck caused by Hans that
Elizabeth and Mary Constance struck up a conversation.

"If you show me your parents, I'll show you mine," was Elizabeth's
opening line. Hearing the lowdown register of the voice coming
from behind her, Mary Constance turned around expecting to see
some fugitive from a reform school recruited on a field hockey scholarship. Instead she found herself looking at a petite brunette whose
appearance brought to mind *cheerleader*. A cheerleader who was
trying a little too hard to look mousy, thought Mary Constance.
Elizabeth's hair was pulled up into a lopsided chignon, and her sly
green eyes were made up, moderately, behind horn-rimmed glasses.
With a touch of dark forest *Forever Evergreen* in the crease and
black mascara. She appeared to be sublimating some truer tendency
to flamboyance.

"What a smart-ass," thought Mary Constance, grinning morda-
ciously. Her first impression of Elizabeth was that there was something about her that just made you want to bite her.

"I'm an orphan," Mary Constance replied, mugging sadly, "I was
raised in a convent," crossing herself to lay the groundwork for future absolution.

Elizabeth had seen Mary Constance earlier in the day saying goodbye to a woman who looked too much like her mother to be anyone
but her mother. But she said, "I'm very sorry to hear that," anyway,
with deadpan sincerity, willing to play anyone's game.

"*Fraulein?*" said Hans, calling Mary Constance's attention back to
the meat at hand.

And Mary Constance sent a look over her shoulder to Elizabeth,
screwing up her face as she mouthed the word "*fraulein?!*" counter-
ing with an audible "begosh and begorrah!"

As they walked together through the dining hall looking for a suitable table, Mary Constance was muttering under her breath that her
"dear old Irish Dad, who fought in 'The Big One,' would keel over if
he heard some old Nazi calling his daughter a '*fraulein.*' Saints preserve us!"

"I thought you were an orphan."

"Oh," Mary Constance thought for a moment. "Well, then he wouldn't keel over, would he? He'd roll over in his grave."

*"Much* more convincing," Elizabeth smiled. She was thinking that Mary Constance's colorful speech mannerisms were a curious counterpoint to the self-conscious refinement of this Upper Alban Hill community. In a place like this it was safe to assume that the ones who talked like juvenile delinquents had the largest trust funds. Being genuinely snooty was more characteristic of the middle class.

Elizabeth and Mary Constance sat together at a far table in the dining hall with six or seven other classmates who had also managed to ditch their parents. Elizabeth noticed that they were all going about getting acquainted rather complacently considering they were only eighteen. They had already worked themselves into a collective snit regarding the accommodations. Throughout the dining hall, the buzz of bees in bonnets was loudest at those tables where Moms and Dads still clung like honey. Elizabeth was observing a little scene at a nearby table featuring weepy parents and a whiny daughter when Mary Constance leaned in impishly and said, "Look at them carrying on like they're sailing for Australia. I know for a fact that these people live three blocks away."

"Mr. and Mrs. Polonious."

"Yeah, right," Mary Constance snickered, delighted by the Shakespearean reference. "There you go now. Off with you, daughter. Get yourself a higher education . . ."

"A rich husband, you mean."

"Do everything in moderation. And mind you: neither a nymphomaniac nor a lesbian be!"

"And above all, daughter, remember this! This is costing Daddy a pretty penny . . ."

*"So don't fuck up!"*

Their laughter drew the full attention of their tablemates.

"How do you know so much about this place?" Elizabeth asked.

"I grew up in this town, sister. I know what people say about Willard girls."

Someone from across the table corrected her robotically: "Women."

Mary Constance bristled with comic indignation. "Yeah, right, 'women,' " addressing the entire table now as the assumed natural leader. " 'Rich bitches' is the nicest thing they call us in this town, so you'd better get used to it, ladies." She went on to inform the out-of-towners about the sociology of the sandwich board at Abe's Tavern, a popular neighborhood bar down the hill where they served platters named after the local universities and colleges. "The Willard" was the most expensive entry on the menu. Rare Roast Beef on a kaiser roll. They called it "the bitch burger."

"Jeez," said Elizabeth, who had been listening like the best student. She pressed her lips together and shook her head to convey the sincerity of a person perfectly content to play the straight man.

"Woman."

"Woman, right."

Mary Constance was saying, "To them, you're either a virgin, a debutante, a lesbian vampire, or a . . ."

"Lesbian vampire?"

"You heard me, sister. And if you know what's good for you, you'll learn real fast how to spot 'em too," she cautioned, tending toward the supernaturally snide side, having been educated by nuns. "This place is crawling with them. The bloodsuckers."

Elizabeth was one of those people who laughed and winced at the same time.

"You're from a small town aren't you, Miss Breedlove?"

She was thinking that Elizabeth's lack of an accent and easygoing manner bespoke a small-town-upstate influence—something about her brought to mind the wry serenity of a Populux motel on a scenic lake.

"You scoff, sister," said Mary Constance, "but I'm a good Catholic girl myself. I've got my crucifix, see . . ." She pulled her necklace out from underneath the Peter Pan collar of the ladylike dress her mother had insisted she wear, holding the cross up under her heart-shaped chin. "There's no way those bloodsucking lesbos are going to catch me unawares. But you, Miss Breedlove! Saints preserve you, lass! We'll have to get you a garlic mattress or something. Won't we ladies?—Where's your room, Miss Breedlove?"

"Ms.," said an uppity voice from across the table, and Mary Constance looked at her in the manner of her favorite tyrant, just as Elizabeth replied, "Fey Five," which commanded all of the attention.

"Fey House? You have a room in Fey House? Frosh don't have rooms in Fey House."

"Well, I do. Some senior dropped out at the last minute and I got her room. A single on the third floor."

Mary Constance crossed herself before she asked, "So which one are you, sister?"

"Well," Elizabeth shrugged, "I'm not rich. And I like boys."

"Ah," Mary Constance brightened, "so you're a nympho."

It just so happened that Dr. Beatrice Brock had been listening in on their conversation from the next table. Unable to contain one of her countless compulsions a moment longer, she leaned back on the legs of her chair, stretched her neck and twisted her jaw so that her face appeared suddenly to spring at them like a jack-in-the-box.

" 'Nympha,' actually, but 'nymph' would be the preferred word." She blinked at them a couple of times like she was playing at being a dipso (dipsa?) and then she smiled neatly, "Dr. Beatrice Brock. English. Medieval, Elizabethan and Victorian, mostly."

They might have guessed.

"I'll be seeing some of you in my Brontë seminar, no doubt," she said brightly, looking at Mary Constance and Elizabeth the longest—though not long enough for them to introduce themselves—before turning back to her own table with a warning to avoid the potato salad if they knew what was good for them.

After dinner, they broke into groups heading back to their assigned dorms for their Big Sister Bashes. Elizabeth found herself in an awkward position, standing in the dining hall between two groups of women: those who lived in Whitman Hall on one hill and those who lived in Bertha Beekman Hall on the other.

Mary Constance lived in Whitman and was surrounded by the classmates who had become instant cronies.

As Elizabeth was trying to decide where to go, her Big Sister, Dusie, approached her. "Sorry about this, little sis," she said, with a sweetly helpless shrug, "that's the one bad thing about being the only frosh in Fey House. Hey, um, by the way," she hummed, "I meant to ask you something . . ."

"What's that?"

"Well. My roommate? Pip? You know? She's a psych major? Well, she needs volunteers for her tutorial experiment, and I'm, like, her assistant? Helping her out on the research part of it? She has these little tests . . ."

"Little tests?"

Dusie's attempt to explain Pip's tutorial experiment proved so convoluted that Elizabeth said yes just to put an end to it. And Dusie positively gushed, she was so grateful, squeezing Elizabeth's forearm warmly, "Thanks so much!"

"Yeah, sure," Elizabeth mumbled distractedly as she heard Mary Constance calling to her boisterously from a distance, "Well come on already, Miss Breedlove, don't *dawdle,"* expecting her to join *her* party, of course, having already designated Elizabeth as her sidekick. When Elizabeth didn't respond immediately, Mary Constance marched over to where she and Dusie were standing.

"So this is your Big Sister, Dusie Hertz?" Mary Constance cooed at Dusie like a kindergarten teacher, "How do you do? I'm Mary Constance McNaught. You're a model, aren't you? I've seen your pictures in the Sunday Supplement."

"Yes," said Dusie, having no idea that she was being mocked, "nice to meet you, Mary."

The moment Dusie was out of earshot, Mary Constance shook her head. "What a kai-kai," she said.

"What's a 'kai-kai?' "

"You really *are* from a small town, aren't you, Miss Breedlove? A 'kai-kai' . . . is a girl who goes 'both ways' until her prince comes along, and then, all of a sudden, she's straighter than your mother."

"No one could be straighter than my mother."

Mary Constance slapped Elizabeth on the back affectionately. "Just remember, sister, here at Willard 'kai-kai' means only one thing."

"What's that?"

"Vampire feed."

"Would you stop with the vampire stuff already?"

"Just trying to warn you, hon," said Mary Constance, affecting her heaviest Westonite accent and snapping her gum, "I'd hate to see you get your boobs sucked off, sister. Not a pretty sight. Greatly reduces your chances of finding a rich husband. By the way, I meant to ask you . . . you have a boyfriend, right?"

"At least."

"Yeah, you strike me as the two-timer type."

"How about you?"

Mary Constance removed her Lady Buxton wallet from her purse and showed Elizabeth a picture of her boyfriend, Vincent, who was good-looking.

"My parents think he's bad news. We have to sneak around. But sneaking around just makes it better, you know?—Did I say 'my parents'? Oh. I meant the nuns at my convent—Come on. Let's go party-hearty with these daddy's little wawas at Whitman. Can you believe this happy camper nonsense? By the way, I meant to ask you . . . Do you play poker?"

Whitman Hall was the biggest dorm on campus, housing freshwomen and sophomores mostly, one hundred and twenty-two of them. Elizabeth accompanied Mary Constance and her entourage to a double on the second floor that belonged to Mary Constance's Big Sister, Trish Macon, and Trish's roommate, Judy Feidelman. They positioned themselves politely on various perches about the room like tuckered-out cats yawning, as if to say, "Now what?"

Judy Feidelman walked in carrying a case of beer shouting, "OK, Trish, you can cut the cornerstones and tiddlywinks bullshit," referring to all of the speeches that had been made that day invoking the school motto. " 'Our daughters are our cornerstones . . . ,' " she bellowed like the antithesis of a cheerleader, and a chorus of Big Sister sophomores responded:

"They get laid!"

And the little sisters seemed considerably relieved to hear it. There was a collective uncrossing of legs.

"We've got a tradition here at WCW, ladies. A little game we like to play the first night in order to separate the girls from the *women!* Isn't that right, Fidel?"

"That's right, Trish," said the young woman who got her nickname because she smoked cigars.

"The name of the game is 'papers, papers, who's got the papers?' "

At that, Trish produced a bag of marijuana and dangled it before them. "Maui Wowie, ladies."

When none of them budged because they suspected this might be some kind of a trap, Trish hollered at them, "Those of you who are mama's girls and frigid bitches and daddy's little deadbeat darlings—those of you who don't know how to party-hearty—better head on over to Bertha Beekman Hall right now, where they're serving warm milk and cookies and playing Old Maid and Go Fish! until lights out. Right Fidel?"

"Right, Trish."

"Now: Papers, papers, who's got the papers?"

And this time, they all scrambled for the door, except for Elizabeth, of course. For the next five minutes, she heard the hurry-scurry of footsteps and activity, her classmates banging doors, searching through drawers, doing a quick-change into clothes they actually wore. And then they reappeared as themselves in a seeming uniform of worn-out jeans and corduroys, T-shirts, flannel shirts, sweatshirts, or some combination thereof—*sans* bras. In their possession was the most colorful assortment of smoking paraphernalia imaginable: bongs and pipes and papers, papers, *everybody* had the papers. Trish passed out beers while Fidel cued up Van Morrison on the stereo. Within the hour, the diehards were down and dirty on the floor playing poker for shots of tequila.

"Ante up, suckers!" Mary Constance growled, holding out a shot glass thick and slick with Cuervo Gold to Elizabeth who had won with a queen high in Five Card Stud. She took a lick of salt, downed the shot, sucked on a slice of lime, and raked in the pot, about five dollars and a couple of joints. She had been on a winning streak, and this shot made her feel like she was going to lose it.

"Gotta go," she said, suddenly rising to her feet a bit wobbly, chuckling, "whoa . . ."

Mary Constance insisted upon walking Elizabeth back to Fey House. Like Mercutio with a band of revelers in tow, she was followed by Helen, Vivian, Gracie and several others.

Because it was such a balmy September night with an ample moon, they found themselves down by the pond behind Fey House, crowded on a bench telling ghost stories. The one about "Fey Ray" became everybody's instant favorite. Mary Constance had heard the tale years before from a couple of Willard women she had befriended in the student union around the pool table where she sometimes hung out after high school waiting for her mother to clock off from the kitchen.

Fey Ray, or, Ray Willard Fey, was the original inhabitant of Fey House. A pipe-smoking flapper from the Roaring '20s, she had married late in life, at least for those days, at the age of thirty-five, and only because she wanted a baby. Her husband, Perry Fey, was a golf pro at the swanky Tumbling Rock Valley Country Club. Nine months after their honeymoon, Ray Fey gave birth to a son. Several months later, she became a widow by rather curious circumstances. It seems her toothsome, athletic husband had died from massive head injuries sustained in a bowling accident.

"A bowling accident?"

"That's right," replied Mary Constance for ghostly emphasis, "A bowling accident."

Elizabeth squinted her eyes against a dope-y curl of smoke floating up into her face. This was just like a slumber party, she thought, except nobody was fighting—yet.

"This is the honest-ta-God truth, lemme-tell-ya. No lie," said Mary Constance, "It happened up there." She was pointing across the moonlit pond in the direction of Fey House. And it did look a bit spooky.

There was a quaint, two-lane bowling alley in the basement of Fey House, paneled in rich hardwood inlay and appointed with brass fixtures. In Ray Fey's day there were no automatic pinsetters, so the players (or their servants) had to set the pins by hand, standing in a little pit up to their waists at the end of the lane. When the bowling ball was in play, the pinsetter sat up on a little plank, legs dangling out of harm's way.

Except for poor Perry "The Pinhead" Fey. On the night of his death he had been hosting a party, serving illegal substances to his guests (booze, that is), and after a whirlwind evening of drinking games, he and his wife found themselves alone in the bowling alley. The servants being among those who were passed out cold upstairs, Perry and Ray Fey were obliged to take turns setting up each other's pins. Ray had been winning, which never failed to get the competitive Perry's testosterone up. He could not stand to be beaten by a girl.

"Woman."

He was also rather edgy because his wife had not slept with him since he had impregnated her over a year before.

Ray was at the foul line ready to roll while Perry was in the pit setting up the pins. Perry gave her the go-ahead, so she bowled the ball just as he jumped for the safety plank. But Perry slipped, taking out the ninepin with his noggin a split second before the bowling ball did.

"Oooh," they all shuddered.

That's what Ray Fey said anyway. And she stood up magnificently at the inquest, a real Willard girl, putting anyone who even dared think foul play to shame by virtue of her ladylike behavior under pressure.

Many years later, a story emerged implicating Ray Fey in an "unnatural relationship" with her lifelong housekeeper and companion, Miss Francine Hamilton, whom she called "Frankie." WCW legend had it that when they were both elderly and cantankerous, Frankie strangled Ray in the closet of the master bedroom, during a fight over whether or not Ray could wear white shoes to a luncheon after Labor Day.

Another legend had it that Ray and Frankie hadn't died at all, but rather, "had gone into the closet to become . . ."

"Lesbian vampires?"

"You got that right, sister."

Sometimes in the night, residents of Fey House would hear disquieting moans, and they would wonder who among them had been taken.

Every Halloween, Fey House was converted into a haunted house and tours were conducted as part of a raucous costume party to which everybody on campus was invited. Even the jaded enjoyed a good scream when Fey Ray sprang from the closet flashing glow-in-the-dark vampire fangs and breasts smeared with "blood," wielding a bowling ball with Perry The Pinhead's name on it. When she threw the ball (which was Styrofoam) it never failed to topple the whole lot of them, bouncing around like bowling pins in fits of hilarity, screeching and squealing enough to raise the pinhead dead.

Despite the exhausting events of the day, Elizabeth did not sleep soundly through the night. She woke at one point with the onslaught of a wicked hangover, feeling feverish and thirsty but too confused by her new surroundings to get up and set out in search of water. She was almost asleep again when she heard hushed voices. Sensing urgency, it took her a moment to locate the source. She sat up in bed, pulling her cotton comforter around her, not from the chill of the open window but for modesty's sake, because she always slept in her *birthday* jammies. Leaning toward the ledge of her open window, she saw Dusie standing on the landing of the fire escape below, wearing nothing but a white T-shirt, underpants, and bobby socks.

Pip was calling to her quietly from the window, trying to coax her back into their room, but Dusie mewled meekly, "Leave me alone."

"Come back inside. Please."

"No."

"Come on, Baby D. I said I was sorry."

There it was again, that oddly demonstrative pet name.

"You're shivering, Baby, come on in."

"So what? Who cares? Fuck you." Dusie's curse, like her aspect, was more tearful than enraged, more self-pitying than spiteful.

Pip stepped out onto the fire escape and took Dusie by the arm to lead her back into the room.

Elizabeth fell back into bed, in an agitated state, but relaxed somewhat when she heard Dusie giggling, only to find herself tensing up again when, after a telling silence, she heard a moan.

# CHAPTER 4

# Feminism, Existentialism and the Menace that Was Freud

The student to faculty ratio at WCW was nine to one, which, as the glossy course book phrased it, made for "close relationships" between students and teachers. Each freshwoman was assigned a faculty adviser, preferably in her major, who would advise her until her senior year, when she would then choose a faculty tutor (oftentimes the same person) who would see her through the yearlong and often grueling process of completing her tutorial. All students were expected to meet with their advisers or tutors at least once a week, so it wasn't long before freshwomen fancied themselves privy to a great deal of information regarding the more interesting (and usually most attractive) teachers.

Although they weren't the only outstanding teachers in the school, four professors emerged immediately as those whose attention the students most wanted to secure. The eccentric Dr. Beatrice Brock taught a seminar that revolved around the Brontë sisters; the lovable but peremptory Dr. Geoffrey Maddocks chalked out a systematic approach to understanding the concepts of Classicism, Romanticism and Naturalism; the provocative Dr. Virginia Vacirca, associate professor of biology, developed a sort of "hands-on" seminar with lots of guest speakers under the title, "Biological Aspects of Sexual Function," and the notorious Dr. Jojo Crews taught a seminar entitled "Feminism, Existentialism and the Influence of Psychoanalysis."

Dr. Brock's seminar was most delightful. Dr. Maddocks's seminar was most difficult to ace. Dr. Vacirca's seminar was most "ace-able, like watching daytime TV talk shows for a grade." But what they said about Dr. Crews's seminar was that it "changed your whole life." And it was into Dr. Crews's seminar that Elizabeth had been bumped because the Brontë had been overbooked.

"But 'Feminism, Existentialism, and the Influence of Psychoanalysis'?" said Mary Constance to Elizabeth. "Of all things to have to contemplate right out of high school."

They were walking through the cafeteria line at lunch during the first week of classes. Mary Constance was laughing because Elizabeth referred to the seminar as, "Feminism, Existentialism and The Menace That Was Freud."

"I'm laughing all the way to the Brontë seminar, sister. I can't believe you've got the notorious Jojo Crews for your adviser."

Seminar teachers also served as advisers for freshwomen, at least until the student had culled enough information about campus politics to choose a more appropriate adviser.

"Why notorious?" Elizabeth asked, as they pushed their trays up to the salad bar.

"Jojo Crews was the first black sister admitted to this 'Fortress of Chastitude.' "

"You don't say?"

"And, as I understand it, she's a radical feminist separatist therapist."

"?"

"I'm not sure exactly, but I think it has something to do with living one's life without penises. God forbid. Jell-O?"

"No thanks."

"And speaking of penises, whaddaya say we go down to WU Friday night and find a couple? I haven't been in this nunnery a week and already I'm gettin' so antsy I'm making eyes at Herr Hans over there—saints preserve us!" She nodded in the direction of the white-haired man as he was busy his task stacking cups and saucers by the coffee urns. The clacking of Buffalo china in his shaky hands put everyone on edge.

"There's a frat mixer down at Sigma Chi with a great band, and Fidel's big brother, Stan, is also having a party. So we've got options, sister. I saw some pictures of Stan Feidelman, by the way. He's very good-looking and super-smart, so they say."

"I thought you said you would never go out with Fidel's brother because he's Jewish."

"Hey, who said I'm going out with him? I'm just hoping he has some nice Irish Catholic friends, that's all."

"You really wouldn't go out with him just because he's Jewish?"

Elizabeth asked this question rather fatuously, knowing she wouldn't get a clear-cut answer. Mary Constance tinkered so much with the tiny mechanism that runs prejudice that Elizabeth could not tell when it was switched on or off. Or else Elizabeth just couldn't believe that anyone who she found charming could also be contemptuous of anyone else for reasons of race, ethnic background, or religion. She didn't want to think that her new friend's seeming prejudice was anything other than froshy posturing. Still, Elizabeth didn't really know. Having been raised in a small town herself, where lovely people turned into foul-mouthed lumpkins, she was extremely sensitive to any discriminatory undercurrent.

"So whaddaya say? Are we gonna party or what?"

It was fine with Elizabeth. She, too, was getting antsy for some male companionship.

"There's slim pickings around this place, that's for sure. Ugh," Mary Constance muttered, referring to the male members of the faculty. "Except Dr. Maddocks maybe. He's cute, I mean, in an aging beatnik kinda way. He's also available, you know, recently divorced. Get this: His wife dumped him for a T.A. at the brother school who isn't even published."

They entered the dining hall and took their seats at what had already become their usual table. Five of the others were already seated and at different stages in their meals, depending on individual course schedules. If they crowded in, they could fit seven or eight women at any given moment. Elizabeth and Mary Constance gravitated to the chairs that allowed them to sit with their backs to the wall, enabling them to keep their eyes on the entire dining hall as they were entertaining at table. Elizabeth wondered what she had in common with Mary Constance that compelled them both to vie for those prime points of observation with more determination than anyone else. Were they both just naturally observant? Or afraid of being stabbed in the back?

Elizabeth certainly was cagey, thought Mary Constance.

And Mary Constance, thought Elizabeth, wasn't one to offer much about her personal experiences either, unless of course, they were made up, and then she had the most wonderful stories. Elizabeth suspected that Mary Constance only told her "personal" stories in order to goad the others into revealing further intimacies about themselves, which she would never let them live down. Trish Macon, for instance, made the mistake of confessing a certain frustration with her boyfriend's lovemaking insofar as he never lasted long enough to satisfy her, and every time afterward that Mary Constance saw the couple around campus, she muttered impishly, "There goes Trish Macon and her boyfriend, the premature ejaculator."

For her inconstancy, Mary Constance McNaught earned the nickname Mary Contrary, which was soon shortened to Contrary.

Elizabeth's seminar turned out to be fascinating because Dr. Jojo Crews was such a dynamo. Frosh as she was, Elizabeth remained suspicious of the radical feminist bent running throughout every classroom discussion, as they tried to make sense of this stuff in the context of their own rather sheltered, if not cushy, lives. But she trusted Dr. Crews, herself, implicitly. She wasn't sure why. Probably her eyes, which seemed to be consistently compassionate. Dr. Crews talked about Simone de Beauvoir and Jean-Paul Sartre and Carl G. Jung and the Menace That Was Freud. She told them that they could, in fact, choose their own destinations.

The concepts were especially enticing as voiced by this most extraordinary teacher, who appeared in class in her chic caftans and silver squashblossom necklaces, a vision of high style and even higher consciousness. She taught students and treated patients and attended world conferences for women, and spoke out against racism and sexism, especially as it was woefully fostered within the family. She was on a rampage against people who blamed victims for being victimized. She helped found rape crisis centers and shelters for battered women and abused children. She wrote articles for journals, as a practicing psychologist, about the crimes against women and children.

And she played tenor sax. Straight-ahead jazz.

In the same sense that a man can be thought of as a *man's man,* Jojo Crews was *a woman's woman.* A worthy role model. Women loved her. And, needless to say, she loved women. She was especially courageous to be openly gay in such a provincial city as Weston. There was a flirtatious aspect to her brilliance, an irresistible quality in a teacher. The downside of this, of course, was that she developed

a reputation for walking the fine line between mentorship and seduction. Dr. Crews herself, felt she had to work much harder than
any of her colleagues to reassure everyone that she wasn't some
"voodoo doctor," as she put it, right up front to the class that first
week, "My Lord, ladies, you would not *believe* the trouble I have
seen," being the first black student enrolled at WCW and, later, the
first black faculty member. And when she said this, she made a point
of looking into each and every one of them as they were sitting
around a rectangular conference table. This was her favorite calming
device. Her training in clinical hypnosis showed. She held fifteen of
them spellbound with one pair of arched eyebrows.

Elizabeth had no problem speaking up in class, but she was a bit
intimidated having Dr. Crews as a faculty adviser, which meant she
had to meet with her once a week in her office across from the psych
lab in the basement of the main classroom building. As Elizabeth
passed the door to the lab, the smell of caged animals made her eyes
tear.

"You get used to it," Dr. Crews said smilingly, inviting Elizabeth
into her office, with its cavelike cool. Elizabeth felt stupefied by her
adviser's increased magnificence in these surroundings. If Dr. Crews
was concerned about people thinking she was a voodoo doctor, she
did nothing to downplay the image. There were primitive masks and
fetishes and other Third World souvenirs from her global travels on
display among countless volumes of books. Earthenware jars exuded
pleasant fragrances that offset the smell of those anxious white rats
and hop-head monkeys.

From where Elizabeth sat in a chair catercorner to Dr. Crews's
desk, she could see through the open door across the hall into the
lab. As the discussion turned to her personal and career goals,
Elizabeth's eyes wandered. She found herself drawn to the distant vision of a student posed at a lab bench. It was her Big Sister's roommate, the enigmatic Pip Collier.

If Pip sensed that she was being observed, she did not acknowledge it, but went about her tutorial business with vivid concentration. At one point she carried a little white rat into Elizabeth's visual
range and proceeded to give it an injection. Within seconds the creature went limp in her hands. She stroked it absently before returning
it to its cage. Back at the lab bench, she peeled off her latex gloves,
washed her hands in the sink, dried off and then stretched her rangy

length in a yawn reaching toward the dropped ceiling. Her white T-shirt came untucked. She pulled on her jean jacket and lit a cigarette before scooping up a pile of textbooks and heading toward the door.

When Elizabeth turned back to Dr. Crews she found herself being scrutinized with a disturbing intensity and felt embarrassed to have been caught not paying attention. She was about to apologize when Pip appeared in a puff of smoke at Dr. Crews's door, looking either haughty or sultry.

"Excuse me, Dr. Crews . . ." Pip started, with a surprising formality considering that she was Dr. Crews's protégé.

Elizabeth assumed that Pip's stiffness stemmed from some aversion she had to being in the presence of a little dink such as herself. Especially when she seemed to recall her surname as an afterthought.

"Breedlove, right?"

Elizabeth caught a curiously private eye exchange between Pip and her mentor, sensing some amusement at her own expense, a payback, perhaps, for that Dickensian crack about Miss Havisham when she first met Pip. Elizabeth was accustomed to being teased about her surname, but not by someone as plainly self-contained as this senior. It was especially difficult to contemplate the subtext in the midst of all these tribal masks. When Dr. Crews and Pip both looked at her, Elizabeth felt like the cornered quarry of Jungian headhunters. In rare moments of shyness such as this, she averted her eyes and found herself studying a feathered and rather phallic artifact on a nearby shelf, wondering if it was a dingus.

Pip stood curtly talking shop with Dr. Crews for a moment, attempting to schedule a tutorial meeting. Then she surprised Elizabeth by addressing her directly again. "By the way," she said, craning her graceful neck in order to look down upon the frosh, "Dusie told me that you were too nice to say no when she asked you to volunteer for my tutorial experiment."

Elizabeth smiled sheepishly, "Yeah, well," trying to think of something clever to say, but no such luck.

So Pip said, "Well. Thanks, Breedlove. I appreciate it."

And Dr. Crews interjected, "How is Dusie?" before Elizabeth could ask Pip what she really wanted to ask, which was: What is your tutorial about anyway? And then she completely forgot her question as she glimpsed on the side of Pip's neck what appeared to be a scratch that had bled not long ago. A lab rat attack perhaps?

As if Pip could sense the focus of Elizabeth's furtive scrutiny, she turned up her floppy denim collar, though offhandedly. Elizabeth felt strangely pleased at the prospect that her own observant eye had made this serene senior uneasy. Intrigued by the deep scratch, Elizabeth was wondering: fingernails, foil, or fangs? Maybe fangs. She shuddered inwardly imagining fangs. From across the hall she heard the resentful rattle of a captive. Something around here was passing strange. It was making Elizabeth shaky. Or else she had been drinking too much coffee. Was it a gnawing or a throbbing in her gut? Lunchtime?

"Actually," Pip continued her cagey conversation with Dr. Crews, "Dusie hasn't been feeling very well."

"Oh, I'm sorry to hear that. Is there anything I can do?"

There was a long pause as they appeared to be in a headlock amidst the masks.

Pip won. "I think you should give her a call," she said.

And Dr. Crews pondered that suggestion for a moment before answering, "Why don't I just stop by? I could stop by Fey House tonight. After dinner." It was not appropriate for a teacher to visit a student's room, but meeting downstairs in the parlor was fine.

"Good idea," Pip said, primed to make her exit. "Thanks."

Dr. Crews called after her, "I'll see you tonight then."

But Pip pivoted in the distance, shaking her head. "Actually no. I'm going out," before walking off in her exquisitely broken-in Dingo boots. Elizabeth figured it would take a decade to get the leather that supple.

Dr. Crews's regulation outstanding WCW jaw seemed to compress somewhat, as if she were chewing down some choice words bespeaking tutorial irritation, but then she turned back to Elizabeth, resuming her role as adviser.

She's a cool one, Elizabeth thought. But not as cool as Pip. In fact they had been awfully cool to each other. Elizabeth could not fathom the seeming distance.

Unnerved by the ever-smiling composure of Dr. Crews, Elizabeth said something idiotic, "Dusie Hertz is my Big Sister," at the same time wanting to slap herself into a coma for being such a frosh.

# CHAPTER 5
## Shuttlecocks

After dinner Friday evening, the frosh dorms became electrified, all lit with the whir and buzz of simultaneous primping, as they plugged into hair-curling devices, blow-dryers and electric razors. The girls were going out. Collectively, they had accepted an invitation from the frat houses of Weston University to come down off that Willard high horse of Upper Alban Hill and party-hearty with the BMOC below. To spare the ladies the embarrassment and anxiety of public transportation, one of the frats was providing a shuttle service between the WCW and WU campuses, including complimentary cocktails and a well-packed bong for passing. These were the guys voted most likely to get laid.

What few straight-laced, self-righteous, goody-goody virgin dinks were still left after a couple of weeks in this seeming school for wayward women, all came to the same conclusion that night: Resistance was futile. Those who had been most sheltered from the common experiences and initiation rites of their peers, namely, sex and drugs and rock and roll, turned feral as bacchantes in a frenzy to make up for lost teen party time.

Elizabeth and Mary Constance were among the group delivered to frat row and then escorted, en masse, into the house of the shuttlecocks. Unfortunately, that party did not live up to its clever method of transportation. Elizabeth and Contrary opted to expedite a mass move to the next house, and they kept on moving, though their numbers dwindled, determined to find a gathering that actually had the right to call itself a party. But they would find themselves in the basement bar of still another frat, standing like everybody else on the edge of an empty dance floor, refusing to be a party to the crime against ears being perpetrated by a live band whose twiggy, tone-deaf frontman kept ordering them to "boogie."

"I hate that word."

"They're idiots."

"Saints preserve us . . ."

"Is it just me, or do all of these guys look like rabbits in pink polo shirts and loafers?"

"Ya got that right, sister."

And yet, eventually, Mary Constance could be seen rubbing up to one of them named Brian in the corner of the hutch, flirting like Thumper. Totally unworthy of her, in Elizabeth's opinion, but she kept this to herself. Even when Mary Constance asked what she thought of him outright as they were primping at the mirror in a dank little powder room, Elizabeth said quite honestly that she did not know him well enough to comment on his character.

"So you hate him."

Elizabeth just rolled her eyes as she glossed her lips with a little retractable Shiseido brush, pretending that the highly skilled process rendered her mute.

"Character? Bah. Who gives a damn about character? I'm not casting a play here, sister, I'm looking for nice buns. I think he's a hunk."

It was obvious that Elizabeth and Mary Constance were attracted to entirely different types, which was much more conducive to an enduring friendship.

"I take it you're gonna hang here for awhile?"

"Yeah, is that OK?"

"Of course, it's OK. Why wouldn't it be OK?" Elizabeth snickered: "We're not going steady."

Mary Constance gave her a playful smack upside the head and explained, "I hate to leave you stranded like this, that's all, you little dink. These are mean streets. You don't know your way around."

"I'll figure it out."

"Listen to me carefully, missy. There are pimps out there who prey on small-town innocents like you. If you end up walking the street in shiny hot pants, I'll never forgive myself."

Elizabeth promised Mary Constance she wouldn't talk to any pimps, wished her luck with the hunk, and left, resolved to live a frat-free life henceforth. She was on her way upstairs, headed for the nearest exit, when an exceedingly drunk lop rabbit in a rugby shirt—

a rebel—came thumping up the stairs behind her to announce that he had a waterbed.

"Really? Your parents must be so proud."

"Huh? Whadja say?"

"I was just leaving."

"Aw don't go."

She went, but again, he stopped her.

"Hey, you're a fox. Foxy lady . . ."

"And you're a rabbit. Rabbity guy . . ."

"Huh?"

"Goodnight then. Nice talking to you. Bye now."

"Hey wait up . . . gotta ask ya . . ."

"What?"

"Wanna screw?" He assumed this straightforward approach would be a real turn-on for any Willard woman, or as he put it in his native tongue: "Aren'tcha all wimenzslibbers?"

As she continued to ignore him, he grabbed her ass, trying to grope her. She was shocked. No one had ever handled her like that before. She doused him with beer from a super-sized paper cup, thinking that *ought* to cool him off, but knowing it would only incense him. And oh my—what a colorful variety of derogatory terms the college boys had reserved exclusively for Willard women. Rabbity guy's cheeks seemed about to go pop as he spewed the entire lexicon. But by then, several of his frat brothers had appeared suddenly to subdue him.

"He's sorry," said one of the brothers, calling up to her, affecting a contrite and knowing cuteness, which was the only reason she gave him pause from the top of the stairs, "You're sorry, aren't you, Wayne?"

The two other brothers who were restraining Wayne joined in: "Say you're sorry, man."

"Yeah, Wayne, apologize."

Wayne said he was sorry, belched, and then promptly passed out. Cute guy let him drop in order to bound up the steps in pursuit of Elizabeth, and then puppied along with her for several blocks until he had permission to call her sometime.

It was a classic September night, not even half past ten, and there were lots of college kids out and about as she crossed the campus of Weston U, headed uphill toward the neighboring campus of Weston

Academy of Fine Arts. When she arrived there, she asked the first student she saw to kindly point her in the direction of the student union, hoping to get a refreshing beverage and just take in the scene. Setting off across a darkened section of the grassy campus quad beyond the range of various outdoor lights, spots and floods, her eyes were directed upward and so she jumped with fright when she felt a soft bump underfoot and heard a growl, followed by an exclamatory: "What the f . . . ?"

"Whoa . . . oops . . ."

"Hey. Ow!"

"Sorry . . ."

"You stepped on my head . . ."

"Oh jeez . . ."

The resonance of his voice was more startling even than the sight of him rising up from the ground like a stage apparition from a trapdoor, this raven-haired lunatic prophet set to upbraid the idiot populace, entered railing, on a roll. It pissed him off to be stepped on, naturally, but as he sat up hunkered on the heels of his black proletarian boots, and rubbed the cobwebs from his inky eyes, he got a better look at her.

"What's this? What's this?" he asked, laughing easily: "Where the hell did you come from?"

His name was Reuben Shockor.

"Shockor, that's right, as in *electric shock*. Not a stage name. Nope. Reuben Shockor. My Hebrew name is Ribs." He stuck out his ribs.

He made her laugh.

"You're an actor."

"Performance artist."

"What's that?"

"I don't know yet. I'm still inventing it. Self-designed major."

He was a junior at WAFA, and a deejay for the campus radio station in the basement of the student union. He pointed to the transmitter on the roof of the four-story building. He liked to take a nap sometimes on the quad before his show, which aired from midnight to four A.M. This was the first time anyone had ever stepped on his head.

"You've got a good giggle," he said.

"I *need* a good giggle," she replied.

He stood up suddenly, brushing grass off the baggy, black gabardine trousers he bought for fifty cents at the Salvation Army store, along with the rest of his Cold War, film noir clothes. Black and white. His entire wardrobe.

"Come on, kid," he said, offering his hand like a gentleman, "I could use a good giggle in my opening monologue."

She followed him into the student union and down into the basement studio. As he cued records and cassettes for his show he kept her supremely entertained with his relentlessly antic disposition. The depth of his voice all but compensated for his lack of heft.

Over the weeks, she saw a lot of Reuben Shockor, usually in the middle of the night. He was too overwhelming a presence for Elizabeth's dorm room because he liked to sing and dance to loud music at all hours, so they spent most of their time together at his place. He lived in the little attic room of a co-op on the WAFA campus. She would sit with him at the studio through his radio show, supplying the occasional wicked giggle on cue, and then they would go to his room and engage in highly provocative but ultimately unsatisfying sex—at least for her—though she enjoyed every maddening minute of it. Between his intellectual hostility and her intellectual frustration it was a wonder they put up with each other for as long as they did. He made fun of her provincial background and she pushed him out of bed. They seemed to spend a lot of time rolling around on floors.

"I feel like I'm in a Lindsay Anderson movie," he said, referring to the cult classic *If*, about a British boy's school that inadvertently breeds terrorists. "Call me Travis."

Then he would be charming and cuddlesome, which made it so much easier for her to dismiss her frustration. And he would read her a bedtime story.

If it was Sunday, they stayed in bed all day, and then she would make her way, weak-kneed and disoriented, back to WCW, walking up through the residential neighborhood of Alban Hill. For all of his anti-heroic posturing and smart-mouth rebelliousness, Reuben was something of a closet gentleman. If it was getting dark, he would escort Elizabeth back to the campus himself. When they parted, they never made plans to see each other again. They just kissed on some cobblestone street corner in front of some old mansion lined with scratchy shrubbery until the residents got nervous or a car came along.

While Elizabeth had no desire to see Reuben more often than she did, she got into the habit of falling asleep to his radio show when

she was alone in her own dorm room, deriving some sort of entertainment from the prospect of waking up in the middle of the night
hearing his voice and not knowing at first whether he was on the
radio or in her bed. She heard the murmuring tremolo of his intro-
duction, "The incredible, but not totally inhuman, Reuben Shockor,
boys and girls . . ." over a crackly forties recording from *The Wizard
of Oz,* "Ha ha ha. Ho ho ho, and a couple of tra la las . . ." before a
segue into the Lou Reed song "Vicious," which he dedicated to "a
certain Willard girl . . . You know who you are . . ."

It occurred to Elizabeth that she might come to prefer Reuben's
presence on the air to his appearance in the flesh. It was easier to get
along with his artful abstraction.

"Sorry I wasn't sexually superlative," Reuben japed, kissing her
sweetly at the door one night, after a surprise guest appearance several hours before his show. "Ta," he said, with a ticklish wave, mocking the more effete WAFA drama twits, and then off he went to work.
Leaving her in the usual clench and dampened sheets, telling herself
to just go to sleep. But after midnight, no such luck, she heard the
telltale bestirring below. Payback, she imagined, for subjecting them
to three-and-a-half hours of Reuben routines.

She tuned him in on the receiver in stereo. His sonorous musings
almost obscured the mystery show of erotic disquietude coming from
down under. Oh those girls. What *did* they do to wrest such sounds
of pleasure? And for so long, too. At first, an easy flow of murmuring
intimacy, conversational sense of movement in equipoise among pillows, a give-me take-me kind of shifting, but then increasing urgency,
some kind of struggle, in hellfire almost unbearable, tossing off the
sheets. The sustained breathlessness, caresses of yeses or pedal
pumping staccato notes: "No, no, oh no, oh please, oh . . . no . . ."
that seemed to beg for what it regrets. At last, the pleas to deities, the
"Oh Gods," and gasping promises of things to come. Simultaneously?

Shuddering, solus, in silence, Elizabeth would sink deeper into
such dreams.

Pip, on the other hand, would be pacing, having left Dusie snoozing,
curled around an infantile stuffed animal, her lamb named Lambikins.
Pip felt her own disgrace acutely. She lit a cigarette and stepped outside, cloaked in an absorbant robe. She leaned on the railing, looking
out over the darkened back yard for the longest time, experiencing instead of the afterglow, a tenebrific reverie. Her fair skin reflected whatever moonlight made it down between the knees of the trees.

# CHAPTER 6
# Tutorial Experiment

The experimental part of Pip's tutorial called for sixty women between the ages of eighteen and twenty-two to be subjected every seven days to consecutive months of tests monitoring thresholds of pain, aggression and frustration. One involved having a finger wired by electrodes to a potentiometer measuring a mild electric shock. Any mention of the mechanics surrounding the experiment made it difficult to recruit volunteers, particularly upperclasswomen who had grown wise to those "psych weirdos who get off on zapping things."

Elizabeth was scheduled to report to the psych lab every Wednesday afternoon at three o'clock. Dusie, who was to administer the tests, was late for their first session, so Elizabeth took a seat on a bench, the sole audience to a whole lot of rats and monkeys. The air was stuffy with the straw they wet in their downed-out aloneness.

Dusie showed up ten minutes later, carrying a duffel bag and an armful of textbooks, which she dropped on the bench next to Elizabeth, babbling apologetically, "Sorry I'm late, little sister," before she stopped and looked over Elizabeth's shoulder, "Hey! That's neat! I didn't know you could draw."

Elizabeth had been absently sketching lab animal portraits on the cover of her notebook, giving them empathetically human expressions. One of the monkeys bore a distinct resemblance to Dusie that Dusie, herself, could not see.

"Is that, like, a cartoon?"

Elizabeth looked up, only slightly annoyed to be kept waiting because Dusie was so easy to forgive. Elizabeth had a hard time trying to reconcile the image of this effervescent daytime Dusie with the leaden late-night Dusie she sometimes overheard. If Dusie was sick or unhappy, it was not immediately apparent. She talked Dusie-maroonie effusively as she unsnapped her denim jacket and peeled it off, like she was on the runway, tossing it to the heap of her belongings. She was wearing a long-sleeved black leotard. "Come on in to the cube . . ." she giggled, playing (badly) at being a ghoul as she led Elizabeth into a cubicle down the hall and shut the door.

In the center of the cube was a small wooden table with two chairs. On the table were a couple of gizmos which looked about as scientific as instruments of torture in a porno pictorial meant to get the captive bunnies to spill their craws.

But first!—a questionnaire.

They took their seats at the table. Dusie put a pen to a clipboard.

"This is in the strictest confidence, OK? We use numbers instead of names, and I'm the only one who knows your number, OK? And, like, I am totally sworn on the honor code not to repeat anything I hear, OK?"

"OK."

"OK, so you're twenty-two."

"Eighteen."

"No, not your age, that's your code number: twenty-two."

"Oh," Elizabeth smiled, feeling vaguely charmed by memories of junior high school slumber parties where she and her chums would stay up all night giving each other sex quizzes from fashion magazines.

"OK. Ready *twenty-two?*"

"Ready."

Dusie scanned a line, and then looked up, pen poised. "Age?"

And there was every reason to believe from her facial expression that she was not kidding. She went on for a couple of pages asking Elizabeth a lot of questions meant to determine if her sexual experiences jibed with her sexual attitudes. At one point she asked, "Are you a virgin?"

"Are you kidding?"

"At what age did you lose your virginity?"

"Five."

"Five?"

Elizabeth told her about a little accident she had had at the age of five involving an icy gym set and a slippery pair of cowboy boots. She had lost her footing and come down hard on a horizontal bar tearing some flesh despite the cushion of snow pants.

"I lost my virginity to a jungle gym," she said. "Fifteen stitches."

"Hoo-boy," Dusie winced. "But when did you lose your virginity really, I mean, to a guy?"

Elizabeth told her.

"OK, now, this is a tough one for most people and you don't have to answer if you don't want. But . . . have you ever had a homosexual experience?"

Elizabeth bounced a blink back and forth with Dusie a couple of times before asking, "Mind if I smoke?"

"No. Not at all. Go ahead. Fine."

As she fired up a cigarette, she muttered, "To tell you the truth, Dusie, I'm not sure what that means exactly."

"Seriously?"

She shrugged.

"Oh. OK. Well. Um, hey could I bum one of those?"

Elizabeth gave her a cigarette, and when she extended her hand again to offer Dusie a light, Dusie took hold of her wrist and held it languorously until her cigarette was more than sufficiently lit. Elizabeth wondered aloud if this qualified as a homosexual experience.

Dusie laughed ha ha and sat back adjusting the brim of her newsboy cap real kai-kai-like. Her prince was a long way off, you know? So why not? Still, there had been a tremulousness to her touch that seemed more the symptom of illness than seductiveness. Elizabeth could not help but think of her in the context of that mysterious passion after midnight.

"Where were we?"

"Homosexual experience."

"Oh yeah. Um. Did you ever like, you know, kiss a woman?"

"Sure."

"With your tongue?"

"Is that really the question?"

"Nope. Just kidding."

"Yeah, well . . ."

"So what's the answer?"

Elizabeth told her.

Dusie put her pen to the clipboard and scribbled down a notation before scanning the page. She looked up momentarily to ask, "Have you ever been raped, Elizabeth?" And there was something very innocent about her then, as she was watching Elizabeth's face. "Well?"

In a moment, Elizabeth mumbled, "I dunno. Maybe."

"Maybe? I don't think rape can be a maybe."

Elizabeth shrugged. "Probably not, but . . . Well, I learned at an early age that the power a woman has over a man is to accept him or reject him."

Dusie nodded, snapping her gum. "You got that right, sister."

"But rejection only works if it's accepted, right? I mean, if he doesn't take no for an answer, and he has it in him to beat you up, then . . ."

"Then you're fucked," Dusie concluded.

"Yes, well . . ."

"Tell me about it."

"I'd rather not."

"Please?"

Elizabeth sighed, thinking Dusie's earnest curiosity was difficult to resist. She was surprised, herself, when she spilled her craw.

The first time it happened, Elizabeth had been out carousing with a group of friends she had known since childhood. They had been drinking at their favorite country bar. She told her old buddy, Fred, that she felt sick and asked him to drive her home, without fully realizing that he was almost as drunk as she was. When she started throwing up in the parking lot, he led her back to a more secluded spot, speaking to her in a soothing tone, and holding her hair out of her face. She was too sick and delirious to sense, and least of all to believe, that this guy she had known for years, purely as a friend and with no sexual subtext whatsoever, would suddenly push her to the ground and force her to have sex with him while she was throwing up. She struggled in vain, gagging and gasping to breathe beneath his 6 feet, 3 inches, 220-pound star fullback frame. The whole time—and it was probably less than two minutes—he spoke to her in the same friendly voice.

"The scary part," Elizabeth said, "was that I really think he believed this was consensual and even *good* sex. Lucky for me he was so drunk he couldn't really get it up, but he kept slamming at me anyway, and missing—thank God, because he came all over my leg and then he told me that he loved me."

"You're kidding me."

Elizabeth shook her head. "He just got up and fastened his pants and stumbled back into the bar. I never told anybody. And I'll bet you a million dollars, he doesn't even remember what he did to me that night because he was so fucked up."

"That's how it happens."

"Yeah, and I mostly blame myself. I never should've lost control like that. Alcohol, man. It's the worst."

"You said it, sister."

The next time, she was kidnapped by an acquaintance named Hansen. Ironically, he had always been like her bodyguard at the clubs when some goon was bothering her. Instead of driving her home from a dance club as promised one night, he took her to his family's cabin on the beach. It was frigid wintertime and so off-season there was no one around. He locked her in a bedroom for five hours, believing this to be a sure-fire way of winning her heart. He told her how hurt he was that she had been going out with this other guy named Zach, whom Hansen considered his best friend.

"He was doing acid, tripping his brains out. Very weird talk, telling these strange jokes that weren't funny. This misogynist and racist stuff that didn't connect to anything else, really disturbing. And then he pulled a rifle out of a closet and pointed it at my face."

Dusie appeared astounded.

"I'll never know if it was loaded or not. It took me hours to convince him that he should put the rifle down. I had to play 'sweet,' you know, how girls have to be . . . And then it took me until dawn to talk him out of molesting me because he saw my 'sweetness' as a come-on, yeah, right, and he kept trying to touch me in these really creepy, coy ways. I felt terrified by him, but I couldn't let him know that."

Elizabeth shuddered to remember it so vividly. Hansen had put the key to the door in his front pocket and invited her to come and get it. Eventually she was able to persuade him that she really cared about him as a friend and that she feared for his life if their mutual friend, Zach, whom she had been dating, found out about this.

He released her unharmed just before dawn. When she got home her parents were waiting up for her. She believed it would only extend the nightmare to tell her parents what had happened. She was grounded for a month. Hansen heard about her sentence and sent her a dozen roses with a note saying he was so sorry he could die. But she never spoke to him, or even looked at him, again. And surprisingly enough, he accepted the banishment with a certain humbleness and discretion, partly fearing the wrath of his friend, Zach, as well as Elizabeth's memory.

"Didn't you tell *anybody?*"

"What's the point?"

Elizabeth was taken aback to see Dusie's eyes tear up. "What's the matter?" she asked.

Dusie was cursing wetly, "That fucking bastard. They're all fucking bastards," trying to dry her face on her leotard sleeve, but not having much success, as the material was water-repellent. Dusie excused herself momentarily and left the cube in order to get a tissue from the women's room down the hall. When she returned, she apologized profusely for her acute empathy.

But Elizabeth reassured her, "It's OK, ah, Dusie. I'm sorry for upsetting you. I don't know what got into me. I never talk about this stuff."

"I'm really glad you did, Elizabeth," Dusie sniffled. Aside from her emotionality, she felt honored that Elizabeth had seen fit to spill her craw right then, to her of all people.

Elizabeth, on the other hand, was feeling mortified that she had revealed so much. The popular notion that "talking about it" always makes a person feel better afterward, like the purging effect of intestinal distress, was nonsense as far as Elizabeth was concerned. She felt much worse for her confessional lapse. She believed she could control her traumatic experiences simply by not telling anyone about them.

It was in this frame of mind that Elizabeth submitted to the electric shock part of Pip's tutorial experiment. Dusie reached for the potentiometer. She asked for Elizabeth's right hand in order to strap electrodes to her palm and middle finger. As Dusie was gazing absently at Elizabeth's palm, she got a strange look in her face that compelled Elizabeth to ask, "What's wrong?"

"Your love-line."

"Love-line?" She had heard of a "lifeline," but never a love-line. "What about it?"

"It's just like Pip's."

"That's not possible. No two wrinkles are exactly alike."

"But it is," she said with a child's sort of combativeness, the abrupt force of which made Elizabeth uncomfortable. "Your hand is exactly like Pip's. Look," she pointed fatuously. "See, you've got this line going down that way, and this one curling up kinda in the corner over there . . . Hey, did you ever fence?"

"Fence? No."

"You should try it. I'll bet you'd be a natural just like . . ."

"Pip. Yeah. I know. Could we just get on with this?"

Dusie hopped to it, babbling, ". . . and then I'm going to turn this little dial here, up a little bit each time from one to ten, see, and you tell me when you just can't take it anymore, OK?"

Elizabeth felt like she was being set up for some science fair exhibit on sadomasochism.

"OK. Ready?"

"I guess."

"Here goes."

The first shock was the dullest tingling sensation, not much more than a hum passing through the finger and the palm, warming up the forearm, making the finger twitch a bit. In fact, the voltage increased on the dial to five before Elizabeth felt any discomfort. Still she sat placidly by, gazing at Dusie, who was, herself, more excited by the electricity, fidgeting half out of her seat in her disbelief. She was turning up the dial to levels no other subject had withstood, and Elizabeth barely blinked.

"I can't believe it!" Dusie screeched, "You're up to seven!"

It had the sting of a Joy Buzzer.

"Eight!"

It was starting to ache.

"Nine!"

Really ache.

"Nine and a *half!*"

And then pain.

"T . . ."

"Stop."

"This is incredible! Incredible! You almost made it to ten! You almost made it to the top! The average is three! Three, Elizabeth! Jeezus! The best Pip can do is eight! She's not gonna believe this!"

"I thought this was confidential."

"Well I won't tell her *who*, but jeez, Elizabeth, er number twenty-two, you're a tough little fucker!"

Elizabeth shook her head, "I'm not tough, Dusie. I can't stand the feeling anymore than anyone else. It's just that I—I dunno—I guess I have a way of turning it off."

"How do you do that?"

Elizabeth shrugged, "I just think about something else."

"Like what?"

She had been thinking about the strange sounds emanating through her floor at night, thinking about how she had to turn those off, to think about something else.

"Like what, Elizabeth? What were you thinking about when you were getting zapped?"

Elizabeth acted quickly to redirect the attention away from herself, which was another talent of hers. "You and Pip fight a lot, don't you?"

"No we don't," was Dusie's snappish retort.

"But I can hear you. At night. You fight."

"We don't, I'm tellin' ya. You're wrong. Pip never fights. She refuses to fight. She's too *above* all that." She had meant to say "superior," but she remembered just then that she was supposed to be conducting a tutorial experiment. "But what am I doing here talking about these things? I just feel like I know you or something. I mean, that's good, isn't it?"

"Sure," said Elizabeth more insouciantly than ever, wanting nothing more than to change the subject, even though she, herself, had brought it up. "So. What's next?"

"We call it The Nerves of Steel test."

It was an upright stand made of wood and metal about a foot tall, like a miniature guillotine with its blade raised to the crossbeam and punctured with three perfect holes of graduating sizes from an eighth of an inch in diameter. The subject was to place the nib of a penlike instrument into each of the holes without resting her elbow or in any other way supporting her arm or hand. She was to hold the point steady for as long as she could without touching it to the edge. If the nib came in contact with the circumference, it would make a zapping sound, no shock, just a zap. It was an interesting thing for Elizabeth to discover the extent of her own tremulousness since she had always fancied herself a paradigm of steadiness. She was quickly zapped.

"Damn," she said, smacking her convulsive forearm down on the table.

"This is Pip's best event," Dusie beamed proudly. "She's got the record. Fifteen seconds."

"That's impossible."

"Nope, you don't understand. She's like a rock, man. Nothing shakes her." She said this with a certain bitterness Elizabeth pretended not to notice as she was cueing up her arm again, putting the tip to the tiniest spot, but a micropuncture with the nerve power of ten, steadily, steadily, licking her lower lip.

She got zapped within seconds, and wrenched against her compulsion to throw the pen.

# CHAPTER 7
# Climbing Ivy

They were three hours into a poker game at Whitman in Contrary's room. That gamester had just raised the pot sky high by tossing in a couple of joints when Elizabeth called her bluff in a game called "Guts." Trish, Fidel, Helen, Vivian, and Gracie had all folded, and it was "down and dirty from now on," according to Contrary.

"Show me what you've got, sister."

And when Elizabeth did, Contrary frowned, "Jesus, Mary and Joseph," before throwing her own hand face down.

As Elizabeth was raking in the pot, there was a knock on the door.

Contrary bellowed, "Whaddaya want?" and they all recognized a frosh named Peevie Johnson whining from the other side. "Phone call for Breedlove."

"Who is it?"

"Security."

"Security?" They laughed collectively, even as they were passing around a joint.

"Is this a bust or what?" Contrary asked, inviting Peevie into the smoky room. Peevie looked unmistakably disgusted with them all, fanning her face with her hand, before telling Elizabeth, "Security caught some guy climbing the ivy to your window."

The announcement triggered absolute hilarity. "Aye," Contrary bellowed in her best Dr. Brockian brogue, "Climbing the ivy was 'e? A regular Romeo!"

Peevie persisted despite the roar of the crowd. "They've got him at the front desk of Fey House. If you don't vouch for him, they're going to turn him over to the city police."

Contrary and her entourage pealed at the sound of that, although she was not too distracted to remember that Elizabeth, The Queen, possessed the largest pot at that moment, and so bid her "to return anon." Elizabeth said that she would. Still, she pocketed the joints.

Contrary gave her the Tudor eye—the one that saw so many queens beheaded for High Treason—before returning to the game at hand, yelling, "Feed the kitty, you mangy cats!"

Elizabeth was acutely aware that she was being dismissed and she did not like the toady feel of it.

She took the shortcut to Fey House through the Japanese maples around the pond, feeling uneasy about Contrary's way of playing games. When she arrived at Fey House, she heard Reuben's voice, as she was coming through the door, before she spotted him. He was standing at the front desk entertaining two rather bemused looking security guards, and a small crowd of residents who had gathered. He beamed at her like Cary Grant, "Ah, there you are my dear, Miss Breedlove. How good of you to come. Would you tell these gentlemen *who* I am, darling?"

Elizabeth blinked for a while at him blankly as if she could not recall. WCW's own Chief of Security, Peter Pierson, stepped in front of Reuben to ask Elizabeth, "Do you know this guy?"

She looked from Chief Peter to Reuben back to Chief Peter as Reuben raised his finger at her and this time his model was Jesus. "Three times you will deny me, my dear. Don't deny it."

And somebody in the crowd giggled.

Chief Peter was impatient. "Look, Miss, if you don't know this guy we've got him for trespassing, attempted burglary . . ."

"Burglary?! Now see here my good man . . ."

There was an outburst from the crowd. A protest was raised on behalf of Reuben's civil rights, or some such, and he received it with smug gratitude. But Security was not moved. And it delighted Elizabeth to perceive in Reuben a certain dread that she might deny him. He sought her eye more privately. She smiled politely. He smiled back. He raised his finger again, musing aloud on the quality of mercy, " '*It droppeth as the gentle rain,*' I read that once above a urinal."

Until Elizabeth said, "Your face does seem familiar," just to make him shut up. "Come on, Shockor," she said, expecting him to follow, which he did at that point, pretending to be contrite and thanking his audience as they dispersed. Turning the corner on the landing up the stairs and out of sight, Reuben grabbed her and she spun around defensively, "Hey."

So he mocked her, "Hey."

"I don't talk that way."

"Sure you do."

"No, I don't."

"Yes, you do."

Within seconds they were tumbling and wrassling up the remaining steps coming down with a thud onto the mustardseed carpeting of the second floor which was scratchy, she complained, but could not contain her giggles as he nuzzled and teased and tickled.

"So. You would deny me, you snotty little *shiksa goddess.*"

Suddenly, the door to Fey Ray's room swung open and Pip stepped out pulling on her denim jacket. Elizabeth found herself staring down the vamp of a worn pair of Dingo boots.

"Hello, Breedlove."

Elizabeth smiled sheepishly, shimmying out of Reuben's grip and rising to her feet, hoping to reclaim some semblance of dignity. But no such luck. By the time she found her footing, Pip had already disappeared around the first landing of the staircase, and Reuben was warbling some Disney cartoon take on Wagner, like Elmer Fudd, "Oh, Bwoon-hilda you're so wuv-wee . . . What's she majoring in? Aryan domination?"

"Reuben, do you *ever* shut up?"

But he had bounced to attention and taken her arm determined to rush her along up the last flight of steps. Once inside her room, he led her more ferociously to her bed with a kiss.

"Reuben?"

"Elizabeth."

"I'm in the middle of a poker game."

"Is that what you think this is?"

"At Whitman. I have to go back."

"No you don't."

"Yes I do."

"Nope."

"*Yes.* Who the hell are you, telling me what to do?"

He sighed hotly into her neck and stood up from the bed with his long white shirttails untucked under his jacket, cotton collar bleached in stark contrast to thick coils of black hair. She anticipated his hostility for pushing her off, but ever unpredictable, Shockor backed off, smiling nicely, pulling a notebook from his battered canvas knapsack and taking a seat at her desk, like a good little squirt.

"You just run along now," he said, "I'll be fine. I've got a philosophy paper due tomorrow."

"Oh?"

"Yes. That's correct. I have to prove the existence of God through rational argument—and I lost His phone number—so it's going to be a long night. Come, come, give us a kiss."

Any sweetness in Reuben (before sex) aroused her suspicion and little else. He pulled her down onto his lap so that she couldn't help straddling him in the chair. Within seconds he was instigating some conflict to heighten the impact of his lust, teasing her with some fantasy wherein she was the *shiksa goddess* who was taboo to him.

But he couldn't help himself.

She did not appreciate the pejorative *shiksa* (though *goddess* didn't bother her) but she didn't know how to tell him this. She was too polite to counter his intimidation with anything other than aloofness, being averse to teasing him, in kind.

"That's right, Shockor, I'm the forbidden fruit. And ouch, you're bruising me."

"You're a smart girl, you know, with great tits and a *massive* ego problem," he insisted, gnawing on her while yanking at the buttons on her shirt, "but your attractiveness makes up for everything."

"Fuck you."

He put his teeth to her breast. She got a fistful of his hair. He lifted her roughly from the chair. They fell together on the bed. She was thinking *here we go again* even though she felt highly responsive. There was that promising level of physical and theatrical thrill, as ever, but she was left all knotted up and tight-fisted and shut down behind a nice little ladylike smile.

"You're really a sweet kid, you know that?"

"Don't ever say that."

"You're sweet. You are."

"Don't be nice to me now, Shockor. I despise you."

"You despise me? She despises me!" He played the abject lover biting on his own knuckles before he segued abruptly, "Let's order out for pizza. What's the number for Antonini's?"

She didn't make it back to Whitman Hall that night to rejoin the poker game, being too busy swallowing her frustration in the face of some artistic genius. She had the most fitful night staring in the dark at a gutted pizza box in the moonlight—some romance—aching with restlessness, while Reuben slept, curled and clawed his way deeper into Rockland.

She found out the next morning that she had lost the bulk of her poker winnings according to some rule invented (of course) by Contrary, stating that the player who leaves the game for more than an hour without telephoning herself officially out must forfeit her "chips" to the pot.

"That's ridiculous," said Elizabeth.

"What are you complaining about? You took off with a fair share of 'chips' last night. So what?"

She didn't know so what. She said nothing. She was not surprised to hear that it was Contrary who had pocketed the pot. Elizabeth mollified herself by assuming that her friend would not cheat her out of her winnings unless she was really needy. And if her friend was really needy, then certainly Elizabeth could overlook some trifling financial loss.

"Boy, you're in a mood," said Contrary, putting her arm around her as they were walking to class. "What's the matter, sister? Premature ejaculators gettin' ya down? What are you doing wasting your time with those Jewish intellectual types? He doesn't even come from money. Right?"

"Contrary . . ."

"Yes?"

But Elizabeth could not bring herself to say it. They parted soon after, coming to a fork in the sidewalk, each in her own unmistakable smiley snit and, according to Dr. Brock's method: very politely.

They met up with each other again before lunch in Dr. Maddocks's expository writing class where they sat in their usual seats in the back by the windows. Twenty minutes into Dr. Maddocks's lecture on euphemisms and specialized diction, Contrary slipped Elizabeth a note, just like junior high school.

Elizabeth waited until Dr. Maddocks turned around to face the blackboard again before she read it. "Dear Elizabeth," it said, "Are you mad at me? Circle one: yes or no."

Elizabeth circled both, refolded the note into a tinier missile and launched it. It dropped onto Contrary's desk. Dr. Maddocks turned around to face the class, glancing at Miss McNaught and Miss Breedlove who were smiling back at him cherubically. He knew full well that they called his class "suppository writing," yet he regarded them more with curiosity than annoyance. Annoyance, to him, was reserved for Dusie Hertz, who sat in the front row fidgeting in her tight clothes when she wasn't babbling some dim-bulb nonsense in response to his lecture. He did his best to stifle the Dusie digressions, but sometimes she really tried his patience, not to mention that of his class. Especially when she was hunkered in her chair, leaning forward on her desk with her chin on her elbows. Half the class would be watching her derriere, wondering at its perfection and love-hating her for it, while the other half would be snickering at her dumbfounding observations. And Dr. Maddocks would be doubly exasperated somewhere in between. He could not think of the last time a student had been so beyond his control who was not also brilliant.

# CHAPTER 8
# Captain Blood

One afternoon Elizabeth became so aggravated by the Nerves of Steel event in Pip's tutorial that she toppled the device, accidentally, during a rare display of explosive temper. She had a long fuse, she explained with effusive apologies, but when she reached the end of it—run for your lives. Dusie remained calm throughout. She was, after all, on the job.

Elizabeth blamed her own hypersensitivity on claustrophobia here in the cube, which Dusie then duly noted on her clipboard.

"Closet-phobia. Hm. OK. How do you spell that?"

You had to love her. Like a sister, which Elizabeth did, quite literally, because her youngest sister, Z, also had a wide-eyed way with words.

"Boy, you are, like, just really giving off a lot of negative vibes right now, Elizabeth. You should eat more yogurt."

"I don't eat *any* yogurt, Dues. I hate yogurt."

"But have you tried the frozen, yet? It's yummy."

Dusie was referring to the machine recently installed in the cafeteria, dispensing frozen yogurt, which everyone assumed was a nutritious and nonfattening alternative to real ice cream. They called it "health food," a revolutionary new way to eat. The more they ate the healthier they would get. Or so they told themselves as they lined up for seconds. The little dinks, in particular, had yet to learn that college was fattening. They could expect an average weight gain of ten pounds in the first trimester.

"Well, ya gotta do sumthin' to get rid of those babe vibes, man."

"Babe vibes?"

"Huh?"

"You said *babe* vibes."

"I did? Oh, I meant bad vibes, but y'know, jeez, man, 'babe vibes.' Far out. Is that like one of those things?"

"A Freudian slip?"

"Yeah."

"I dunno. I think you better save that question for Pip. And that's F-R-E-U-D-I-A-N," she added, because she knew that would be the next question Dusie asked.

"Well, ya gotta do sumthin' to get rid of those vibes, man. Like how 'bout exercise? What d'ya do for your workout?"

"My workout? What's a workout?"

"Exercise, dumb bunny. Where did you come from anyway? Outer space?"

"You guessed it."

"A workout is like exercise . . ."

"But with more fashionable outfits."

"Oh, so you *do* know. You're such a little teaser."

"Must be the babe vibes."

Dusie giggled, but she returned to high seriousness: "You always do that. How come?"

"Do what?"

"Teasing, like jokin' around about everything."

"I dunno, Dues, maybe you should jot that down."

"See? See what I mean? You just did it again."

Dusie was on to something—not that her observation of Elizabeth's relentlessly defensive wit was profound or original, but simply that Dusie was the first person ever to ask her about it. Her open-faced and genuine concern made Elizabeth feel strangely compelled to spill her craw. For all of her Dizzy Miss Dusie behavior, she paid a lot more attention than most people when they were supposedly paying attention. Moreover, she had nothing at stake academically or intellectually in Elizabeth's world to find her intimidating. On a purely sentient level, Dusie was a veritable empath. Unknown to Dusie, she could have asked Elizabeth anything then and received the kind of straightforward, honest answer no one ever got. Dusie, however, remained fixated on fitness.

"'Cause I'm being serious here, little sister. I'm older, OK? And I'm a model, y'know, so I know these things."

"Dusie, you're a year older than me."

"Exactly. So I'm just warning ya. If you don't take good care of your body right now . . . like, *today,* even, don't come cryin' to me when you're, like, thirty, and your boobs are down to here."

"I understand and will obey. I read a lot of big books. Does that count as exercise?"

"Huh?"

"Big? Heavy? Carrying? Lifting? Like up and down on shelves?"

"Ohhhhh, OK . . . like pumpin' iron y'mean?"

"Yes, Dues, it is exactly like pumping iron."

"And that's how ya got, like, muscles in your legs, too, huh? Pretty amazing."

"No, none of the above. I'm telling you: the only exercise I ever get these days is from faking orgasms. Really *incredible* orgasms, too. And it's quite a workout, I assure you."

Dusie actually got that one. "I never did that," she said.

"You never faked an orgasm?"

"Nope."

"Wait a second here. Are you saying that you *always* have an orgasm when you have sex with somebody?"

"Oh no, no way. Is that what you thought?" Dusie guffawed, "Are you kidding? I never *ever* had an orgasm with a guy. Ugh. And a lot of girls aren't that great either, but at least you can make 'em get better. You can, like, show 'em, y'know? And they don't go all limp on ya, like, totally useless . . . But I never fake it. Uh-*uh*, no way. I got no problem tellin' 'em they can't do it for shit. Like, I go: 'Man, you can't do it for shit.' Just like that."

"And how do they react?"

"Ah, y'know guys, they always wanna go out again. Yeah, *you* know, right. You can kick 'em in the teeth and they keep comin' back."

"Yes, well . . ."

"Are you surprised I've been with guys? Me too. But, last year, when I got here I was kinda, I dunno, lonely 'cause, um, girl trouble y'know, and shit, especially here. Nobody would talk to me 'cause I was a model, so it was, like, I'm automatically stupid or something. Right? Women. Sometimes they're just so friggin' frigid . . . at first, anyway, it's hard to make 'em like you. But calling me kai-kai, y'know, 'cause I went out with some jerks 'cause the girls wouldn't pay any attention to me. And all I wanted was a girlfriend so bad, y'know? Sometimes I was with guys just by accident, being totally shit-faced. The blowaways. *You* know . . ."

"Blowaways?"

"Yeah, like, a blow job when you just wanna make 'em shut up and go away . . . leave me alone . . ."

The blowaway. The fake-out. The mercenary blowjob.

"Guys, jeez, they think it's like such a big deal, y'know, like you're so *into* them 'cause you put their dick in your mouth like, for two seconds. Big deal! They don't even get it: it's such a *put-down*, you're shutting 'em out, like, really saying, you can't touch me you dumb jerk, I'm not in your arms. You're not coming inside, so, just, like, go away, man. Blow away."

This time it was Elizabeth who said: "Wow." Dusie had her moments of vision.

"But, thank God for Pip, man, that woman saved me from those jag-offs. First time she kissed me? Wow, it was like . . . whoa, y'know? Nobody is ever gonna kiss you like Pip. Ask anybody."

"Really Dues, *anybody?*" Apparently Pip was a popular guest for spin-the-bottle.

"I like it that you call me that: 'Dues.' I'm used to Baby D."

"What does that mean, Baby D?"

Dusie laughed. "Well, the 'D' doesn't stand for Dusie, that's for sure.

"What then?"

"Babydyke."

"Oh."

"I got that from the models. When I first started modeling for Gimbels, the older girls used to call me 'Babydyke,' because I was always hitting on them. They couldn't believe I was only 15. Hey, I'm a flirt. What can I say?"

Dusie brightened like a camp counselor, "Hey, I know what you need. You need to work off that negativity. Come to fencing practice with me."

This was an invitation that Dusie extended every week. But today, for some reason, Elizabeth accepted.

"It's a great way to relieve tension," said Dusie, with no uncertain amount of glee at having successfully enticed Elizabeth into something.

"Yeah, right," was Elizabeth's reply, as they left the psych lab together walking to Fey House so that Elizabeth could pick up the appropriate gym clothes.

"Don't you believe me?" Dusie asked.

"Oh, I dunno. Fencing just strikes me as a sport meant to *increase* tension, not relieve it. That is, unless you actually *kill* somebody. And then, I guess, well, that would be a relief."

"Huh?" Dusie puzzled momentarily, but then she lost interest and skipped off the sidewalk down a grassy embankment toward the pond like the perfect schoolgirl in braids. Elizabeth followed, though without skipping.

"Isn't it wonderful!" Dusie cried, panting and pointing as she came to a rest on the edge of the pond to consider the koi fish. Some hyper-drive of happiness had overtaken her, which made Elizabeth wary. She sensed that the revelation of her own companionable side was the reason for Dusie's delight. Elizabeth looked around to see if anyone she knew had spotted her with this frolicking babydyke, relieved to see that the coast was clear. At the same time she was angry with herself that the thought would even occur to her. Was she really *that* insecure?

Onward and upward ho! climbing the hill to Fey House, Elizabeth was breathless from cigarettes because Dusie insisted on showing her a "secret" shortcut. Leaving all of civilization behind, they stepped off a lovely landscaped sidewalk into the wilds, straight up the cliffside bolstered by boulders the size of a truck, obscured by the overgrowth of moss and weeds, an impressive variety of ivy, and probably rattlesnakes indigenous to the area.

Dusie scolded Elizabeth for being so out of shape all the way up and into Fey House, then the staircase, and—merciful heaven!—into the master (or would that be mistress?) bedroom. Elizabeth collapsed into the nearest chair, while Dusie disappeared into the haunted closet to "scare up some whites," which evoked from Elizabeth a breathless laugh, assuming Dusie was making a ghostly Fey Ray joke when, in fact, "whites" was just the term for fencing clothes.

Eventually, Elizabeth recovered enough to growl: "Doesn't bode well for fencing, does it? I mean, if you also have to use your legs."

"Are you kidding, man? It's *all* legs," Dusie replied in earnest, bustling about the room, going through a chest of drawers Elizabeth suspected belonged to Pip, from which she withdrew a brand spanking new pair of white cotton athletic socks. One size fits all, Dusie reassured her, unless Elizabeth had freakishly small feet. "Hm . . ." Dusie cocked one eye as she gave professorial pause to observe Elizabeth's feet. Within seconds, from across the room, she ventured an educated guess.

"Seven."

"Damn!—You're good."

"I know!" said the perky wardrobe mistress of the master bedroom, skipping back into her closet.

Dusie was rummaging around in there talking about who knows what because her voice was muffled. Elizabeth recognized the sound of shoe boxes toppling to the floor, followed by a clack, clack, jangle, snap, crack!—dammit!—as Dusie stepped through a minefield of hard plastic retail store hangers. But then (uh-oh!) *"Whoa!"* cried Dusie, as something heavy dropped and rolled. Had she discovered the murder weapon? The bowling ball?

In the meantime, Elizabeth was, well, not so much snooping as taking a little stroll about the big room with the high ceiling, carved wainscoting and dark wood. Having become more familiar with the other college houses—houses? hell, who were they trying to kid? they were mansions—all along winding Deerborn Way, she could appreciate the striking difference in style. Fey House, in particular, stood out because there was nothing fussy or fancy about it, being relatively rustic, woodsy, with a kind of hunting lodge ambience and—dare she say it?—a masculine air. Not girlie.

"Girlie" was the word that came to mind when she found herself standing at Pip's dresser, surprised that her personal effects were pretty typical girl stuff. But then, what did she expect? A shaving kit? Jock strap? Dog tags? She slapped her idiot forehead. Her eyes were drawn then to an easily recognized bottle of perfume. Blue Grass. A classic, and with an atomizer yet. How girlie can a girl get? There was some sort of seal or official stamp of France, and the card of a store bragging about being from Paris. She also observed that the bottle had been placed like a paperweight on a little gift card. And—oops— it seemed to have popped open a bit, as she was admiring the bottle, to reveal a brief handwritten note—*damn*—in French.

She had had enough high school French to recognize a few words, but not enough that she wouldn't need to look them up later.

*Que faites-vous?*—something something *C'est pénible*—was it?—followed by—*Je suis puni pour*—something—and then *Je t'aime, ma chère*—signed only with an initial she could not identify.

But, my gosh, she thought, that was one lovesick French poodle. Did Pip have another girlfriend? Is that what she heard them fighting about all the time?

There was no offense in casually regarding the objects displayed on a woman's dresser, and girls had universal clearance to sample each other's perfume. She spritzed a little on her wrist and her eyes closed automatically, imagining a misty thicket; she replaced the bottle on the note exactly as she had found it, and glanced toward the closet to see a Frisbee come flying out the door.

When Dusie followed, she found Elizabeth studying one of several photographs Pip had prominently displayed, featuring a quartet of handsome guys.

"Pip's brothers," said Dusie.

"She has four brothers?"

"Yep. Best part is she's the baby."

"Pip has four older brothers?"

"Yep. How spoiled is that, huh?"

"She doesn't strike me as spoiled."

Dusie did a dry spit take.

They stopped by Elizabeth's room to pick up her white tennis shoes, T-shirt, and whatever stuff she had that was suitable for swordplay. Dusie caught a glimpse of Elizabeth's "wet bar."

"Whoa. Look at that. Cocktails. Par-tay."

"Guys. They come bearing gifts of drunkenness."

"Blowaways?"

Elizabeth laughed.

"May *I?*"

"I dunno, Dues . . . isn't there a warning on the label about operating heavy machinery and swords?"

"Not swords, remember? They're called *foils,* like aluminum foils."

"Aluminum foils. Fine."

"I won't get drunk. Come on, don't be such a fo-dee-dote."

"Hey. Be my guest."

Dusie selected Southern Comfort, which she drank straight from the bottle, then cradled against her breast like her stuffed Lambikins as she flopped back on Elizabeth's bed, enjoying its daytime function as a window seat with lots of big soft pillows.

Two-and-a-half ounces of Comfort later, Dusie was spilling her craw about her girl trouble.

"I love her so much. And she won't even try. Can't commit. Nope. Sorry. Wants to be with other women. Can't live with me. I'm not smart enough for her. Won't take me out. Doesn't wanna be seen with me. It's just killing her right now, y'know cause everybody knows now, about me. She hates that. She wanted me to be a secret."

Somehow that one statement seemed hard to believe, though Elizabeth had no idea why. She was getting a different take on Pip.

"I tell her I love her and she just *pushes* me away . . . yeah, right. She doesn't push me away when she needs to get *laid*. Then it's all ooh baby baby baby can't get enough of me . . . whoa, man, I mean, wow, you just have no idea." Big sigh. Bigger swig. "You're lucky, y'know, you don't like women. They're way worse than guys. I mean, they will eat you alive."

"I dunno, Dues, I don't . . ."

"That's right, little sister." Dusie was looking back at her right now, pursing her lips on the bottle for one more swig, "You do not know. You have no fucking idea."

At the gymnasium, Dusie led Elizabeth into the equipment room, where not only did they find a jacket that fit her but breeches, too. There were three different lengths of foils, and Dusie suggested Elizabeth start with the shorter one, of course, French grip. Who was Elizabeth to object? Right now she was Dusie's little slave of swordplay. Dusie tossed her a mask and showed her the pose, how to hold it in the crook of her left arm, balanced on her hip. She followed Dusie into the locker room, which was lively with dancers peeling off damp leotards that they dropped onto benches before stepping into the misty shower room with its vaulted ceiling and mosaic tiles in an Old World pattern. It was an enchanting echo chamber, a seeming catacomb of arches set meticulously, wall and ceiling alike, with spotless shining tile. And the sounds. The mirthful urgency of entrances and exits being made intermittently on the staircase leading up to the gymnasium, shouts, hoots and hollers or cursing and kissing off all mockery, and banging metal locker doors, a click of a lock, the random toilet flush, and a faucet squeaking on and off like an anxious laugh.

They went to the farthest alcove on the end where Dusie's locker was and Elizabeth's new locker would be, since there were plenty available.

"Nobody comes back here."

"Why not?"

Dusie gave Elizabeth the dumb bunny eyeball.

"Oh great," Elizabeth groused when she figured it out, "that's just great. It's not enough I'm the only straight one in Fey, now I've got a lesbian locker."

Once dressed, Dusie gave her head a little runway model kind of practice shake, checking herself out in the wall-to-wall mirror, giving her sumptuous chestnut coif a little finger fluffing. Surely, she had the kind of hair that merited its own salon products.

As they started up the stairs, Dusie told her to take special care because the tiles got terribly slick, and nearly everyone had slipped or taken a spill at some point.

"This is the *gym?*" Elizabeth practically gasped before a vision like nothing she had ever seen or even imagined unless it was the Temple of Diana. She was so taken aback that Dusie starting laughing and took her by the hand to pull her along across the gorgeous wooden floor inlaid more intricately than the foyers of some neighboring mansions.

In one far corner were the archers who had just come inside to escape the rain, setting up their targets and falling in line to await the command of their instructor, Captain Bly. Seriously. Retired from the service. "Nock," she bellowed, "Draw, Anchor, Aim, Release." Then the rapid-fire thwat thwat sound of arrows when they hit the target. Or not. Uh-oh.

In the opposite corner, dancers were lined up at the brass bar along a mirrored wall listening to their instructor count. And then, the fencers, those strange white creatures with dark mesh faces in another corner with their own wall of mirrors. But only a few were faceless, because most were novices, who practiced their lunges and footwork unarmed and unmasked.

Elizabeth followed Dusie to the fencer's mats, joining the other latecomers doing stretching exercises, reminding each other not to rush the warm-up because lunging was exceedingly strenuous.

"Don't want to pull a muscle," said one.

"First week," said another, "you'll wish you were dead."

"Well, I'm looking forward to that."

The fencing instructor, Poins, emerged from his office then, so

the novices sat up to watch as he gathered the team around to pair
them off as opponents for some "dry bouts," which were informal
contests, scored visually instead of electronically. The four *hand*
judges were positioned at each corner of the fencing strip, or the
*piste,* as it was called, a six-foot-wide, forty-foot-long mat that ran par-
allel to the mirrored wall. Coach Poins assumed the role of "president," the person with the final word on whether or not a hit was
judged to be proper or improper.

"We hate him," someone said, referring to Poins.

"He hates us . . ."

"He hates women . . ."

"So do I . . ."

"Sexist pig . . ."

"Lousy teacher . . ."

"Good coach for the team though . . ."

"Speaks French . . ."

"Yeah, you'd think he was from France . . ."

"But Hays found out . . ."

"He's from Altoona."

It was true. Poins did despise the lot of them, with precious few
exceptions. As far as he was concerned the novices could all just
go off and slice each other to bits. It annoyed him to no end that
the first thing the little imbeciles did when they got a grip on a foil
was to swing it around in a mad dash for some imaginary staircase
from which they would jump onto a chandelier, ride across the
meadhall, fly through a chink in the palace wall, over the moat to
a little village about a mile down the road, land on the roof of a
thatched hut, and bounce into the saddle of a roan mare, with a
risible *Yodel ho!* or some such nonsense they had seen so many
times in movies.

They all watched as two foilists in whites from head to toe, with
mesh-faced masks, a single glove and their own personal foils, positioned themselves on the *piste* to begin the bout. The only thing
Elizabeth could grasp at all was the salute, which was cool, she
thought, because they always saluted, first their opponent, then the
hand judges and then the president.

She was told that it was best for the inexperienced eye to fix on
the movements of a single foilist, which was probably good advice in
general, but entirely unnecessary in this particular bout, it seemed,

because there was only one fencer whom she, or anyone else for that matter, *could* watch. Such was that fencer's command of the sport.

"How come she's doing it that way?"

"She's left-handed, dumb bunny."

It appeared she was one of the few whose padded cotton breeches actually flattered her lean frame and long legs, not to mention, her glorious sartorius. She lunged with the speed and extension of a cheetah.

As she hit her target, Poins called out "Halt!" immediately stopping the action. The fencers returned to their engarde lines while Poins confirmed with the hand judges that the hit was proper. It was and so she scored a point.

"Whoa."

"Yeah."

"Wow."

The bout resumed, this time demonstrating the foilist's defensive skills, which were in fact, her greatest strength, though she barely seemed to move at all. Elizabeth was baffled by the teasing asides then, the telling snickers, giggles, eye rolling and elbow-nudging. Elizabeth was informed that this particular fencer was most admired competitively for what was known in the sport as "fingerwork."

"No kidding . . . "

"Yeah famous fingers . . ."

"Uh-huh."

"Phew . . . yeah . . ."

"I wish . . ."

"The best."

"You should know . . ."

"Eat your heart out, bitch . . ."

"Yeah . . . that too . . ."

The refinement, dexterity, and strength of this foilist's fingerwork, her mastery of defensive parries, could make a mawkish old coach weep. And lord knows how many women.

After winning her bout, she pulled off her mask, raking her fingers through her hair as she came swaggering over. Face flushed a golden rose and barely winded.

"Hello, Breedlove."

Elizabeth felt stupefied in Pip's presence. Fortunately, she wasn't required to speak just then, as Pip turned to Dusie: "Where have you been?" and she sounded kind of pissed, maybe even jealous. This seemed inconsistent with all those things Dusie had been telling her about Pip's indifference.

"We were just hanging around Fey House, me and my little sister here. Talking, like, some pretty heavy shit, too, right, little sister?"

"That is correct."

"You know, Pip, like, a *deep* conversation? With, like, topics?"

Staredown.

Dusie was palpably pleased with herself for securing Pip's complete attention. In fact, Pip's unblinking regard was unnerving as she said: "Your doctor called. You missed your appointment."

"Oh shit!" she cried, "Shit. I forgot. Shit. Daddy's gonna be so pissed."

Her psychiatrist charged for no-shows, and reported any absenteeism to her father, who happened to be his golfing buddy. As Dusie yammered on about the doctor, Pip redirected her attention to Elizabeth, asking her if she had ever fenced.

"No."

"Stand up."

She stood up, yes, m'am. Pip looked her up and down, supremely amused—or something—she was chuckling either way: "You wear the whites well."

"Thank you," and because Pip was still scrutinizing, she asked, "What?"

"Why did I think you were taller?"

Elizabeth directed Pip's eyes downward to consider her lowly white leather tennis shoes.

"Flat. Actual size. Does it matter?"

"Not at all. The smaller the target, the harder it is to hit. And, if you also happen to be fast, then being . . . *petite* is an advantage. In fact, I have never lost a bout so badly as I did to a Brandeis woman, who was about your size."

Elizabeth raised her fist for a quick soul salute to all persons of rarefied stature.

"She brought me to my knees . . ."

Pip extended her open palm, asking for Elizabeth's hand. It wasn't until she had it nested in her own that she seemed to realize she was still wearing her leather glove on her other hand. "First rule," she said, putting her fingertips to her mouth for the purpose of removing the glove with her teeth and then just letting it drop to the mat: "Don't do that."

Grins.

Elizabeth seemed entranced by the gesture but she was really scrutinizing Pip's sensuous lips remembering what Dusie had said about her kiss. She was roused from this reverie when Pip traced lightly up and down her thumb and forefinger causing a tremor along Elizabeth's fault line.

"Manipulators," Pip said. "These digits are called 'manipulators.'"

"Uh-huh."

Then Pip touched the other three fingers: "Aids."

"Will you name my toes, too?"

Pip smirked, rolling her eyes, and then turned to Dusie, commanding her to assume the position, lower her mask and help her demonstrate the basics. She was surprised to see her stagger.

"Have you been drinking?"

"Who are you? My mother?"

Pip sighed heavily, lowering her foil to indicate she would not proceed with Dusie in this condition.

Unmasked, Dusie was mopey. She shuffled away, headed for the water fountain. Pip looked after her for a moment, as if she might follow, but returned instead to Elizabeth, who braced herself, expecting some sort of reprimand.

"Cocktails before dinner?"

"Not I."

"She can't drink," said Pip. "She's on medication."

Although Elizabeth perceived a certain underlying hostility in Pip's tone, she could not tell to whom it was directed.

"You seem fairly . . . flexile, Breedlove. This shouldn't be too difficult for you. Here," Pip said, sidling up to her in fencer's poise, back foot at a habitual right angle, "this is how we stand." Elizabeth noted Pip's use of the royal We. Pip assumed the position and Elizabeth attempted to mirror it. Pip raised her foil. Elizabeth raised her foil. But she could not get the grip right.

"Fingers up," Pip said, "Here . . ."

She stepped behind her, placed her hands on Elizabeth's shoulders and turned her.

"Real Rule Number 1: Fence forward. Never sideways like you see in the movies."

"Fence forward," Elizabeth repeated the rule obediently like a good little dink.

"I fence left so I'll have to . . . reach across—if you'll pardon me . . ."

"Ah, yeah, sure."

Elizabeth tried to be a pliable doll but she was not accustomed to being handled by a woman.

"See," said Pip, being so blasé about it herself, "it should feel like this."

Because Pip was half a foot taller, Elizabeth felt challenged to outreach her grasp. The formidable senior cupped her steady hand, still ungloved, over the frosh's tremulous one, enclosing her fingers around the foil grip firmly before twisting her wrist ever so slightly thumbs up.

"It feels awkward at first."

"Yeah, well . . ."

"But it becomes second nature."

"Uh-huh."

Pip sniffed, curiously: "Your perfume . . . do you wear Blue Grass?"

"No, actually," she answered quite truthfully, "I wear Joy."

Pip turned Elizabeth effortlessly toward the mirrored wall so she could see for herself the proper form. No vampire there, Elizabeth thought, for she could see Pip's reflection well enough. An acute pang of regret surprised Elizabeth when Pip released her and dropped back, as if she were unimpressed by the equipoise she had demonstrated.

Pip proceeded to demonstrate the most basic moves in very slow motion. Elizabeth caught on quickly. All the while, she was aware that Dusie was keeping a petulantly watchful eye on them. When Elizabeth chanced a glance in Dusie's direction one more time, she found the tip of Pip's foil at her breast, but held her ground, feeling the pressure of the foible against her heart, despite the padding.

"See how the blade bends about five or six inches? That's how deeply it would penetrate your flesh."

She looked down at her breast.

"Never take your eyes off your opponent, Breedlove."

"Yeah, well," she chawed, "I'll try to remember that . . . *Captain Blood.*"

Impressed by Elizabeth's flinty nerve, and pleased to be likened to the toothsome Errol Flynn, Pip withdrew her weapon and gave the little dink a *touché* in the form of a full-fledged laugh.

*   *   *

Elizabeth automatically followed Pip into the locker room where they passed Dusie on her way to the shower. The way she glowered at Pip made Elizabeth feel politely obliged to step aside, allowing them the illusion, at least, of a private conversation. But even after Elizabeth found her new locker in the last row and doffed her whites, she could not help but overhear:

"Look, I'm sorry about that, B.D, but I'm not fencing with you if you're drunk. You could get hurt."

"You mean worse than this? I don't think so."

"You shouldn't be drinking."

"Fuck you. Who are you? My friggin' mother?" Dusie stalked off to the shower, tossing her towel over a hook outside the entranceway, shaking her ass as she always did when she was in high dudgeon.

Pip's appearance around the corner startled Elizabeth, who felt more naked than she actually was.

Impact noted in Pip's wan smirk as Elizabeth reached for a towel and wrapped it around her torso. Pip regarded her for a second, absently unbuttoning her fencing jacket from the high line on the right down the inside line, exposing a white cotton T-shirt underneath, which she peeled off unabashedly.

Elizabeth was intent on averting her eyes as she headed for the showers, feeling so self-conscious, thinking: if Pip and Dusie were attracted to women, then this was no different from being naked in a locker room with naked guys.

Pip was used to awkward reactions from straight women and smiled to herself, sauntering into the shower a moment later, self-possessed as that rare person who has confidence in the pleasing appearance and ability of her own body. Her skin was nearly as flawless as Dusie's. And Dusie looked as if she had been airbrushed.

Dusie was in the conditioning phase of her daily hair care ritual, chattering to Elizabeth about which shampoo and rinse she preferred and why. Pip chose a showerhead on the opposite wall and turned her back on them both. Dusie got soap in her eye and cursed, rinsing frantically soliciting assistance, but neither Pip nor Elizabeth would indulge her. Unable to milk her crisis any longer, Dusie fell silent and sulked, soaping her breasts. The weird sensuality of the misty scene proved too much for Elizabeth. She was out of there and dressed in record time. Passing the showers on her way to the door, she overheard Dusie speaking sharply to Pip: "You're unbelievable man. You're, like, what? Jealous now? You're actually jealous, aren't you? Un-fucking-believable."

That night, Elizabeth was awakened by the sound of Pip's car pulling into the parking lot behind Fey House. It was 2:20. On a school night. Even half-conscious, Elizabeth found herself entertained by the prospect of Pip getting grounded, muttering to herself: "You're in big trouble now, missy." She didn't even have to lift her head from the pillows to be afforded an overview, but simply turned her face to the window and opened her sleepy-winking peepers. The floodlight was bright back there and seemed attracted, as most people were, to Pip's car, a classic '65 Mustang she had inherited from one of her brothers. Very cherry red and highly buffed to outshine all others. Pip got out of the car wearing her black leather motorcycle jacket, which was a shocking sight back then on anybody other than a Hell's Angel, and she wore it well. For a moment, she just leaned back against her car firing up a cigarette and gazing up at the house. And then Elizabeth could have sworn Pip spotted her, because she raised her eyes, it seemed, and stared right at her, sending a stream of smoke her way. Elizabeth dropped back, closed her eyes, and drifted off.

She was aroused again soon after by the sound of Dusie's rage. When she showed no sign of letting up, Elizabeth pulled on her jeans and a WCW sweatshirt and climbed out the window, presumably to put an end to it, herself.

Dusie was on the attack, screeching: "How can you do this to me, Pip, how? What don't I do for you? I would do anything for you. Anything you want. And you go out cruising like I don't even exist? Damn you. Why do you have to have other girls? What do they do for you that I can't do? Huh? Tell me. Say something, goddammit." Dusie grabbed one of her fashion magazines and hurled it at her: "You're fucking heartless."

Whoa.

Elizabeth was having second thoughts about entering into this particular fray. If a fray can be one-sided, because Pip wasn't saying anything. She was packing a little duffel bag calmly until Dusie pounced, clawing at her so ferociously, she ripped the breast pocket from her oxford cloth shirt. Pip was pushing her away when she spotted Elizabeth at the window. Pip broke her own rule never to take her eyes off her opponent and got cold-cocked as a consequence.

Dusie slapped Pip so hard she split her pretty lip. All three of them were stunned. It was Dusie, however, who broke. Sobbing, she threw herself at Pip's feet, begging for forgiveness.

At the first sign of peace and quiet, Elizabeth, who already had Pip's attention, also managed to get Dusie's.

"Ah, excuse me? Dusie? Hey Dues? Over here . . ."

"Oh," said Dusie, snuffling and sniffling, "Hi Elizabeth . . ."

She seemed more relieved than surprised to see her, and they both watched her like a couple of kids waiting for direction. Pip with her fingertips on her bloodied lip and Dusie hiccupping pitifully.

"May I?" Elizabeth asked, requesting permission to enter, and they nodded in unison.

She hopped into the room like a little bird that forgot to go south, and the weather was turning quickly. She helped herself to a cigarette from a box of Marlboros that was sitting on the arm of an overstuffed chair in which she took a seat and said, "You don't mind if I watch, do you? I mean, I'm wide awake now."

"Oh man, I'm really really sorry, Elizabeth," Dusie sniveled.

Pip, on the other hand, appeared too mortified for words, and stepped into their private bathroom tending to her wound, while Dusie went over to the bed and flopped down. And Elizabeth appeared to doze with her eyes open, transfixed on the big, old freestanding mirror in the corner.

Standing at a porcelain sink with brass fixtures, Pip took off her shirt and leaned over the sink to splash cold water on her face. There were fresh scratches on her back. It wasn't until she turned and reached for a towel, that she realized she was being observed in the mirror. Her eyes met Elizabeth's there. The little dink showed no fear, not even when the would-be vampire tasted a drop of fresh blood on her lip and staunched it with the tip of her tongue. Pip went from the bathroom to the closet, emerging a moment later wearing a black turtleneck and pulling on her jean jacket whose denim was worn like doeskin. She picked up the duffle and an armful of books, looking over at Dusie lying on the bed despondent, she said: "You know where I'll be."

"Go to hell."

Pip's pained expression indicated that she was already there.

Then she turned to Elizabeth. "I apologize," she said, "for keeping you up, Breedlove."

"Yeah, well . . . don't worry about it, Pip, I'm a speed freak."

"I hope you're kidding."

Something about having seen this royal senior trounced to speechlessness by a babydyke had emboldened Elizabeth. "I'm always kidding," she replied.

"It's true," said Dusie from across the room.

After Pip left, Dusie resumed her mewling and puling, making it difficult for Elizabeth to leave.

"But I love her so much . . ."

"You *hit* her."

"Didn't you ever love a guy, like, so much you wanted to just, like, kill him for being with somebody else?"

"Honestly? No. But I had a boyfriend who felt that way about me. He wouldn't let me break up with him. He followed me around town, every party, every date. If he couldn't find me, he would lurk in my yard, in the dark, waiting for me to get home. He screamed and shoved and grabbed and punched and cried and trashed things."

"Well, that's not good."

"No, it's not. But he said he did this because he loved me. He loved me so much, he said, he could just kill me for being with someone else. He broke my ribs, he shoved me down stairs, on two separate occasions."

"Wow."

"He thought this would make me love him. Do you think I loved him for this?"

Dusie shook her head.

"Do you think you can slap Pip into loving you?"

"Are you saying, like, you don't think she loves me?"

Elizabeth sighed. Dusie sobbed.

"Aw, come on, Dues, you deserve a lot better than this, and you'll have it, too. I know you will. Someone who loves you as much as you love her."

Dusie threw herself upon Elizabeth, needing her shoulder to cry on, but Elizabeth had never been comfortable comforting anyone like this. She gave Dusie a couple of mechanical back pats, saying "There, there," and then set her off to the side. But Dusie came back for more, clutching at Elizabeth each time she attempted to pull away gracefully.

"Ah, Dues?"

"Hm?"

"What are you doing?"

She was nuzzling her neck.

"I have to sleep now," she said robotically, "or I will die. Sorry Dues. Gotta go. Sleep or die."

But after she had stepped through the window, she paused, momentarily framed there.

"Say, uh . . . Dues?"

"Yeah?"

"Where did she go anyway, at three o'clock in the morning?"

Dusie crawled into bed, pulling the covers up over her head, mumbling, "I dunno."

"Then how come she said that you would know where she'd be?"

"I dunno, please don't ask me that, OK."

"I only meant . . ."

But what had she meant? She stood there a moment longer, watching as Dusie reached for her lamb named Lambikins, and turned out the bedside light. She returned to her own room without saying another word.

# CHAPTER 9
# The Jungian Cave of Dr. Crews

Dr. Maddocks flagged down Dr. Crews one day in the crowded hall outside his office by waving a fresh batch of his students' papers like a semaphore over their heads as they milled about between classes.

"Well, hello there, friend," he bellowed to Dr. Crews, "how the hell are you?" at the same time shooing away a half-dozen little hangers-on who wanted to talk sophomoric shop. "I'm glad I caught you, Jo. Do you have a minute?"

But Dr. Crews gave him the brush-off. "Sorry, Geoff, but I have to prepare for my next class."

Dr. Maddocks knew that her next class was Abnormal Psychology, so he could not help wondering what those preparations might be. His idea of preparing for an abnormal psych class would most likely involve still another attempt to read *Finnegan's Wake.*

"Please, Jo. This is important."

Dr. Crews stopped and looked into his face as if she were scanning his brain. What she perceived compelled her to stay.

She followed him into his office and watched as he went about the process of making a fresh pot of coffee while he talked. "As you know, I have Dusie Hertz in my expo class—my *word,* she's a pretty young woman." He turned unexpectedly then to catch the expression on her face, but that psychotherapeutically practiced countenance revealed next to nothing. "Dusie, yes, what about her?" She met his gaze without flinching. She had fended off more homemade knives than Dr. Maddocks had ex-wives.

"Your Miss Hertz has been . . . "

"What do you mean *my* Miss Hertz, Geoff?"

"She *is* your patient."

"She *was* my patient."

"But you still keep an eye on her."

"I still keep an eye on her. Yes. Of course."

He kept an eye on her. She kept an eye on him, too.

"There's really no reason for you to be so defensive, Jo."

It was true, she thought, there really was no reason for her to be so defensive. She attempted to explain, "Dusie Hertz is a special case, Geoff. Her parents brought her to me for therapy when she was fifteen. She was my first case of anorexia."

Dr. Maddocks could not help but reflect upon Dusie's voluptuousness now. "Obviously you've cured her of that."

Dr. Crews shrugged modestly and explained that Dusie's parents had initially refused her professional services. The referring physician had not mentioned to Marshall and Eva Hertz that his old classmate from Tulane, "Jo Crews," as he had referred to her, was a woman *and* black. He had made the mistake of recommending Dr. Crews solely on the basis of her impressive work with self-destructive teenagers.

Upon meeting Dr. Crews, the Hertzes were too cowardly to come right out and say that they would prefer not to have their daughter "saved by a black woman." Instead, they fumbled through some lame-brained excuse about how Dr. Crews wasn't *doctored* enough. Presumably, they wanted a psychiatrist with full prescription writing capability.

Dusie, however, wanted Dr. Crews. And she jumped at the opportunity to drive her parents crazy on this point, refusing to talk to any other trained professional. When the Hertzes said no, Dusie's seeming determination to starve herself intensified. One night she put her fingers down her throat and ended up in the hospital being fed through a tube. Upon regaining consciousness, she refused to open her mouth for anything or anybody but Dr. Crews.

Dr. Crews could not share any more Dusie stories with Dr. Maddocks without violating doctor–patient privilege, and certainly, he respected that. But he could ask for her insight as a fellow teacher, handing her a paper that Dusie had turned in that morning.

When Dr. Crews read the title aloud, "The Influence of Marilyn Monroe on the English Language," she could not help but chuckle, considering Dusie's most endearing side.

Dr. Maddocks's eyebrow was arched as he asked, "Let's just put aside the most obvious question: 'How did this young woman come to be a student here when she's barely capable of maintaining a substandard academic record?' The point is, she has been disrupting my class. She blurts out whatever pops into her head during my lectures, and she completely monopolizes class discussions, making the most absurd connections between points of exposition and *Marilyn Monroe,* for heaven's sake. And while I admit that the young woman can be amusing, adorable even, nothing that I say or do to gain control of the situation seems to have any effect. I called her into my office this morning after class, and I tried to talk with her about it, but . . ." Dr. Maddocks pushed aside a pile of papers and texts on his desk absently as he paused. To Dr. Crews, he appeared to be disproportionately distressed, and she wondered what was really bothering him.

"Well, she burst into tears, Jo. And you know I really *hate* when that happens. I'm not an ogre. I wasn't scolding her, for pity's sake, I was just asking her to please exercise a little self-control. She told me I was just as bad as 'those macho a-holes who murdered Marilyn,' and then she ran out the door." He turned up his palms as a man most baffled by the behavior of women for the very fact that he was constantly surrounded by them. "I'm concerned about her. She's on academic probation from last semester. I don't want to flunk her, Jo, but she's turned in only one of the last four assignments. And that bizarre, incoherent treatise is not acceptable. The best I can give her is a 'D' for 'it's a doozy.' "

Dr. Crews was empathetic, "You want me to talk to her?"

"Would you?"

"I'd be glad to."

Dr. Maddocks gave a grateful nod.

"Is that all?" she asked.

He shook his head, cleared his throat. "Actually, no, Jojo. There is something else."

Right again, thought Dr. Crews, without deriving any pleasure from her insight.

"After Dusie ran out of my office this morning, I went downstairs looking for you and . . . well, I saw you in the lab."

"And?"

Not even a skip in her blink. The woman was that cool. She knew where this awkward chat was headed, but she was not about to volunteer anything.

"You didn't hear me at the door, but I wasn't spying, I can assure you . . ."

Damn those stealth Hush Puppies of his.

"And?"

"I saw you make a pass at Pip Collier," he said, "and, clearly, you were rebuffed."

Dr. Crews did not budge, but the fact that Pip's rejection was so obvious to Dr. Maddocks really stung her.

"How long has this been going on?" He sounded like a cuckold.

"May I?" she asked, referring to his pack of cigarettes. He gave the pack a little shake for her to make her selection and produced a Zippo lighter from the pocket of his cardigan, bearing the little torch for her. He was reminded that she only smoked when she was tense.

"Thanks."

He fired one up for himself. The lighter lid snapped back with that clipped metallic clink only a Zippo can make. He was content to wait for her answer because he knew she always did.

"It happened last year. It was brief. Extremely brief. It's over."

"Define 'over.' "

" 'Over,' meaning . . . it's over for her."

She was palpating her high forehead with one hand from temple to temple where the veins were most protuberant, as if to smooth them down.

"I'm so in love with her."

"Oh, Jo . . ."

"Please spare me the sanctimonious posturing, Geoff. I'm already painfully aware of the damage I've done . . . She despises me."

He remembered one fellow, years ago, a newly hired doctor of philosophy and an acutely handsome young man who had seduced a student and fallen obsessively in love with her. When the student eventually rejected him, the philosopher shot himself in the head in the office directly above Dr. Maddocks's. It was after class hours and few people were in the building when he heard the shot. He found the fellow face down ensanguinating a pile of student papers on Schopenhauer. There was a sealed envelope on the desk, addressed to a student Dr. Maddocks recognized immediately as "the love object." He pocketed the letter before the others arrived and later delivered it to the young woman personally, in the privacy of his own office. When she recognized the handwriting on the envelope, she got hysterical and Dr. Maddocks was left with the most unpleasant task of being unwittingly obliged to tidy up another man's mess, which he greatly resented.

So Dr. Maddocks was well aware of the consequences of falling in love with a student, and he was more concerned than incredulous. It also bothered him that Dr. Crews had not trusted him enough to tell him about her feelings at an earlier stage, so that he might have persuaded her not to make this mistake. But then, he had never found it easy to hear any details regarding her love life. It was a topic he was happy to avoid, not because of her homosexuality, but because of his own discomfort discussing sex, in general. Which is why she teased him sometimes, calling him "The Puritan."

They had no time to discuss the matter further but made plans to have dinner that evening. Dr. Crews left Dr. Maddocks's office and went downstairs to her own office, shutting the door, which she rarely did, feeling so ashamed and upset. She went through the motions of pulling out her notes for Abnormal Psych and reviewing them, but she couldn't concentrate. She was heartsick over Pip and worried about Dusie. Pip could take care of herself, she had made that painfully clear. But Dusie was a different story. Dr. Crews had spent several years trying to help her survive her teens.

They weren't five minutes into their first therapy session when Dr. Crews knew that Dusie had been sexually abused, though she said nothing overt to that effect. According to Dusie, everybody was always trying to shove something in her face, or ram something down her throat. Her father was always ramming his opinions down her throat. Her mother was always shoving fattening food in her face. And her stepbrother, Bram, well, it took weeks of therapy before Dusie felt safe enough to say what it was exactly that Bram was always shoving in her face and ramming down her throat.

Her earliest memory of this abuse involved being held captive in a closet in their basement playroom by Bram, a ten-year-old, who was intent on teaching her, a five-year-old, how to perform fellatio to his satisfaction. Dusie told Dr. Crews he had threatened to kill her pet rabbit if she ever told. The abuse continued on a regular basis until he went away to Pulver Military Academy in the Midwest at the age of fourteen.

By the time Dusie entered WCW, Bram was out of the picture almost entirely. He was Lieutenant Hertz, now, of the U.S. Marine Corps, stationed in Camp Lejeune, North Carolina, when he wasn't off to some Third World locale, which he was not at liberty to name, doing what task exactly, he was not at liberty to say. Since his only alternative was Vietnam, he was considered to be lucky. In truth, he was disappointed to be missing out on the action. Unknown to him, his wealthy, influential father had seen to it that his son would never have combat duty in Vietnam.

"Too bad," Dr. Crews muttered when she heard how lucky Bram was.

It was a blessing at least that he rarely visited his family in Weston, preferring to spend time with their parents at their vacation home in Hilton Head, South Carolina, which was more convenient to Camp Lejeune, and had excellent golf courses. So Dusie was mostly spared. Mostly. At least she had fair warning in advance of any homecoming so she could arrange to be somewhere else entirely or, at least, to have a companion.

Seeing Dusie cured of her eating disorder, and ensconced, safe and sound on campus, Dr. Crews suggested it was time to terminate therapy and Dusie agreed. Just knowing that her good buddy, Dr. Crews, was nearby in case of an emergency, was bolstering.

The problem was that Dusie did not really know if she wanted to be in college at all, let alone this one. At WCW she felt like a Barbie Doll among so many brainy women, most of whom had not a jot of good fashion sense, but seemed intent on making themselves look as "blah" as possible. She missed the company of models and others in the fashion industry who were always up on the latest—the *dernier cri*—an expression Dr. Crews taught her to pronounce with the utmost sophistication. And while she had tried to maintain her friendships with local models she worked with, she soon discovered that there was no relationship beyond the work. College and couture seemed mutually exclusive. But Dusie's parents had insisted she attend WCW. So there she was.

Feeling out of place on campus that first semester made her too dependent on Dr. Crews, who considered it necessary to complete their psychotherapeutic "separation," but was not sure how exactly, given the unique circumstances. Ironically, Dusie had never felt so estranged from women as when she found herself at Willard that first year living with six hundred of them. Her loneliness made her dreadfully vulnerable to the relentless pursuit of Dicks from the brother school and every other male in Greater Weston who had seen her modeling underwear in the Sunday Supplement, or her senior high portrait in a bootleg copy of *Mugs & Plugs*.

Dr. Crews came to believe that aside from Bram—and possibly because of him—Dusie's mental health was most seriously jeopardized by guys in hot pursuit. So she decided to make an exception to the rules, as well as the law, and take Dusie out to the gay bars and clubs, the only unambiguous setting in which to meet women.

As it went, Dusie's lesbian debutante party-for-one proved a smashing success, particularly with the debonair Dr. Crews as her escort. The popular professor knew everybody, and introduced Dusie to scads of lovely ladies, any one of whom Dr. Crews trusted to treat her with respect and admiration.

After one such evening of club-hopping bacchanalia, both Dr. Crews and Dusie had a bit too much to drink and ended up back at the professor's place, a roomy second-floor apartment duplex not far from the WCW campus. There was no lascivious intent, it was simply too late for Dusie to get back into Fey House without causing a commotion, because first-semester frosh were not allowed dorm keys for some reason. So Dr. Crews invited Dusie to crash on her couch.

Unbeknownst to Dr. Crews, somebody had already crashed on her couch. Pip had dropped by earlier (she had her own key) and dozed off hugging Volume 5 of *The Collected Works of C.G. Jung*. When Dr. Crews and Dusie came staggering through the door giggling and shushing each other riotously, Pip was not amused.

"Well, well, look who's here . . ." Dr. Crews was palpably pleased to see her and could barely contain her enthusiasm in French: *"Je suis très content de vous vois, ma chère . . ."*

"Hey, Jo . . ." Pip yawned and rubbed her eyes to get a better look at Dusie, or so it seemed from where Dr. Crews was standing, or, swaying rather.

"Dusie, honey, may I present my protégé, Pip Collier," Dr. Crews drawled, which was always a tip-off that the professor was tippled.

"Hi," Dusie beamed, adding a little wave.

Pip had heard a lot about Dusie from Dr. Crews and certainly had noticed her, in passing, around campus.

"Hello, Hertz," she said, with that look on her face Dr. Crews recognized as attraction, and would not be above exploiting, if necessary, for her own pleasure. The little bundle of boob was unconscious within minutes of settling on the couch while the willowy psychotherapist went urgently down the hall in the direction of the master bath, groaning, "Oh Lord, I think . . . I'm going to be sick . . ."

The retching proved more purifying than anything, and when it was over, it really was over. None of that malingering queasiness for this dame, she joked, speaking to Pip from the private bathroom adjoining her boudoir. Firing up the shower, she stripped down and invited Pip to join her for a thorough laving—for old times sake—"How long has it been now, sugar?"

"Since what?" Pip asked without any real curiosity because she knew full well. She declined the shower invitation and took a seat or rather leaned on the edge of a tremendous antique brass bed, with sturdy bars at the head and the foot for securing willing captives, figuratively or literally. Pip was the former sort, who took no pleasure in being bound, but would graciously oblige the submissive request, unless the objective was to inflict or suffer pain. Pip didn't play that. Tonight, she was thinking, Oh hell, here we go again, in the very position she had hoped to avoid. She had dropped by with the intention of trying once more to put an unequivocal end to this whole regrettable affair. Her repeated requests for nontherapeutic separation were not being met.

After her bracing shower, Dr. Crews seemed considerably more sober. As she was drying off, she could see Pip's profile reflecting her way in an array of mirrors placed throughout her otherwise tastefully appointed bedroom. She liked to watch herself with women making love in the decorative surroundings of art nouveau, the organic fluidity and serpentine curves. Beyond the foot of the bed in the corner stood an enormous, full-length antique mirror whose angle was easily adjusted to the touch and revealed as much as a body, or anybody, could bear. She loved it that Pip was not intimidated by mirrors, unlike most women. As a matter of fact, Dr. Crews had yet to discover what, if anything, intimidated Pip in bed.

As Dr. Crews sashayed around the room, it was Pip's turn to watch, which she did in hopeless quietude, even as she appreciated how divine Dr. Crews appeared in the buff. Such a girlie-girl, Pip always said, entertained by the vision of her going about her toilette, all that ooh-la-la, as she sat at her vanity, palming her lovely skin with lotions from Paris: the top secrets of her international balminess. And here in the wee hours of this particular morning, she was visibly tremulous at the prospect of getting "laid, relaid and parlayed," as she said.

"So what do you think of her? My pulchritudinous charge."

Pip took her time answering, sensing the game was afoot, and yawned, stretched her arms above her head, dropped them again, and said:

"I think that her beauty deserves a better word."

"Do you want her?"

"You say that as if she's yours to give."

"All I asked is, Do you want her?"

"What if I did?"

Dr. Crews caught Pip's eye in the mirror and shook her head conveying therapeutic forbearance.

"That look," she said.

"What look?"

"The look you always get when you catch me in the act of being a mere mortal. My, oh my," she added, with a tsk-tsk, "I must be such a disappointment to you, *ma chère.*"

As Pip did not dispute this or offer her any reassurance whatsoever, Dr. Crews could only conclude:

"You have no tolerance . . . no tolerance."

Skin care completed, Dr. Crews climbed on the bed, slinking toward Pip on her hands and knees until she was right behind her and then she sat back on her heels, hunkered. Taking Pip by the shoulders, she held her steady while she kissed the back of her neck ardently, reaching around the front to unbutton Pip's shirt, pulling it to bare her shoulders, which she grazed with her teeth to create shivers from one side to the other, and most polarizing: the thrill straight down the middle. All the while, she was murmering in French about how much she missed her, craved her, intended to devour her. She seemed only vaguely aware of what Pip was also trying to tell her:

"Jo . . ."

"Hmm . . ."

"We can't be together . . . not like this . . ."

"But we *are* together like this, my love . . . Look," she said, referring to their reflection in the vanity's mirror, expressing her sloe-eyed dreamy appreciation, feathering her long fingers over Pip's breasts. The striking contrast of their skin never ceased to fascinate either one of them.

"White sugar . . ." Dr. Crews called her, which would always make Pip smile even when she frowned. Like now.

"*Très belle* . . . so beautiful together, look at us sugar, . . . aren't we a fine couple?"

Pip could not disagree with the visual assessment. But she had come over this evening hoping to talk, she said.

"It's four o'clock in the morning. . . Give it up, sugar . . ."

She sighed haplessly, dropping her head back against the collarbone of her captor, who sucked on her tender neck, while presuming to instruct her in her own feelings:

"You want this . . . you want this as much as I do . . . *allons . . . ma chère . . .*"

What was the use? Pip thought, yanking off her boots, standing and turning to face Dr. Crews, who unbuckled and unzipped and otherwise stripped her down to this: yes, m'am, at your service.

Then she climbed into bed, giving Dr. Crews, who was a bit overanxious to have her now, a gentle shove back against the pillows, kneeling between her legs.

The protégé-cum-paramour's tutelage had turned into bondage.

# CHAPTER 10
# Blowaways

When Pip woke up the next day in her mentor's bed, it was mid-morning and Dr. Crews had already left for class, leaving her a cute note stashed in her boot. Pip walked down the hall following the aroma of coffee, assuming Dr. Crews had left it brewing for her. But when she stepped into the kitchen, she was startled to see Dusie sitting in the breakfast nook, perusing the lingerie ads in the "ladies" section of *The Weston Gazette,* looking for models she knew.

"Good *morning!*" Dusie chirped. "I made fresh coff . . . oh," she stopped, seeing that Pip was naked, then giggling. "Whoops!" Dusie was unfazed, as she explained, because models are used to being naked around each other. And then she added, "You have a nice body, um, Brit, is it? Sorry, I was, like, so blasted last night." Pip couldn't help but find her matter-of-fact manner endearing. She was also struck, as everybody was, by the realization that Dusie was the most gorgeous woman she had ever seen in the flesh. It was actually difficult *not* to look at her.

After that night with Dr. Crews, Pip was resolved to end the romantic and erotic aspect of their relationship. Dr. Crews was not amenable to this resolution, so Pip soon found that she had to avoid her mentor entirely, except for classes, labs, and tutorial meetings. Because Pip would not talk to her privately, Dr. Crews increased the number of missives she sent to her by in-house mail. When Pip did not respond in kind, Dr. Crews became even more aggressive, seeking her out at various places throughout the campus, cornering Pip in a testy or cocky manner, almost within earshot of others.

One morning, Pip and her classmates had just settled in, waiting for Dr. Crews to make her entrance, but instead of going directly to the lectern, she went down the aisle and handed her a book in front of the other students. Pip looked up into her teacher's face, waiting out an internal adrenaline storm, pleading silently, "Please don't do this to me, Jo, please. You're mortifying me."

And Dr. Crews just smiled down upon her pet so easily, with some cleverly contrived insight into her student's character, as if she could re-create her. The book, J. Huizinga's *Homo Ludens,* was from Dr. Crews's own library.

"What's this?" Pip asked, trying to sound casual, aching from a sense that everyone in the room could see the sordid extent of their affair in this pretense to formality.

"You mentioned the other day you were having trouble finding it. You may borrow my copy."

"Oh. Right. Thank you, Dr. Crews."

"You're quite welcome, Ms. Collier."

Pip knew full well there was a letter stashed in the book, but she was not able to refer to it for the hour and twenty minutes that she sat there. When the class ended, she bolted out the door. She headed across the quad and down the grassy knoll to the pond where she took a seat on the bench to read the letter, feeling like a courtier, trapped at court, in dreadful conflict with Her Majesty, The Queen.

Pip rose from the bench and circled the pond on stepping-stones before striding up the hill toward Fey House, which she entered by the side door. She went up the secondary staircase to the third floor and knocked on Dusie's door. Getting no response, Pip headed downstairs, but as she arrived at the second floor landing, she bumped into Dusie ascending.

"Oh," said Dusie, "Hi," and she stepped aside. But Pip bandied with her, pretending she didn't mean to block her way until the teasing made Dusie giggle. As Dusie proceeded up the steps, a piece of paper slipped from a notebook she was carrying and Pip scooped it up. She saw that it was a list and read it aloud:

"Six pairs of jeans, four Levi's, two Lee, one pair of white sneakers, one pair of Gucci loafers, one pair of Mario Valentino, one pair of old, old Botticelli boots . . ." She paused to consider the boots that Dusie was wearing. "Are those the old, old Botticellis?"

Dusie snatched the list back, "Hey! Gimme that, jeez . . ." pretending to great pique when she was truly delighted, especially when Pip followed.

"Are you following me?"

"Yes. If you don't mind. I'd like to see your closet."

"My closet?" Dusie squeaked.

"I've never known anyone who had six pairs of jeans," Pip said. "Six pairs of jeans intrigues me."

Dusie shrugged, acting as if she wasn't totally "blown away" that Pip wanted to see her closet, of all things: something so personal.

"Do you want to keep modeling?"

"Yeah. So? That doesn't make me stupid."

"Who said you were stupid?"

"Everybody says models are stupid."

"Did I say that?"

"Nope."

"Then not *everyone* says models are stupid."

As Dusie entered her room, dropping her books on a chair Pip held back in the hallway.

"Well, come on in," Dusie beckoned cutely, opening the closet door. "Don'tcha wanna see my closet?" She pulled a joint from her cigarette pack and put it between her lips. "Wanna get high?"

Pip closed the door behind her and grinned when she saw a half-dozen pairs of blue jeans strewn about the room as if they had sprung from a gag can of peanuts.

Dusie followed Pip's eyes to the snapshots she had stuck in the frame of the mirror above her dresser, drawn to a Hertz family portrait in particular.

"That's my stepbrother. Bram." There was a resemblance except that Bram had inherited blond hair and blue eyes from a different mother, which gave him an arctic aspect.

"I hate his guts. I hate him so much, once when we were kids I stuck a pencil in his head."

Pip mulled that over for a moment before she asked, quite plainly, "Did you kill him?"

Dusie shook her head, tickled by Pip's drollness. "He's got a really hard head."

Seeing that Dusie was getting loopy, and feeling pleasantly buzzed herself, Pip reached for the smoldering joint, took a hit, and then dropped it into the ashtray.

"I'm sorry," Dusie said. "I get stoned really quick because of this medicine I have to take. Hey," she brightened, "wanna see my portfolio?" And before Pip could say yes or no, Dusie was opening the big black book on her desktop, flipping through the pages, describing every shoot. From the clips Pip could see clearly that Dusie was a beauty already at fifteen when she appeared in newspaper advertisements for downtown stores like Gimbels and Saks, posing for the Sunday Supplement in some polyester peignoir that she wouldn't have been caught dead in at a séance. She said the modeling itself was boring, but she loved being fussed over by fawning makeup artists and hairstylists and seamstresses, especially when they were attractive women.

"Can I ask ya sumthin?"

"Go ahead."

"Y'know the way you kinda make yourself look like a boy? Or not a boy really, but not a girl either. I mean. It's kinda like you don't want anybody to notice that you're really pretty."

She mistook the expression on Pip's face for chagrin and apologized haphazardly. "That didn't come out right. I'm sorry. I hope I didn't hurt your feelings."

"Dusie," Pip said, with an easy smile and unexpected tenderness, "you could only hurt my feelings if you *meant* to hurt my feelings."

"Huh?" And then she figured it out. "Wow." She turned abruptly toward a chest of drawers, fussing fatuously with various and assorted sundry items, everything under a layer of talc as she was given to dusting herself profusely with baby powder. She picked up a natural bristle brush and put it to her hair as she was standing in front of the mirror, brushing her luscious glory straight back, wondering how long Pip would just stand there watching her like this. Pip never volunteered any information about herself. When she eventually spoke it was to ask Dusie if she was making her nervous, and Dusie replied: "No. Or yeah. Oh, I dunno, man I just think you're so . . . fucking sexy."

She turned back to face the mirror, extremely flustered.

"Boy, I'm hot. Aren't you hot?" she asked, rather suggestively, in light of the fact that she was taking off her sweater.

Pip had appreciated the easy relationship that Dusie had with her clothes, today's outfit being a pink, pin-striped, oxford cloth shirt over a white undershirt, half-untucked, looking cozier than her unmade bed.

"Remember that night," Dusie was saying. "Dr. Crews and I got drunk off our asses? Jeez-us-bejeebers, we were trashed."

"I'm surprised you remember *anything* from that night."

"Not much from the night. But the next morning? I remember that."

"What?"

"You. Standing there. Buck naked. It really blew my mind. I've been thinking about you ever since."

"What have you been thinking?"

"That I wanna, like, um, see you buck naked again?"

Pip just grinned.

"Didja ever think about me?"

"As a matter of fact I have."

"What do you think?"

"That I wanted you to see me buck naked again."

Pip was thinking this was going to be even easier than anticipated. She moved in closer, leaning on the edge of Dusie's desk, in order to appear nonchalant and to have Dusie within easy reach. Dusie was leaning against her dresser.

"Why are you looking at me like that?" Dusie asked.

Pip responded by brushing the side of Dusie's face lightly with her fingertips, tracing slowly down her neck, which made Dusie all a-quiver.

"Maybe I should go," Pip said, moving her hand up the other side of her neck to her face.

"Why?" Dusie asked vacantly, too sensually enthralled to think.

"Because if I don't," Pip murmured more intimately as she pulled Dusie closer, "then I'll have to kiss you."

Even if it hadn't been such a long time since Dusie kissed a girl, she would have forgotten it all in an instant anyway since Pip took her to a whole new level. There were moments that night when Pip had to stop and check to make sure nobody was getting hurt from all this roughhousing. They were into multiples when Dusie just broke. Pip sat up, turned on the lamp beside the bed, and asked, "What's the matter? Why are you crying?"

Dusie said she had never experienced a pleasure so intense in all her life that was not also associated with pain and shame. And then she spewed the whole ugly truth about her abuse at the hands of her stepbrother. Sometime later, Pip got dressed and left, feeling no undue amount of disgust with herself for having bedded such a troubled girl merely because she was so gorgeous.

Her car was already parked in the lot behind Fey House so she got in and just drove with no particular destination in mind, only to find herself inevitably in the neighborhood of Dr. Crews. Seeing her lights on, Pip rang the doorbell. In a moment, an inside stairwell was illuminated for her mentor's descent in a sashless red kimono billowing all the way down, her bare legs flashing through elegant silk folds.

"Pip?" She was clearly thrilled to see her.

"Jo. May I come in?"

Pip brushed past her going up the stairs into the living room. It was clear from the disarray, that she had been correcting papers, listening to John Coltrane. The aroma of freshly baked sweet potato pie mingled with percolating coffee, and incense. Pip submitted to an embrace, even mustering some memory of tenderness, until the nuzzling turned passionate and then she pushed off. Dr. Crews eyeballed her suspiciously because she smelled like baby powder.

Pip walked around the dining room table, removing from her breast pocket the letter her mentor had given her earlier that day. She read from it aloud before Dr. Crews could stop her, that is, if she would have stopped her.

" 'I care about you, more than you know and much more than I should.' " She paused to look into her teacher's face. "What do you mean?"

"You know what I mean."

"No, I don't. You always think I know what you mean. I don't always know what you mean, Jo."

Dr. Crews was mum, so Pip read on, " 'Please don't outsmart yourself and drive me away. It would grieve me. Perhaps you, too. But know that when there is a winner, no one wins, least of all the winner. I guess we're both so used to being pursued.' " Pip looked up from the letter again at Dr. Crews, who appeared strangely pained as she was also grinning.

"What do you think I'm trying to win?"

"You tell me. You're the compulsive competitor."

"I'm not competing with you."

"Of course you are. You compete with everybody. You're still competing with your brothers."

"You read too much into me."

Dr. Crews just shook her head, realizing the futility of trying to explain.

" 'I miss you painfully.' "

All Dr. Crews could say was, "But I do. I do miss you painfully, Pip. Why are you so angry at me for telling you how I feel?"

"I'm just trying to understand this."

"By avoiding me? For weeks and weeks? Not returning my phone calls? Ignoring my letters? That's how you're trying to understand me?" She seemed surprised herself, by her emotionality: "I'm in love with you, Pip. I love you. Do you have any idea what that *means?*"

But Pip did not want to hear it. She walked into the living room and took a seat on the arm of the couch, brooding. She noticed the saxophone sitting pretty in a chair as if it paid rent.

Dr. Crews was saying, "You think that if you don't let yourself love me back, you're winning somehow. You're very young that way, *ma chère* you truly are. I know you so well"

"Stop telling me what I think. You don't know what I think. That's part of the problem, Jo."

Pip hated that Dr. Crews indulged some fantasy that she could read her mind and guess her motives and predict her behavior: that she could leaf through Pip's hidden agenda, like there was something psychic about it. For this, Pip turned on her, bitterly, "You *must* know I was with Dusie Hertz tonight. Since you know me so well. Did I enjoy myself?"

After a wrenching sort of silence, Dr. Crews said honestly, "That would explain the baby powder." She went into the kitchen, calling back to Pip, "Would you like a drink? Can I get you something to eat? How about a piece of my sweet potato pie? It's still warm."

"No, thanks."

Alone in the kitchen, Dr. Crews slammed her fist down so hard on the counter that her lithograph of *Sojourner Truth* bounced off its hook in the adjoining dining room and slid down the wall. She lost half the ice cubes she threw at her glass, and took a hit right off the top of the Scotch before pouring it. When she stepped back into the dining room, she was carrying her cocktail and a sliver of pie on a little plate for Pip. She handed it to her as if she had asked for it and sat down on the couch beside her. While Pip ate the pie, Dr. Crews seemed to lose herself in the music. She picked up her sax and started to play along with Coltrane a song called "Soul Eye," which she thought of as their song.

Finishing her pie, Pip said, "I'm not used to your anger."

"I'm not angry, Pip. I'm disappointed."

"You know that hurts me worse."

"Yes. I do know that."

"You expect too much from me," Pip said.

"I just want you to get what you want, honey."

"Then why do you get so jealous and possessive?"

Dr. Crews made a tragicomical face. "I've peeled you off too many bimbos in too many bars to have any illusions about your libido, lover." She took an eager gulp of Scotch. "Just look out for those biker dykes who hang out in The Backroom, Pip. You never know where those chains have been."

But Pip wasn't laughing. She felt wretched. Dr. Crews watched her for a long time, quietly but for the clatter of cubes as she threw her drink down as if she'd been taking lessons from Beatrice Brock. And then she put her hand on Pip's knee, whispering, "You once told me that you loved me, Pip."

Pip looked down.

"It used to be great. Wasn't it great?"

Pip wanted to shout, "No! It wasn't great. Not for me," but once more she found she could not.

"Talk to me."

"I can't talk to you, Jo."

"How can you say that?"

But Pip wasn't talking, so Dr. Crews rose, shaking her head sadly as she stepped backward slowly toward the hallway leading to her bedroom. The embittered teacher considered her reticent student a moment before she said:

"I can almost hear how bitterly you'll talk of this part of our lives when it no longer exists."

"If I'm bitter, it's only because it didn't have to be this way."

"You're saying it's all my fault? How could you?"

"I didn't seduce *you*."

"You didn't stop me."

"I didn't know *what* to do, so I did nothing."

"Nothing? You made love to me. We were lovers. In the purest sense."

"I did it because you made me feel special and I wanted to be close to you. I guess I thought that was the only way."

"You make it sound as if you think I *victimized* you."

Pip looked at her then and said so quietly, "Maybe you did."

Dr. Crews was crying.

"I just hope that you won't forget me too much, and that you will eventually forgive me . . . just enough." And then she turned, "Please, forgive me," and walked down the hallway. In a moment, Pip heard her close her bedroom door.

# CHAPTER II
# The Family Hertz

As the spring term came to a close that year with the same sort of shutting of a private door, all personal correspondence between Pip and Dr. Crews ceased. In class or the lab as at any campus event where they happened to meet, there was no personal conversation. They appeared friendly enough but strained with mocking formality. They went so far as to express academic hostility with smarmy Socratic badinage, going brilliantly back and forth in front of the class arguing whatever point. In no time, it appeared to their more perceptive peers that they were indulging in an intellectual feud. For those times that Pip outdebated her in class, Dr. Crews retaliated at her tutorial board meetings by grilling her on her premises and evidence every step of the way.

They didn't communicate much over the summer break, except that Dr. Crews dropped Pip a postcard every so often from some exotic place as she was traveling. When she returned from her trip, she was delighted to find a message to call Pip, assuming she had been missed, until she got Pip on the phone and realized that Pip only wanted a favor. Pip wanted information on an incoming freshwoman named Elizabeth Breedlove, whose picture she had seen in an advance copy of *Mugs & Plugs*.

Over that summer, Pip had become more involved with Dusie. Her rational resolve not to carry on like a fool for the girl had become something of a bitter joke every time she found herself looking to get off. She wouldn't call Dusie for a week or two. But then she would bump into her at some bar or club and she would be grinding Dusie into the wall, hating herself for the sordid abandon, and hating

Dusie more for being so compliant. She tried to make it up to her by caring for her mental and physical health, helping her to find some balance and self-discipline by teaching her how to fence, assisting her with her reading assignments, that sort of thing. But it seemed more like barter than friendship.

Pip found that Dusie could be delightful when she wasn't in breakdown mode. That summer before Elizabeth came to WCW, Dusie said she felt "happy at last" because of Pip, certain that she was in love. As the fall semester approached, she expressed her desire that she and Pip would room together. Pip had already agreed to room with a classmate who needed an on-campus address to keep her parents off her back while she lived with her boyfriend. But Dusie put on a tight turtleneck and convinced the campus-housing director to switch her into the room instead.

Before that point, their relationship, as Dusie referred to it, had progressed smoothly, at least by her estimation. She was especially pleased when, after pressing Pip about the fact that they never saw each other outside the realm of bars and the WCW gym, Pip started asking her to accompany her to dinner and concerts and films.

Pip knew it was a mistake to encourage such companionship simply because she felt guilty. She worried about her own manipulativeness in the service of her tyrant libido. Most troublesome to her was Dusie's willingness to be debased, not that Pip obliged or indulged this, but Dusie made it clear that she really needed to feel forced somehow. The intensity of Dusie's neediness increased to the point that sometimes she would lash out at Pip in a rage when she came, then crash into sobs.

"Dusie, why do you do this?"

"Because it feels so good," Dusie sobbed. "I can't stand it."

"You hit me and kick me and bite me because it feels good?"

Dusie screwed up her face, slick with sweat and tears. "Huh? Yeah. That's it. I guess."

"Did you ever hit Bram?"

"Are you kidding me? He'd kill me."

Pip felt obligated, as a student of psychology, to try to help Dusie exorcise what she deduced were the demons of her stepbrother, Bram. That was the only reason why, in the third week of August, Pip accepted Dusie's invitation to spend the weekend at the Hertzes' cushy suburban home, giving in only after a great deal of prodding and begging. Pip had hoped to avoid this sort of thing, being understandably leery about walking into any situation where she was not free to be honest about her sexual orientation. Sitting at the bar in The Titan one night, Dusie pleaded with her to accept the invitation.

"There's a swimming pool and a tennis court and . . ."

"It sounds like you're trying to sell me on Club Med."

"Huh?"

"Never mind. I just want to know one thing."

"What's that?"

"You're not going to use me to 'come out' to your parents, are you? Because someone did that to me once, without giving me any warning, and it was a nightmare."

"I wouldn't do that to you, Pip," she whined. "I swear. Never, never-never. Cross my heart and hope to die . . ."

Pip only agreed to come because Dusie told her that her stepbrother Bram would be home visiting.

"Please, pretty please don't make me be alone with him."

"Won't your parents be there?"

"No!" she screeched, "You don't understand! My parents are *never* there, even, y'know, when they're there."

As it went, the Hertzes were very friendly to Pip, having no reason to believe that she was anything more to their daughter than a college chum. And because Mrs. Hertz assumed all college chums bunked together, she put Pip's overnight bag in Dusie's bedroom. "I'll just leave you girls to your fashion magazines," she said insipidly. "Dinner will be served in an hour," and then she went downstairs.

Dusie rolled her eyes as she shut (and locked) the door, muttering irascibly under her breath: "Jeez. Can you believe her?"

"She seems nice enough."

"She's a bitch and I hate her and she's so fucking phony it makes me sick!"

Pip should have known better than to say anything nice about Dusie's mother.

"She thinks all college girls sleep together. I mean, really sleep? Can you believe? She would never think, like, love, um, you know? Do you know what she said to me once? She said she didn't understand what being a 'lesbian' meant. I tried to explain it to her, y'know, but . . ."

Pip mused, "I'm really sorry I missed that."

"She said she couldn't 'imagine how girls do it.' I mean, if she can't imagine it, then it doesn't really happen, right? Or like, with girls it doesn't really count or something? Like, unless there's a dick around, it's not really sex?"

Dusie could be difficult to follow, but sometimes she made a lot of sense. At least her feelings about people were never ambivalent, "I really hate her for that."

She pulled a *Playboy* magazine from beneath her canopied bed of white lace and tossed it to Pip: "Check out Miss August. What a fox."

Pip obliged her methodically by picking up the magazine and flipping through it as she continued offhandedly to query Dusie, "Maybe you hate your mother because she didn't protect you from your stepbrother."

"How could she? She would never believe me. I tried telling her once. She slapped me in the face and called me a 'sick child' with a 'filthy mind' to be having these 'sick fantasies' about Bram coming on to me, and I didn't even tell her hardly anything. I mean, like, I just said something about him trying to touch me funny or . . . I dunno what I said, but she just blew up, like she always does. She said what was I doing to him to give him these ideas? Wearing tight jeans? Going without a bra? Showing off my body? And then she said I was just trying to ruin her perfect marriage or something like that. She always turns it into herself. Like I'm jealous of her and Daddy? Can you believe that shit? She's so fucking selfish. Hey, promise me something please, please, please. Just don't let him be alone with me."

"I won't."

"You're so good to me, Pip. You're the best friend I ever had."

"No, I'm not. Please don't say that."

Bram Hertz arrived just moments before they were to sit down to dinner. He took a seat at the table directly across from Pip, and she caught him looking at her with an intensity that made her regret all the more that she had ever gotten involved with Dusie.

"I don't know about this women's lib stuff," he said, spitting corn as he was drilling a cob, "It just looks like you girls got yourselves some bad haircuts, if you ask me."

"Nobody asked you, dickhead," said Dusie and her mother scolded her for using such language at the table, but to no real effect, in the pitiful manner of a parent who has never even commanded, let

alone earned the respect of her children. "What are you talkin'
about, Bram? What about your skinned head? You look like a dork."

"Hey, I don't have a choice, you know?" he snapped back. "And
I'm proud of it," he saluted with a smirkish bravado and returned to
his original point, "We've got some chicks in the service. They're all a
bunch of lezzies, if you ask me. Pass the corn. They want combat
duty. Right. Like I want some ball-bustin' carpet-muncher covering
me with a grenade launcher. Right."

"Bram!" said his mother as if she had never heard such talk, while
their father laughed literally, "Ha ha," like his boy had really gotten
something over on the girls.

"What?" he replied, straightening in his uniform. "Oh, that's right,
not in front of the company," turning directly to Pip, "sor-ry," he
smiled. He looked like a distortion of Dusie.

Pip knew that Bram was unaware that she had heard about his cruelty to Dusie. She also knew that Bram found her attractive, as men
often did, assuming that their own desire canceled out any possibility
that she wasn't interested in them. As she caught him looking at her
with salacious intent, she scowled, which he took to mean that she
was coming on to him. In truth, Bram had never met a woman like
Pip, and he found her pretty, despite her "bad haircut." Her full, blunt
blond bangs obscured her eyes in a sexy way, and emphasized the
compelling sensuality of her mouth, especially when she scowled.

"So where ya from, Pat?"

And Dusie shouted out, " 'Pip,' not 'Pat,' dork-brain."

"I'm from the suburbs of Philadelphia."

"Oh?" said the perky Mrs. Hertz. "The Main Line? We have friends
from Devon, don't we, Marsh? The Stiwtin family. Do you know
them? Sterling and Lillian Stiwtin?"

Pip blinked thoughtfully just to be polite before she said no, while
Dusie blurted out, "Of *course* she doesn't know them, Mother. You
always think everybody in Philadelphia knows each other. Do you
know everybody in Weston? And why do you always have to ask
Daddy if you know somebody somewhere? Don't you know yourself,
like, if you know them or not? I mean, why do you have to ask
Daddy?" But the real reason she was perturbed was because she felt
her mother was being pretentious in bringing up the Stiwtins, who
were even more full of themselves than her parents.

"I defer to your father, young lady, because he's my husband."

"Oh, cut me a break," Dusie groaned.

"See," Bram piped in, "that's what you get when you send 'em to girls' schools. This women's lib bullshit."

When the main course arrived, Dusie complained that the ham was too fatty and salty and made such a fuss that her mother got up from the table and went into the kitchen to make her a hamburger. Pip had never seen anything quite so extreme as this mother whose lack of true affection for her daughter caused her to indulge her infantile demands in place of real caring.

After dinner, Bram took Dusie aside for a moment, to ask her if Pip had a boyfriend. And Dusie just split a stitch laughing:

"Bram, you are such an asshole."

"You're just jealous, that's all," he sneered at her, giving her a painful little pinch just to remind her as Pip entered the room.

That night, after their parents had gone to bed, Bram was challenging Pip to still another round of darts in the pool house.

"We used to have some great parties here, man," he said, trying to impress Pip while Dusie thwarted his effort at every turn.

"Yeah. Tell her about the time the cops came 'cause the music was so loud? And they pulled right up to the house and you and your stupid, drunk friends were running around the front yard trying to pee on each other . . . bunch of assholes."

"Bullshit! What do you know? You were blowing Beau Garvey in the laundry room."

"I was not!"

"Was too."

"Was not!"

"Was too. He told me."

"He's a liar. I wouldn't blow Beau Garvey if he was a, um . . . If he was the *last* rubber raft on, ahh . . . ummm, a sinking ship!"

Pip had never heard such a foul-mouthed exchange between siblings, not even in the suburbs of Philadelphia. The scene rendered her speechless. She simply stared at them until they stopped and Bram resumed the dart game. When Dusie stated for the "millionth time" that she was "sleepy as a noodle" and wanted to go to bed, Bram shrieked, "So go to bed already. Judas Priest!" blowing the last round in a dart game called "baseball."

Dusie looked at Pip, who shrugged ambivalently as if to say, Go ahead, so Dusie went to bed.

After Dusie left, Bram said to Pip, "What was that all about?"

Pip took aim with the dart, ignoring him.

"She has to get your permission to go to bed?"

Pip threw the dart.

"You're a strange chick, you know that? Being friends with my sister. She's a nut case."

Pip gave him a look out of the corner of her eye that she reserved for chuffs.

"What are you . . . studying her or something? Like, for some psychology project?" He sniggered, considering himself a wit.

Pip's dart hit the mark for maximum points. "I win," she said.

Bram appeared stupefied, being all the more attracted to Pip for her skill at games. "I gotta take a leak," he said, walking to the door of the bathroom. "Don't go away."

Pip smiled wanly. After he left the room, she went to the bar and filled a shot glass with whiskey. When he emerged from the bathroom a moment later, she challenged him to another game with the suggestion that the winner would do the shot. The militant gleam in his eyes indicated the extent of his thrill at the prospect of playing drinking games with her.

"Oh darn," Pip said flatly when she lost another game by one point.

"All *right!*" Bram clapped, reaching for the shot glass and swallowing the whiskey in one gulp. He let out with a loud "Ah," and smacked the empty glass down on the bar, wiping his mouth with the hem of the T-shirt he had changed into after dinner. It was a Rolling Stones shirt with the *Sticky Fingers* logo: a big red mouth with a distended tongue. "Lez go again," he beamed, slurring his words.

They went again. During the game, Bram said, "I heard you're a pretty hotshot fencer. I've done a lot of fencing myself. Mostly sabers."

"Oh," Pip smiled, "the *real* swords," and Bram completely missed her sarcasm until she added, "I'll bet you're quite a swordsman."

It was evident from Bram's beaming face that he had gotten quite a rise out of her statement. He was about to make a pass at her when he reeled back suddenly complaining of extreme dizziness and barely made it to the couch before passing out. Pip continued to throw darts for another five minutes, until she heard him snoring, then she turned off the lights and left the pool house.

The weekend went relatively smoothly. Bram had such a bad hangover the next day that he was almost docile. He lounged by the pool for the most part, leering at Pip and Dusie in their bathing suits, and then he went out in the evening to the local tavern.

The only nocturnal disturbance was Dusie awakening from a bad dream in the darkest hours, needing Pip to hold her.

# CHAPTER 12
## Down and Dirty

As much as Elizabeth was mesmerized by Dr. Crews and entertained by Dr. Brock and variously attracted to or put off by a handful of other professors, she found herself most intrigued by the seeming odd man out, Dr. Geoffrey Maddocks. He was the odd man out because he had a gaggle of groupies like anybody in his position, but he discouraged such adulation, especially in the younger, more cuddlesome ones, by being erudite and gruff. Those who made it into his small but intimidating retinue were most often upperclasswomen with intellects that wouldn't quit. A "B" from Dr. Maddocks, they said, stood for "Best," as in the best grade anybody could get from him. And most students (particularly freshwomen) found him terrifying or whined about how impossible he was to impress, but Elizabeth, for one, was resolved to work her way past that terror.

While his colleague, Beatrice Brock, would liken the college's ambience to the royal court with all of its accompanying intrigue, Dr. Maddocks behaved more like a knight-errant passing through an enchanted forest, under some banner of chastity, who gets bonked on the head and comes to in a castle filled with buxom succubae that he must resist. And, by God, he does!

In Dr. Maddocks's expository writing class, Elizabeth and Contrary sat in the back by the windows behind their broad-shouldered classmate Vivian. Dr. Maddocks was showing a certain delight in the occasional comment made by "Ms. Breedlove," and even rewarded her at times with the knowing "Ho! Good question!" or "Exactly!" When he turned his back on the class to scribble on the blackboard, Contrary leaned toward Elizabeth whispering, "Breedlove's a brownie-noser, Breedlove's a brownie-noser, brownie-noser . . ."

And Elizabeth's wicked chuckle would not shush her.

"Why don't you just blow him now and get it over with?"

"Why don't you just kiss my ass?"

"The line's too long."

"Why don't you two just shut the fuck up?" grumbled Vivian, the most cantankerous frosh. "I'm trying to get some sleep."

Which made them laugh and caused Dr. Maddocks to turn around, hoping to be let in on the joke. He didn't mind a little sideshow in his class now and then, as long as he was also entertained by it. Unfortunately, on that particular afternoon he was wearing a new pair of chinos with a fly that proved defective. It wouldn't stay zipped and he forgot to check it that last time he was at the board, so he inadvertently became the entertainment. Seeing seventeen young women all beaming up at him bright-eyed and riveted, he assumed that his lecture was going over very well and tossed his chalk up in the air as he paced and talked, feeling elated finally to be astounding them. Because no one had the nerve to tell him that his underpants were showing.

"So, Elizabeth," said Contrary, later that evening, "I see your five and raise you five. None of us had the nerve to tell the poor guy xyzpdq. Are we a bunch of bitches or what?"

"Yes, we are," said Elizabeth, folding her hand. "He should flunk each and every one of us."

Contrary laughed, raking in the pot.

Elizabeth was rubbing her weary eyes even though it was only eight o'clock.

"What's the matter? You feel OK, sister? You look a little peaked." That was good old Mary Contrary: always the first to notice the slightest downturn in a gal's appearance.

"I feel great," Elizabeth insisted, as she dealt the hand for five card draw.

Contrary regarded her more closely as she rearranged the cards in her hand. "No, seriously, you're lookin' kinda pale, sister—Lemme see your neck."

The others laughed.

"Play poker," Elizabeth answered.

"You've been wearing turtlenecks a lot lately," Contrary said, and, addressing the whole lot of them, added, "Ever notice how the girls over in Fey House always wear turtlenecks?"

"Contrary," Elizabeth sighed, tolerantly, *"you're* wearing a turtleneck."

"No, this is a *mock* turtleneck. It's just acting."

The high delectation eventually subsided as they played out the hand, which Elizabeth won. The cards were passed to the next dealer, Helen, whose favorite game was "guts." As Helen dealt the cards, Contrary rolled a joint (from Helen's bag, of course), lit it, took a drag and passed it to Elizabeth.

"Dr. Maddocks always wears turtlenecks. He's probably the King of the Lesbo Vampires."

"Ohhh . . ." said Vivian, the official curmudgeon of the group. "So *that's* why he wants our blood." A poli-sci major, Vivian felt lucky to get a "C" on a paper from Dr. Maddocks, which made him "a pompous ass," in her opinion.

"Tell us, sister," Contrary continued, still intent on teasing Elizabeth, though Vivian was next on her list. "Was Dr. Maddocks wearing boxers or briefs? You can always tell a man by his underpants."

"Boxers I think," Elizabeth whispered on an inhale of dope, giving Contrary a very private look meant to convey privileged and confidential information in regard to her *idol* Dr. Maddocks.

Contrary was most likely to needle people when they were ahead in the game. And poker wasn't the only game she and Elizabeth played. There was the additional challenge on the academic battlefield inspired by Drs. Brock and Maddocks, whose rivalry had an insidious influence. Contrary had become attached to Beatrice Brock's perspective like heather to Heathcliff and Cathy. And it seemed that, in order to be Dr. Brock's favorite, one had to dislike Dr. Maddocks. Contrary insisted that her aversion to him had nothing to do with the fact that she had yet to ace a single assignment in his class. She kept getting "B for Best," and far worse was the minus he sometimes attached to it. It was especially maddening to Contrary that Elizabeth had more than one ace in the hole.

"Damn," said Contrary throwing down her cards when Elizabeth wiped her out. "I don't believe it—three bullets. Hey, where do you think you're going? You don't want to be a party-pooper, now do you?"

"Please don't sing the song . . ."

Contrary got hold of Elizabeth's shirttail, tugging cutely. "Ladies, from the top . . . *Every party has a pooper, that's what we invited you for—party-pooper . . .*"

"God, I *hate* that song," said Elizabeth.

"One more deal, huh? Whaddaya say? Everybody else wants to keep on playing, right, everybody else?"

Everybody else agreed.

Elizabeth sat back down, while Contrary beamed brashly, "Feed the kitty! If you're strapped for cash, ladies, throw in your garters! Whose turn is it to make the beer run?"

And it was only after Contrary had won back some of her money that she allowed Elizabeth to leave peacefully. "Good night, sleep tight. Don't let the lesbo vampires bite."

Elizabeth made her most world-weary face and yawned.

After Elizabeth had gone, Contrary continued to play cards with the others for another hour or so, instigating all sorts of speculation on Elizabeth's private life while professing concern for her. Shaking her head and sighing at one point like a senior citizen looking for a little attention, "I don't know about that girl. I hate to say. I'm worried about her. She's getting awfully involved with that Angry Young Jewish Genius down at WAFA. The lunatic on the radio who thinks he's Lenny Bruce?"

By this time, they were all familiar with the "incredible but not totally inhuman" Reuben Shockor.

"Yeah, we know," Gracie snapped. "He's got horns."

"Well, really, Gracie, who could tell with all that hair?"

"Is he one of the rich ones?" Vivian asked. Coming from a family of self-important WASPs herself—one of the rich ones—she perceived the good fortune of others as grabby.

"Would you guys stop it already?" Gracie simply had to protest, shy as she was. After all, she said, "my boyfriend is Jewish and I don't like hearing this kind of talk. You ought to be ashamed of yourselves."

"Oh, lighten up, Gracie—begosh 'n begorrah, lassie, we're only joshin'. We love the Jews, don't we, Viv?"

"We do?" replied Vivian and no one could tell whether or not she was kidding.

"But this guy, Shockor," Contrary continued, "he's a piece of work—lemme tell ya. I think she's got some weird, sadomasochistic thing going on with him. All they do is fight and fuck."

"Sounds normal to me," sighed Helen, as that fairly described her relationship with her own boyfriend. As a matter of fact, Gracie saw Helen's comment and raised it five, referring to her own relationship with her boyfriend, Alvin.

"Yes, but Elizabeth is the only frosh I know who has her own copy of *The Story of O.*"

"*O?*" Vivian responded wryly, firing up a pipe packed with hash. "I wonder if she'd loan it to me."

"I mean, just look at how fast she signed up to get zapped by those Frankindykes in the psych lab."

"Hey," Gracie finally spoke up, because she was also a volunteer subject for Pip's tutorial.

"Well, really, Gracie," Contrary apologized, sort of, snidely, "you do it for science. Right? What does Elizabeth do it for?"

After a thoughtful silence, Vivian answered, "Art," and everybody laughed.

"Hey, I love the sister, you know. But I'm just saying that she's got this strange fascination for the sleazy side of things. Those weird little drawings of hers? Looks like the ugly consequence of LSD if you ask me."

While Contrary was leading the round-robin trashing—all in good fun, of course—Elizabeth was behind the library making out with the young gentleman whose character had been called into question, Reuben Shockor. He was groping her against a parked car, a rather beat Volvo, which turned out to belong to Dr. Maddocks. Elizabeth didn't realize this until Dr. Maddocks himself appeared beneath the streetlight jangling his keys and humming a song from *The Student Prince,* which he had directed once in summer stock for a local community theater. Hearing his approach, Elizabeth and Reuben both turned involuntarily toward him, though their legs remained entangled and Reuben's hand had slipped a bit down the back of her pants, which made it difficult for her to step away from the vehicle quickly.

Of course Dr. Maddocks was a sport, "Well, hello there," he said easily, exchanging a few friendly sentences with Elizabeth while deliberately ignoring Reuben. He could not resolve what he knew of Elizabeth's studious side with this vision of her up against a car being manhandled by some raven-eyed WAFA punk whose foreplay included a recounting of passages from *Gravity's Rainbow*. At least, that's the novel that was sitting on the hood of his car. Dr. Maddocks handed it to Elizabeth, joking that he found Thomas Pynchon "brilliantly incomprehensible."

Reuben made a bozo face behind his back mouthing the words "brilliantly incomprehensible." He did not respond nicely to being ignored, nor was he accustomed to having his intellect overlooked in deference to some froshy girl.

As Dr. Maddocks got into his car and drove off, Reuben jammed his hands into his pockets, mocking the man under his breath, something to convey professorial bafflement while Elizabeth just smiled.

"He's smitten."

But Elizabeth scoffed.

"He is. He'd like to nail my testicles to a wall. He would. Fucking girls school. You spoiled little twats with your horny old Harvard English professors. You get an 'A' for the shape of your ass and you think you're a real intellectual."

Elizabeth glared at him, "What did I do to deserve that?"

"You don't want to know."

"Yes I do."

"It's 'brilliantly incomprehensible.' "

"And you're the center of the universe."

When his retort was harsher still, she turned her back on him and walked away, which caused him to shout after her until he lost sight of her around a nearby dorm.

"And you're snotty. A snotty little . . . *snot*. And you're so . . . fucking manipulative. You are. Oh yes. But you're yanking on leashes that aren't attached!"

# CHAPTER 13
# Bloodlust

Elizabeth went to fencing practice two, sometimes three times a week, and for no good reason she could ascertain. She didn't know what she was doing or why she should want to do it. Nothing about it gratified her competitive need for measurable results. Was it too much for a novice to expect to have some sense of Winning? Losing? Standing still? With nearly two months of instruction behind her, she still found it all too esoteric to grasp.

Who *thought* of this stuff? The only thing she had any chance of mastering in her lifetime was the salute. Oh, and she really liked the jacket. Everybody looked good in the jacket. Not true of the breeches. Most women would not even bother to try them on, and gave thanks to the goddess of sweatpants. The more familiar of the novice stretchers whom Elizabeth befriended had become a sort of Greek chorus in a tragicomedy on women and their weight:

"Oh sure . . . just what I need: heavy cotton padding for my butt and thighs . . . "

"They make my legs look like friggin' sausage links . . ."

"And white yet, they have to be white . . ."

"Oh, yes, right, skintight white pants . . ."

"Can't have too many skintight white pants, right ladies?"

More mumbling dissent, grousing, growling . . .

And then, there was the prospect of wearing these fattening whites before a wall of mirrors. It was enough to make them want to fall on their foils.

Footwork was the first thing they were taught starting with the stance, *en garde,* or the less pretentious "on guard." Nearly all novices felt awkward or, in Elizabeth's case, ridiculous at *en garde*. It took some getting used to, keeping one's back foot constantly at a 45-degree angle, and then lowering the center of gravity by squatting. Squat had never been a position Elizabeth would use to do anything if she could help it—certainly not in public. In this regard she felt quite fortunate to be closer to the ground.

Only team members had permission to fence on the *piste* without permission from Poins. But sometimes, when the team was performing drills and Coach Poins had that sadistic twinkle in his eyes, he would give a couple of novices the privilege of being terrorized and humiliated by him phrase-by-phrase on the *piste* in a little "conversation of blades."

It was late December just before the holiday break, when Poins ordered Elizabeth and another frosh named Lindy, who was terribly shy, to the *piste* for one of those "blade conversations"—as Elizabeth would refer to them, taking pleasure in distorting the terms just to be obnoxious. Tit-for-French-tat. It was really awful for her and Lindy to have their wretched incompetence exhibited on this veritable stage.

But while they were being brutalized by Poins to the point where they both just lost their will to live, Elizabeth and Lindy shared an out-of-body experience or something because suddenly their blades quit their bitching and became fluent. Elizabeth actually felt herself making some kind of a move on purpose—maybe—and then another, and another, until the inevitable: Oh my gosh, what a rush.

*Bloodlust.*

It happened to the best of them. Even pacifists could be spurred on by the visceral thrill that the sport still retained from its dueling days of old. When Elizabeth assumed the "right of way," meaning the offensive, she took the opportunity to attack and missed the target, Lindy's torso, just as she *expected* she would—"*Voilà!*" She had actually *strategized;* Elizabeth's plan was that her aggressiveness would cause any blustering novice to recoil instinctively. Lindy, however, executed a respectable defensive parry. Elizabeth took advantage of the moment to attack, but damn, foiled again. That was when Elizabeth's alter ego emerged from the primordial ooze.

Or else she was getting her period.

As Lindy tried opening the distance, Elizabeth gave chase, remembering how she had seen Pip do it, accelerating to close the space before lunging. When she heard Poins call out: "Halt," she knew she had hit the target. Right on.

Problem was, she did not stop, but pressed on relentlessly, forcing poor Lindy back until she stepped off the mat. Elizabeth cried, "Aha! Out-of-bounds! Prepare to die!"

Lindy panicked, emergency adrenaline giving her superhuman strength, as she pitched her foil to the rafters and fled screaming bloody murder to the locker room door, flung it open and slipped on the steps, bouncing all the way down on her cotton-padded bum, unharmed.

Meanwhile, the foil Lindy had hurled to the high heavens was on its way down, as if to avenge her, aimed directly at Elizabeth, who stood there unaware in the face of Poins's vein-popping upbraiding. Throughout the gym all other action came to a halt with onlookers being riveted by the scene, yet helpless to intervene. When Poins suddenly realized what was coming down, he jumped back to save himself, which was an instant tip-off to Elizabeth, who spun just in time to see the fateful foil stopped dead in the air, barely an arm's length above her head.

"Hello, Breedlove."

*Holy shit,* sang the Greek chorus in unison, with tragicomic masks agape: Now *that's* fingerwork. While the other girls clasped their hearts and sighed, *My Hero*.

Pip had caught the errant blade—by its grip, no less—with her bare hand, and held it aloft like Excaliber, momentarily, for the full theatrical effect, especially considering she had her own blade in her other hand. She gazed upon Elizabeth with a deadpan aspect that belied something truly dazzling in her eyes, and slightly twitchy, those lips which indicated some greater private mirth in play. It made Elizabeth weak in the knees; a swoony kind of thrill she never felt before had become, in the instant, all she ever wanted to know.

*Whoa.*

As she lowered her arm, Pip brought down the house, as well as the foil, turning the stunned witnesses into a real live audience, who broke into applause and cheered *bravo!* Pip, herself, was entertained by her teasing teammates, as they all fell into line and raised their foils in unison, to salute her. She pivoted neatly to face them, returning the gesture doubly because she used both foils. Afterward, she presented the flying foil to Elizabeth, who could not resist going for her own big laugh when she let it drop like a hot potato.

No one felt like resuming practice, and it was dinnertime besides, so various groups rapidly dispersed, in noisy camaraderie, streaming into the locker room, until only a few remained, scattered to the far corners. A half-dozen devoted fencers from the team, having confirmed that Poins had, indeed, fled the building with a migraine he blamed on Elizabeth, doffed their padded whites and played some hoop at half-court in their undergear.

Pip and Elizabeth remained in the same place, oblivious to the locker room exodus, and eventually found themselves relatively alone still standing face to face.

"You caught that with your right hand."

"Um-hm," Pip nodded.

"But you're left-handed," pointing to her jacket, Elizabeth said: "buttons on the right means you fence left, right?"

"I think so." Pip laughed. "What you said."

"So you're ambidextrous?"

"Um-hm." She held her steam blade up for consideration. "This foil, Italian grip, very rare" and, she neglected to add, very pricey. "See the crossbar? It's the only ambidextrous foil made in the world." She had three of them.

"Hm."

Pip offered Elizabeth her fancy foil, but then quickly retracted, teasing her, about her bloodlust.

"You're not going to hurt me, are you, Breedlove? Because— here"—this time, she did surrender her weapon to Elizabeth, raising both her palms—"See? I'm unarmed. Defenseless."

"Defenseless? You? The dashing swashbuckler, Captain Blood? Who saved me from the fateful foil of my foe?"

"I'm at your service, Breedlove."

"Indeed?"

Elizabeth had been turning the foil over like a barbeque skewer or something:

"So, ah . . . I'm still curious about something, Pip."

"What's that?"

"That first time I came to practice you were showing me the grip, remember?"

"I do."

"And you had turned me in that direction because you said you fence left. Right?"

"Um-hm."

"But you *can* fence right—right?"

"Of course."

"So, you really didn't have to, ah, you know, . . . do that little . . . tango hold, did you?"

"Not really. No."

"Oh. So, you were . . . what? Just making a fool out of me?"

"No, Breedlove. You're nobody's fool."

"What then? Taking advantage?"

Extra long pause.

"Defensive parries."

"Defensive parries?"

"Um-hm. You really need to work on those parries, Breedlove."

Pip walked toward the mirror, and seeing that Elizabeth did not automatically follow, said provocatively, "Come here."

When Elizabeth stepped up, Pip moved her much closer, so their eyes could actually meet there.

"What's the rule?"

"Fence forward," she said lowering her voice kind of close to her ear, enough to feel her speak as to hear, and she shivered.

"Whoa."

"Hm?"

"Nothing."

"OK, Breedlove, I'll parry right with you this time, OK?" Pip's grip, made her fear she would lose hers.

It was startling to look in the mirror, but every time she looked away, Pip would manually adjust her again practically whispering in her ear:

"Fence *forward*."

And Elizabeth was mesmerized just repeating and no longer so startled to see herself in Pip's arms. Now it was compelling and she couldn't look away.

"OK, Breedlove, I'll parry left with you this time, and remember, it's ah . . . a bit tricky . . ."

"Yeah, I remember . . ." Tricky.

"But, I didn't quite do it accurately that time, you see, because I didn't drop my elbow . . . like this . . ." The reason she hadn't dropped her elbow before was because it required her to press against Elizabeth's left shoulder blade, and also to slip her right arm around Elizabeth's waist.

"... so we don't lose our balance ... and fall over ..."

"Uh-huh."

"Which is a bit more intimate, yes?"

"Oh, yes."

Of course, Pip had never lost her balance or fallen over in her entire life. There was nobody more firmly planted on the ground. But in order to drop her elbow "for accuracy's sake," she also had to "... lower the center of gravity a bit, like *en garde,* see ... to compensate for differences in height ... or, well ... "

"Or what?"

"Your breast ... kind of ... gets in the way ..."

"Huh ... well ... my breasts have been getting in the way ... since I was fourteen."

"Oh?"

"Uh-huh ... I hate it ..."

Best to let that one pass, distracted as Pip was by the sensation of her right leg leaning against the back of Elizabeth's left leg. They were close enough to make Elizabeth's balance dependent on the rake of Pip's leg as her body automatically followed its natural inclination to lean back. And the scent of Blue Grass made her woozy. Pip, too, seemed a bit breathless from the proximity ... And now she was murmuring, with her lips almost touching Elizabeth's ear, "You see, Breedlove, this is what I would have done ... if I wanted to take advantage of you."

"Uh-huh ..."

*"Corps-à-corps."*

"What's that?"

"Body-to-body. It's illegal."

That wrested the low-down laugh from Elizabeth that got to Pip something like a depth charge. "What? You mean, like ... the fencing police are gonna ... burst through the skylights and ... bust us?"

Pip laughed quietly, "Maybe," as she reached across to close her grip on Elizabeth's grip, "defensive parries."

"Oh ... yeah ..."

Pip turned her wrist, "Keep your fingers up."

"Looks like we're ... doing the fencer's tango."

She was hard-pressed to hide what her thick cotton jacket could not, the hyper-charge of her heart. When Elizabeth felt them both throb, she panicked, uh-oh. She said something about how she had to be somewhere and turned to skip away, but then stopped: "Oh, yeah. Pip?"

"Uh hm?"

"Ah . . . Thanks for, um, you know, saving my life."

And then she fled for her life.

Elizabeth walked into the shower room, submerged herself completely under steaming water and attempted to scrub herself clean of the underlying sensuality of the place while at the same time reveling in it.

When she returned to her locker she found Pip sitting on the bench untying her shoelaces, and stepped around her without a word.

"Breedlove? I thought you had to be somewhere in a hurry."

"I'm getting there."

She went about the business of drying herself, turning her back to Pip, without realizing this just afforded the best opportunity to sneak a peak. As Elizabeth put on her socks and had to stand to pull on her snug jeans, Pip couldn't help but notice—what's this?—that she wasn't . . . wearing underwear. Laundry day? Suffering a momentary lapse, she got caught looking this time.

"What?" Elizabeth asked, offhandedly, pulling on her boots, with her towel hanging around her neck to cover her breasts.

"I didn't say anything."

Elizabeth decided to take a cigarette break and straddled the bench in Pip's direction. Emboldened, no doubt, from the *corps-à-corps* upstairs she watched Pip, in profile, stripping down to her skivvies.

"Pip?"

"Yes?"

"May I ask you something . . . personal?"

"Sure."

"Why do you . . . um . . . live with Dusie?"

"It wasn't my choice."

"It's not your choice to sleep with her?"

"It's . . . complicated."

"But she hits you. Why do you put up with that?"

"I don't know. Why don't you ask her yourself? Since you're such bosom buddies now."

"What? Are you jealous?"

Pip turned snappishly. "Yeah, I'm jealous."

"What do you care what she does?"

"Look, Dusie hits me because she can't help herself. She's not well."

"So you're her nursemaid?"

"Maybe in a way I am. She's very fragile. I can't just kick her out."

Elizabeth lit a cigarette because it was difficult to keep looking at Pip's face when she was standing there in a man's sleeveless white undershirt, very brief underwear cut really high on the hip and droopy white jock socks. And she didn't look anything like a man.

"I think you feel guilty."

"Why would I feel guilty?"

"Because you used her. And you're still using her."

"Now what could you possibly know about that?"

"I live upstairs, remember? I have ears."

"Well, I live downstairs, remember? And I have ears too. But you don't hear me accusing you of using the men you use. Do you? Because that's really none of my business, is it?"

Pip stepped over the bench where Elizabeth sat and straddled it herself, so close that their knees almost touched.

"May I?" she asked, referring to Elizabeth's cigarette. Elizabeth nodded, transfixed as Pip removed the cigarette right from its perch on her lower lip, and took a long smooth drag, looking dead center into her eyes. She replaced the cigarette in the exact same place she found it, and smoothed her hair straight back with both hands as if she actually knew how much that gesture would enchant Elizabeth.

"Do you know what I think has gotten in the way of everything since you were fourteen years old?"

"What?"

"Your boyfriends."

Elizabeth could only shake her head slowly, galvanized by Pip's restraint, her little tug of the towel around Elizabeth's neck sent serpentine shivers down her spine, as the towel slithered from her shoulder and slipped down over her breast to her thigh. And she dropped her eyes.

Oh hell.

Speak of the devil.

Dusie's voice arrived like a newcomer to the inferno as she called out urgently for Pip. She hadn't seen her all day, was she down there? "Hey Pip? Pip? Is anybody down there?"

Pip rose from the bench retreating smoothly but endeavoring to steady her breath backing up toward her locker without taking her eyes off Elizabeth's. Putting her palm to her forehead, Elizabeth felt her own pulse throbbing.

"Hey . . ." Dusie whined awfully as she turned the corner into their little cave. *"Hey,"* like a clueless little kid left behind in hide-and-seek who suddenly realizes she was deserted on purpose. Stopping short when she saw the two of them, half-dressed or undressed. Not knowing who was coming and who was going.

"What's goin' *on* here?"

Elizabeth suddenly remembered that her knees had bones and stood quickly reaching for her bra. She pulled her shirt out of the locker, buttoned up without bothering to tuck in the tails, and reached for her jacket and books. Dusie's eyes went to slits when she recognized the effort being made to cover for a certain breathlessness. And Dusie was "no dummy," as she said:

"What the fuck is going on? Pip? Look at me."

She grabbed at Pip, who eluded her by sidestepping. "Don't you dare pull away from me, man." She kicked the lockers cursing first at Pip and then at Elizabeth, tears welling as she felt so betrayed: "What are you doing to me? How could you do this to me? You're supposed to be my little sister, you back-stabber."

And then she *sprang* at Elizabeth, shoving her into the lockers before Pip caught her from behind. When Dusie's arms were restrained she started kicking.

"Stop it," Pip said. "Just stop it, for chrissakes, calm down."

She saw the anguish in Pip's face and read her lips, "Go. It's OK." Elizabeth hesitated. "Just go." And she walked slowly backward before turning the corner, hearing Dusie call after her, "It's not OK. It's not. Better watch out. She's settin' you up. She's just playin' with you."

And then she heard Pip say, her teeth clenched, "So help me God, don't touch her. Don't you ever touch her again."

"What about you, Pip, huh? Can I touch *you* again?"

"No . . . don't . . ." but her protest was more like a last gasp, because Dusie already had a good grip, deft and dexterous down there below the practice floor.

"Oh my God . . . oh man," said Dusie. "You're such a fucking liar. Nothing going on back here? She gets you this hot, huh? What a little teaser. Oh sure, like you're gonna push me away now, like I don't know you, man. You need me here, don't you? Huh? How about here?" Pip cried out sharply. "Look at you, you just wanna get off. Yeah, she gets you hot and who's gonna finish you off? Huh? That's right, you close your eyes, you go ahead and pretend she's me . . . 'cause that's as close as you're gonna get, Pip. She is never gonna do for you, not like me, not like this."

To illustrate her point, Dusie dropped to her knees and finished Pip off.

# CHAPTER 14
## Boy Crazy

The week of finals before Winter Break found the WCW campus in a state of suspended "Uh-oh!" as grade point averages and going home for the holidays loomed. How to pass linguistics and what to get mother for Christmas became so much the collective preoccupation that no one seemed to care or even to notice how slowly Hans (dressed like Tiny Tim) served the smoking bishop at the traditional WCW Christmas dinner. Across the campus, Willard women could be seen muttering to themselves more than usual, strung out on everything from caffeine to pizza. Bickering broke out among roommates, chums, lovers, and teachers as everyone scrambled to make deadlines—or excuses.

After Elizabeth completed her finals, she went home for the holidays to be with her family in her hometown of South which was—and this was only part of its charm—three hours due North. In fact, it was located as far North as a body could be without driving into Great Lake Erie. The Breedloves lived in an extraordinary, historically protected and lovingly preserved Victorian home just off the park in the center of town. Big front porch with a swing on the same side as a lilac bush of tremendous size and age, whose pleasing fragrance could make them woozy while swinging on a hot summer day. All of which was currently under two feet of sculpturally drifted snow, like everything else. In South they never wondered if there would be a White Christmas; they were more likely to be concerned about the possibility of a White Easter.

Elizabeth got a ride home from her primary hometown boyfriend, Matt Manfred, who was a junior at a downstate college renowned for its champion wrestlers. Matt was there on a wrestling scholarship and seemed destined to qualify for the Olympics. While he truly had God's Bodykin, he was no dumb jock. His intelligence and charm were palpable, and he was the paragon of the athlete everybody loves. They drove home in his cute little orange sunshine MGB. Roads dry. Blue skies. But it never failed: when they drove under the first sign for South, the big fluffy snowflakes would start falling, turning the world outside the windshield into a winter wonderland.

When they got off the main highway, a car pulled up behind them, honking disruptively and flashing its high beams. They finally pulled over, and realized it was Elizabeth's sister Z in her boyfriend's unfamiliar car. The youngest of the four Breedlove sisters, Z popped out waving her hands in the air. The look on her face said everything at once: I love you, I've missed you, Thank God you're home and, well, we've got a little problem back at the Old Breedlove Place. She pulled Elizabeth aside and they chatted conspiratorially.

One of the guys Elizabeth had been dating in Weston had decided to drive up and surprise her for Christmas. He was sitting in their family room at that very moment, enjoying an Irish coffee with Dr. Breedlove, who had the grin of concerned cordiality pasted on his face. Her mother was buzzing around the kitchen with her other sisters—the oldest was back already from her sophomore year at the Rhode Island School of Design.

The Breedlove house was large and had many entrances. She could make out goodbye with Matt at the back door without the men in the family room near the front door even knowing she was home yet. Then she could come in, greet her family, glare at the unannounced guest from Weston, and push him out the front door before her mother started re-stenciling the dining room.

Oh, those Breedlove girls. The minute the boys were all gone, the family knew this was going to be another one of those stories they told every year, the ones that left everyone in such torrents of laughter that there was nothing to do except refill the wineglasses.

Dr. and Mrs. Breedlove were inseparable as a couple, secure in their rejuvenating love, and maintained at all times a unified front that their children could not corrupt. There was none of that pitting Mommy against Daddy behavior that Elizabeth was now confronted with almost *hourly* at WCW, where the daddy's little wawas were really starting to give her the creeps. Later that evening, after her father was asleep and the Breedlove girls sat up talking, she regaled her mother and sisters with stories of the girls who called home every five seconds. A couple of her poker pals were required to call their daddies—and daddies only—when it came time to schedule classes for the next semester. And one of them, the daughter of a State Supreme Court justice, had already been told that she would be going to law school even though her one dream in life was to be a pastry chef.

The only time Elizabeth went home was during the usual college breaks, and she talked with her mother on the phone occasionally. She and her sisters *did* exchange letters, but they rarely talked on the phone. The Breedloves weren't phone people. They lived for body language and nuance, and they could be so intense with each other that casual phone conversations seemed insulting.

In fact, Elizabeth was perceived as something of a freak for not having her own private phone installed in her room. Elizabeth and Contrary figured they were the only ones on campus who ever used the pay phones available in every dorm. For that matter, they were also among the few residents who didn't have their own personal television sets or mini-fridges. Contrary admittedly would have had those appliances if she could have afforded them. Elizabeth, on the other hand, just had no use for them. In fact, she was certain that such possessions would make her feel even more crowded by life. The Breedloves were all small but wiry, a family of spectacularly fit and splendidly sexy elves. Almost everyone they knew was taller than they, and Breedlove girls loved nothing more than to be lifted up, while dancing, while lovemaking. They had a tendency toward, as Dusie would say, closet-phobia.

Her hometown, South, was also a party town, a summer lake resort that refused to stop being festive when the boat people left. Elizabeth went to a couple of parties every night that she was home, careful to dodge the hometown guys she had left behind, who were still infuriated with her for believing in life after high school. One particularly feral former beau caught up to Elizabeth on Christmas Eve at a Yuletide celebration and found her in the company of another former beau. He pulled her out onto the Victorian porch of her family home, heaped with snow and decked with elegant garlands, to steal a kiss redolent with Irish whiskey under the mistletoe before pursuing her halfway across town (it was a small town) howling like a lovesick animal. For his grand finale, he shoved her down a flight of icy stone steps outside a Gothic seminary where hundreds of revelers had assembled inside for Midnight Mass. Fortunately she fell into a soft snowdrift and nobody inside heard them shouting at each other because of the spine-tingling majesty of an all-male choir singing "In Excelsis Deo" to a full house of tipsy, sentimental townspeople.

It had not been a romantic homecoming for Elizabeth, and she was anxious to return to WCW for Interim, a time when students could spend January on campus taking a special monthlong course, or doing an internship, or—for those good-time Willard gals—enjoying an extended holiday until the first week of February, when the spring semester began.

Elizabeth and Contrary had opted for the intensive course work with their respective favorite teachers. Elizabeth signed up for Dr. Maddocks's "Myth and Archetype," while Contrary opted for Dr. Brock's "The Victorian Poets." For all of the "party-heartying" that had gone on the first semester, the two brownie-nosers' greater competitiveness was revealed in their nearly perfect first-semester grades, which arrived during the second week of Interim. The real test had been the teeth-gnashing discovery that each had been deprived of straight As by the other's mentor.

But they still had done better than most.

"Do you know what Helen said to me?" Contrary asked. "She said, 'Well, of course you and Elizabeth got straight As. You're *English* majors. All you have to do is *read books* all day.' "

Elizabeth rolled her eyes, but was more tolerant of Helen, a chemistry major who held to some popular prejudice of dunderheads that a C student in the sciences was equivalent to an A student in the Arts and Humanities.

"I mean, I love Helen dearly, truly I do. But she's such a Philistine!"

Because so few students were around, Contrary and Elizabeth had the run of the recreational facilities in the student union, Willard Hall, which was the grandest of the grand mansions, given to the college by the family Willard, who had always been the reason WCW was so well endowed. Willard Hall had been the home of the great patriarch and progenitor of all things Willard in Weston, Randolph H. Willard. If his portrait hanging in the foyer was accurate, Elizabeth and Contrary estimated he had died at the age of one hundred and sixteen.

With the poker gang temporarily disbanded during Interim, Elizabeth and Contrary had been enjoying the richly paneled, un-apologetically macho front parlor with its ridiculously massy antique pool table with leather pockets. A real plus was the privacy afforded by the double drawing room doors which slid so smoothly out from the walls on their tracks, and met so perfectly that few intruders had the nerve to knock. Sometimes it was just the two of them, other times Vivian and Gracie and her boyfriend, Alvin Decker, and what few others of their gang were around during Interim. The only game they ever played was eight ball, which Westonites called "slop," but they could hold the table as long as they liked or unless someone else, not easily daunted, dared to assert her righteous turn.

In workaday excursions here and there on campus, in the weirdly quiet dining hall especially, Elizabeth avoided Pip, in passing, or any-where near approaching. These tactics of evasion were a real chal-lenge in such a small space, especially Fey House, and Elizabeth seemed to be developing an uncanny ability to know exactly when Pip was just around the corner.

Dusie was away. For Interim, she was doing the same in-depth study she did every year at this time, a week skiing in Aspen, a week on the beach in Boca Raton, and two weeks in whatever exotic island location the catalog companies had chosen that year to make sure their bathing suits were photographed in the best light.

As for Elizabeth's participation in the weekly tutorial torture, she was mercifully spared any close encounters in the lab. Obviously, she concluded, Pip wasn't keen on bumping into her either. The senior had secured another one of her lab rat minions to run Elizabeth through the test. It was a lot less stressful process, and much quicker with Marla, a prematurely stern and rumpled junior who never said anything beyond what was strictly required during the test. Without the Dusie distraction, Elizabeth was considerably more successful at her nemesis, Nerves of Steel Test. But surprisingly less tolerant of being electrocuted.

She sought further escape by serial dating. But no matter who she was out with, she always seemed to run into Pip. One date-guy was escorting Elizabeth to his car parked behind Fey House, when Pip pulled in, parked her cocky little Mustang and started walking toward them. There had been snow, and the path shoveled on the sidewalk was only wide enough for walking single file. Elizabeth just kept telling herself to avert her eyes, don't look directly at her—as if Pip were an eclipse—while the date, a gentleman, walked at a polite distance behind. Elizabeth's avoidance technique failed when she realized that Pip was playing chicken with her on the sidewalk, hands stashed in the pockets of her navy pea coat, collar turned up like that sly expression of hers that Elizabeth could not decipher. The spy coming in from the cold.

When it became clear that both Elizabeth and Pip would rather collide head on than be chicken, they called it a draw with their private eyes, then stopped dead in their tracks for a face-off.

"Hello, Breedlove."

Change in tempo.

"Hel-lo, Captain Blood."

With a flick.

Hit. There it was. Ha! Halt. Hand judge raises her palm, yes, indeed, a proper hit. Elizabeth had made Pip laugh, so she stepped aside to let Elizabeth pass, taking care not to trip the date—whoops! watch out for that ice patch there, sorry.

On another evening, Pip's arrival actually proved advantageous. Elizabeth was just outside the side door trying to untangle herself from some jerk while maintaining that certain level of "niceness" according to established kiss-off policy. She had given the guy a chance to save face: Just take the goodnight kiss and go away now with some dignity. Because the next level was, "Get the hell off me," followed by the swiftly executed duck and cover to the inside, with the immediate slam of a really heavy metal security door. And oh what a sweet sound it was: the big bang clang and the little automatic lock going click.

On this particular evening, Pip was coming down the side stairs when she saw the utter exasperation on Elizabeth's face just outside the door and flung it open, knocking the guy on his ass.

"Oh. Pardon me, Breedlove, I'm *terribly* sorry, I didn't realize you were out here," holding the door for Elizabeth to scoot inside, and strolled away snickering.

"Hey," the guy yelled, "you pushed me." Turning toward the door, he said, "She pushed me."

But Elizabeth was already halfway upstairs, laughing all the way, realizing: damn, she came to my rescue again.

One unexpected development and pleasant surprise was the success of Elizabeth's most ambitious date thus far including dinner at a slow-food restaurant and a play at the city's respectable repertory theatre on the North Side, The Weston Public Playhouse. To up the odds of getting laid, it was *Macbeth.*

Even Contrary was impressed: "He's a bloody genius. Obviously. *The play's the thing, wherein I'll capture the . . . booty of Elizabeth, The Virgin Queen.* Eight ball in the corner pocket."

One clack, neat.

"Very nice."

Contrary raised her hands triumphantly hearing the hurrah of her imaginary spectators, "Ahhhhh . . ."

"Rack 'em up."

Leaning over the table, poised to break, Elizabeth was undermined by Contrary's perfectly timed line—"Have you ever even *seen* an uncircumcised penis?"—which caused her to knick the cue so pitifully she collapsed face-first on the baize, groaning.

"You are wicked, Contrary."

"Hey, it's a fair question."

"Don't go there, sister. Just don't."

"Cripes, you are so uptight. Lighten up already. I'm happy for you. Hey, you know, I think he might be the one who actually makes it to the third date. Ooh, that was a nice shot."

"Uh-huh."

"Anyway, all I'm saying is—and I believe I speak for *all* of the people here in the tristate area—that we want you to come home from a date, just *once,* with a radioactive afterglow, you know? Matted hair, last night's makeup, mascara bulls-eyes, shirt on backward, temporarily blind and a wicked case of cystitis—the kind you get from a screaming orgasm nonstop from midnight to dawn."

Poor Seth Grossman. That was a tall order to fill for a junior at Princeton who was home on an extended holiday.

"Princeton yet."

"Eat your heart out."

"Speaking of hearts: I see your ten and raise ya ten."

"That's it for me," said Elizabeth, "I'm out."

"Whaddaya mean? Where d'ya think you're going, sister?"

"I dunno," Elizabeth shrugged, reaching for her coat, "I think I'll take a walk down to WAFA. I'm restless."

"A walk? Are you nuts?" Contrary cried, "It's freezing out there!"

"Freezing?" she scoffed. "Bah! You call *that* freezing? Where I come from we eat blizzards for breakfast."

"You mean you're from The Lesbo House of The Living Dead where you eat—oh never mind," Contrary sighed in her most meddlesome motherly way. "Please don't tell me you're walking down to WAFA to see Shockor."

"I might."

"Oh, Christ, I thought that was over."

"Hey, it never really started, you know, so how could it ever really be over?"

"You're such a romantic," Contrary smirked. "Well, Godspeed. Off with you then . . ."

Elizabeth had not seen Reuben in a month, not since their big fight about nothing. Contrary excused herself from the game to accompany Elizabeth on her way down the long hall, which had that special Interim hollowness about it, with half the inhabitants gone. Contrary pulled Elizabeth into the communal bathroom.

"OK, what's going on? Talk to your mother," she beckoned. "You've been moping around like a lovesick teenager. Who *is* this guy? Who is it? And don't tell me it's the 'incredible but not totally inhuman' one either, because my poor old heart can't take the strain of that. Is he married? Is that why you're being so mysterious?"

Shrug.

"Do tell. Oh please. Please, please, please. You mad wag! You pint pot! You slut! You know, if you don't 'fess up, I'm just going to assume it's your manservant, Dr. Maddocks. It *is* Dr. Maddocks isn't it? Ooh, this is so exciting!"

But Contrary could not get Elizabeth to ante up any portion of her secrets.

# CHAPTER 15
# Full on the Mouth

Reuben was sitting cross-legged on the floor with his friend, Albert, a painter. They were working on a "performance art" project. Between them was a stack of *National Lampoon's*, an empty jar of Musselman's apple butter, the crumbly remains of toasted waffles, a bottle of Southern Comfort, a pot of tea, and a bag of homegrown. Reuben looked even more severe than Elizabeth remembered. His lush black hair fell forward over his face like the pen and ink scribblings of an Angry Young Illustrator. He said he had a sore throat, growling more hoarsely than usual, and his neck was wrapped in a long wool scarf like a "tallith with zizith—that's 'prayer shawl and fringe' to you, my little *shiksa goddess*. I trust you had a very white Christmas up there in Ya Ya Land? Come, come, give us a kiss."

Elizabeth frowned at the sound of *shiksa*. It was one of the names she had decided she did not want to be called anymore, and she was immediately disappointed in herself for allowing it to pass. The eloquent speech she had been rehearsing to deliver at this moment was reduced to a mere stutter. And mostly because he seemed genuinely happy to see her. In fact, he was especially affectionate. "Hey kid," he mused more intimately, as if Albert could not hear, "What are you doing here?" pulling her down on his pointed knee blowing dopey smoke rings into her face, nuzzling playfully.

"What's this? What's this?" he teased, gesturing toward her hair, neatly knotted at the back of her head in a style he detested. "Why so marmish?" He tugged at the chignon annoyingly until it was so straggly that she was forced to let her hair down. "Next thing you know you'll be wearing sensible shoes and a Cross Your Heart bra. There.

That looks much better," he smirked triumphantly, rewarding her with a kiss.

Elizabeth suspected that Reuben's positive demonstrativeness was mostly for Albert's benefit. Albert was gay. And despite Reuben's occasional posturing for art's sake, he was actually mortified that anyone might think he was a homosexual.

In light of what Elizabeth had been going through lately, power-dating to overcompensate for her own seeming ambivalence, she was all too happy to indulge Reuben in any flagrant heterosexual display. She lay across his lap like a cat, listening to his dopey dialogue with Albert, knowing full well that if Reuben ever heard her talking to her girlfriends like this, he would call them "insipid twats."

As far as she could glean from their inane dialogue, Reuben and Albert were angry that there were people in the world who didn't recognize their brilliance and pay them handsomely for it.

Reuben was grousing, "My backsliding thought of the year is . . . if I spent all of my time doing idiot's delight, trying to get into law school instead of this express thyself shit, I could be independently wealthy in five years."

As Reuben paused, Albert had time to build a sort of sentence of his own, "That's like, ah, one of the things about life, um, that just . . . you know, it's, like, the only thing that can get you down, man."

Elizabeth rolled her eyes to the slanted ceiling where there was a film poster of *A Clockwork Orange* with Malcolm McDowell as the bad boy, Alex, leering with one mascaraed eye and holding a stiletto. It had been Elizabeth's focal point many times when she and Reuben were in bed. She looked up at it now from where her head was resting in Reuben's lap, musing, "What is it with boys?" even though she had seen the movie four times herself.

Reuben invited Elizabeth to accompany him and Albert to the Fine Arts building to see Albert's paintings. He worked in acrylics, photorealism, mostly portraits. Indeed, Albert had acquired his own WAFA notoriety for responding to a Fine Arts instructor's assignment to do a portrait of his father, a prominent Weston City Councilman, by painting a portrait of his mother with a screw through her head.

Albert also had done a life-sized portrait of Reuben, which astounded for its meticulous rendering of the Shockor edge.

"What's this? What's this?" Reuben pretended to be mortified when he saw the likeness. He mugged and blinked and deadpanned at the canvas as if he had never seen it before. He had, in fact, posed for it. "What do you think, my dear?" querying Elizabeth with an imaginary pince-nez. "Frightening isn't it?" he scoffed, biting his fingernails operatically. "Dorian Gray. Awk. Come on. Let's get out of here. I feel so old."

He was twenty.

After he had kissed off Albert, he groped Elizabeth in the stairwell beneath a graffito: ANDY WARHOL SCHLEPT HERE (written in what looked suspiciously like Reuben's own boldfaced hand), murmuring, "Ahh . . . female, female, normal, wholesome, white bread, wheat futures! Praise the Lord! Be true to your school . . ."

"I don't think Albert likes me."

"Why should he? You've got better tits."

Outside on the quad he invited her to hang out the rest of the night with him at the station, but she was adamant about wanting to return to her dorm. She had changed her mind about sleeping with him again.

"I don't *believe* this. What is this? I don't understand you and Your People. Your silver gravy boats and your Miracle Whip. Your incurable frigidness . . ."

As they walked, her mood was of little consequence to him since he seemed, as ever, more intent upon rehearsing his shtick than anything else. Only when his lines failed to get a laugh did he turn on her, " . . . and you're *strangling* in self-control . . . and you haven't got *one* fucking real emotion to show for all of that fucking little hot snot girls' school self-control . . ."

He seemed intent on walking her back to WCW, but she told him she would rather go it alone.

"Besides," she said, "it's almost midnight. You'll be late for your show."

"So what? What's it to you? I'll be late for my show. So what? Big deal. It's just my *job*. It's just the *only fucking way* I can stay in this fucking Dingdong school—short of blowing Mister Tweety in admissions like Albert does. But hey, fuck my job, right? Sure. Right. I really think that this is the *time* and the *place* for us to have a little *mother–daughter* on why *you* just can't stand to be touched by *icky* boys."

"You really hate women don't you?"

"I threw up on my mother's milk." He actually had been born with some malabsorption disease. "I was a pale, querulous child."

"Reuben, you are *still* a pale, querulous child."

"Right. At least I have an excuse. An organic excuse. But you . . . You sit around with a bunch of rich bitches indulging your Gertrude Stein phase, playing poker and spitting on the floor, thinking you're so fucking subversive and intellectual—hoo-ha!—just because you parody boys. Badly. Ten years from now you'll all be married to guys who *golf!* You'll go shopping every day out there in Dingdong Village, and have lunch at the club, chasing Valium with vodka because you can't get laid by your own husbands."

Affecting her most insipid country-club-lady under the influence of Valium, vodka and a potentially lethal dose of too much politeness, Ms. Breedlove bid Mr. Shockor a very pleasant good evening and a "Well, dear, to hell with you, too." But, of course, she should have known he would be impervious to an attack of good manners.

"Hey."

"Hey."

Unable to slip his wiry grip or resist her natural inclination to follow the lead of a good dancer—Reuben being among the best—she was easily twirled into his arms and dipped for a kiss. A deep one. He certainly was The Make-out Man, and she enjoyed a momentary indulgence, but not enough to justify a sleep-over. She pushed off him the same way she would a little boat from a dock, a bit wobbly as she drifted farther out, but then she got her sea legs and set course.

"Hey, kid," Reuben called out: "Don't forget what your friend, Officer Shockor, says . . ." but he was distracted by a car that was slowing down to get around him in the street. Flashing his high beam into their low, he raised his index finger sagaciously.

"Drive drunk," he said, "Face traffic with confidence."

He looked back in time to see Elizabeth disappear around a bend and hollered: "And button your fucking coat already, wouldja? Jeezus. You're a warm-blooded mammal, remember?" But he gave up, "Ack," waving her off, grumbling to himself: "Go ahead and freeze your Nordic ass off, you snotty little . . . er . . . snot . . . you. Ha! So there."

In truth, he was not comfortable with the thought of her walking back by herself, and under any other circumstance, he would have escorted her whether she liked it or not. But the Shockor Show must go on, and so on he went, however perplexed—maybe even a little disappointed—as to why she had paid him a visit only to brush him off.

*   *   *

It was only four blocks to the WCW campus but they were side streets, some of brick or cobblestone, which followed random paths of least resistance over and around the hills. The big old houses were set back from the street, tenebrific among the antique trees, stone walls and dense hedges. Add ice to the mix and the sidewalks were treacherous, if not untraversable, as well as desolate. Elizabeth had her coat wide open, as usual, paying no attention whatsoever to the bitter chill in her uphill stride, but being very careful not to hit an icy patch unaware. What an irony it was to feel so utterly alone here in the city, when she had grown up roaming the countryside to her heart's content, the open roads and stepping-stone creeks and lakeside cliffs, so far from the madding crowd, and yet she had never known this feeling. Lonely. So this was it, she said to herself, this was lonely. It was a feeling she could have lived without.

She had felt the first pangs before she even set out. It started the moment she set foot in the tremendous WAFA classroom studio with the skylights high above, pipe easels set in a circle around a wooden platform for the model. When she looked at the paraphernalia of art, she realized she was lonely for a part of herself.

Elizabeth was an Olympic listener: she always focused with the same genuine interest and concern to the outpourings of her kith and kin, acquaintances, even strangers. But she did not experience or seek the experience in reverse. She did not know how to let people listen to her, in part because she was easily disappointed the moment someone seemed not to share her level of rapt attention. So what she might have said emerged instead in her artful abstractions, her drawings and paintings, which she had picked up again after a long period of visual quiet. Nobody in Weston knew much about it. She tried not to keep the stuff lying around for the same reason she wouldn't leave a diary or a journal lying around. Her artwork was private.

But she had recently found out that WCW students could take classes at WAFA, which had a nationally known fine arts program that she otherwise would never be able to get into. Every instructor was at least a prominent, if not a famous artist. It was an amazing opportunity, except for that pesky little intimidation factor. To have the balls to sidle up to an easel with those intensely talented art students. It would take her a long time to buck up for that Nerves of

Steel Test. In the meantime, she could take basic art classes at Willard. They did have a rather cute Art Department. But then everyone would know about her secret avocation.

Approaching the campus, she began to sprint, full speed ahead up the stone steps into the floodlights behind the library, running out onto the open quad, doing the hundred yard dash like the tomboy she had been before the impediment of breasts and bitterness and too many cigarettes.

As Elizabeth emerged from a path kicking through some rather peevish snowdrifts, she noticed a low glow from the skylights of the gym and was drawn in that direction wondering was it possible? But no, she thought, not on Saturday at midnight. Maybe it was just Security making their rounds, checking about the grounds for guys looking for some ivy to climb. Pip was *always* out Saturday night, especially at the witching hour, but doing what and with whom Elizabeth could only try and fail *not* to imagine. Or so it was on those restless weekends when she went to bed in the wee hours, trying not to wonder where Pip was, and had to keep twisting away from the window, telling herself to stop this pointless vigil over an empty space in the spotlight out back where Pip always parked her car.

Pip was illuminating the gym, and Security had already been by to make sure all was well, locking every door but one. Pierson was fond of her, with utmost reverence, and took great care not to get caught admiring her workout uniform, always a skimpy white T-shirt, and droopy gray sweatpants, low-slung to show off abdominal ridges. But it was not like Pip to be here this late, and never on Saturday night. Priding himself on being a professional and keen observer of human nature, it was obvious to the chief that Miss Collier had had a big fight with her boyfriend.

For hours Pip had worked herself into a trance performing drills with an odd-looking contraption set up in the corner, a mechanical arm rigged with a foil. Frustrated to distraction and worse: an unfamiliar feeling of out-and-out loneliness, a big gravid nothing in the gut. It stayed with her even when she was out and about in the company of friends or just hanging by herself cruising one of her haunts. She couldn't even flirt. Earlier tonight, she was invited to join a private party already in progress at one of the clubs and she recoiled like a rookie from the first stranger who reached for her through the dark. From there she just drove around and around spiraling Upper Alban Hill until she arrived at this precise moment.

Lonely. Longing. Lunging.

All in the effort to exorcise via exercise the face of a woman who put her at such a loss. Damning all the straight women of the world who play dyke for sport. The ones who freaked out when their fantasy turned into a reality they could not believe existed and did not actually want.

As she thrust the hell out of the machine, her repetitive motions and stance seemed more robotic than the mindless metal opponent she would puncture like a sieve, envisioning each and every one of Elizabeth's lousy dates, whose footsteps she heard overhead, being forced to endure the telltale tones of her toying with boys. Or the silence, which was worse. Now, there was this new guy—Princeton, she called him. She had overheard McNaught in the cafeteria line last Saturday telling her little gaggle of followers that Elizabeth had gone out with "her new, improved Jewish genius, and we're talking tall, dark and handsome Seth Grossman." And by no means a gross man. He appeared to be quite refined, savvy, charming. She was always laughing demurely haha hahaha. Bastard. Willard girls were suckers for Princeton men. Two of Pip's brothers had gone to Princeton, and they got almost as many pretty girls as she did.

Almost.

Last night, Pip caught sight from her window of Elizabeth and Seth on their way out and he was holding her hand—damn him—and worse, she was wearing a dress and (gulp) heels. He's a dead man, said Pip, to the windowpane, which was the term she and her crowd gave to a person of either sex who was smitten. The dead man opened the car door for her and—oh hell—it was a Mercedes. And they rolled on down the road. Pip was betting that this would be the mate date. Heels, for chrissakes, how could Pip blame him? She was grateful simply to be spared the grossly engrossing sound of it above her, because they did not return to Fey House that night. Princeton was just too tall, dark and handsome, no doubt, for such a little girlie dorm bed. After all, how could there possibly be room for Elizabeth *and* his penis, assuming he was well-hung—whatever the hell that meant.

It was midnight. The polls were closed, the votes were in, and the result was unanimous: this evening set the record low in Pip's entire social life. She decided to quit while she was ahead. She gulped down ice water at the fountain and then stuck her whole face in, as she often did, using the front of her T-shirt as a towel. She gathered up whatever stuff she had lying around, tossing it all into her equipment bag, taking care to tidy up after herself, discarding all the empty Gatorade bottles and countless wads of gum wrappers that would pile up around her in no smoking zones. With her equipment bag in one hand and her steam blade in the other, she set off across the gleaming wood court, shuffling in her defeat.

She was reaching for the handle of the locker room door when she heard the familiar clang of the outer door in the main vestibule, which was way on the other side of the gym—that's how noisy it was. Turning toward the sound, she anticipated the entrance of her buddy, Pierson, or one of his deputy dogs, except those guys lumbered, and these footsteps were sprightly.

But soft! What sprite through yonder gym door breaks? It is . . . What?

Breedlove?

Wow. So, that whole witching hour thing was for real, after all. It had to be because Elizabeth just appeared—right over there—out of thin, or rather, arctic air, striding the blast as it followed her, with her wind-tangled hair whipped back. She came in hot haste from clear across center court, in daring defiance of the *no shoes with hard soles* commandment—the saucy minx!—and hers were those Italian city slicker boots with heels.

Pip was stricken by this vision of Elizabeth, who was closing the distance between them swiftly, giving Pip no time to speculate on the reason. She saw the blood-rushing ruddiness of Elizabeth's face setting off, or setting free, the green ferity in her eyes. And so it was instinct that informed the senior foilist's intellect to drop everything she was holding—now—including her fussy Italian foil. She didn't even flinch to hear it fall *kerplunk* on the floor. She dropped it all in that split second she sensed Elizabeth's acceleration into the lunge and did not deflect the hit but rather stepped right into it, imagining it slit the viscera as she felt the vital heat inside bleeding out, and could have died when she caught her and Elizabeth kissed her.

Full on the mouth.

Surprise collided with manipulation, and the impact set them off on a wonderful wayward course kissing and turning, tilt and whirl, a loopy tango to the locker room door.

And *oh dear, my gosh, good God, oh Lord, children cover your eyes, ladies, run for your lives!* for what bodice-ripping ban-the-book kind of lesbian lust was unleashed that night. But there was nothing mysterious about it. The objective became acutely obvious. And there were so many ways to reach it. Intent on proving that a kiss is *not* just a kiss.

It was dark on the slippery stairs, as they descended kissing. Pip had Elizabeth up against the wall polishing the tiles while sliding slowly down. Pip knew Elizabeth's need to be pleased had never been vaguely fulfilled and thrilled like this at last she was compelled to rush ahead of herself. So Pip controlled her, stayed her hand when she reached down, caught her by the wrists, pinned them to the wall above her head, and teased her breathless with words, *"No-no . . . sorry . . . Breedlove . . . not on the first date . . . I'm not that kind of a dyke . . ."* which wrested a low-down giggle from Elizabeth, *"just kiss . . . that's all . . . for now . . . just kiss . . . like this . . ."*

"I'm slipping . . ."

"I've got you, Breedlove . . . I won't let you fall . . . just kiss me that's all . . . see? . . . no hands . . ."

Just legs. And kiss. Like this.

"Oh God . . ."

She felt the glissade, the breath-quickening, the pressure of Pip's legs, one that braced, the other uplifting . . . and on so many levels. At the bottom of the stairs they paused to lose the boots and shoes and socks and—yikes—the shock of that cold tile underfoot, stepped up the pace. More urgently tugged and yanked each other's clothes off, let the stuff just drop. Like a couple of coupling babes in the woods they left a trail of clothes in case they got lost and had to grope their way back to that long-forgotten place where they had been before the kiss. As if such a return were possible.

They stumbled back against a sink where Pip would free her from those tight jeans, wiggling a bit, pulling them down from her hips. That evoked that glorious gratitude expressed to deities. Laundry day it was. Elizabeth reached for the single string that held those sweatpants so magically. One little tug and they dropped straight down.

Pip took Elizabeth's hand to lead her into the darkened shower room. Feeling along the wall, she turned on three showerheads in a row, and aimed them at a single point dead center of the back wall

creating a waterfall. Waiting for the steam to rise, and water temperature to become exactly right, Pip pulled Elizabeth up against her bare
skin still dry, *corps-à-corps,* handling each other roundly up and
down. Followed by the slow walking turn around right into the drink
to be drenched. Pip leaned Elizabeth back against the water wall,
slightly lifted, never slipped, shimmed her legs, and shift, embraced,
allayed her fears. She would not let her fall.

Elizabeth shinnied up her, throbbed, the long, slow crawl, called
out, "Pip," and gasped, "I can't," clawed her shoulders, drawing
blood. Pip wrapped her arms around her neck, saying, "you can."
Their hearts pounded. I can't, you can, she could, she did. One sharp
cry collapsed in shudders on her thigh, as Pip gave in to moaning,
told her, "Hold me . . . tight," with all her might, then going gone,
she groaned, Oh God and then the surge.

And that was just the kiss.

# CHAPTER 16
## Quite Contrary

Contrary was on her way to the library early Sunday afternoon when she saw Elizabeth walking somewhat listlessly up the icy sidewalk.

"Elizabeth?"

"Mary?"

"Jesus Christ, what happened to you? You look . . ."

Elizabeth pulled her collar up around her neck.

"PMS?"

"Yeah, that's it."

"Medic! Hurry! Good God can't you see this woman needs chocolate *stat!*"

"Uh-huh."

Elizabeth resumed her little shuffle with Contrary asking her, "Ah hey there, sister, where you headed?"

"Bookstore. Cigarettes."

Contrary stopped to block Elizabeth's way, took her firmly by the shoulders and turned her in the opposite direction: "Bookstore. That-a-way."

"Ah . . . yes . . . it's all coming back to me now . . ."

"What the hell is the matter with you?"

"Sleep. Need."

"Up all night being guilted by your Jewish genius?"

"Slumber party cancelled."

"Don't tell me. Could it be? I'm seeing some of the signs. Hm. No leftover mascara but pretty bloodshot, dear, and ooh, yeah, indeed, very bruised lips. Good kisser, huh? Nothing like a good kisser."

"You can say that again . . . and again . . ." and her voice ended with a whimper.

"But you always said The Sandwich is a great kisser, a real make-out man."

"That he is. But Mary."

"Yes, dear?"

"Don't call Reuben a sandwich ever again or I will have to bite you."

"Speaking of which. Lemme see your neck."

Elizabeth stepped back beyond Contrary's reach. Opening the distance between them.

"You must have suckerbites all over your neck. You do, don't you? Come on. Let's see."

"Mary."

"Elizabeth."

They regarded each other smartly as the daughters of Contrary's favorite tyrant, the winter wind freezing the Tudor pink in their cheeks, breath turning to cloud of court intrigue full in the face.

"On second thought . . . You're white as a ghost. Are you feeling flu-ish? Seriously. It's going around." Her motherly side emerged as she pulled off her mitten and put her palm to Elizabeth's face. "Holy shit. You're burning up."

Elizabeth was hypersensitive to the touch and jerked away, but Contrary got her arm in a stronghold anyway, intent on dragging her, if necessary, back to Fey House.

"What for?"

"You're sick. You're going back to bed."

"Sick? Are you kidding? I *never* felt better in my life."

"Obviously, you're delirious."

"That I won't deny."

Elizabeth allowed herself to be walked back to Fey House and obligingly complied as Contrary bossed her into going back to bed.

"Now you just lay there and stay there, missy. Hear me?"

"Yes, Mother."

"Don't you make me worry about you. You've got to take better care of yourself. You're burning the candle at both ends."

"Yes, Daddy."

"You've got some crazy look in your eye. Now sleep."

* * *

And she slept through dinner. It was dark when she woke, in a febrile weakness of limbs and disorientation so intense that the throbbing in her temples made her imagine she had just had a little stroke, while the throbbing below the neck recalled the most erotic. She vaguely recalled a dream in which she had begged some feminine animus for mercy. Otherwise, nothing was more disturbing to her than waking up in the darkness without knowing if she should be getting up or going down. She groped for the bedside light, reeling from the feeling of poignant emptiness that is the consequence of circadian upset, with her gradually awakening awareness that she was still shaking and aching in the afterglow of a fantasy turned into a reality that she definitely wanted to handle.

She looked at the clock. It was 6:15 P.M. She heard a soft knock on her door, and stumbled on kitten-bones to answer, checking her reflection in the mirror. Egads.

"Hello, Breedlove."

Pip leaned against the doorjamb, her pea coat unbuttoned. She had just gotten in, didn't even stop by her room first to reconnoiter or toss her coat. No time. She had to see Elizabeth.

"Thank God it's you."

"Who were you expecting?"

Shrugged, "You," and gave that little lopsided laugh.

They were both thinking the same thing: every time I lay eyes on you, somehow you're even more beautiful, and how is that possible?

"You look like a Laplander.

"You look like a kitten."

Elizabeth pulled her in by her lapels, locking the door behind her, eager to embrace. She slipped her arms inside Pip's coat around her waist, reveling in the newfound solace of this place, turned away from the jarring background noises of the dorm, in full swing at this hour, after dinner, the jarringly energized, hallway volley of voices ping-ponging off walls, and then the clashing telephones and battle of the stereos.

But always the inevitable equivocator came knock-knocking.

It was Cynthia from across the hall who answered the floor phone, in passing, then rapped impatiently on Elizabeth's darkened door, not even waiting for a response, because they so rarely got one: "Hey, Lovebreed, yoo-hoo, are you in there? Phone for you. A Mr. Grossman, I believe."

"Oh hell.'

Pip was disappointed that Elizabeth would even consider opting out of this embrace for a phone call from Princeton—the swine—and was reluctant to release her. Elizabeth excused herself with a skittish dip.

This was the first time Pip had been in Elizabeth's room and she felt uncomfortable making herself comfortable without the proper invitation to do so. She was, after all, a Willard girl, too, so she remained standing, leaning against Elizabeth's dresser casually observing the objects on top: the usual girlie stuff, but not too much. She picked up the little black heart bottle of Joy de Patou, lifted the red stopper, brought it to her nose and smiled. That's it.

She knew nothing about the Breedlove family, except for the fact that Elizabeth had three sisters, but there was no mistaking the snapshot of the Breedlove girls, arm-in-arm. Someone had written on the back: *The Fearsome Foursome*.

She was pleasantly surprised that Elizabeth did not still have "a bazillion pictures of her boyfriends" fringing her mirror, as Dusie had described it to her way back in the fall. There was one, however, which was more troubling perhaps than seeing dozens. This guy must be something special, thought Pip, to make the cut from a bazillion to one. She leaned in for a closer look, and, of course, the first thing she couldn't help noticing was his Apollonian physique—wow—clad only in a lifeguard tan and a pair of snugly cutoff jeans. What a body. Such a warm smile, too, with impish dimples, twinkling green eyes, sandy blond hair. Hm. Looked familiar somehow. Reminded her a little bit of one of her brothers.

When Elizabeth returned, they started making out again and flopped onto her little bed like a couple of teenagers, except their groping and pawing was gratifying, even with their clothes on but — what else? A knock on the door.

Pip's limpid eyes opened into Elizabeth's and neither said a word, calming themselves by nuzzling in the limited intensity light that had been folded to an afterglow so low it was barely perceivable to anyone on the other side. Elizabeth didn't respond to the knock, but put her lips once more to Pip's, half-listening in dreamy distraction as the messenger lingered momentarily in the hall, scribbling off a note and slipping it under the door before clogging down the corridor.

Elizabeth rose from the bed like a slow loris moving across the room to retrieve the note. She groaned, "Oh no, not again."

The note said, "Jeff Johnson stopped by."

"Who's Jeff Johnson?"

"He's one of the Dicks who crashes our poker games."

"You're a regular femme fatale, aren't you, Breedlove?"

"Hey, don't be laying that on me. I went out with him one time. Did not have fun. Politely declined any further invitations until we were in double digits. Which forced me to avoid him, won't take his calls. And how does he respond? He starts showing up here. And because I don't want him here, he will call me a bitch. And he'll tell the Dicks, Breedlove's a bitch. And that's as good as the scenario gets for me. If he stays away. If not, I call Security. So. How—I ask you—does that make me a femme fatale? I didn't invite him here."

"You didn't invite me either."

"That's true," she replied. "I conjured you." Then a most unexpected, tender follow-through: "You belong here."

She certainly liked the sound of that, but still she had that gnawing need to know certain things such as: "How many are there anyway? Boyfriends, I mean."

Elizabeth shrugged, feeling awfully on the spot. "Two or three," but then, that wasn't exactly true, "Okay, four, maybe five . . . *ish* . . . Nothing serious. Obviously. It's not like I'm sleeping with all of them. Or even most of them. In fact, at this particular, shall we say, Interim, I'm not sleeping with any of them. What's that look?"

"Who's he?" Pip asked her point-blank, referring to the solitary photograph stuck in her dresser mirror.

"Matt? Hm. How can I explain . . ." she appeared to be talking to herself, so Pip sat placidly by, "I guess you could say he has been my official boyfriend for a while."

"I see."

"No, you don't."

As if to illustrate this point, Elizabeth took the snapshot of Matt and put it in a drawer.

"But since you brought up the subject, how many girlfriends do *you* have, exactly? That is, not including everybody's favorite baby-dyke who shares your bed."

"Not anymore."

"What do you mean?"

"Dusie's not coming back. She's dropping out. I got a letter from her a few days ago. Seems to be having the time of her life jetting from ski resorts to tropical beaches, visiting old friends, meeting new ones. I guess she's been getting lucrative modeling jobs—what are they called?—photo shoots?"

"That's fantastic news . . ."

"I meant to tell you last night, but I kept getting . . . distracted . . ."

"What about the other girls?"

"What other girls?"

"Dusie kind of led me to believe that you have other girlfriends. I suspect there's at least one."

"Why would you 'suspect' that, Breedlove?"

"Oh, I dunno, I was just remembering that night I dropped in on you two lovebirds having a slapfight. You packed as I recall. And you left. Where did you go?"

Not even lovers for twenty-four hours, and already Elizabeth had begun the process of assassinating all existing and/or prior sex slaves. And Pip was loving it.

"I stayed with a friend, an ex-lover."

"Where did you sleep?"

"If you must know . . . I wanted to crash on her couch, but she wanted me in her bed, so we were up most of the night discussing why that wasn't going to happen. Again."

"I repeat: So where did you sleep?"

"On the couch."

"Oh."

"She woke me up early the next morning . . . made me breakfast in bed . . . before she went to work . . ."

It was the truth. Literally. Pip, of course, being the breakfast.

Hm. Elizabeth pondered the potential ambiguities and decided to let it slide this time.

"Yes, well . . . As long as you didn't take any showers."

Pip smiled at her with the memory of last night, still feeling the imprints they left on each other with every touch. And the shower had served as prologue to the swelling theme, inspiring quite a passion play, back in the master bedroom of Fey House.

"What time is it?"

"Eight o'clock."

"Let's go out."

"Out?"

"Oh. I'm sorry. I forgot." Pip said, so snidely, "You can't be seen with me in public."

"That's not true."

"Sure it is, Breedlove. Everyone knows I'm a dyke. If we're seen together, they will assume we're doing it."

There it was, Pip observed, that old familiar look of utter homophobic panic.

"Don't worry, Bree," Pip held up her hand like a good, heterosexual Girl Scout, "I promise not to mortify you in public, or identify you, in any way, shape, or form as "Queer Like Me."

"That's very gracious of you, and I thank you, Pip, but there's only one reason I don't want to go out. I'll give you a moment to think about it."

Pip brightened then and reached for her. And it was back to the passion pit.

They had just begun to make out on the bed again, so they were still dressed, luckily, because it was time for another interruption, as annoying as a knock-knock joke.

Again, they were in suspended animation, except for the great effort it took them both to suppress all that panting.

"I know you're in there, Sleeping Beauty. Open up! It's chowtime." It was Contrary, doing her boisterous Falstaff act. "Come on, pint pot, open up, you ticklebrain! I know you're in there. I can see that teenie-weenie little yellow light."

Bang bang bam, kicking the door with her foot because she was holding a cafeteria tray. "Open up, sister, or I get the housemother."

"Wait just a minute!" Elizabeth called out, checking the buttons and zippers. Pip opened the window to make her escape, and oh what a bitter chill it was. As she went outside, Elizabeth pleaded at the window doing her Juliet act: "I'm sorry."

"Not to worry. I'll just have to forget that part where you said I belonged here."

"Oh man . . ."

And down the fire escape she went, in order to spare Elizabeth the trauma of knowing what she knew about herself.

Contrary stepped into the room with an operatic display "Brrr . . ." as Elizabeth had shut her window only seconds before unlocking her door, making a great pretense to grogginess as if she had been aroused from hibernation.

"It's as cold as a witch's tit in here," Contrary said. She crossed herself, and then hollered, "Dear Lord, you have the window wide open! It's frigid out there. Have you taken leave of your senses, lassie?"

She was carrying a covered tray of food she had lifted from the dining hall and she set it down on Elizabeth's desk, shoving papers aside, ordering her to eat.

"What is it?"

"Eggplant parmigiana."

Elizabeth made a face.

"With extra garlic. I figure you need all the garlic you can get around this place." She pulled her crucifix out from under her sweater and passed it around the room, circling once in a benedictory manner.

"Would you puh-leeze cut that out . . ." Elizabeth flinched at the glinting gold, trying not to laugh, and then proceeded to pick at what little food on the tray she deemed edible, feeling miserable about banishing Pip, but not knowing any other way.

"Eat more."

"I'm not hungry."

"Are you stoned?"

"I am perfectly straight." She couldn't help but wince at the sound of that. How odd to have one's perspective so suddenly altered.

"You're looking better. You've got some color back in your face anyway—What's this?" Contrary asked, picking up Pip's pack of cigarettes from the floor beside Elizabeth's bed. "Have you switched, or are you sleeping with the Marlboro Man now?"

"The Marlboro Man. I like his chaps."

"Uh-huh."

"That's all I could get out of the machine last night."

"I see. So what are these?" Contrary turned from Cheshire Cat to House Dick holding up Elizabeth's pack of cigarettes, which had been sitting on the night table beside an ashtray filled with the butts of both brands.

"I found them in the pocket of my bathrobe," said Elizabeth very coolly. "Would you kindly refrain from poking through my personal effects like my snoopy boyfriends, for crying out loud?"

"I dunno—You're a mystery to me, sister."

"How so?"

"Your love life for one thing. How do you do it? I mean, you juggle a dozen of The Dicks . . ."

"Now there's an image."

". . . And I can't even handle one of 'em, well, okay—two of 'em then. How do you do it?"

"I'm 'boy crazy,' remember? Aw, now, what's the matter Sister Mary Constance? Did you have another fight with Vinnie?"

"Nope."

"Problems with Brian?"

"Just the usual stuff. You know, I'm a saint. He's a jerk. And how come you're letting Jeff Johnson go, by the way? He's supposed to be a catch."

"He's an ass. He still thinks I owe him a blow job for taking me out to dinner."

"You mean you don't? Jeez—and all of these years of thinking I've been getting off easy . . . so to speak."

"Uh-huh."

"I just bumped into Jeff Johnson downstairs."

"You didn't tell him I was here, did you?"

"Not to worry. I sensed the scam. I told him you were down at WAFA dancing nude for your Jewish boyfriend's Performance Art piece. He took off so fast he forgot to ask me which theater."

"Thanks."

"Don't mention it. Oh, and you're gonna love this. You should have heard what I told Andrew Gordon the other night when he asked about you."

"What?"

"I told him you were secretly engaged to Jeff Johnson."

Elizabeth laughed.

"Say. By the way. I meant to ask ya: Do you have any hooch to mooch? I'm wiped out."

"Middle drawer. The film can."

"I know," Contrary brightened as she was riffling through Elizabeth's desk. "It's Dr. Maddocks, isn't it? You're having a wild, passionate affair with Dr. Maddocks. Has he kissed you full on the mouth yet?"

"Perish the thought."

"Did he remove his cigarette?"

"Contrary . . ."

"Or better yet, did you remove his cigarette? Say? Doesn't Dr. Maddocks smoke Marlboros?"

"You know damn well he doesn't."

Elizabeth could not wait for Contrary to leave so she could go downstairs in search of Pip. She made her way down the escape. There were lights on in the room and a John Coltrane album playing on the stereo. She did not see Pip, but the sound of water running in the tub was a clue. She waited until the water stopped, because she did not wish to startle Pip, but as she stepped up to the open door, it was she who was startled.

What a vision she was in repose, stretched to her loveliest limits in a big old claw-footed bathtub, illuminated by the random flickering flame. She opened her eyes and turned her face, with a lazy smile, in the slo-mo voice of the bathtub drawl and said, "Hello Breedlove."

Who was speechless.

"What's the matter?"

"You startled me."

"I startled *you?*"

"What you do to me. The sight of you. I . . . I never experienced this sensation before . . ."

The sensation was one of pure physical arousal in response to the mere sight of another human being who is the object of desire. So this is what all the fuss was about. So this was what all her previous experience was lacking. The glorious helplessness of impulse. Still dressed and not touching, but this rush and pulse, this urge for the surge.

So when Pip said, "Come here, kitten," she was already there, stripped to her claws.

# CHAPTER 17
## The Kai-Kai

Going out together had been an issue between them since that
first night Elizabeth put Pip out like the cat when Contrary
stopped by. Except there was no immediate reason to agree on a resolution or set policy regarding going out because all they wanted to
do from their first kiss in late January until the approaching Ides of
March, which was the beginning of spring break, was to stay in. And
staying in to be inside out, wide awake in a wet dream doused.
Elizabeth dropped down and slipped into Pip's bed most nights,
slept entwisted blissful nest of interlocking limbs and fingers and
scissored legs; and licks of quiffs at napes, tips of tongues, and lips
and teeth that tug. Up down over under top bottom. Everything in
between the in-betweens of women imagining such things. After
which: girls just *gotta dance.*

And that romp led to certain bars and clubs.

There was Dawn's on the North Side, a long-standing blue-collar
tavern with a pool table in back, located on the most unlikely street
between an abandoned steel mill and a cannery. It was doubtful any
man had ever set foot in there, unless he delivered cases of beer, and
not many college women either, assuming the place was rougher
than it was. No guys were allowed but how ironic that was. Just to
walk into Dawn's a gal really had to have balls.

And then there was Weston's first feminist bookstore, Blue-
stockings & Daughter, which had opened a year ago on the South
Side and was quickly developing a reputation as a great (and safe)
place to "talk." This was the euphemism used by those feminist patrons and customers whose delicate sensibilities would not tolerate

the insinuation that they would go there to pick up women just for sex. This, in turn, offended the strong sensibilities of other feminists as a contradiction that was downright Victorian held by swooning prigs. Either way, there was a lot of "talking" going on there. A lot of yak and chatter, bitch and blather.

Lately, there was much excitement as a new coffeehouse was about to open for business on the South Side with a clever unforgetable name: Outskirts.

But the only place where women could dance together—really together—unfettered and without fear was The Titan, undoubtedly the best dance club in town, with a state-of-the-art ear-busting sound system controlled by a real live deejay, along with strobe lights and, on special occasions, cloudbursts of confetti or balloons or sex toys. Ahead of important societal trends as gay clubs always are, The Titan had installed Weston's first disco ball.

The club was on the seedy side of Alban Hill, a neighborhood once so grand but where the only remaining evidence of that was The Titan building itself, a three-story town house built during Prohibition to look like a private residence as a front for a posh speakeasy. Once the world was safe for drinking again, it became a private club for gay men exclusively until 1969 (wink) when women were invited to join.

The entranceway was an experience unto itself. Bouncers checked cards while members and guests either tittered or recoiled from the terrarium containing a real live hairy tarantula named Tiny Tim. Inside, Elizabeth observed the crowd. It was mostly men, with a small sampling of women, all clustered in booths along the sidelines, looking surly while watching a smaller gang of mercurial females whirl like bacchantes on an elevated floor that was elaborately lit from below. Colored lights pulsated in time to a Michael Jackson song. The women appeared in all different shapes and aspects, and Elizabeth tried to figure out where Pip fit in, cloaked in the fabric of which subculture? And then, of course, she wondered about herself. For the first time in her life, she did not know how to react to a smile. She watched how smoothly Pip moved through this world, the same way she fenced, and was determined to secure the same kind of self-assurance, but not by imitation, by complement.

Elizabeth recognized quite a few faces from the college, but she was careful not to acknowledge anyone, at least not overtly, having been forewarned that patrons and their guests were not to be discussed in the presence of civilians. On the way to the dance floor, they stopped by a booth filled with Pip's senior sister pals who gave Elizabeth the collective stink-eye, having long since become accustomed to seeing their friend out and about with some little dink sex kitten kai-kai bimbo-type in tow. They were wondering when she would find herself a nice, appropriate dyke and settle down.

As Pip affably declined their invitation to join them, the most incredible thing happened. She held Elizabeth's hand. She could just hear her old pals cluck about that as they set off for the dance floor. Growing up, Elizabeth and her sisters and friends had always held hands and danced together, in a tribal manner, not cheek-to-cheek, and no one considered it suspect. But this, for some reason, felt *shocking*. This was the most intimate, sexual, public display she had ever known.

After a few tunes, Elizabeth asked where she could find the "ladies room." Pip got a funny look on her face and insisted on escorting her there herself. And Pip felt obliged to recount its back story. When women were first invited to join The Titan, few did, because they found it insulting that there were no separate but equal restroom facilities for them, and they did not appreciate sharing the men's rooms, especially given that the stalls were always being used by the guys for sexual encounters. So the club responded by converting one of the larger men's rooms into a "ladies lounge." The ladies were positively delighted by the décor, which was very Fred and Ginger—not only plush, but a veritable shrine to pink.

Pip told Elizabeth she had been at the bash The Titan put on to celebrate its grand opening, with their usual too much ado, with printed invitations to attend The Maiden Flush. Pip was just a little dink, herself, back then—if Elizabeth could imagine such a thing—among a gaggle of Willard frosh who were the guests of upperclasswomen. She witnessed the ceremonious presentation of a gigantic pair of scissors to the person who got the honor of snipping a large paper strip "seal" affixed diagonally across the door that said: "Sanitized For Your Protection."

While playing docent, Pip neglected to mention the various *theme party* rooms located most discreetly in the labyrinthine hallways and stairwells in the rear of the building—except to say she would not want to get lost back there. There was one lounge exclusively for women which they called, simply, "The Backroom." Female membership had skyrocketed that first year after The Backroom was opened, and the Puritan feminists were aghast, as usual. Their protest had lasted only seconds, as they were headed off by Backroom enthusiasts who suggested they go form a sewing circle to embroider Scarlet letters for everyone. Pip wasn't sure exactly how she would describe the ongoing, largely anonymous orgy going on in The Backroom to Elizabeth without being drawn into a discussion about her own experiences back there.

They sat at the bar of a cozier, calmer room off the dance floor, having a couple of beers and enjoying an ineffable closeness in front of other people, heightened by an almost giddy sense of being free from the vigilant care taken otherwise in public not to appear too familiar. What was liberating here was not simply that they could touch each other freely, but that they did not have to think about it one way or the other. Therein lies the true freedom, said Elizabeth. She had never realized until then how exhausting it could be just maintaining a façade. And, of course, Pip's easy answer to that was to "stop maintaining a façade."

To which Elizabeth replied: "I wish it was that simple."

"It is that simple."

To demonstrate how simple, Pip leaned in closer to give her a brief, but soulful kiss.

It would have been a perfect evening had the mood not been ruined when Dr. Crews appeared out of the blue, literally, entering the room with a flash of strobe from the adjoining dance floor, parting the crowd with her statuesque verve. She had seen the kiss. She had never seen Pip kiss any other woman like that before.

"Hi there," she beamed, in her least attractive manner, which was glib, politicky, and tipsy. "Well, well," she said, extremely sarcasticly. "What a surprise, Pip, to see you out here. You're usually holed up in The Backroom." She sidled up to the bar, or rather she swiveled in place like a gear between Pip and Elizabeth on barstools, nudging her protégé's hip with her hip.

Pip barely turned to acknowledge her. She said simply, "Hey, Jo."

"Hello, Dr. Crews," said Elizabeth.

"Say, Pip," said Dr. Crews, "do you suppose that the occurrence of two surprises in one night constitutes a syndrome?"

"Maybe," Pip muttered. "But don't worry, Jo. You'll sleep it off."

Elizabeth was taken aback by Pip's seeming disrespect and Dr.

Crews's biting response, "Am I acting drunk? Am I *embarrassing* you, my dear? Oh, I am so sorry. And to be carrying on like this in front of Lizbeth—my advisee—can you forgive me Lizbeth? I was very impressed by your final, by the way."

"Thanks," said Elizabeth. She had never seen Dr. Crews outside the ivory tower before, and here in the sleazy elegance of this club she appeared somehow mordant. She stood a little too close and she grinned a little too purposefully. Which is not to say she wasn't riveting, as ever. At least, Elizabeth was listening studiously as Dr. Crews delivered what sounded like an impromptu lecture on the subculture.

It seemed harmless enough until Dr. Crews asked, "Do you know why Pip brought you here, Lizbeth? I mean to this place. The Titan, as opposed to say . . . Dawn's, downtown?" Dr. Crews's eyebrow arched in the direction of Pip's cold shoulder. She didn't wait for Elizabeth to answer the question, because she wasn't really speaking to Elizabeth. "She brought you here because it's the only place that's safe for kai-kai. Isn't that right, sugar?"

Sugar?

"Do you know what a 'kai-kai' is, Lizbeth?"

"Jo, please," Pip interjected, but Dr. Crews ignored her.

"It's spelled 'K-I-K-I' actually. Some people say 'ki-ki,' meaning 'neither-nor.' AC/DC, you know, 'bisexual.' I first heard the term in Buffalo, of all places," musing somewhat bitchily, which wasn't like her, ". . . probably before you were born, girl."

Only Dr. Crews could get away with *girl*. She went on to explain that ki-ki was a pejorative term meant to stigmatize a woman who didn't conform to the strict code of butch-femme. She had written a term paper on it. The fifties were so conformist that even "the sisters" enforced masculine and feminine roles upon each other. Dr. Crews preferred the spelling "kai-kai," and pronounced it with a long 'i,' being Jungian, because she associated it with "The Kai-Kai," which is the title of the epic history of Easter Island, "the place with the big stone heads." Only a handful of the natives can still recite The Kai-Kai, and it involves the story of a female cult of white-skinned virgins who were said to have practiced cannibalism at a cave called "Ana Kai Tangata, The Cave Where Men Are Eaten." It was Dr. Crews's theory that there was a direct etymological link between the Kai-Kai of Easter Island and the ki-ki of the American lesbian community. And that link was a French writer named Pierre Loti, who visited Easter Island in the late 1800s. Pierre Loti became mystified by the legend of the man-eating virgins, and it was Dr. Crews's belief that when Loti returned to France, he introduced the term "kai-kai" to Parisian cafe society, where it came to designate a female bisexual, and eventually was Americanized into "ki-ki."

"It's just a theory," Dr. Crews emphasized, as her hand dropped lackadaisically to Pip's thigh as if it knew the place well. Elizabeth noticed that Dr. Crews touched Pip a lot, absently, in a manner so familiar she seemed unaware she was doing it. Pip, however, appeared acutely aware, and shifted away stiffly every time her mentor leaned closer.

It occurred to the frosh, at last, what was going on between the professor and her pet. Academic rivalry did not explain this underlying tension and hostility, as she had originally presumed. There had been no theoretical falling out. Clearly, this was a crisis of the heart—an emotional imbroglio. She regarded them both in a whole new light.

Elizabeth overheard Jo say, "*Tu n'as pas peur me dire?*"

And Pip's put-upon reply, "*Je ne sais pas que vous dit.*"

At the sound of French, Elizabeth rolled her eyes, muttering into her beer, "*Here* we go . . ." She could see it wasn't Pip's fault. She endeavored to maintain their native tongue until she got so frustrated she snapped.

"Jo, *please* . . ." Pip proceeded to tell Dr. Crews how awful and obnoxious and rude she was being—in French. Pip kept looking over at Elizabeth from helpless hell, while professor swivel-hips practically shoved Elizabeth, her very own advisee, right off the stool.

"OK, that's it for *moi!*" Elizabeth said, squeezing in just to tell Pip she was going for a little walk. She ended up back in the Ladies Lounge, trying to understand what the hell was going on in her life that she was here, now, among these strange boys and girls, feeling possessive toward a woman and becoming privy to an extremely disillusioning aspect of her teacher's private life.

She shut the faucet off. From the farthest stall came the unmistakable sound of lust against a cold marble wall. By the time Elizabeth had combed her hair and returned to the bar, Dr. Crews was gone. Their conversation continued as if she had never been there. She didn't ask and Pip offered no explanation.

Leaving the club later, they had to walk through a line of police officers who were posted there periodically around closing time to keep the peace because local homophobes had been known to show up with baseball bats. The cops formed a stone-faced wall between departing patrons and street traffic, cracking only occasionally when confronted with the more flamboyant personalities and outrageous ensembles on parade. It did not escape Elizabeth's notice that there was a rapid eye movement between Pip and one of the female cops, an attractive redhead whose hair was in a French twist under her hat. The split-second glance indicated that they weren't supposed to recognize each other.

Walking through the parking lot to Pip's car, Elizabeth asked, "You knew that cop, didn't you?"

"I hope it wasn't that obvious, for her sake."

"It wasn't really. I don't think anybody else noticed. But I noticed. I notice some things."

"I'm sure you do."

They got into the car.

"What's her name?"

"What's the difference?"

"Just curious."

Pip's response was a bit coy for someone who was usually direct, "That would be indiscreet, wouldn't it?"

"Don't you trust me?"

Pip's uncertainty was communicated by her silence as she put her car into gear and roared out of the parking lot, leaving the cops in a cloud of exhaust. At the first red light, she said, "Novak."

"Novak?"

"Yes, Novak. That's her name."

"What's her first name?"

Pause.

"Officer."

Laughed.

"Wait a second, you're *not* trying to tell me you don't know her first name."

"Lynn. Maybe."

Elizabeth took the liberty of tuning the radio to the Reuben Shockor Show. After Pip pulled her Mustang into the parking lot behind Fey House, she cut Reuben off with no uncertain irritation, and said, "We have to talk."

"So talk."

Pip's hands were resting on the top of the steering wheel and she was looking straight ahead through the windshield, as if she were still driving.

"There's nothing between us, Breedlove."

"Between whom? You and Officer Novak?"

Pip looked at her, hoping for mercy maybe. Unable to speak.

"You and Dusie? You and me? Or are you telling me that there's nothing between you and Dr. Crews?"

"It's a mess," said Pip, "It's so over. It's been over for a long time, Bree, I swear to God, you have no idea how hard this has been. She just won't let go of me."

"Do you love her?"

"Of course I do, as a mentor and I . . . I idolized her, maybe even had a crush on her for a while when I was a dink, but who doesn't? But I never wanted to be her lover. And I've never been in love with her. She says I seduced her. That I tempted her. But I was shocked the first time she touched me. I didn't stop her. I didn't know how. I was afraid I would lose her completely. And now . . . I'm just . . . so ashamed. I don't expect you to understand."

"You had an affair with Dr. Crews. Wow. Dr. Crews is in love with you. Jeez, you know, it's a bit daunting for a little dink like me. I'm sorry, I . . . What can I say?"

Elizabeth got out of the car in that agitated state and went into Fey House, assuming Pip would follow. But Pip sat there in the driver's seat going nowhere for a while, feeling miserable, with her forehead on her hands on the steering wheel. Elizabeth returned sometime later, startling Pip when she opened the door. "You're going to freeze to death out here, Pip. Come on," she said, pulling her out of the driver's seat and into a definitive embrace. "It's OK, baby, I understand." Her voice on Pip's neck sent a hot shock through the bitter chill. "I understand . . . Come on, let's go inside."

Lying in bed in the dark sometime later, Elizabeth said, "Pip?"

"Hm?"

"What's The Backroom?"

# CHAPTER 18
# Mentor-cum-Tormentor

Dr. Crews was at her desk correcting midterms on the last day of class before spring break when Elizabeth appeared in the doorway.

"Excuse me, Dr. Crews?"

"Yes, Elizabeth?" she replied, obviously recognizing her advisee by her voice because she had not looked up until she heard Elizabeth's hesitation. That merited a glance, which appeared enlarged somehow by her chic reading glasses. Immediately, she recognized the official yellow form in Elizabeth's hand.

"You want to change advisers."

Elizabeth's answer was "Yes," but sheepishly, and she was shuffling in place, eyes darting every which way, even when she asked, "How did you know?"

"I'm a voodoo doctor, remember?"

"Oh. Right." Elizabeth's smile bespoke her distaste, in general, for encounters such as this.

Dr. Crews reached for the form with a crisp authority. Noticing that Dr. Maddocks had already signed it, Dr. Crews chuckled fondly and offered encouraging remarks about the appropriateness of that match.

"After all," as Dr. Crews explained it, "I was never intended to be your adviser. Ours was to be a temporary relationship from the start," Dr. Crews concluded, but the level of her scrutiny remained, a kind of circling before the dive and swoop. "So I'm not personally offended . . . if that's troubling you."

"Well, it does make me feel better to hear that, thanks," said Elizabeth, stepping up to the desk.

The silence that followed was relieved only by the sound of Dr. Crews's salient signature being etched in triplicate. Elizabeth cocked her eye running an instant handwriting analysis, confirming what she suspected: it was Dr. Crews who sent Pip the perfume from Paris along with the note that Elizabeth had espied on Pip's dresser last fall. She had, in fact, looked up what few phrases she had remembered from that day and, however paltry her translation, she had gotten the gist of it. *"Que faites-vous?"* Dr. Crews had written: "What are you doing?" then *"C'est pénible."* "This is punishment . . ." and *"Je suis puni pour . . ."* meaning: "I am being punished for . . ."

Something. But for what? Frankly, Elizabeth didn't give a damn. She made her own judgment regarding the offense and figured Dr. Crews had it coming. Elizabeth wished only that Dr. Crews would accept the fact that her one-sided *affaire de coeur* with Pip was *fini*. It was time for Dr. Crews to go quietly, give up the ghost, make like a tree and leave, see ya later alligator, yer outta here.

*Au revoir.*

And scramez-vous. Is that French enough for you?

"Hm?" Dr. Crews queried without looking up.

"I beg your pardon?"

"I thought you said something . . ."

"Ah . . . no. I don't think so."

But then, maybe she had. More likely Dr. Crews was toying with her, trying to keep her in an insecure, subordinate position. It was dawning on Elizabeth that she had power over this powerful professor. She concentrated on a single phrase intently to put that voodoo telepathy of Dr. Crews to the test, thinking:

*Pip is mine.*

As Dr. Crews handed the form back, Elizabeth received it with a felicitous *"Merci."*

And what a kick it was, too, being the little dink who could cause so much confusion in the dread professor's otherwise placid face.

*"Parlez-vous français?"*

Because, of course, if Elizabeth did speak French, then she would have understood the conversation between Dr. Crews and Pip that night at The Titan. Clearly, that made the professor uneasy.

But Elizabeth felt satisfied by this little test run of sorts, and answered her question with a deliberately uncouth "Nope."

Realizing that she had been played, Dr. Crews flashed her devil-may-care grin. And her authority was quickly restored when she commanded Elizabeth, in the guise of a friendly invitation, to shut the door and have a seat. She wanted to clear the air, she said, but Elizabeth was chary, reminding herself, *Pip is mine.*

After removing her reading glasses, Dr. Crews rested her elbows and clasped her hands in front of her on her desk like a perfectly self-contained parochial schoolgirl. And when she spoke, she dropped all of her usual disarming flourishes, the self-ironic huck and jive, the indiscriminately flirtatious terms of endearment—all of the honey-girls and Lizbeths—and the Jungian implications of, well, *everything.* Elizabeth half expected her to get up and go about the room removing all of the masks.

Instead, she said plainly, "I believe I owe you an apology, Elizabeth, for my inappropriate behavior the other night at The Titan. I had too much to drink, which is no excuse to subject anyone to a pedantic lecture on the Kai-Kai of Easter Island."

"It wasn't so bad. Actually, I find your theory compelling."

"Maybe so, but I apologize also for conversing with Pip in French. She was justifiably livid with me for being so rude. Will you forgive me?"

*"Mais oui."*

Dr. Crews matched her arch regard.

"Now then. Let's be real."

*"Real* is fine with me."

"I won't insult your intelligence by pretending that I'm not a little jealous when I see Pip with other women. I happen to be a one-woman woman myself. My cruising days are over," she smiled wanly. "But Pip . . . that girl, she's a regular Backroom bulldagger. I knew that when I fell in love with her. She has always been brutally honest about her . . . ravenous appetite. As I'm sure you know."

She knew damn well Elizabeth did not know.

"Lord knows I tried to explain this to Dusie, to warn her, but you know Dusie. She sees what she wants to see."

"Don't we all?"

"Is that rhetorical?"

"You tell me."

Dr. Crews withdrew the schoolgirl pose to lean back in her swivel chair. Elizabeth also noticed the gradual return to verbal flourishes. She figured she was just about due for her French lesson.

"I've seen them come and go. They all get hurt. You have no idea how many."

"Bazillions?" Demonstrating that she could bat eyelashes with the best of them: blinkety-blink.

Dr. Crews leaned back in her desk chair beneath the mask of an Ashanti shaman. The coolest student would chill to a sweat in this Jungian Cave of Dr. Crews. But Elizabeth did not sweat. Or perspire, rather, the preferred Willard girl way. She was cool.

"And I'm just another one of the millions getting in your way?"

"You're not in my way."

Smug, too, thought Elizabeth. I can do that.

"Well, you certainly are going out of your way to tell me I'm *not* in your way."

Dr. Crews rose from her chair.

Oh, now, of course, it's the height thing, Elizabeth thought. OK, you're tall.

"What I'm trying to tell you, Lizbeth, is the truth, the reality, because I respect your intelligence and Pip is obviously . . . fond of you."

"Fond of me?" Lizbeth scoffed. "You think *that's* the reality? I sleep in her bed every night—as I'm sure you know, since she's so brutally honest with you about all of her other women. And hey, if that's how she makes love when she's fond . . . well, jeez, I better get the hell out before she thinks I'm *swell* and fucks me blind."

So there, she thought: *Pip is mine.*

Ooh. That rattled her. There was no outward sign, of course, but Elizabeth knew.

Behind the steely mask of this professor of psychology was a flash fire, which her steady voice belied.

"You have quite an ego, Elizabeth, so you may find this difficult to hear, let alone to accept, but you are not unique . . . in the greater scheme of things . . ."

And *scheme* certainly was the word.

"I know Pip makes you feel very special. It's part of her charm. And Lord knows she has quite a talent for 'making love,' as you called it, not unlike her talent for fencing. She's a competitor. Her pattern of seducing straight women—kai-kai, which is the same thing—is about competition. It gives her some kind of a sexual thrill to *win* over the type of woman who men chase after. I do believe I am the only full-fledged, out-and-out, one hundred percent genuine *dyke* that Pip has ever had any kind of serious relationship with."

"What about Dusie?"

Dr. Crews shrugged: "Too soon to say. She could go either way."

"And yet, here I am, younger than Dusie . . . You know next to nothing about me . . . but you've already got me typed and filed away."

"Oh? Are you trying to tell me you really *are* a lesbian, Elizabeth?"

"No. I'm trying to tell you that my sexual preference is not decided by you."

"I do know something about you, Lizbeth."

"What's that?"

"You're nobody's fool."

"Meaning?"

"She's playing you for a fool."

"Maybe *you're* playing me for a fool."

Dr. Crews scoffed: "I was just trying to spare you some heartbreak, girl, but I can see it's already too late, isn't it?"

Elizabeth swallowed hard against the biliousness rising up inside.

"You're hopelessly in love with her . . ."

Dr. Crews shook her head slowly to convey her condolences. "It's always the same. Every year. The game: seduction. The target: you. Do you know what she calls her targets?"

Elizabeth wasn't taking any questions at this time.

"Virgins."

"I . . . never . . . I never heard her say anything like that."

"Well," Dr. Crew smirked triumphantly, *"you* wouldn't."

Elizabeth felt ill. It took her a moment to regroup. Somehow she managed: "I hate to disappoint you, Dr. Crews, but there may be a break in the pattern here, because Pip didn't seduce me . . . I . . ."

"No?" she replied, raising her eyebrows. "Funny. She told me that she was going to seduce you . . ."

"I came on to her . . ."

"You think?" and here Dr. Crews laughed, which could only seem gratuitous considering she already had Elizabeth doubting her own senses.

". . . last summer . . ."

"What?"

"Last summer . . . she told me she would seduce you . . . before she even met you, Elizabeth."

"I don't understand . . ."

*"Mugs & Plugs."*

*"Mugs & Plugs?"*

"She was quite taken by your photograph. She showed it to me and then tore out the page just to . . ."

Hurt me. Dr. Crews had not said this out loud, but Elizabeth heard it loud and clear.

"She tucked it in the breast pocket of her jacket, her jean jacket, fencing side, no doubt, over her heart. Such a Romantic, that girl. I wouldn't be surprised if she's still carrying it around. You are the virgin sacrifice."

Elizabeth reached for her cigarettes.

"Do you think your status as the only frosh in Fey House is due to some random selection process? I know you were told that, but really, what are the odds that Pip would pick you for a target and then just happen to find you've been assigned the room right above her head?" Dr. Crews appeared keenly entertained by Elizabeth's palpable distress, as she watched her former student and advisee go through half a dozen matches trying to light her cigarette.

"Of course, I got you bumped into my seminar so I could keep an eye on you."

Elizabeth struggled desperately, but kept it all to herself. She did not possess the experience and knowledge to effect a counter-manipulation just then. Not on such a grand scale as this. And furthermore, she lacked the will since, even if only a fraction of what Dr. Crews had just told her was true, it was appalling nonetheless. And thank God for that knock on the door because she could not bear to hear anymore.

"Come in," said Dr. Crews.

It was Pip.

"Well, well. Speak of the devil," said Dr. Crews, and the three-way silence that ensued was like a congress of the deaf and dumb and blind. Dreading the worst of all possible reasons Elizabeth would have that horrified look on her face, Pip asked, "What's the matter, Bree?"

"Bree," Dr. Crews muttered under her breath. "Isn't that sweet."

But Bree couldn't speak. She was shaking her head as she picked up her stuff and hastened to make her escape. As Pip got hold of her arm, she jerked it violently away and looked back with her high intensity green-eyed glare, angrier than Pip had ever known her to be. Then she was gone in that flare.

"Jo," Pip said in a dreadful whisper, "What have you done?"

"I put an end to the *manigance.*"

The trickery. The scheme. The game.

"You didn't," said Pip, her voice so diminished she couldn't even hear it, herself.

"I just did you a favor, *ma chère.* My love . . ."

"You just . . . you just betrayed me."

"I betrayed *you?* Well, isn't that a fine how-do-you-do? As I recall, you came to me, just to punish me. You wanted access to that . . . that . . . *minette.* I got you that. On a fucking platter. Table grade, too, isn't she? Hm? A real honey-fuck. I did that for you, just so you would stay . . . friends, at least, as you promised. Instead, you fall in love with her. And you can't even tell me that. You could have told me that."

There was nothing Pip could think to say, so entwisted was she in this *manigance* that it choked off her voice entirely.

"So, Pip," said Dr. Crews in conclusion, "we're in the same place now."

Which was exactly where Dr. Crews believed they both deserved to be.

"No," Pip whispered, shaking her head, "we are not the same."

"Yes," she nodded, "we are."

Master mind-fuckers and corrupters of virgins no less.

But Pip got the last word in protest as she turned and left in search of Elizabeth:

"No," she said, "I am not that. I never was. And what Elizabeth and I have in love is something you can't stop. She knows the truth in my heart, Jo, and you don't. *You never did.*"

From across the quad, Pip could see Elizabeth nearing the pond and gave chase.

"Don't touch me."

Pip backed off circling, having forgotten the no-touching-in-public rule. She seemed to be pawing her hair until she had a fistful, as if she would rip it out at the roots.

"I don't know what she told you, but please, just give me a chance to explain."

But what was she going to say to stop the inevitable devastation of self-incrimination? Had she corrupted and crushed this love of her life?

But wouldn't you know it? Here comes Mary Constance.

Pip grit her teeth to keep the curses from escaping when she heard "Here comes Mary Constance," as irritating as the singsong treacle of an ice cream truck.

"Shall I dive into the pond and hold my breath until she's gone . . . or I drown?"

Elizabeth muttered the cover story under her breath, "We're on our way to fencing practice. We just stopped down here to, ah . . ."

"Smoke a joint . . ."

Pip to the rescue, as usual. She had already produced the handy prop and was firing it up when Contrary stepped into the scene, inhaling deeply, hoping the smoke would muffle the shrill alarm that had gone off inside.

"Excellent!" said Contrary, accepting the offering with a huff and a puff and tentative nod in Pip's direction. They had never been formally introduced. "Ah, you're the fencer. The one who sticks it to The Dicks on May Day."

Being several inches taller, Pip looked down her patrician nose at Contrary, *au contraire,* chewing gum between her front teeth slowly turning, on a spit of sorts. Every so often it would snap.

"Well, it certainly is an honor to meet you, Pip."

"Likewise . . . McNaught."

Snap.

Pip stuck around long enough to suck the joint down to a roach. And then she addressed Elizabeth on the subject of fencing practice, forcing her angry lover's eyes to answer her own, so that she might glimpse what she knew, surely, to be pure and true in Pip's heart before it sank in the muck.

"Are you coming?"

"Ah . . . I dunno, Pip . . . maybe. Later. You go ahead. I'll catch up."

Sinking, sunk, stuck.

"All right, then . . . See you later, Bree . . ." Pip slipped, trying quickly to recover the "d" that got stuck, but finding only " . . . love."

As Pip turned to walk away, it was Contrary who called her back. "Hey, Pip?"

"Yes?"

"Do you play poker?"

Pip shrugged. "I know the basics."

"Yes, indeed, I bet you do," Contrary turned brightly to Elizabeth. "Only a card sharp would be that humble."

"I'm no *sharpie,* McNaught. But I do tend to pick up games quickly."

"That would explain your friendship with Elizabeth."

"Does my friendship with Elizabeth need to be explained?"

Snap.

Contrary looked from Pip to Elizabeth, speechless for once. She would have felt humbled had she not been distracted by the pack of Marlboros in Pip's breast pocket. She made a big show of asking for one. "Thanks," she demurred, which meant, "Look out, here it comes."

But clearly, the games Contrary played didn't faze Pip in the least. She was quick on the draw with her lighter, and Contrary leaned in closer to the torch: "How gallant . . ." and puffed until she smoked.

"There's a game tonight in my room: Whitman 206. Friendly, penny-ante stuff . . . we have some fun. Why don't you join us, Pip?"

"Maybe I will," Pip replied, with her jaw set so pretty in the hood of the WCW sweatshirt she wore beneath her jean jacket, as the weather was still chilly.

Contrary marked the smoothness with which Pip pivoted on her mink-oiled Dingos and set out along the stone path around the pond. "Damn," she said, as she watched Pip walk out of earshot, "She still looks thin in a million layers. I hate her."

Pip was one of those mesomorphs whose clothes always hung just right, while the rest of the world felt their own weight. Being cursed with a "lousy metabolism," Contrary constantly complained that her clothes felt "bulky." She never could have worn those clothes in which Pip always looked so "goddam handsome." It was hell sometimes for women like Contrary, who would starve themselves and never look one ounce lighter, being forced to sit in the dining hall with women like Pip who could eat like horses, dress like cowboys and never look bulky.

"Well, isn't she the haughty one?"

Elizabeth shrugged, watching Pip until she disappeared around the corner of Willard House.

"You are vampire feed, sister."

"Don't worry about it."

"Don't worry about it? The sun's going down and you're hanging out at the pond with, not just any old lesbian vampire, but Count Collier, herself, the highest ranking dyke in Fey House, and you say, 'Don't worry about it'? You poor innocent—I know you think you were just smoking a joint, but that's not how it looks "

"Really? Well, how does it look?"

Contrary drew in her breath. Seeing that Elizabeth was in no joking mood, she opted for a safer answer. "It looks like you're even more of a babe in the woods than I thought."

"I can take care of myself," said Elizabeth, getting crispy, "and stop calling her a dyke."

"Isn't that what they call themselves over there in Fey House?"

"I don't know, or care, what *they* call themselves. *They* can call themselves anything they want. *You* can't."

"Says you."

"Yeah, says me."

"OK—whoa!" Contrary shuddered as she backed off: *"Excuse me."*

For a while they both held their tongues. Contrary flicked a dead cigarette butt into the pond in defiance of its pristine quality, and then she said more pacifically:

"I have this theory about you . . ."

"What's that?"

"You've spent most of your life hanging out with guys, right? You never liked doing girlie stuff, right? I'll bet you never even got into a slapfight at a slumber party, for instance."

"I went to slumber parties. I did girl stuff."

"Yeah, but you never got into a slapfight. I know. You were the one in the big horn-rim glasses, like Little Miss Diplomat—you and Shirley Temple Black. You were the one who was always trying to get those screaming bitches in the baby doll pajamas to 'be reasonable.' "

"Well . . . yes, I guess."

"So were they? Were they ever reasonable?"

"Come to think of it, no," Elizabeth realized, scoffing. "It probably just seemed that way because they were all cried out."

"Exactly."

"Your point being?"

"My point being, you don't know women. You don't know the difference between a woman who wants to be your friend . . . and a dyke—oops—who wants *you* to be her sugar-pants!"

Contrary's focus on Elizabeth's face was astute, wondering was it possible? But no, it couldn't be. Elizabeth was the most confident man-eater she had ever seen. Therefore, it must be her bleeding heart liberalism, some goody-goody, small-town, upstate way of counting a token of each "type" on her tidy little ark.

"So, you have a homosexual friend now? How nice. How good of you to adopt a lonely lesbian, Sister Elizabeth. Did you give her a lovely fruit basket for Christmas?"

"Why do you persist in this? Someone as intelligent as you? A lover of literature? Is this the way you have to talk down there in The Valley to be tough? To elevate yourself because you feel so put down?"

"Hey, I'm just kidding, OK? Lighten up already, will you? You know I love all peoples, be they white, be they black, yellow, green, whatever . . . Jeez, what's the matter with you? You're so touchy lately. I mean, fuck ya if ya can't take a joke! See, this is what being friends with lesbians does to you: it makes you hormonally unbalanced *every* day of the month."

Contrary had never seen Elizabeth so down in the mouth.

"Oh hey, come on, hon, if I really had anything against your friend, Pip Collier, would I ask her so nicely to join us for poker?"

"Yes."

"So, sue me. We need some fresh blood. And what better donor than a real Fey House vampire, huh? I'm getting tired of winning the same old markers off the same old rubes, you know? I'll bet she comes from some bucks."

"I dunno," Elizabeth shrugged, "probably."

"What does her daddy do?"

"I dunno. I don't . . . know her that well."

Contrary snickered, "Maybe he's The Marlboro Man."

Elizabeth caught her eye in a sidelong glance.

Contrary shook her head, "You're a mystery to me, sister."

"Yeah, well . . . I'm a mystery to me, too."

# CHAPTER 19
## Feed the Kitty

Elizabeth skipped fencing practice in order to avoid Pip and went down the hill with Contrary and a gaggle of others to celebrate the official start of spring break. Most of them were leaving the next day for two weeks. To avoid any possible confrontation, Elizabeth didn't even return to her room to drop off her books, but went instead to hang out with Contrary and Helen in their room until the poker game got under way.

Unfortunately, someone had broken the poker gang rule and invited a couple of boyfriends. They weren't the problem. It was the tagalong guys who always came with them from the brother school. A carload of the Dicks showed up at Contrary's room, including her roommate Helen's boyfriend, Todd, and Gracie's boyfriend, Alvin Decker, the physicist. Those two were familiar and welcome, but Elizabeth blanched when she saw Andrew Gordon and Jeff Johnson, the Dicks who had been vying for her attention. There was also some strange guy no one seemed to know, not even the guys who brought him, named Douglas Marbles.

To kick off the spring break celebration, the boys had decided to celebrate by chewing some magic mushrooms. "Now that's what we call 'bringing the bridge mix,' isn't it, girls?" Contrary said snidely, doing her very pleased yes indeedy Dr. Beatrice Brock routine, because poker and mushrooms were not a good mix at all. A plastic baggie filled with dried-out caps and stems of organically grown psilocybin was passed around. Both Elizabeth and Contrary declined. But those who had no qualms about participating in a mass hallucination washed down the mushrooms quickly with beer in order to beat the gag of that godawful bitterness and spooky consistency, "like shriveled skin," Decker said.

Within the hour they were getting off.

Jeff Johnson slipped his hand over Elizabeth's knee while Andrew Gordon bared his poetical side, endeavoring to impress her with an intellectual engagement that was only made tolerable by the assurance that he was sure to forget it all the moment he entered medical school.

"This is the last time we play poker with the guys," Contrary mumbled in an aside to Elizabeth, when the tripping poker players were taking another break to laugh hysterically about God knows what.

"I hate the way guys play games."

"I hate it worse the way girls play games when the guys are around."

"I know whatcha mean."

It was true. The girls did play differently when the boys were around, which was to be expected. But why did it seem, like, more often than not, the boys brought out the worst in the girls?

Back on the floor acting as dealer, Contrary became increasingly irascible on the issue of sex and games. She was losing more money than she could afford to lose, which was none, really. Elizabeth noticed her friend's pique, and the next time the kitty was high, and it was down and dirty, she folded, as if she had been bluffing when she had, in fact, been holding a flush.

There was a knock on the door and the Dick who was crawling around on the floor closest to it was expected to answer. That was Douglas Marbles, the guy whom nobody knew though he behaved as if he had known them all for years, so no one had the heart to ask. He reared up on his knees to reach the doorknob. There stood Pip, looking fabulously rakish in her black leather biker jacket with the silver studs and zippered cuffs. A bit of self-parody on her picaresque adventure out there in the hinterlands of heterosexuals.

"Wow," said Douglas Marbles, still on his knees before this hallucination.

Contrary welcomed Pip gregariously, waving her inward with a gee whiz of good will, clearing a spot on the floor beside her own wonderful self by pushing over a lesser player, telling him it was his turn to make the beer run. She introduced Pip around.

"And, of course, you two already know each other."

"Hello, Breedlove."

"Pip," she replied, with a perfunctory nod.

Pip mustered a grin, pretending as if it didn't pain her to see Elizabeth toying with two lap dogs like a languid mistress. And it was only after the multiple conversations resumed that Pip ventured a glance in Elizabeth's direction.

Nobody noticed anything unusual about the exchange because they were so out of their minds. Pip didn't catch on until the first deal when Alvin Decker complained that his cards were "too large"—obviously his hands were shrinking—and couldn't they "switch to the micro deck?"

Otherwise, they all played on rather typically, arranging and rearranging their hands and placing their bets. Pip kept glancing at Elizabeth as if to ask, "Is this really you? Are these really your friends?"

But Elizabeth would not look back, and in fact, was unusually quiet. She folded her cards at one point and went to the stereo to put an end to the Linda Ronstadt record, and switched over to the radio because it was after midnight, tuning the receiver to WAFA–FM just in time to catch Reuben's intro:

"The incredible, but not totally inhuman, Reuben Shockor, boys and girls. Before we begin tonight's polka show, I'd like to put an end to the ugly rumor that Patty Hearst is carrying my love child . . ."

Contrary guffawed. He was a funny guy; she gave him that. Elizabeth reached for her coat, mumbling something about needing some fresh air.

"Are you feeling okay, sister?" Contrary asked Elizabeth.

"Sure. I'm fine." And then she left, and Pip could not follow without betraying her trust. Pip stopped staring at the door Elizabeth had just passed through when she heard Contrary, the Cheshire Cat, reminding them all to, "Feed the kitty."

Feed the Kitty, indeed.

So Pip fed the kitty, being forced to endure Contrary's teasing remarks about Elizabeth.

"Well, we all know where Elizabeth's going, don't we ladies?"

Snickers all around.

A quarter of an hour later, Contrary excused herself to go to the bathroom, after which she went to the pay phone way on the other end of the hall. She put in a call to the Reuben Shockor Show and was taken aback when he answered his own phone. She asked him if he would take a request.

"Depends on what it is," he replied.

" 'Whipping Post,' " she said, "Allman Brothers Live at the Fillmore East."

He laughed.

"All twenty-two minutes of it."

"Yeah sure, I could use a nap."

When she returned to the room all of the Dicks and other trippers were gone, having followed Decker outdoors to "listen to the resonance of the Red Giants," which had something to do with the stars.

"Thank God they're gone. Now we can play some cards, gentlemen."

The girls had some fun round-robins, one of which dealt with their general consensus that guys were pretty much all hopeless when it came to fondling a woman's genitals. While Pip was certainly entertained, she had nothing to contribute until Contrary said, "Say, Pip, may I ask you an extremely obnoxious, offensive, tasteless, tactless, appalling personal question?"

"Sure," Pip replied, with perfect comic timing, which impressed and tickled the lot of them.

"Have you ever been with a Dick?"

"Define 'been with.' "

"Not 'Dick'?"

Pip smirked over her hand ha ha, but in a moment she answered quite frankly. "I've had only one such experience."

"Ooh, this is so exciting. Do tell."

"Junior high. A make-out party. I got stuck with a boy and decided to find out what all the fuss was about."

"Ooh, this is so exciting. Do tell."

"We kissed."

"Did you get to first base?"

"I believe so."

"Second base?"

"I'm not sure, what is it?"

"I really have no idea. Ladies?" she queried them but they were all similarly confounded. "How did you find the kissing?"

"Well, in the interest of science . . . not totally terrible. I've had worse . . ."

Helen was confused: "But I thought you said this was the only guy you . . ."

"She's talking about girls, you ninny . . ."

"Oh. So, you're saying girls can be bad kissers, too?"

As all of the women in the room expressed confidence in their superior ability as kissers, Contrary suggested that Pip kiss each and every one of them and be the judge.

"It's a titillating proposal, McNaught, but . . ."

"I feel so rejected."

"Me too."

"Yeah."

"Sorry, ladies . . ."

"So tell us about the Dick."

"Well, it was the strangest thing because, I felt it through his jeans, and was somewhat intrigued . . . by the mechanics of it all."

"The word is 'penis,' Pip. Can you say 'penis'?"

"I don't think so, no. Do I have to?"

"Of course not, dear, please . . . proceed."

"The next thing I know, he opened his fly and it was like one of those pop-up books for kids, you know. It just seemed too . . . lively."

She wasn't sure why this made them howl, but she was pleased to be considered amusing.

"And now tell us, please, did he fondle your genitals?"

"I believe he thinks he did."

"How would you describe the experience?"

After a pause, and in her acerbic style, Pip said, "Well, it kind of felt like he was washing his car . . . and I was the sponge."

This wrested screams of hilarity. It was true they cried, so true! And how ironic it should come from her, after only a singular experience.

When "Whipping Post" came on, it had the effect Contrary wanted, insofar as the poker gang all lost it: they were floored with raucous laughter. Contrary let Pip in on the joke, explaining that whenever Elizabeth was visiting Reuben at the station during his show, he would put on "Whipping Post" because it went on for so damn long, they could have a wild "make-out session," rolling around on the floor of the little record library, which seemed carpeted for this purpose.

Pip turned pale.

"Are you okay?" Contrary asked with genuine concern.

Pip managed to mask any further sign of her heartache by contending that she was not much of a drinker, and was feeling rather queasy at the moment. But she still felt the necessity of staying a while longer, even to the bitter end of that interminable song. That turned out to be even more excruciating, which she wouldn't have thought possible, because when Reuben returned, not only did he sound sated, he made good on his promise to Contrary that he would tell his listeners that the song had been a special request for "Mother Superior and all of the sisters up there at the Willard Convent for Women. Don't forget to feed the kitty, girls." Naturally, Reuben had a field day with *that* one before segueing into Bruce Springsteen's instant classic, "Kitty's Back," which they cranked up.

Pip said she had to call it a night shortly thereafter and headed back to Fey House with a heavy heart, wanting to uproot any plant life that crossed her path as she made her way across the green, cutting through shrubbery like a twister.

# CHAPTER 20
# Weight Check

Pip watched Elizabeth from across the dining hall having lunch with that motley bunch of juvenile delinquents she called her friends. Those party-hearty-*plus* Willard girls, down and dirty. The whole lot of them, coffee hop-hopheads, who could command, mobilize and ignite the entire dining hall and still have a chance to reach the nearest exits before the emotional velocity broke the sound barrier.

But to Pip, they were just little dinks looking for a food fight. They sat in that smoky corner, an alcove really, with the ambience of the backroom of a bar. Pip and her friends sat at the opposite end of the dining hall, near the door. So nobody got in or out of the dining hall without being checked out by the Dykes of the Roundtable.

Pip watched as Elizabeth and Contrary rose and set off down the widest aisle dead center of the dining hall. It was on this runway that all Willard women were perused, judged on their appearance and then, of course, on their appearance. Any walk down that aisle, from a saunter to a dash, could mean only one thing:

Weight Check.

It was Elizabeth and Contrary's turn to make the coffee refill run, and they were juggling cups and saucers like gum-cracking diner waitresses. There was no way of getting around it: they had to pass Pip's table. Elizabeth tried not to look, but instead she caught Pip's frown and promptly tossed it back. She was trying really hard not to notice the glowering faces around Pip at this little ladies luncheon in progress. A few had spotted her at The Titan and considered her a shameless kai-kai. In fact, she could have sworn she heard someone say it. Sanctimonious bitches.

Contrary went to the dessert counter to place an ice cream cone order with Hans, while Elizabeth stepped up to the coffee urns. As she stood there filling cup after cup, she shivered suddenly as every follicle on her nape pricked up, and that could only mean one thing: Pip was standing behind her. But not so close as to be indiscreet.

"Hello, Breedlove."

"Ouch," was her reply, as she splashed hot coffee on her hand. "Yeah, ah, hi."

Not exactly the reaction Pip was going for, as she had been aching from Elizabeth's absence last night. Of course, there was absolutely no outward indication of this. She just stood there looking down at Elizabeth with her usual insouciance and perfect posture, which sometimes made Elizabeth feel Pip was *being* taller than she was on purpose.

"How was your evening?"

"Splendid," she lied, borrowing one of Dr. Maddocks's favorite words, before remarking, "but, hey, Pip, I heard you were the life of the party last night. Miss Popularity. Contrary told me that Douglas Marbles is smitten. I think he's gonna ask you to the prom."

Pip was not amused. But Elizabeth wasn't playing this one for laughs.

"See, Pip, that's what happens when you fraternize with, well, frats. Mixing with the mixers. Next thing you know, you'll be kissing icky boys and they'll be crowning you Queen of the Maypole. And we all know what *that* means," Elizabeth whispered. "*Penises*. Welcome to my world. All for penises and penises for all."

Elizabeth's manic blathering was meant to prevent any reasonable conversation from taking hold. The more relentless the jest, the more volatile the aggression. Then—look out below!—because the jokes fell flat, collapsing under the weight of her true emotions.

But Pip retained her silence, in stone, always the foilist holding her zone. She considered this antic disposition of Elizabeth's, playing out her own little Hamlet here, more pathological than manipulative.

Finding Pip's nerve as unnerving as her own yammering must have been, Elizabeth made a biting interrogation out of a simple "What?" and caught her breath.

"I was just waiting," said Pip, "for you to say something real."

Pip was visually vivisecting Elizabeth's every move. She was also doing battle with that horrible green-eyed monster Jealousy chewing and jawing its way through her viscera, engorging itself. She had never encountered such a beast as this. There were a few women in her past who had evoked some jealousy, but now she realized those were merely slights to her vanity or pride, compared to this. All her effort to cage it before escaped just failed.

"Did you fuck him?"

The saucer that Elizabeth dropped did not break, but rather bounced and spun like some jerky drunken toy. She looked Pip so fully in the eye then, and with such indignation that even the devouring beast looked up from its Filet of Pip's Heart.

Whether this Desdemona was true or false, or an essay question, Pip the straight A student, 4.0 average, Phi Beta Kappa, did not know the answer. And so she got her first F, from Elizabeth in the form of a resounding "Fuck You."

So Pip just—*quit* her.

Returning to her table just long enough to collect her stuff, without saying anything to her tablemates or even glancing at any one of them, she headed for the nearest exit. Four years of square meals at a round table together, what *didn't* they know? They gave her a moment of silence, in solidarity, a sisterly reverence. And then in their highly codified and esoteric feminist, lesbian, separatist secret language that was just beyond the comprehension of any heterosexual, they said, "Yep."

"Uh-huh."

"It's love."

"Um-hm."

"Definitely love."

A big sigh all around for love.

"The dink?"

"Not the dink."

"Yep."

"Bow-legs?"

"Pussy-cat."

"Sugar-pants."

"Trouble."

"Capital T."

"Table grade."

"Het?"

"Kai. One hundred percent Kai."

"Poor Pip."

"Yeah, phew."

"She's a dead man."

"Um-hm."

"Big time."

"Yep."

At that moment, all doubt was put to an end most dramatically, as their attention was redirected toward the kitchen where Elizabeth emerged, sans coffee cups. They watched her bandy-legged swagger ass all the way back to the table, murmuring quietly among themselves, esteemed judges in this Miss—or Ms.—WCW pageant. There were conflicting opinions on how she should be typed. But they agreed to disagree. And the ass always passed.

Back at her table, Elizabeth collected her stuff and made a beeline for the nearest exit, which was, in fact, the farthest. And damn, she had to walk past the band of bulldaggers again. What was next? The bathing suit competition?

And they had to give her credit, too, for as much as they protested the particulars of her private sex life—about which they knew absolutely nothing—she did exhibit a certain derring-do. Instead of just passing them this time, Elizabeth stopped short, as if to reposition the shoulder strap of the heavy canvas WCW book bag she had slung over her back. When *Pow,* without warning, she turned right into the awesome force of their collective stare. Took it full in the face, without flinching, or even turning the least bit pink in the cheeks like most dinks. Not a blusher, she. And then, of course, there was the matter of her mouth being, well, did they dare say?— pretty—and titters all around regarding their theory of women's mouths. While eyes were windows of the soul, mouths were . . . but wait, what was *this?* Did she just give them *the kiss-off?* Yes, indeed, Elizabeth had kissed her fingertips and flicked it at them. Executed just as Contrary had taught her, Weston-style, by those girls whom the nuns deemed fresh.

Prompting another round-robin:

"Damn . . ."

"She's good . . ."

"Real good . . ."

"Could work."

"I'm seeing it."
"Love?"
"Could be . . ."
"Balls?"
"Definitely balls . . ."
"Yep."

The little scene between Pip and Elizabeth had not escaped Contrary's shrewd eye either. While waiting for Hans to scoop, she had noticed a certain intensity over there by the big shiny metal tanks of joe. Elizabeth's back had been to her, and she could only see Pip in profile, but both were clearly vexed. Pip's eyes were smoldering. A minute later, she heard the saucer drop and turned, as did everyone else, with no real urgency toward the minor commotion. No breakage, no applause. She did not know who had dropped the saucer, but she thought it odd that neither of them picked it up or even seemed to notice it as they were face to face now in some kind of a showdown. She had what she called her "radar" for tracking distant discussions, picking up blips from a sudden change of course or a pending collision. And these two were bleeping Mayday . . .

Mayday . . .

Why? Well, she had her theory.

"What was *that* all about?" she had asked Elizabeth after she caught up to her.

Elizabeth just shrugged, same as ever, unbothered, no problem. A little suspicious that, but otherwise a quick recovery.

"I failed to report for my tutorial experiment yesterday. But hey, jeez, oh, man, I just realized I've gotta run. I'm out of here in an hour and I'm not even packed." She wished Contrary a lovely spring break.

"What about the joe?"

"Sorry . . . gotta go."

When Pip pulled her car into her space behind Fey House later that Saturday afternoon, right beside a rather adorable Triumph Spitfire in British Racing Green, she had a hunch this car would be taking Elizabeth away from her for the next two weeks. And sure enough, as she walked through the house to the main staircase, she was taken aback to see an attractive and natty gentleman in his prime, with blond hair, blue eyes, and a boyish face standing at the reception desk asking Marla to please place a call upstairs to Elizabeth Breedlove. As Pip turned on the landing to get a better look at him, Marla called up to her.

"Yes?" she replied, leaning over the banister.

"No one's answering on three, would you please tell Elizabeth that her father is here to pick her up?" Pip could not help but beam at that, especially as Dr. Breedlove was offering her his charming gratitude.

But Elizabeth had already spotted his car, and was coming down the stairs right toward her, carrying her suitcase, completely distracted.

"Hi, Daddy," she called down to him over the banister, which caused her to stumble, "Whoa," right into Pip.

"Oh, jeez, excuse me, ah . . . Pip. I'm sorry."

"It's quite all right," Pip replied.

"Well, ah, have a nice . . . break, wherever you may be."

"Thank you, Breedlove, same to you . . . up north in South."

Elizabeth gave her the snidely-eye, muttering under her breath, "Ha ha Captain Blood."

Out back, as Elizabeth waited for her dad to put her stuff in the car, she looked up at Pip's window to see Pip standing there at the panes, looking grouty, staring down at Elizabeth. Both of them were in disbelief that this vision would be all they had to carry them for the next two weeks, not even knowing if it was over between them or not.

# CHAPTER 21
## Whipping Post

And what a miserable spring break it was. Elizabeth saw Matt, but felt too anxious to relax and have fun, particularly if it involved any sexual activity—and, naturally, it did. Matt, being a sensitive guy, perceiving her subtle evasions, asked her if there was someone else. And for once, she could not lie to a guy. Yes, she said, there was someone else, but that was all. Being a gentleman, he did not push, and most incredibly, they continued to go out and enjoy themselves. They went to a few movies and parties and hung out with familiars at their legendary roadsides, and danced at a couple of popular clubs. They could do this because they never felt that heart-busting passion.

Upon returning to Willard, she found Pip's room dark and vacant. Even the window was locked. First day back to class, in the dining hall, no Pip. Second day, same thing. No Pip. Third day, she was due in The Cube for the last time—thank God—and got there early being eager to end it. She paced the perimeter like a round peg in a square hole. Next time around, when she made the turn toward the open door, she stopped dead. Pip was standing there in the doorway with her hands in her pockets, as self-contained and motionless as a Calder stabile. It appeared that her expression had not altered at all since Elizabeth saw her last. Pip made the same observation of Elizabeth. Neither was anxious to break the silence of two weeks for fear of making matters worse. Even the customary *Hello, Breedlove* was too risky.

Pip took the first shot in the sulky girl showdown.

"How's your . . . *official* boyfriend? The grappler. Manfred?"

"He's fine," Elizabeth replied, taking her time: "How are all the *virgins* on the Eastern Seaboard?"

Given that intro, Pip thought it best to close the door for privacy's sake. Elizabeth was relieved, despite her closet-phobia. She ignored her impulse to bolt.

"I have only one thing to say to you, Pip. And it's the answer to that insulting question you asked me before the break, even though you don't deserve it. I should let you ponder that one forever. But I won't. I did not 'fuck him,' Pip. Or anybody else. But, hey, thanks for all your confidence in me, *lover.*"

"I'm sorry," Pip said, humbly, hanging her head, though there was great jubilation and dancing in the streets of her mind.

"I'm out of your sight for one night and you automatically assume I'm jumping into bed with someone else? Why is that, Pip? Is that what you would do? Head on over to The Titan to fuck a dozen women—anonymously for chrissakes—in that . . . *bull* pit."

"I really am sorry, it was just so hard for me to watch you walk out that night and not be able to go after you . . . like torture . . . and then, lying there all night . . . not knowing where you were . . . not having you there in my bed . . . for the first time in how many weeks? I miss you . . . painfully . . . please forgive me, Bree."

Elizabeth had to turn her face away unwilling to show she had missed her so terribly, too.

"Why did you do that? Were you afraid I would call your bluff? Do you think I went there to *out* you in front of your poker pals? I just wanted to see you before you left for two weeks. Even if I had to sit there for all eternity pretending I don't know you."

"Where do you get off trying to guilt me for making you pretend anything, Pip? According to Dr. Crews, our whole relationship has been based on pretense, from day one."

"I don't know what Jo told you, but it's bullshit."

"Bullshit? Really? Let's see . . ."

At that, Elizabeth approached Pip, who really had no idea what she was up to until she reached out and unbuttoned the left breast pocket of her jean jacket, thinking godammit, Jo, how could you? There was no point in trying to stop her. Pip could do nothing but stand there watching, like a dishonored soldier being stripped of her stripes. Elizabeth went pale when it was just as Dr. Crews had described it: unfolding the page Pip had torn from *Mugs & Plugs*.

Elizabeth held the page before Pip like Exhibit A. But she said nothing.

"What does this mean, Pip? What the fuck does this mean?"

Pip seemed determined to withstand the derogation in silence lest she incriminate herself any further. She did flinch, however, to see Elizabeth rip the picture into confetti, letting it flutter to the floor without taking her eyes off her.

"You ordered me from a catalog? You were just flipping through and saw my picture and said, 'Hm, she's kind of cute—I think I'll send away for one of those.' And I arrived Special Delivery, didn't I? Right to the room *above your head* . . . right to your . . ." She grabbed one of her notebooks from the table and hurled it at her, ". . . bed."

Pip was shaking her head, no, that's not true, but she could not offer an alternative explanation.

"You set me up. All of you. You're all liars. Lying and pretending every step of the way. Dusie tried to tell me that day she caught us in the locker room. 'She's just setting you up,' she said. I remember. She knew. Did you do this to her, too? Was she one of your 'virgin' experiments gone bad? What kind of twisted little . . . mind-fucking sex games have you been playing here? You and your lover, Dr. Crews? What am I? Your tutorial?"

Pip thought it best to let Elizabeth spew first to see what she knew and where she stood.

"Well, I don't play that. I don't like your little game, Pip. I think it's fucking sick. I don't want to play with you anymore."

She picked up her stuff and stepped briskly to the door, grabbing the knob, but Pip pulled up behind her faster, "Wait," she said, "please don't run away, please not again . . ."

As if she could. Pip put her left hand to the door, braced to keep it closed, and Elizabeth felt her lover's hard body pressed against her back, and all she wanted was to go slack and be with her without all of this "Manigance . . ."

"Listen to me, please . . ." Pip murmured miserably, with her lips just behind and below Elizabeth's ear, the erotic parotid, causing shivers every time. "This is not a game . . . or a tutorial experiment . . . I did *not* order you from a catalog. You are not a trophy, a subject, a pawn, or any other object or objective . . ."

"I have to get over this," said Elizabeth. "What have you done to me? I don't know this feeling, never felt this before. What's happening to me? I can't get you out of my mind. I try and I try. I missed you so much I thought I would die."

"Why? Why do you try? Why can't you just let it happen?"

"I can't. I just can't. I feel like it's all going to come crashing in on me. I don't trust this feeling. How can I trust you?"

Pip kissed her neck, feint left, feint right, this way and that and right up and down the middle, grazing lightly with her teeth, whispering, "Don't you trust this?"

Elizabeth had the shakes.

"Let go . . ." said Pip softly, referring to the doorknob.

She released her grip on the doorknob, all swoony, leaning back into Pip, who embraced her from behind with an erotogenic precision, handling her up and down, holding her tighter, lowering the center of gravity for leverage, her long strong legs pressing steady to the inside.

Elizabeth's claustrophobic panic, cornered as she was then in The Cube made her balk, "No, Pip . . . I can't do this Pip, let go," but Pip just tightened the grip to make her more secure. Her voice was sonorous, a murmuring and then moaning inevitably from some great distance, which was Elizabeth, because Pip was tugging at the stays, buttons, zippers, anything that blocked the progress of her fencing hand.

Then Pip turned her around, lifted her to face her face, leg sliding like a side of the blade, watched her dreamy eyes, burrowed with her thigh, and higher, rising, made her climb the wall.

"I had your picture in my pocket over my heart . . ." Pip was saying. "I've looked at it a million times . . . because I love you . . ."

"Oh God . . . Pip . . . I . . ."

"I fell in love with you that first day when I saw you in the mirror. I didn't know who you were. And then I fell in love with you every single time you caught my eye. And you know that's true. I know you do. Please . . . just let me . . . love you."

There was no arguing against Pip's palmy persuasion. All she could do was say "yes, anything, anything . . ." and hold on, for the trembling, unbelievable, it went on so long. She got lost, and she bit Pip's neck to keep from crying out, but barely stifled the sound. The lab rats and monkeys in the lab next door sensed it all and went kind of wild.

\* \* \*

Andrew Gordon had been calling Elizabeth every other day since the last poker game. Several weeks later, when she still had not answered or returned any of his calls, he sent her a poem he appeared to have scrawled in his own hand, affecting the calligraphy-like effect on parchment paper.

"Oh jeez . . ." Elizabeth muttered under her breath as she stood in the crowded post office removing her mail from a quaint brass box.

Looking over Elizabeth's shoulder, Contrary's guffaw promised more of the same at this lovesick Dick's expense, "Ooh . . . Lord Byron . . . ," as the curious gathered 'round for Contrary's dramatic reading:

*"She walks in Beauty, lik (sic) the night . . ."*

From the midst of the laugh riot that followed Contrary's image of Elizabeth as this Beauty who would "lick sick" the night, a round-robin ensued:

"I think it's so sweet . . ."

"You would. He's a chauvinist pig if you ask me . . ."

"Byron? What a wimp . . ."

"Yeah, a Real Man would've sent Keats . . ."

"Hey, I'll take the Dick if you don't want him . . . bitch . . ."

"Did she just call me a bitch?"

"Slapfight slapfight yippee . . ."

Under the din, Elizabeth studied Contrary's face more closely, noticing that her laughter was sardonic, that is, fake, belying some greater distress. She took the letter back from Contrary, folded it and stuffed it in her pocket, waiting until the crowd broke up and rattled away before she asked, "Did you have another fight with Brian?"

"Not a fight exactly. More like Armageddon."

"Hm."

"He gave me the old 'I think we should see other people' routine. Uh-huh. Meaning that sleazeball's been seeing someone else. Uh-huh. That's what he told me last night. Can you believe? Right in the middle of trying to finish my fucking Keats paper for Beatrice too — that jerk. I threw the book at him. And then the typewriter. Thank God it's not electric. My mother was right: stick to the manual. Less to repair. Didn't even put a dent in it."

"Did you kill him?"

"Brian? Yeah."

"Good."

Contrary sighed, "It's Gloria Spencer. Can you believe?"

"Not Gloria Spencer."

"Uh-huh. The one with the face like an inflatable doll."

"What are you going to do?"

"Pop her cheeks with a hatpin."

"Did you tell Brian about Vinnie?"

"You know I tell nobody but nobody about Vinnie. Nobody but you and Father Gregory."

"So why are you so mad at Brian?"

"I can cheat. He can't. I have my double standard to uphold, you know."

The more Contrary joked, the more she choked against her increasing emotionality, ducking through an arbor to get off the main path as she and Elizabeth walked toward the dining hall for lunch. They found momentary solitude in the garden of Japanese maples behind Fey House where Contrary burst forth with a great deal of fragmentary information beyond The Brian Betrayal, adding things about her father being sick and her mother barely being able to support the family and her feeling guilty for having sex with Brian, and Vinnie, too, because she was "basically a good Catholic girl, you know?" And then she did a flip-flop, damning her religion because men had invented it and she couldn't handle men, and how the hell did Elizabeth handle so many of them without getting hurt, when she couldn't even handle one of them, and was hurt all the time. And after she had gotten this off her chest, or rather, off her enormous breasts, as she had put on a little weight recently, she whined about her weight.

The usual.

"Oh . . . yeah . . ." she added, "and I think I'm pregnant."

But Elizabeth had already guessed that.

# CHAPTER 22
# 19th Nervous Breakdown

It had been blessedly convenient that Dusie decided to drop out of college, and did not return to share the master bedroom in Fey House. And her decision had been mature, reasonable, entirely her own. Going back and forth from snow bunny to beach bunny in the company of goodtime friends, attractive models, made her cheerful. She switched modeling agencies in New York and immediately started getting more serious shoots in more exotic locations for more astonishing fees. She sent Pip and Dr. Crews postcards, which she signed with a little happy face dotting the "i" in Dusie.

It was certainly therapeutic that her stepbrother, Lt. Bram, had been shipped overseas, stationed somewhere in the Middle East for much of the year.

By late April, Dusie had finished all of her sun-drenched location sittings. The summer catalogs and magazines were already laid out by then, and in the day-for-night world of fashion it was time to come back to the East Coast to prepare for the spring shows of woolens and furs for the fall collections. On her first free weekend, she decided to fly in to Weston to visit her family, and then drive up to WCW ostensibly to pick up the two rolling racks of clothes and all those shoes she had left in the closet when St. Bart's beckoned. She did have an ulterior motive, however. Maybe if Pip saw how mature and independent she had become, she might take her back. If reason didn't work, she could always try showing Pip she was "brown all over" and see what developed.

The first thing she had not counted on was to find her stepbrother visiting when she arrived at her parents' home. It was a surprise, they said, knowing how tickled she would be. She went into the powder room and threw up. He trapped her later that night when their parents went out. They got into a fight. It seemed like everything that had been right these past months was suddenly all wrong. The next day, she fled into the city, with the intention of seeing Pip. But her original plan to be cool and mature "had gone to shit, because of Bram, that shit." Still, she was determined to try.

When she arrived at Fey House, Pip was not there. So she decided an even better approach was to wait for her in the tub. Soon the room was wafting with peach kernel oil, part of weekly care packages Dusie used to get from her mother, overflowing with all those Crabtree & Evelyn products she had left piled in their decorative wicker basket in the bathroom. When Pip finally got home, she smelled the peach kernels and realized the day she knew would come had come at last.

When Pip walked into the bathroom, Dusie rose from the bubbles to greet her. But she knew from the look on her ex-lover's face that it did not bode well.

"Hey," said Dusie, like a little kid picked last to send over in a game of Red Rover. "You act like you're not happy to see me or something."

"I'm sorry, B.D. I meant to write. I really did, but I just . . . well, I was so busy, you know, ah, with . . . the tournament coming up, I've been working out at the gym a lot and . . ."

"Yeah, sure. I understand." She slid back into the tub and started to cry.

Pip could not stand it when Dusie cried. When Dusie cried, she generated some sort of "psycho-electromagnetic" force, and strange things would happen. Pip would rather Dusie took slugs at her outright than to sit there sobbing, stirring up electrons, causing lights to flicker and objects to break in odd ways, and even triggering freakish reactions in innocent bystanders, usually those in the service profession. A perfectly nice waitress, for example, would start out friendly enough, but caught up in the whirlwind of Dusie's quantum whine, would suddenly rear like a double-headed Hydra when Dusie asked for sugar substitute. Naturally, she was oblivious to this effect she had on people. When someone got short with her, Dusie was puzzled. "Boy," she would say, "what's with her?" Dusie, of course, never saw herself as the generator of these "negative vibes." It was always someone else who was getting her period.

Today she wailed, thinking of all the time she had spent away, assuming that she was doing something "mature" allowing Pip "some space," hoping this would "improve their communication." The pop psych recipe she had gotten out of the fashion magazine she worked for now registered as a Big Mistake; she *knew* she shouldn't have bothered reading the articles. Panicked by the realization that she had already lost Pip, without ever really understanding that she never really had her, Dusie reverted to the one thing about herself that she believed her lover could not resist, which was, naturally, The Body Beautiful.

"You didn't even notice how good I look," she said, pouting like a haunted high fashion doll winding down from a trying shoot and excessive medication, but all the more photogenic for the dreamy lack of focus.

"I noticed."

"I'm brown all over."

"Yes, I can see that. Very nice."

Dusie traced her own collarbone down over a gold cross (minus the little corpus, being Presbyterian) that she always wore on a gold chain. She licked her sunburned lip. "Aren't you just a *little* bit happy to see me?"

"Maybe you should dry off and get dressed."

"But why?"

"We need to talk."

"Not me. I need to *fuck.*"

"Well, maybe I need to talk, okay?"

"OK, so we can fuck first and then talk."

"Just talk."

"You and me? Just talk? Oh yeah, right, sure, Pip. Like, I'm supposed to believe that." Dusie all but guffawed. But Pip's affect remained somber.

"Aw, come on, Pip—look, I wanna show ya something really neat," she said, standing up, " . . . I went to this salon? And got, like, this bikini wax—whoa. The wax stung, but the woman who did me? Like, she practically *did* me." She twirled around cutely and even bent over slightly. "See?" At a time when women were daring to suggest that there were political implications in every cosmetic affectation, the appearance of a significantly, but not wholly denuded Dusie— "That would just be too weird, boy"—was all the more compelling in a house full of women who made a point of not shaving. It would have caused a riot (or at least a stimulating round-robin discussion), had it not been for the fact that Dusie was such a doozy.

But, the sentient appeal of Dusie at her bath was no longer compelling to Pip. Still, she had a responsibility to her, owing her honesty and compassion, and maybe even an extensive apology. Dusie was sitting in a little pool of bubbles with her face in her arms and her arms on her knees sobbing. Pip leaned on the edge of the porcelain sink, watching her without saying anything until Dusie blew her nose into a bubbly washcloth, redolent with peach kernel.

"I'm sorry, Dusie. I really am. I never wanted to hurt you."

"Oh shut up, Pip. Don't you dare give me that line—'you never wanted to hurt me.' That's what *guys* always say. It's so bogus."

"But I *am* sorry. Just trying to tell you that I'm sorry."

"That's a lie. You're just trying to tell me that you don't want me back. Well, all right, fine. Fine! I'll leave already and you can go back to having the whole fucking room to your whole fucking self! You selfish . . ." In her rage she slapped absently at bathwater, making waves. "You are the most selfish dyke in the world."

A wooden hairbrush with natural bristles fell from somewhere behind Pip and clattered to the tile floor. When Dusie splashed more purposefully, Pip deftly caught her flailing arms, attempting to settle her down and getting soaked in the process. But Pip was beyond noticing the chilling unpleasantness, having lapsed into her "secure the patient" mode, recalling an internship she had done her sophomore year at a state psychiatric hospital where it was part of the job to perfect methods of restraining people quickly to keep them from hurting themselves or more important, yourself. In Bedlam, it was best to sharpen reflexes rather than try to find some system by which to predict irrational behavior. That was something Pip had learned in an understaffed ward filled mostly with career inpatients, with whom you might think you've developed a rapport until—*pow*—they threw the sucker punch from a dead start during which they had been smiling so nicely into your face.

Dusie was slippery when volatile in peach kernel oil and these old tile bathrooms were remarkably treacherous. Pip could barely control her. Her mindless thrashing was punctuated by a weeping so violent that she practically gagged. Eventually she broke into the most disturbing high-pitched mewling, especially at the mention of her stepbrother, Bram.

"Dusie, what happened? What did he do? Did he hurt you again?"

Dusie's eyes opened looking dolorously down. "It doesn't hurt anymore, Pip."

"Oh, no, no, don't say that . . . That's not possible."

"He says I'm his whore. I think I'm your whore, too."

"Dusie, for God's sake. You're not my whore," Pip snapped. "You're nobody's whore. Your stepbrother is extremely sick and dangerous. And he has used you and abused you in the worst possible way. And this has got to stop."

"At least he *wants* me!" she shrieked more weirdly. "Bram wants me. He does. I know he does. And that's more than you do. I mean, you never even said you loved me, Pip. Not once, not one fucking time. So—so, I mean, like, maybe that means *you* used me, you know? Worse than Bram."

It was a horrifying thought, but possible. Pip was not one of those women who subscribed to some puritanical presumptuousness disguised as a feminist ideal that women were, by nature, above all of this.

"At least he remembered my birthday."

"Dusie, don't be pathetic."

"You should see what he gave me for my birthday. You didn't even remember my birthday. Not even a fucking Hallmark card. You know how much that hurts me?"

Pip felt the sting of Dusie's words, but all she could say was that she was sorry. As Dusie had become abnormally docile, Pip pulled her gently from the tub and wrapped a big towel around her, drying her off like a kid. Dusie stared up at her, blinking oddly.

"Does she do you, Pip? Does she give you what you need? Does she go down on her knees . . . huh?" she asked weirdly, putting her fingertips to a place on Pip's sinewy neck just beyond her ear, a fading mark, roseate. "Little bloodsucking bitch. She got to you, didn't she? Ha!" She was laughing like crazy, "Haha, Pip, hahaha," and she didn't quit haha-ing until Pip gave her a little shake, but then she seemed so out of it anyway. She shut up momentarily to consider the haunted glaze of Pip's irises, the translucence of her skin, which indicated to Dusie that Pip was hopelessly enslaved.

"Elizabeth Breedlove," said Dusie calmly, for once, which was the best indicator of her pending electric storm. "First time I saw her, I thought, Here she comes—the little bitch who's gonna take Pip away from me. And I was *still* nice to her. I was *still* a good Big Sister. And you! You . . . fucking . . ."

Dusie slapped Pip so hard across the face from a dead start that she knocked her back into the closet, staggering dumbstruck into two rolling racks of clothes. Perfect example of how professionally honed reflexes can't always save you either.

"I hope she eats you alive!" Dusie cried, pouncing on her. "I hope she eats your fucking heart out! I hope she sucks your fucking heart right out of your fucking throat!"

Strange anatomically, but effective in getting a big reaction from Pip, who held Dusie tightly, closeted amid a ridiculous array of hanging clothes and hooks. They werre up to their shins in overturned shoe boxes, Pip was aware of the absurdity—not to mention the Fey Ray legend—but said slowly, calmly, "Dusie. Listen to me . . . I'm not your mother. Or your father. Or your stepbrother. Or your shrink. Or your lover anymore either. And I'm going to add 'friend' to that list of things I'm never going to be for you, Dusie, if you don't stop acting like a two-year-old."

Dusie went limp then and doubled over, gagging inconsolably. "That is the cruelest thing—that is the cruelest thing you ever said to me. I can't deal with it. I just can't deal with it, please . . . Don't do this to me. Please. Not now, please, I need you."

Her distress was such that even Pip felt sorely defeated by it, enough to put in a call to Dr. Crews, who told her to bring Dusie over to her place. Pip pulled her car up to the curb in front of the therapist's duplex, and helped Dusie out of the vehicle. Dr. Crews stood on the front porch with a natty lady who appeared to be leaving in a hurry. Dr. Crews introduced her as Nikki Golden, an old Willard chum, though Pip had already deduced that—Willard girls being able to spot each other at a remarkable distance.

Dusie brushed past the others, somnambulating up the stairs to Dr. Crews's place.

When Nikki Golden was gone, Dr. Crews mused, "She's a lovely lady. Isn't she lovely?"

"Yes, Jo, she's lovely, but Dusie's . . ."

"And to think that she dropped by out of the blue, just to talk and have some of my sweet potato pie. Hmm . . ."

"Jo, what about *Dusie?* She's in bad shape. I feel like such a failure."

"Relax. Everything will be all right. We'll put her in 'Crews control,' OK? Leave everything to me. You know the best thing you can do for her right now is to go away."

Crews control.

*   *   *

At nine o'clock, she called Dr. Crews to see how things were going with the little patient, and was reassured that Dusie was "an absolute pussycat." Dr. Crews had just given her the equivalent of about five therapy sessions, not to mention dinner. Presently, she reported, Dusie was taking a bath.

"A *bath?*" Pip asked. "She already took a bath. How many baths does she need, Jo?"

But Dr. Crews had dropped the phone and dashed to the bathroom. She burst in to find Dusie curled up in the bathtub. She had made some scratches in her wrists with a rather dull pair of cuticle scissors. Dr. Crews was relieved to find the wounds superficial as she applied first aid, but she was concerned about the fact that Dusie seemed intent on feigning unconsciousness. There was no way she could have been unconscious from such peevish wounds, and she showed no sign whatsoever of having ingested too many drugs, prescription or otherwise. Not only were her pupils responsive, but her eyelids clamped shut violently when Dr. Crews tried to open them.

"Dusie, come on, talk to me," said Dr. Crews, exercising the power that never failed to rouse even the most stubbornly withdrawn patients. She pulled her out of the water, amazed at how light she was for such a tall girl, realizing that models must be made out of marshmallow. Dr. Crews was taller and certainly more substantial, so she wrapped her in a beach towel, picked her up and carried her to her own bed. She replaced the telephone receiver, assuming that Pip was on her way over.

Dr. Crews took a seat on the edge of the bed. "Dusie? You don't have to open your eyes if you don't want to—that's your choice—but I know you can hear me. If you don't talk to me, Dusie, I'm going to have to call Dr. Valentine because he's your doctor now, not me, and I'm walking on thin ice tonight as it is, having you here. Dusie, please."

Dusie remained unresponsive. Dr. Crews sighed.

"I can't treat you anymore. I'm not your doctor, honey girl. You've put me in an awkward position. It's a matter of professional ethics. If you're not well enough to talk to me and tell me that you didn't really mean to hurt yourself, Dusie, then I'm obligated to call your doctor. And he'll call your parents and they'll put you in Weston Psych. Is that what you want? Dusie? They'll put you in four-point restraints and sedate you. Is that really what you want?"

Dusie would not open her eyes, but tears were evident, welling up in the tremulous corners. Dr. Crews heard Pip let herself into the apartment—she had never returned the spare key—and, in a moment, appeared in the bedroom, with a supremely perplexed expression on her face when she spotted the gauze around Dusie's wrists. Being reassured by Dr. Crews that the wounds were minor and no overdose was likely, Pip leaned over Dusie and coaxed her to open her eyes, but Dusie remained petrified.

"What does this mean, Jo?"

Dr. Crews picked up the phone and started to dial, but Pip stopped her hand.

"You can't."

"I have to."

"Her parents will have her committed."

"Obviously that's what she wants."

"How do you know?"

"Do you think she's unconscious?"

Pip put her thumb to Dusie's eyelid gently attempting to pry it open with no success. "She's conscious. Aren't you, Baby D? You can hear me."

It seemed so absurd and yet Dusie's withdrawal became more serious when each attempt to bring her around failed.

"Can't we just let her sleep it off or something?"

"Do you think this is a *joke?*"

"Do I look like I'm laughing? Do you think I need this?"

"Well you'd better get used to it, because this is like a slow night in the life of a clinical psychologist."

"Maybe I'll go into research."

Because no suicide attempt, no matter how ineffectual, was to be taken lightly—especially a first attempt—Dr. Crews called the odious Dr. Valentine, who recommended that Dusie be admitted immediately to Weston Psych. Pip helped to get Dusie dressed and down the stairs and into Dr. Crews's Karmann Ghia, but she didn't go along for the ride.

# CHAPTER 23
## Weston Psych

Dusie came out of her funk at Weston Psych, feeling downed out and sick to death of having people ask her questions, particularly her parents who were hanging over her bed threatening lawsuits. First and foremost on their list was the "black radical lesbian feminist separatist therapist," who they held "directly responsible for this," their daughter's latest "nervous breakdown." They wanted to know, first of all, what was Dusie doing at Dr. Crews's apartment?

Dusie finally cracked during the inquisition, her face all screwed up like her demons, bursting forth in the midst of a screamfest with her mother over her favorite soft drink. Mrs. Hertz could never remember Dusie's preferred cola.

"Coke or Pepsi! Coke or Pepsi!" Dusie cried, and for a moment, it was conceivable that a whole generation could have been driven to madness by this choice alone.

"I always kept a variety of soft drinks in my home," Mrs. Hertz insisted to a baffled orderly who had been swabbing the floor, while Mr. Hertz ignored them all. Mrs. Hertz was so embarrassed by her daughter that she clenched her teeth to keep from screaming as Dr. Valentine and Bram walked into the ward together, discussing the ninth hole at Tumbling Rock Valley Country Club.

Bram took both parents under his massive military arms, squeezing their shoulders to reassure them that they all must work together through this, their grief, at the prospect that poor Dusie was "totally wacko."

"I am *not* a wacko!" Dusie shrieked. "You're not going to make me out to be some kinda crazy like poor Marilyn! I won't let you! I won't! As Dr. Crews is my witness! So help me God."

"Who's Marilyn?" Mr. Hertz asked.

"Monroe, Dad, you're so out of it," Dusie squeaked.

"Marilyn Monroe?" her father puzzled, almost pitiably, turning to his wife. "She's talking about a movie star who's been dead for a decade and she says *I'm* out of it?"

Standing at the foot of her bed, Bram turned up the spotlight on Dusie like an evil gynecologist, focusing on the subject of her alleged "homosexuality."

"It's true," she screamed. "I'm a lesbian! Put *that* in your pipe and eat it!"

"Oh . . . Dear . . . God," said her mother as if she was spitting up her words into her endless supply of purse-sized tissues.

"That's impossible," said her father. "You're too pretty to be a, well, er, uh, whatever you call it. Obviously, you've been brainwashed."

"I want Dr. Crews," she started to cry, and a passing orderly drove a hamper of dirty linens over Dr. Valentine's foot. Overhead fluorescent tubing flickered oddly. "I don't want *him* anymore for my doctor. He's evil!"

"Dusie?" Dr. Valentine protested, still hopping somewhat, though braced against the pain like a professional, "I thought we got along marvelously."

"Marvelously my ass. You said I had 'penis envy.' Penis envy? Can you believe that?" she asked the orderly, who shook his head, before turning back to Dr. Valentine. "You tried to make me give you a blowjob to get over my 'penis envy.' You did—He did!"

"Now, Dusie, you know I did no such thing. You're just projecting your own latent desires . . ."

"And you said you'd love to see me 'do it' with another 'chick,' too, you sleazy dickhead, like you begged me for the details. You asked me if we used a dildo! A dildo! Can you believe this guy? He calls himself a doctor. He really thinks women can't 'do it' without dildos! Like, is that hysterical, or what?" She was laughing weirdly.

Dr. Valentine attempted to huff and puff his way out of this fine mess while Dusie continued to make her demands. "I want Dr. Crews to be my doctor. She used to be my doctor. She's the only person who even cares anything at all about me. The only person in the whole world. If you don't get me Dr. Crews," Dusie warned, "I'm gonna, like, demand my constitutional rights, you know? And, ah, get a lawyer! That's right! I have my rights! I'm not a minor! I have the money Grandma left me!"

"Oh dear God, she is completely out of her mind, Marsh. Do something for God's sake. My poor baby. My poor sick child. Dusie, sweetheart," Eva Hertz turned to her daughter, weeping. "Where do you come up with such things? The things that come out of your mouth. God knows you didn't learn that from your father and me. Why do you say such terrible things about yourself? Where do you get these sick fantasies? You're only twenty . . ."

"I'm twenty-one! I was twenty-one last week, Mother! Don't you remember? You had a birthday party for me. And besides, what's age got to do with it? I've been making it with girls since the second grade."

She was looking at Bram who was shaking his buzz-cut head condescendingly like "poor Dusie, she's so deranged."

"Why does she *say* these things?" Mrs. Hertz asked Bram, as if Dusie were no longer there.

"It's the 'Feminism' talking," he said with great authority. "She hates men. This is what they teach 'em at those girls' schools."

"You shut up, Bram! You just shut the fuck up or I'll stick another pencil through your head! I will!"

There it was: the threat. It was just what Dr. Valentine needed, a good solid "phallic" threat to support his case for flaming penis envy—and cancel out those horrendous accusations Dusie had made about him.

"Your daughter is obviously a threat to herself and to others."

"You're a threat to me and to others, you phony bastard!" Dusie was screaming so loudly that orderlies were called to fasten her restraints and Dr. Valentine upped the dosage of her medication. Somewhere in the building, an elevator stopped between floors and several depressed patients rapid-cycled into mania.

As Dr. Valentine led Mr. and Mrs. Hertz out of the ward, Bram lingered bedside a moment longer, watching his stepsister struggle helplessly against the indignity. One nurse held her still while another lifted her hospital gown and turned her over just enough to expose a portion of her shapely haunch, which she swabbed with a disinfectant and injected with a hypodermic needle.

"There, there," said the nurse nicely as Dusie calmed down, whimpering herself to unconsciousness. The other nurse covered Dusie and stroked the hair from her face. When she noticed that Bram was still standing there, off to the side, with a creepy gleam in his eyes, she ordered him curtly to leave.

# CHAPTER 24
## Shrubbery

The last class that afternoon for both Elizabeth and Contrary was Dr. Brock's "Elizabethan Drama," an absolute must for those English majors most likely to go "bloody daft" for hardcore Anglophilia. Because here was Beatrice at her best, or at least in context; her anachronistic eccentricities, her revelatory details of everyday life for rustic and royal alike were a scream. One lecture in particular on the table manners of courtiers, followed by her answer to the big question no one would be so indelicate to ask regarding the bathroom habits and facilities left them rolling in the aisles. She could have taken this act on the road.

As for the drama Queen herself, Elizabeth's name alone created a seeming mother lode of material for Contrary's repertoire of gibes and retorts made at her friend's expense. It was almost too easy to be gratifying. Almost.

"Where's the challenge?" Contrary asked, with her full-service shrug, one of the more operatic affectations she had in stock. This one she pulled from the trunk packed with purgatorial angst, assuming the position and appearance of some dreamy Saint So-and-So in extremis, whose face she recalled from parochial school days when she and her girlfriends traded little portraits of saints like baseball cards. She had only a vague recollection of where they got them, mostly from nuns, sometimes for good behavior, or on holidays or at Mass or funerals. Whatever special occasion called for giving children little pictures of people being burned at the stake and pierced through and through with arrows and drawn and quartered and— God knows what kind of torture they would think of next.

As for the cards, the bloodier the martyrdom, the higher its prize.

"It was kinda horrifying," was Contrary's conclusion. She had been sharing this memory with Elizabeth as they were winding their way down Deerborn Way headed off campus. Their destination was a place called the Free Clinic. A sort of radical, feminist, semi-separatist, younger first cousin of Planned Parenthood. The clinic had the advantage of being conveniently located, within walking distance of the campus, and it offered walk-in pregnancy testing. The only inconvenience was that women were expected to bring their urine specimens in a proper glass container, and it had to be refrigerated until delivery. Sounded easy enough, except for anyone who lived in a dorm. Then, even scaring up the right jar became the quest for the Holy Grail. As for refrigeration, sure, there was a refrigerator on every floor in the dorm. But on any given day there could be dozens of identical plain brown paper bags, taped and initialed, some promising mayhem if raided. (The most dreaded scavengers, of course, being the ones who were stoned, with the munchies.) But, no matter how it was packaged, obscured, disguised, even sealed like plutonium, the sisters could spot the specimen every time; they always knew when there was a urine sample with your name on it.

All this humiliation just because the Free Clinic required a sampling of that first refreshing pee of the day.

"But how can this be?"

"How, indeed."

They pondered this for yards. Especially Elizabeth, who had a brain that threatened to explode if she couldn't find a syllogism to resolve something that struck her as illogical.

"That would imply that morning pee is more pregnant than evening pee. Does that mean you really *can* be a little pregnant?"

Contrary shuddered just to hear the word.

"Sorry."

They were trying their darnedest not to talk about certain things, fearing a debate might turn ugly on issues now, suddenly, hanging over their heads, threatening to burst with more relevance to their lives than they could absorb. Like water balloons to wanton boys.

They reached the end of Deerborn Way, the gateway in and out of the campus, and stood side by side in an uncharacteristic silence that was, ultimately, more threatening. Contrary in crisis. Elizabeth in love.

At least, in Contrary's case, they both knew precisely what it was that they couldn't discuss. They also knew that it was possible they wouldn't have to broach the touchy subject of abortion at all. If the pregnancy test was negative, then no discussion would be necessary, so there was no point in starting one now.

But love, such as Elizabeth felt then, the head-spinning, knees-giving, gut-grabbing, heart-stabbing, mind-churning rush of love that was crushing inside, was some method devised in cruelty to extend and sustain the slow burn of martyrs.

The sensation of stepping through the arch from the serene green of the campus into the gritty city always startled. Even when they knew what to expect: a suckerpunch of noise and exhaust from Weston's biggest, baddest bully, The Boulevard. And this street had to be crossed. Four lanes of traffic mostly speeding to beat the longer lights of major intersections, with busy commuter bus lanes on either side. No intersection, light or crosswalk near here, making them wonder if resentful Westonites made a sport of targeting Willard women as trophy roadkill.

And so they waited for the first sign of anything resembling a lull, toeing the curb like relay runners doing their twitchy dance, at-the-ready, anxious to get their grip on that baton. And here it came.

"OK. Ready, get set," said Elizabeth, "Go!" and she was off like a sprinter, safe on the other side before Contrary could shriek, "Run for your lives!"

Elizabeth had never seen anything quite like Contrary's slapdash running. Miss Limbs Akimbo, flapping her arms like one of those big wannabe birds that Mother Nature has grounded for no apparent reason. Elizabeth was not given to screaming like other girls under any circumstances, but she did, on occasion, peal with laughter, as she did when Contrary, with no sense of brakes, plowed into her. Neither of them could recall ever having laughed quite as hard or as long in their entire lives.

They could not immediately regain their composure, or get their footing to escape from the spindly runt of shrubbery Contrary had plowed them into. And the more they struggled to disengage, the harder it became to get up, compounding and prolonging the hysterics, which was making other pedestrians a bit nervous. Although, one fearless passerby was clearly amused as he caught some of the airborne giggles and carried them away.

"He was kinda cute," Contrary said, pulling Elizabeth and herself upright at last. And had it not been for the appearance of that puny shrub just sitting there looking so . . .

". . . so . . . very . . ."

"Flat?"

"Oh, dear."

Silence.

"There goes our Charlie Brown Christmas."

That did it. Another laugh riot ensued.

They were still giggling when they arrived. The Free Clinic was a veritable gynecocracy of, by, and for . . . We, the Women, staffed entirely by volunteers, providing birth control services to women who either could not afford private care or felt uncomfortable in the predominantly male medical mainstream. Roe v. Wade was only a year old and while the clinic was not equipped to perform abortions, it made referrals and adamantly upheld a woman's right to choose her own biological destination. Located in the basement of an old Protestant church in an Alban Hill neighborhood designated "funky," its discreet side entrance opened into a stairwell spackled and painted in-utero pink.

When told that her result was negative, Contrary snarled at the nurse practitioner because she knew the result was wrong and she could not wait another day or two to repeat the slow and obviously unreliable urine test. Since it was a founding precept of the Free Clinic that nobody knows a woman's body better than the woman, herself, Contrary was told there was a relatively new blood test available that was much faster and accurate, but it wasn't free. If she was willing to pay the eight dollars, then they would prick her finger and provide the result in an hour or so.

"Well, why didn't you just tell me that in the first place?" she snarled. "Don't you think I'd rather give you eight bucks than carry a jar of pee around all day?"

Unfortunately, the length of a Free Clinic "hour or so" wasn't determined by the Earth's rotation around the sun, but by the more feminine moon, so Elizabeth and Contrary were still waiting long after twilight. They had smoked all of their cigarettes, finished off the complimentary beverages, and read all of the walls, which were covered with quotations from famous feminists handwritten in a Day-

Glo rainbow. The psychedelic scrawl, and the clash of orange and fuchsia modular, sponge furniture, led Contrary to designate the decor "postmodern morning sickness."

Every time Contrary was summoned from the waiting room, Elizabeth would go upstairs to a pay phone to call Pip, an absurdly inefficient system starting with a polite request to the switchboard operator, would she please ring the second floor of Fey House, and after so many rings, if no one felt like answering the phone, that was that. She had made plans with Pip earlier. They were going to meet at the gym to do some fencing and then go out to a Lina Wertmuller film at an offbeat theater downtown. Unfortunately, Elizabeth had neglected to mention to Pip that she was going to the clinic with Contrary, because she had no idea the appointment would last an eternity.

When Contrary finally emerged from her last consultation, she found Elizabeth dozing on a worn-out copy of *Our Bodies, Ourselves*, which made a comfy pillow. She gave her a nudge and Elizabeth opened her eyes.

"Are we out of here?"

"We're outta here," Contrary replied. And Elizabeth did not have to ask.

It was too late for them to make it back to the campus for dinner, so they walked to Abe's Tavern for a bite and a beer. Contrary was also sorely in need of a pleasant distraction, which could be found in the attractive form of a rookie bartender, Vaclav Masaryk, from Czechoslovakia. He had been working at Abe's since Christmas break while attending graduate school for engineering at Weston University. While he flirted with everyone, Contrary appeared to be his favorite. She spoke for most women when she declared Vaclav "awfully good-looking."

Maybe too good-looking, Elizabeth thought, the first time she heard him introduce himself as "The Lion of Prague," a title he had acquired when he was an undergrad at the university there.

When Contrary caught Elizabeth rolling her eyes behind Vaclav's back, or rather "his very cute buns," she pounced. "You little bitch burger, you're just jealous because he's madly in love with *me*. You want everybody in the world to be madly in love with you, and when one little guy from Czechoslovakia doesn't slobber all over you, you consider him suspect."

"Not true. I'm the one who said you'd make a cute couple . . ."

"But?"

It was a loaded question Elizabeth would not answer.

Contrary persisted, getting increasingly agitated, "What? You don't think I could keep a guy like that interested?"

"That is *not* what I meant at all. I'm just a little concerned that he could be a *green card groom*."

"Well then, you had better choose your words very carefully, my dear, because you're talking about my future husband." And she wasn't entirely kidding. Vaclav made no secret of his plan to acquire citizenship by marrying an American girl, preferably a wealthy Willard woman since they had inspired the "bitch burgers" he was serving. He had observed that Americans took their sandwiches very seriously. Surely they would not associate WCW with the priciest platter if it weren't true.

Otherwise, he was an intelligent guy.

Naturally, Contrary was supremely pleased that Vaclav seemed to favor her above the other bitch burgers. On a good night, she would flutter around him like a fan in the hand of a southern belle. In this pretense of affluence, Contrary convinced herself that she was not letting Vaclav believe she was an heiress so much as a Willard woman, being loathe to appear a vulgarian. Tonight, however, Contrary was not in a flirtatious mood, although she kept an eye on Vaclav from where she and Elizabeth sat in a distant booth. She admitted she could never seriously consider getting involved with "a guy like Vaclav anyway," presumably because of her provincial family and their patriotism. American girls did not date communists.

"To American girls," Contrary said, raising her beer mug in a joyless toast, "We have such complicated lives."

"Complicated lives? We're still teenagers, for chrisssakes. Choosing our own destinations." They had both just turned nineteen.

"Yeah, and we're going straight to Hell."

"So get thee to a nunnery."

"Oh sure. Like I don't have enough testy dykes around me already."

Elizabeth deadpanned and redirected, "So, what about Brian?"

"If I didn't need the money, I never ever would have told him. But, a hundred and fifty bucks, man, that's a lot of penny ante. I figure if I have to get my guts sucked out, then the least he can do is chip in.

And then I never want to see that little dickhead again. Can you believe he never even asked me if I used birth control? I just realized—you know—I've never had sex with a guy without using birth control."

"Me neither—come to think of it . . ." Elizabeth had another revelation that she did not share. As long as she was with Pip, she had no use for birth control. Although, she wasn't about to have her IUD yanked out.

"Which is, man, so unfair, you know? I have *always* used birth control devices and been sexually responsible. Mature. I'm so damn mature I feel like I'm thirty years old. Actually, when was I a teenager? Was I *ever* a teenager? Were you ever a teenager?"

Elizabeth mulled it over before concluding, "I'm not sure. I don't think so. Although, I do recall some kind of teenager thing around the age of fourteen. But look on the bright side. When we're thirty, maybe we'll feel like we're nineteen."

"Assuming that would be a good thing."

"Are you kidding? We'll still have a whole decade to look forward to our sexual peak."

"You maybe. I'm never having sex again."

"Yes, well."

Elizabeth followed Contrary's eye to Vaclav who was mixing and moving at top speed because the place had gotten crowded.

"I can't have a baby."

"You don't have to have a baby."

"I can't drop out of college. How could I do that to my family? They would think I was a total failure. It would just kill my mother. You have no idea."

Elizabeth did have some idea, but she kept it to herself.

"But how can I have an abortion, for chrissakes? My brother is a priest."

She crossed herself, as she always did, at the mention of her brother. Her eyes were welling and her throat was swelling, a sure sign of the pending onslaught of sobs, so she took a moment to collect herself. Willard women do not cry in public.

"Look," said Elizabeth gently, "this is happening to *you*, Mary Constance, not your parents or your brother, or anybody else. This isn't about them. This is about you and what's best for you in your own life," leaning in closer as she directed her voice beneath the din, "and no one in your family ever has to know."

Contrary sighed, the control over her emotions restored. "Swear to me you won't tell anybody. Please. Promise me."

Elizabeth promised, although she privately inserted a little clause that allowed her to make one exception in regard to Pip, whose confidence was unimpeachable.

"You know how I don't talk much about my family?"

"You mean, aside from the fact that you told everyone your parents were dead?"

Contrary shrugged to indicate this prior subterfuge had served its purpose and was no longer of consequence. "You know I only said that to escape the *Snobbish* Inquisition during orientation. It kept them from interrogating me, like they do, making such a big deal about who your parents are. That's one of the reasons I liked you right away. You were the only person who didn't ask me what my daddy did."

Elizabeth wondered what the other reasons were.

"All I wanted was to be accepted or rejected *as is*. For who I am. Without any back story or pedigree."

"Me, too. As is."

There would never be a right moment for Elizabeth to tell Contrary what *as is* meant to her, but this was probably as close as she could get, and the immediate mood gauge was reading acceptance, so she gave it a here-goes.

"Contrary, there's something I need to . . ."

But Contrary was too preoccupied and cut her off with an odd request, "Go ahead. Ask me what my daddy does."

"What? Oh. OK. I'll play. What does your daddy do?"

"He's 'in steel.' You notice I always say he's 'in steel'?" which would be the discreet and proper Willard way of saying that your daddy owns a steel mill."

"Yeah, so?"

"It's not a lie," Contrary argued, although Elizabeth wasn't challenging her. "My father is a mill hunk, a steelworker. At least, he used to be."

"Yeah, so?"

"You didn't grow up in Weston, so you don't really understand the social hierarchy, or the geographical one. There's up here and there's down there. This city is so vertical. You know how whenever someone asks me where I'm from, I tell them 'The Valley'? They assume I'm talking about the green one out there in scenic Tumbling Rock. But I grew up in the gray one. The Mill Valley. Way down yonder where the River of Slag meets the River of Sludge to form the Mighty Polluted."

She went on to explain how her gray valley was once a nice, tidy, working-class neighborhood peopled by proud immigrants who had every reason to believe their quality of life would just keep improving. That was back when Weston was the steel capital of the world and being a mill hunk meant something. Powerful unions. Good pay. Great benefits. But then everybody got greedy, assuming their jobs were secure, as indigenous to Weston as steel itself. There were strikes, then layoffs, then more strikes and layoffs, until the mills started shutting down one by one, moving to other countries to exploit cheap nonunion labor.

"And now my dad . . . he just sits there being sick and pissed off at the 'foreigners', and harassing my poor mother, who kneels and prays to a statue of the Blessed Virgin, who is a 'foreigner,' by the way, and so is that little guy in the little red shoes—what's his name? Oh yeah, The Pope. Can you believe I actually said that at the Sunday dinner table?"

"No."

"It's just that everyone at Willard has this daddy thing, you know? They hate their mothers and worship their fathers."

"I love both of my parents. You know the thing that's most amazing to me is that I actually *like* them, too."

"You're very lucky."

"I know."

"You can't imagine how it feels to lose respect for your father. I mean, the guy worked in a coal mine when he was fourteen years old, for chrissakes. He fought in 'The Big One,' he calls it, or WWII, when he was twenty. And now he just . . . sits there."

"What your dad is now isn't the sum total of what he was. Can't you carry the respect forward?"

"Hey, I try, you know?"

There was nothing Elizabeth could say but, "Sorry."

Contrary said that the only good thing to come out of her unfortunate circumstances was her good Catholic school education, paid for during the more prosperous Steel City years, which led to a scholarship to WCW.

"So you should be proud of yourself," Elizabeth said.

"For what? Being a charity case in the land of daddy's little wawas? Look at this," she said, motioning toward her gray wool coat hanging on a hook over the booth, "I've been wearing this same ratty coat since the eighth grade."

"You're the only one who would notice."

Contrary sank deeper into the corner of the booth looking like a downcast kid who knows too much about grown-up troubles.

"I think you give people a lot more credit than they deserve for being observant, Contrary. And they're not all wawas up there either. I'm not, anyway. My family isn't rich."

"Compared to *mine* it is. Your dad's a doctor. That alone gives you a certain automatic cachet. You can sit anywhere you want in the dining hall. You can table hop at the princess tables, JAPs, CAPs or WASPs, or hell, you could sit with the grody-roadie Deadheads, your biker dykes, the field hockey team . . ."

"And you can't?"

"Please."

"You think everything at Willard is about money."

"That's because I don't have the luxury to spend four years of my life pretending that it's not. My scholarship will only cover me until junior year, and then I'm on my own."

"Well, my parents will only cover my tuition until I graduate, and then I'm on my own. So what's the big difference between your situation and mine? A couple of years? The irony is that you'll get a head start supporting yourself while the rest of us will be scrambling to catch up. Besides, you could get a student loan. And there's work-study."

"Ah, yes, work-study. Nothing separates the wawas from the wannabes more expediently than work-study."

"Meaning?"

"Two words: Food Service. About ninety-nine percent of the work-study jobs are in the cafeteria. Which means that I can look forward to bussing *your* trays, and scraping the slop off *your* plates, and picking the soggy cigarette butts out of *your* coffee cups, and polishing *your* table with Lemon Pledge so you can see yourself . . ."

"Is this fair?" Elizabeth laughed. "Do I really deserve this?"

"Nope. But it's not fair I'm broke either. And what did I ever do to deserve wearing a goddam hairnet in front of the whole world and the dining hall?"

"A lot of students put themselves through school on work-study, Contrary. There's no shame in it."

"Then you wear the goddam hairnet."

"I would if I had to."

"But you don't have to and that's just the point, isn't it? Look, I know you mean well, but you can't possibly understand where I'm coming from here. The utter humiliation of it all. My mother used to do Food Service."

"So?"

"At *Willard*. She worked in the Willard kitchen. That's right. You heard me. My dear ol' Ma served daddy's little wawas their fucking French toast."

"Ah," Elizabeth brightened, "now I understand . . ."

"Do you know what the worst part of it is?" said Contrary. "The worst part is that the Willard girls—those bitches—they were so perfectly lovely to my mother. See? See what I'm dealing with here? They were *nice* to my mother. And she worshipped them, second only to her statue of the Blessed Virgin. Every damn day I had to hear about their ladylike manners and their classic clothes. Enough to make me gag. How could I not despise them? I despised them so much I wanted to be one of them just to spite them . . ."

Contrary excused herself then to go to the ladies room and Elizabeth watched and waited until her friend's curly blond bob was all she could see before she set out on her own quest to the pay phone. But, this time, Contrary spotted her and asked her, offhandedly, who she had called.

"Reuben," she lied, "We were supposed to go to a movie down at WAFA tonight."

"Surely, you jest."

Elizabeth just shook her head hoping to drop the subject.

"Are you serious? You broke a date just to listen to me bitching and whining and crying boohoohoo in my beer like a pantywaist wawa for getting myself knocked up by some jerk?"

Elizabeth shrugged, trying to hide her agitation about not getting through to Pip. Obviously, she thought, Pip had gone out, and probably to The Titan for the annual May Day party, arguably among the best events of the year. With the obvious frollicking around the Maypoles and making daisy chains and crowning the May Queen, some considered it even better than Halloween. Damn. She was stewing as she always envisioned Pip, in these jealous moments, with a giggly gaggle of green girls. Grrrr . . .

"Ground control to Major Breedlove . . ."

They had arrived at the part of the evening when each of them agreed that the other had had enough to drink and presumed to take her home. By the end of their second semester, the little dinks understood the importance of never deviating from the wackiest directions. For instance, there was no getting back to the college from Abe's at night, on foot, without getting hopelessly lost and circling the same couple of blocks until all hope was lost and one simply sat down to die. Only then, would it dawn on them to look up where they would find the beacon—O wonder!—the secular Star of Willard shining down to guide them the rest of the way. The highest point in that part of the hill being the steeple (nondenominational) of the WCW all-purpose chapel.

"What do we do next? I forget . . ." Contrary asked, when they were well into the block-circling part of the trip where absolutely nothing looks familiar. "What city is this again?"

"Aren't we supposed to make a survival pact or something? Like, whoever dies first is automatically lunchmeat? Guilt-free . . ."

"Didn't we already do that?"

"Uh-uh. That was last time . . ."

But pause—something familiar. They both saw it and gasped.

*The shrub that dare not speak its name.*

"Shhh. Good God Almighty. We do not speak of the shrub. We must never, *ever* speak of it. We will be punished in due time. Why start now? Until then, you must remember: we're forsworn . . ."

"Forsworn, yes, of course, fivesworn, sixsworn . . . whatever it takes."

"They will separate us. Try to turn us against each other by telling lies like you squealed or I squealed. Don't believe them. Don't crack. Remember: the only truth between us is *our* truth."

"Yes, Leopold. Wait a second, am I Leopold or Loeb? I can't remember."

"I dunno. I forget. Which one has the superior intellect? Because obviously . . ."

"I do."

"You?! Why you?! Why do you always get to be the mastermind?"

By the time they were on the campus grounds, the vigorous walk in chilly air had been significantly sobering. They proceeded in silence mostly because Contrary was crying, but ever so quietly, looking positively beatific in the low glow of faux gaslights. When they got to the fork in the road down by the pond, instead of saying goodnight, they stepped to the pond's edge to collect what few thoughts they had left.

"Sorry you missed your date."

"It's really no big deal, Contrary. It's just one night. What the hell? How much can you miss?"

"He's gonna be pissed you stood him up. Just blame it all on me. And after you perform The Fellatio of Forgiveness, he'll be sending *me* a thank-you note. "

"That I would like to see."

"Speaking of thank-you notes . . . um . . . I can't tell you how much I appreciated your company today . . . the way you dropped everything just to keep me laughing, man . . . all that comic relief. I mean, you really, like . . . I dunno, you know? Just . . . thanks."

"Sure. Anytime."

"I better book before I start blubbering again, good night."

"Good night."

They turned and walked in opposite directions until Contrary heard Elizabeth calling out: "Hey, sister?" so she stopped in her tracks to look back:

"What?"

"You run like a girl."

Affectionate smart-ass nods and snickers as they proceeded once more in different directions until Elizabeth heard Contrary calling out: "Hey, sister?" so she stopped in her tracks to look back.

"What?"

"You don't."

# CHAPTER 25
# Broken Time

It was around nine o'clock when Pip got tired of fencing with the machine. She was pissed. Where the hell was Elizabeth? They had made a date. One line kept playing through her brain as she perfected her perfect parries, one through eight and back again, over and over: She stood me up, she stood me up . . . and that desolate sensation made her feel that her heart had been suckered into the tempo trickery of *"broken time."* She couldn't believe how lonely she felt, here in this place that always had been her sanctuary, her comfort zone. But then, she had never been in love like this. Breedlove. Instead, she was forced to face that lovesick woman with a weapon in a wall of mirrors.

She stood me up.

Pip went to the water fountain to cool down, only because the water wasn't deep enough to drown in, drinking her fill and then cupping her hand to catch some of it, splashing her face and hair and the back of her neck. She pulled up the front of her white cotton undershirt to dry herself, slicking her wet hair straight back across her crown. On her way to the locker room, she heard the noisy door at the main entrance clang open and then close. Assuming it was Elizabeth she headed eagerly in that direction, but then stopped suddenly when she perceived the hesitancy of heavy footsteps, which told her this was someone unfamiliar with the place.

She didn't recognize the intruder at first because the gym was only lit from half-court. But when he stepped into the light she realized.

"Hertz," she said scornfully.

"Nice to see you, too, Penelope." He did seem extremely pleased to see her, stopping short a distance she automatically determined to be a measure of twelve or thirteen feet to ogle her in a clingy wet T-shirt.

"That is your real name, isn't it? P*enel*ope? But what does everybody call you? Pat? Pen? What does my sister say? Pet?"

"What are you doing here, Hertz?"

"I was just in the neighborhood . . . visiting my seriously fucked up little sister—yeah—and . . . I just thought I'd stop by and say hey, see what's happening with you."

"How did you find me here?"

"Why do you think they say 'Send in the Marines'?"

"What do you want?"

"Hmm. What do I want? Let's see . . ."

What was that look on his face? He was leering. No one had ever looked at her like that.

"How 'bout we have a friendly little chat? Pat."

"Look Hertz, as scintillating as I'm sure that chat would be, I'm sorry I have other plans. I'm waiting for a friend."

He was looking at her with that same puling Dusie puss when she didn't get her way. Then, his entire aspect changed.

"Hey, look, man, I just wanna understand the chick, OK? I never saw her like this before. She's saying crazy things, making up stuff. I just thought maybe you could put it in some kind of perspective for me, OK? You being her best friend and all, she says, and, you know, like, her roommate?"

Pip was taken aback. He sounded genuinely concerned. Was it possible?

"She's really freaking out the parents, man, like, now she's telling them she's a lesbo? Like, sure, right. A gorgeous fox like that? We're supposed to believe this?" He eyeballed her more intently for some telltale reaction and got none. "See, my theory is . . . I think she'll say anything just to get a rise out of them. She digs the attention. And she really hates her mom, my stepmother. Totally, man. She knows this little psycho act just kills her poor mom. "

Interesting, she thought, how possessive he seemed of both Dusie and his stepmother.

"I have to tell you something honestly though, Pat, and I told my sister the very same thing. I really don't believe there's any such thing as a chick who doesn't need men. Period. Any chick who thinks she doesn't need a man just hasn't been with a *real* man. Yet. I'm talking about in the sack."

"I know what you're talking about."

"I think a real man could set any lesbo chick straight."

Pip took her time before responding to that one. "Then you must believe that's true of men, too. Gay men."

"Huh?"

"That a real woman could set any gay man straight."

He laughed nervously the way insecure, homophobic men do, protesting way too much and professing extraordinary ignorance. "Hey, man, I wouldn't even know where to *begin* thinking about something like that."

"Of course you wouldn't," she said, with a tolerant smile.

"Guys with guys?" The very thought of it made him shudder apeishly.

"But, obviously, you've given a lot of thought to women with women."

"Shit yeah! Who hasn't? I mean, any normal, red-blooded American man. That's why we buy *Penthouse*, man. Two chicks together. Yeah. I'm all for that. I mean, as long as they're not dykes or anything."

He wasn't kidding, but Pip couldn't help but laugh at that absurdity. Of course, Bram assumed she was laughing *with* him and was greatly pleased they were getting along so well. Levity aside, he also wanted to appear highly intelligent.

"But getting back to your question, Pat . . . I don't personally know any so-called 'gay' guys, but if I did, I would kick the shit out of them."

"Oh. That's right, I forgot," Pip replied. "You're a marine. Everyone knows there are no gays or lesbians in the military."

"Damn straight. Fuckin' A." He scratched his scalp, dipping slightly to check his reflection in the distant mirror-paneled wall. His frosty Teutonic blond buzz cut and chiseled features had a kind of clean-looking sheen that brought to mind Deutschland. "You know something, Penelope? You should try smiling more. You're a lot prettier when you smile. You've got those dimples." Seeing his comment had the opposite effect, he tried to come up with something quick to delight her anew. "I know you're a libber and all and you don't believe in, like, guys giving chicks compliments, but I gotta tell ya, you've got a great bod, man, and you know it. You show it. I really dig that. You know, a lot of guys, mostly grunts, they get turned off by chicks with muscles. Not me, no ma'am. You've got it all, man. Nice ass, great legs . . . could be a little bigger on top, but, hey, going bra-less like that is a real plus. I'm all for you chicks burning your bras. Hey, I'll light the match. Yes, *ma'am*. That's the only good thing to come out of this women's lib shit, if you ask me."

The look of utter incredulity on Pip's face defied description. She had never been subjected to this sort of salacious vivisection. It was especially confounding because he seemed genuinely to believe that she should be pleased, flattered by his appraisal.

"You know, I was just thinking. Since I'm gonna be in town for a little while, and I was just wondering if, maybe, you would or . . . we could, like, go out sometime?"

"Why?"

"Man," he said, trying to chuckle off his embarrassment, "you sure don't make it easy for a guy, do ya? I'm trying to ask you out."

"Out? You mean like . . . a date?" she laughed. "You *must* be kidding."

Wrong thing to say. Noticing her other foil, the sleeker French grip Elizabeth preferred, lying near the fencing strip, Bram picked it up and scoffed, pronouncing it a "sword for pussies . . . But, hey, that's a fine blade you got there, huh? What is that? Never saw one like that before."

He raised the foil and taunted her. "Hey, Penelope, how about a little 'conversation of blades,' huh?"

"I really don't have time for this, Hertz. I told you. I'm expecting someone . . . any minute now. We're going out."

He spit her own words back at her. "You mean, like . . . a date?" blinking dumbfoundedly, mocking her. "As far as I can see, there's nobody here but you and me, Penelope."

"I won't fence without gear."

But he replied with those seven words women dread:

"I won't take no for an answer."

She had never been alone before with a man who would not take no for an answer. She had heard about men like this and wondered how Elizabeth would handle him. The clinical lessons and mind games Pip had learned in her major from Dr. Crews seemed ludicrously useless to her now that she was actually alone with a frightening, volatile man.

"Come on, tough girl. Show me what you've got."

As he peeled off his leather flyboy jacket, his skintight undershirt revealed a more formidable musculature than Pip remembered from the past summer when he had seemed a bit bloated from beer. Presently, he was pumped. At six feet two inches or so, he was packing two hundred pounds, none of it fat, a veritable spokesmodel for the Marines. Noticing her noticing, he flexed and stretched a bit, admiring his reflection again in the mirrored wall. While he was hooping the foil through the air like any amateur and moron, making that wind-whipping sound, she discreetly removed the little protective rubber button from the tip of her foil.

"Shall I get you a mask?"

"You think you're gonna hurt me, Penelope? Get real."

"On guard."

He may have had some training in sabers, but he was a fool with a foil. He seemed to think it was bullfighting. At one point, he charged so erratically that he nearly knocked her off her feet.

"You play dirty, Hertz."

"Hey, I play in the *real* world, with *real* weapons, against *real* men . . . not stuck-up chicks in girls' schools."

"You play dirty because you don't know *how* to play the *real* way, Hertz."

His eyes crinkled like the stale frost of freezer burn, as it took a while for him to thought-process that truth and its implications. Yet, all he had to show for it was an old standard:

"Hey, don't talk reality with me, sweetheart, until you get through boot camp. I'd bet a million bucks you wouldn't get past the fuckin' haircut. And this . . ." he scoffed, raising the foil, "this thing is a joke. You call this a weapon? Shit, man, this is just a big fucking knitting needle."

"On guard."

Tolerating a few more minutes of this macho nonsense, his foil tip poked too perilously close to her face—again—so she showed him a dirty trick of her own and deftly smacked the blade right out of his hand. It flew, hit the glossy floor and slid quite a distance. She was hoping he would retrieve it, which would give her just enough time to put herself on the other side of the locker room door and lock it. There was a campus phone in the equipment room, so she could call Security.

"Ooh, I'm impressed . . ." he whined, circling around. Spotting his bomber jacket dropped beside the *piste,* she snagged it with the tip of her foil and whipped it into his face. Stopped the braying, at least. But a whole new grin slithered into place. Snapping to attention, glassy-eyed, he saluted her thank you, m'am for galvanizing him. And, in fact, he was so palpably aroused even Pip could tell.

"That's a clever trick . . . chick. What else can you do for me?"

When he took one giant step toward her, she raised her foil dispassionately, like a mechanical arm, holding her ground, wondering how long she could keep him at bay with sheer attitude.

"On guard," she said impassively, thinking the prospect of another would-be bout might compel him to fetch the foil. But he was not taking the bait.

"Look, Hertz, this little cat and mouse game is growing tiresome. I really don't have time for this. Why don't you just say what you came here to say?"

Even in reflection his steely blues displayed no depth. "I think you have plenty of time. I think you got stood up." He could not have known how painfully accurate his assessment was, yet he seemed to know exactly.

"You got stood up, didn't you?—*Pip.*"

It was the strangest thing to be frightened by the sound of her own name.

"Dyke."

"Yes, Hertz, I'm a dyke. So what? Get over it."

"I told you I don't believe in dykes."

"What you believe has nothing to do with me."

"Don't be so sure. Pip. I know more about you than you think."

"You know nothing about me, Hertz."

"My sister told me some shit."

"No, she didn't."

"No? Then how come I know you never did it with a guy?"

"You're a genius, obviously."

"I *knew* it. You never did it with a guy. So what do you know? Because chicks don't count, man, so that makes you a *virgin.*"

"That makes you a fool."

"You're a real bitch, you know that? You really fucked up my sister, man, what you did to her."

"What I did to her?"

"That's right."

"What about you? What did you do to your sister?"

"I did nothing to her. Did she tell you I 'abused' her?"

Pip affected her privileged and confidential face.

"And you believe her? Look at me? Do I look like a guy who can't score with chicks? Get real. Like I'd waste my time on that little psychobitch. I've had more chicks than this school!"

"Why would she lie?"

"Why? Because she's a little liar, that's why. She's totally out of her mind. It's no wonder either, the way you and that bulldyke, Crews, have been filling her head with all of this women's lib shit about her being *abused* when she was a kid. But I think you're the ones who abused her. You put her in that nuthouse."

For the first and last time that evening, he turned his back on her. When he looked at her again he seemed more pathetic than ferocious. "You just . . . you can't possibly understand, man, about me and my sister."

"So help me to understand."

"It's not what she says. It's not what you think."

She almost had him, almost reached him through that therapeutic chink. "What is it then? Explain it to me."

"She never thought there was anything wrong with us being together. Not until she got a little too skinny and my parents freaked out and started sending her to shrinks."

"A little skinny? She was starving herself, Hertz."

"Oh, bullshit. She wasn't starving. She couldn't eat because she missed me so much when I went off to Pulver," referring to the military high school he had attended. "And then she ended up here with all you bulldykes telling her she's a dyke too, just to get into her pants, man. You got her all confused. About the reality."

"Whose reality is that?"

"Hey listen, I'm her big brother, man, she worships me. If that makes you jealous, well . . ."

"I have four big brothers, Hertz."

"So you know what I'm talking about."

"In fact, any one of them or all four together would kill anyone who hurt me. They always looked out for me. That's what a real brother does."

"That's because you really *are* a dyke."

She brought him back on track. "If Dusie worships you, why does she say such terrible things about you? That you molested her? That you threatened to kill her pets? Why would she say these things?"

"Hey, man, you're the headshrinker-in-training here. You tell me. Because I say she's totally whacked from giving head to you headshrinkers. And I *never* killed her stupid rabbit either. She never even *had* a rabbit. I mean, does it ever occur to you man-hating lesbo-libbers that the deep dark secrets some crazy chick like my sister tells you might not be totally true? Huh?"

"I always take that into consideration."

"And where do you get off, bitch, accusing me, when you treated her like your little whore? You just chewed her up and spit her out?"

"Look, Hertz. I'm not proud of the way I treated Dusie. I didn't mean to hurt her, and I'm really sorry about . . ."

"Sorry? You're *sorry?* What you did to my sister put her in the fucking nuthouse. But who's getting blamed for this mess you made? Me. She's telling my parents and everybody else in the whole world that it's all my fault. That I did this to her. I want more than 'sorry,' from you, bitch. You're not getting away with *sorry.* "

"Don't threaten, me, Hertz. I *will* cut you."

"Oh, yeah, sure babe—look at me—I'm shaking in my combat boots . . . Dusie thinks you're so tough. Tough Chick. Yeah, right. Like you could take her away from *me?* So what you get all the pretty chicks up here, you're all so fucking lonely and desperate without men around. No competition. Screwing chicks doesn't make you a man."

"There are plenty of men around here, Hertz. And I don't want to be a man."

"Well, you should."

He grabbed at her outstretched foil.

"Don't you dare try to command my blade . . ."

She turned abruptly, which surprised him. She made it to the locker room door enough to fling it open wide, as he rushed her—she spun and slashed his face. But she quickly realized she had been too tricky, she should have run him through. He grabbed her foil with one hand, as he was clutching his bleeding cheek with the other, and kicked her down the stairs.

# CHAPTER 26
## Mayday! Mayday!

Dr. Crews was snoozing on the Naugahyde couch in her office on the sixth floor of Weston Psych listening to her favorite jazz show on the radio, pleasantly adrift with Sonny Rollins in "St. Thomas," when a knock on the door broke the spell. An orderly named James told her that Dusie had just been captured while attempting to escape, in a highly agitated state, demanding to speak to Dr. Crews. James was honored to be asked to escort her back to the isolation room where Dusie was being held in four-point restraints, gnawing on the rubber bit in her mouth.

"Nurse? Ah . . . Hukapoo—is it?"

"Macadoo."

The unexpected appearance of Dr. Crews startled and thoroughly unnerved Nurse Macadoo, who could not abide her. And Dr. Crews wasn't so fond of the nurse either, which is why she always pretended not to know her name.

"What's going on?"

"Miss Hertz had a nightmare."

Dusie shook her head, "No no no . . ."

Her eyes were cracked wide open as those chestnuts her mother prepared according to the Hertz family Yuletide tradition, putting them in the microwave on the setting designated for *Roasting on an Open Fire*, as the family gathered to watch them explode because Mrs. Hertz didn't know the shells had to be split.

"The patient has been babbling nonsense all day about her mother's chestnuts blowing up and Coke or Pepsi."

"Nurse Macadoo," said Dr. Crews, setting her stone jaw, "kindly put *down* the syringe and back away from Ms. Hertz. Your presence is agitating . . . her."

Dr. Crews helped herself to Dusie's chart.

"She is *not* your patient."

"She is now," said Dr. Crews, who was surreptitiously communicating with Dusie and James in the universal language of eyeballs.

Nurse Macadoo said, "I beg your pardon?"

Dr. Crews said: "Miss Hertz has informed me that she is firing Dr. Valentine, and asking me to take over her treatment."

This cued James, who pulled the rubber bit out of Dusie's mouth so she could say:

"Tell that asshole Valentine he's, like, fired, man. *Big time*. I want Dr. Crews to take over."

Mission Accomplished.

"And I just might sue his spongy ass, too. You tell them that. I'm getting out of here. Lemme outta here," and James had started to do just that because Dr. Crews had given him the eyeball signal to commence with her liberation. He helped her to slowly sit up.

And indeed, Dusie appeared to be in control, while evil Nurse Macadoo was reduced to the sputtering of buts. All of which gave Dr. Crews high hopes of getting Dusie out of here and away from that cur, Valentine, and calling it a day. Even if it meant giving her temporary shelter in her own home. She did, however, note the urgency in Dusie's roasted chestnuts, knowing she could not keep her from exploding much longer, and endeavored to dispense with Macadoo.

Without looking up from Dusie's chart, she was acutely polite as she asked the nurse to please get Dr. Valentine on the phone.

"Dr. Valentine is not on call tonight."

"Then call his service. Have him paged."

"No can do," said Macadoo.

People who used that expression "no can do" deserved to be slapped upside the head, thought Dr. Crews, but she restrained herself and repeated her request.

"Is this an emergency? Because Dr. Valentine is at the opera."

This time, Dr. Crews did look up and right smack dab into Macadoo's eyes, which were colorless like the rest of her, as common looking as cement.

"I don't care if Dr. Valentine is *in* the fucking opera."

That sent her off with a huff and a puff.

"Finally," Dr. Crews said, moving closer to Dusie while asking James to keep a lookout for the enemy.

"I'd be honored," he grinned, and stepped just outside the door to allow them some privacy.

Dusie hit the ground running though she managed to keep her voice down. She told Dr. Crews that Bram had just paid her a visit, maybe an hour before. Acting really weird, even by Bram standards.

Dr. Crews was exceedingly careful then not to show any doubt to Dusie, but she did find it difficult to believe that Bram could elude hospital security. But then Dusie was in a private room, not a locked ward, and it was near a secondary stairwell that the staff used, providing access to the parking lot of the Weston University hospital complex. Given Bram's military training in covert maneuvers, it was quite possible that he had penetrated the perimeter.

"Not a dream . . . he was here . . . you gotta believe me . . ."

"I believe you, honey. What did he say to you? Dusie, did he touch you? "

"No, no, no, no, no, no  . . . omigod . . ." she started to sob. It was wrenching, but in no way psychotic.

Dusie said she had been roused from her Thorazine stupor by Bram, who had clamped his hand over her mouth. He had a frightful gash across his cheek, which had been staunched for a while since it had begun to get encrusted. He was proud of it, he said, looking forward to the wicked scar. And, man, he said, he had earned it, too, because she had fought him "like a fucking tiger." He took off his leather jacket to show Dusie that his upper arm had been pierced all the way through with a foil, but it didn't hurt one bit and no major damage had been done, he was certain. He appeared to have ripped a towel into strips to use as a tourniquet.

"I'm sorry oh no, oh God, this can't be happening . . . omigod . . . it's all my fault . . . I never shoulda told him. Why did I tell him? Why? Why? Why? Stupid. It was so stupid."

"I'm sorry, honey, but I don't understand. *What's* your fault?"

"I told him this morning . . . oh God . . . I told him . . . oh no, I just blurted it out . . . 'she's my lover' . . . I said . . . 'and I *love* her' . . . he went *apeshit* . . ."

Still not getting it, "Dusie I'm not sure what you're saying . . ."

" . . . she cut him . . . I saw it . . . Pip did . . . she slashed his face and stabbed him . . . Omigod . . . oh no, he showed me . . . pulled his shirt up to show me his, oh God, I can't believe this is happening, he was all scratched up . . . ."

Dr. Crews was saying, "Calm down, just calm down, honey," now as much to herself as to Dusie.

But Dusie was ferocious with determination, pleading to be released immediately.

"Get me outta here . . . please . . . I gotta find Pip. If Bram had done anything to hurt Pip . . . I'm gonna kill the bastard . . . gotta help me, please . . . I'm gonna kill him."

James cleared his throat to signal that Nurse Macadoo was bearing down fast.

"Dr. Crews?"

The nurse stood in the doorway looking pretty proud of herself for having gotten through to Dr. Valentine after all, and so quickly, too. James had not heard her approach because she was wearing the sneaky soft-soled shoes of her profession. She arrived in time to hear the patient say, "I'm gonna kill him," and now she noticed Dr. Crews seemed palpably distraught.

"Dr. Valentine is holding for you, Doct-tor Crews. Line four. You can take it in Dr. Madison's office."

Dr. Crews went to her colleague's office across the hall and shut the door, leaning back on it, exhaling as if she had been holding her breath forever, forcing herself to buck up, telling herself: Think. She had to think. Her hands were shaking as she picked up the receiver and spoke to Dr. Valentine. In her most mechanically clinical tone, she informed him that she was taking over the Hertz case at the patient's request.

"I won't agree to that," was Dr. Valentine's reply. "Her parents are friends . . . ."

"Her parents are irrelevant, Valentine. Dusie Hertz is no longer a minor. She's not psychotic. Dr. Madison is here and he will confirm."

"She's incapable of making decisions for herself. But she's a very sick puppy . . . ."

"Don't you dare call her a 'puppy.' She is a young woman and . . . ."

"She threatened me . . . ."

"*Oh?* Tell me, Linton," using his first name as superciliously as he always did, "did she threaten you before or after you coerced her into performing fellatio?"

"I never . . . That's preposterous. It's a lie, a fantasy. Obviously the transference is incomplete. She's still acting out her Oedipal . . ."

"Do you know what you can do with your 'Oedipal,' you fucking Freudian freak? Do you think I'm going to stand by and watch you do any more damage to this woman than you already have? It's criminal."

"Are you accusing me of criminal . . ."

"I just might."

"You watch it, Crews. You accuse me? You? I'll come after you like . . ."

"I'm not afraid of you, Linton. What are all these prescriptions you've been writing for her. Valium?"

"Is indicated . . ."

"Percodan? Why the hell would you give her Percodan? And you've doubled the dose of Thorazine, even though she's not psychotic."

"Hey—you were the one who called *me* to admit her, remember?"

"It was my duty to do so."

"And you've got balls, lady, playing doctor, questioning my medical decisions. Who do you think you are? What are your qualifications?"

"I'll tell you what I am qualified to do, you pompous-ass scumbag. Dusie Hertz asked me to tell you. You're fired, Valentine. She wants me to take her case, and I'm getting her out of here before you kill her."

"You can't do that. You have no authority to discharge her."

"That's why you're going to tell Dr. Madison to sign the discharge paper for you."

Dr. Madison, the psychiatrist on duty that night, was chummy with Dr. Crews and also considered Dr. Valentine to be "a sleazeball."

"I most certainly will not."

"Listen carefully to me Linton. You had sex with Dusie Hertz when she was a minor. Not only is it unethical, it's statutory rape."

"She's a hysteric and delusional. Who—besides some ball-busting bitch like you—is going to believe her? You have no proof."

"No? Then how would I know that you're a little uncircumcised prick, with a crooked appendix scar, and a birthmark on the inside of your upper left thigh that looks like a turtle?"

He said nothing, but she could hear him hyperventilating.

"I also happen to know for a fact that there are others. Also minors. You'd be amazed at how many patients I've inherited from you, all of the damage I've had to undo because of you, and guys like you.

I'm sick to death of you arrogant, sexist pigs. I could make a career of being the bitch who busted your balls, Mister *Doctor*. So don't fuck with me."

Dr. Valentine took her good advice and instructed Dr. Madison to discharge Dusie immediately under the care of her new therapist, Dr. Crews.

It was after midnight when Elizabeth returned to Fey House. It had been a long day of being a good friend to Contrary and she was fully prepared for a long night of making it up to Pip. There was no light under Pip's door, and after she had knocked for a while, identifying herself quietly, she gave up, feeling dejected. She went up to her room, but there were no messages from Pip on her door or anywhere. Elizabeth surmised that she must be awfully mad not to leave a note, not even an angry one. But when she went to the window, she saw Pip's car, parked in its usual spot.

She could not possibly be at the gym—not for six hours—even with the May Day Tournament being only two days away on Saturday. Assuming Pip had gone to the The Titan with a group of women, probably from Fey House, and, indeed, the place felt eerily abandoned, Elizabeth resigned herself to sleeping in her own bed for the first time in months. She flopped down and closed her eyes, drifting off.

But she heard a noise. What was that? She sat up. Sounded like what? Coughing? After two semesters of studying the sounds below she could identify just about anything. She sensed distress. Vomiting? Oh, jeez, she thought, poor baby must have had too much to drink. Not a drinker that girl. Always preferred to smoke pot because, as she said, "It doesn't make anybody sick or stupid—a danger to herself and others like alcohol does."

Elizabeth opened the casement window wide and crawled outside. It was pretty dark down there but for the reading light by the bed, not strong enough to show under the door on the other side. There was also a light from the bathroom, but the entrance was around the corner. The window was ajar for her, but she always knocked politely on the thick glass anyway before jumping from the sill to the floor, unless she saw Pip right there at the desk or in bed and then she would slip in ever so quietly.

"Pip?" she called out several times and got no response, that is, until she heard Pip kick the bathroom door shut and lock it.

"Aw, come on, Pip, at least give me a chance to explain, please. I am so sorry, but I've got a totally righteous excuse. Come on, baby, please don't shut me out." Elizabeth explained the whole thing until she heard Pip retching again. Then relief and heavy breathing followed by the sound of faucets as she was obviously washing up. Elizabeth heard the medicine cabinet door open and the distinctive sound of tablets being shaken from a vial. More water, then footsteps toward the door. She spoke in a gravelly voice greatly enervated:

"Bree?"

Elizabeth was thrilled to hear that Pip did not sound angry.

"Do you have any aspirin?"

"Aspirin? Ah . . . sure, yeah . . . I have some . . . upstairs."

"Please . . . could you get it?"

"Sure, of course—baby, what's the matter? You sound awful. How much did you drink?"

No answer. In a moment, a repeat of the washing, during which Elizabeth noticed that Pip's books were scattered on the floor just inside the bedroom door, as if she had dropped them immediately upon entering. She gathered up the books and stuff, and noticed the messages she had left, each on its own little piece of paper ripped from a message tablet affixed to Pip's door. They were all balled up and flung hither and yon.

"Bree?"

She returned to the door, asking Pip to please unlock it. But Pip would neither open the door nor offer even a vague explanation.

"Dammit Pip, just open the door. You're sick. Let me help you."

But all Pip would say was that she needed Elizabeth to get her some aspirin.

So Elizabeth gave the door a little kick just to register her own anger and went upstairs in search of aspirin. When she returned, she found Pip sitting in a chair in the darkest corner, with one elbow propped on the chair arm resting her forehead on the palm of her hand. She had turned on the architect's light that was clamped to the edge of her desk and directed the light down and away from herself, just enough to illuminate the rest of the room. She appeared to be suffering from a wicked hangover, already in progress, with a headache that made her extremely photosensitive.

She did not talk nor did she acknowledge Elizabeth's greeting as she came in through the window. So Elizabeth offered empathy. "Hey, I know the feeling . . ."

But Pip did not even look up at her. And then she turned her face away when Elizabeth went to give her a light buss. OK. Fine. She *was* mad after all. Because her lips met Pip's cheek then instead of her mouth, Elizabeth noticed that her skin was cold. Straightening, she placed her hand on Pip's forehead and found it cold and clammy as well.

"You've got the cold sweats, poor baby."

Noticing Pip had zipped up her hooded WCW sweatshirt all the way to the top she asked: "Do you want me to close the window?"

At last, some kind of a response, though not much, as Pip slowly shook her head: negative.

Elizabeth fetched Pip a glass of water to wash down the aspirin and watched as Pip seemed to move in slow motion and rather oddly, using only one hand. The other one was burrowed deeply in the pouch of her sweatshirt.

Pip had not looked at her directly the entire time and now she rested her head back on the chair and closed her eyes. She kept them closed even when she eventually spoke from far, far away:

"You stood me up," she said.

"I did not. That's not fair. I told you what happened."

Pip certainly sounded drunk; most of her words came forth haltingly and the others never emerged at all, simply floating away. Elizabeth had never known her to be so remote.

"I waited for you . . . Bree . . ."

"Well, I'm sorry, but I . . ."

". . . waited and waited . . . you never showed . . ."

"Aw come on, man. I said I'm sorry, what more can I . . ."

"You stood me up . . ."

Exasperated, the penitent took her plea of innocence to her knees, seeking Pip's lap so she could rest her head there like a kid. Pip would always stroke Elizabeth's hair when she assumed this position, but not tonight.

"How many times do I have to say I'm sorry? For chrissakes, come on, Pip, give me a break, it's been a long day. I told you what happened. You saw all my messages. You know I couldn't just leave Contrary like that. She needed me. You would have done the same thing, and I wouldn't have *crucified* you for it."

At the sound of the word "crucified," Pip's face became briefly contorted in expressing something unfamiliar to both of them: something terrible, maybe even horrifying. It appeared she might throw up again, but then she settled back, mumbling: "I needed you . . . I was so alone . . . so alone . . ."

Elizabeth stood up and stepped away, and began to pace haphazardly: "Why are you making such a *big deal* about this? Don't you *believe* me? Do you think I'm *lying* to you? Like I'd use Contrary's abysmal situation as an excuse?"

Since Pip would not answer, Elizabeth started free-associating. "Or maybe you're feeling a little *guilty* about something, yourself? Maybe that's why you can't look me in the eye. Is that it? Where were you, Pip? The Titan? That must have been some Maypole party, eh? To get you this wasted. Did you go back there? You went back there, didn't you?" The dread Backroom. "*Fuck.* Just *tell* me."

Elizabeth was at the end of her rope when she declared: "You really better say something, baby—seriously—because I'm thinking the worst things right now."

Nothing. Jeez, thought Elizabeth, maybe she's asleep. Did she pass out? But no, there, see: she opened her eyes again, staring still as distant as a Laplander.

"So *this* is The Silent Treatment, huh? You know what I think? I think maybe we should call it a night. We've both had too much to drink and it's late. Let's sleep this one off. Obviously, you want to sleep alone . . ."

That brought her around to a whisper, at least. Elizabeth had to lean in close to even hear: "No, don't leave . . . please . . . don't leave me . . . I need you . . . I need . . ."

"What do you need, baby?" She was back on her knees only this time she was between Pip's knees looking up at her, "Tell me what you need. Anything, *anything*, just talk to me, Pip, please . . . I can't bear your silence . . ."

But then she jumped because someone was knocking, a soft, late night kind of knock, but persistent, possibly urgent.

"No." Pip said, with the most animation so far. "Don't answer. Don't."

They kept perfectly still through subsequent knocks, but then they were startled to hear a key turn in the lock. The intruders turned out to be Dusie and Dr. Crews. When they saw Elizabeth and

Pip they stopped, suspended in a peculiar silence and confusion, like apparitions caught in the act of trying to haunt the place. They both looked from Pip's face to Elizabeth's as if they expected some kind of answer when no question had been asked.

Until Pip, drained and strained as she was, asked it:

"What the hell . . . are you doing here? . . . busting . . . into my room . . . Jo? Dusie?"

Well, now that they saw her and she looked all right, sort of, they weren't sure *what* to do.

"Pip? Are you OK?" Dusie stepped toward her cautiously, trying to see her better in the dimness, with one eye cocked. "We're just here to see if you're . . . OK," speaking as if in code.

"Why is it so dark in here?"

"Do not touch . . . " Pip hissed, "that switch . . ."

"Why are you here?" Elizabeth asked, which rankled Dr. Crews. Who did she think she was?

Dusie bossed Elizabeth, poking at her with her index finger, "Stay out of this, you little back-stabber."

"Dues, I don't even know what 'this' is to stay out of it."

"This . . ." she spat, impatient with Elizabeth's ignorance, "is . . . this!"

Elizabeth turned up her eyes and palms to the ceiling.

"And don't you 'Dues' me either. You *lost* that right."

Dr. Crews approached Pip tentatively, "Honey? Are you all right?"

Pip addressed her then in a voice scraped of all excess to raw outrage like nothing Dr. Crews had ever heard.

"Is there no limit to your intrusion into my life, Jo? No end . . . to your violation of my privacy?"

Dr. Crews and Elizabeth turned on each other then, with Elizabeth daring to get in her face. Until Dusie interrupted them both, snapping:

"Shut up. Both of you. I don't have time for this bullshit. I gotta talk to Pip in private, so just back away. Back away . . . that's it . . . back . . . farther . . . farther . . . OK . . ." She turned her back on them to thwart any lip-reading effort and dropped to her knees before Pip the same way Elizabeth had earlier, except that she had no problem securing Pip's eye. In a whispery voice neither Elizabeth nor Dr. Crews could hear she asked several questions about Bram. But Pip looked thoroughly confused and did not seem to understand what

Dusie was talking about. When Dusie asked her where she had been that night, Pip replied with no uncertainty, that she had been right here with Elizabeth.

"Before that. Where were you?"

Pip looked as if she knew the answer, but then paused, strangely puzzled, and said: "I dunno . . . can't remember."

"He threatened you, didn't he? He told you if you said anything he would kill . . ."

"Who?"

"Bram."

"I don't understand."

"It's OK, Pip, don't be scared. I won't let him hurt you again. I promise, Pip. I know you cut his face. And you stabbed him, too, right here, in the arm," Dusie cuffed her upper arm to illustrate, "I saw it with my own eyes, Pip. So I'm gonna need that foil, okay? Was it the steam blade? Is it here? No? OK, um, so I'll have to take a wired one . . . I'm really sorry, y'know, but I have to . . . Don't worry, I'll take out the wire like you showed me, OK? I think I can remember."

Most incredible of all in this curious encounter was that Pip's flat affect never altered the entire time Dusie was talking to her, and Dusie understood the answers regardless, though without knowing the specifics. She found out what she needed to know purely by touch, her hands on Pip's legs allowing her to read the response like a lie detector. When Pip said she did not remember, a subtle shift and tightening in her sinew told Dusie that her body remembered everything.

Dusie cried a little, an empathetic outpouring and apologia, burying her face momentarily in Pip's lap. Observing this from across the room, Elizabeth felt the prickling and crawl of jealousy up her back, especially when she saw Pip remove her hand slowly from the pouch pocket to stroke Dusie's hair. What in the world could Dusie have said to Pip that would elicit this tender display?

Dusie got up, shaking off the tears, wiping, sniffling and—what else?—disappeared into the closet. She seemed uncharacteristically lucid. When she reappeared, she was holding one of Pip's prized foils for competition, and Elizabeth immediately turned to see Pip's reaction. But Pip just looked vacantly at Dusie before dropping her head back against the chair and closing her eyes again. Elizabeth, now aghast, turned to Dr. Crews, who seemed equally unimpressed that Dusie was now armed and swearing that her stepbrother was never going to hurt anyone again.

"That's *it* for him."

Dusie seized Dr. Crews's car keys from the desk where they had been dropped and instructed everyone emphatically and unequivocally: "If anyone ever asks you—*ever*—whose foil this is? It belongs to me, OK? Got that everybody? *Mine.* This foil is mine. Pip gave it to me, see, that's all ya know."

She turned once more in Pip's direction: "Pip?"

Pip opened her eyes to see Dusie executing the fencer's salute in perfect form, followed by the touching declaration: "I love you, Pip."

Elizabeth stood rapt in disbelief, utter disbelief, as she heard Pip say, "I love you too, Baby D."

At that, Dusie took her leave and went unto the breach.

Dr. Crews remained mute, standing at the window, dividing her time between looking out of it and staring at Pip with indecipherable sighs and fretful gestures, wringing her hands and rubbing her temples.

No help there, thought Elizabeth, who went after Dusie instead, catching up to her in the parking lot.

"Dusie, what the hell is going on? What are you doing with Pip's best foil, for chrissakes?"

Dusie grabbed her by the collar, practically choking her.

"I knew you were trouble the first time I saw you, you sneaky little, two-faced bitch, you . . . kai-kai . . ."

The extra spit she put on "kai-kai" demonstrated a level of contempt Elizabeth would not have guessed she had in her.

"I love her. Do you hear me? I love her. Do you even know what that *means?* Huh? I would do anything for her. What would you do for her? Nuthin', that's what. You've got nuthin' but smart-ass answers, little *sister* . . . Like it's no big deal that that guy in your town, like, pointed that *gun* at you . . . your 'friend'? Funny stuff. Ha Ha. You let 'em get away with it. So did I. You did nuthin'. I did nuthin'. Well I'm not doing nuthin' anymore."

"Dusie, what the hell are you babbling about?"

"My stepbrother, Bram, he told me he was fencing with Pip tonight."

"What?"

"Pip says she can't remember what happened. She's really, like, fucked up, man, drunk or high or something, I dunno, but she's out of it. He did something to her. I know it."

"Dusie, what are you saying? I don't understand . . ."

"I think he . . . oh God . . . I think he raped her."

"Oh my God . . . oh no . . . it can't be . . ."

"And now he's gonna die."

Elizabeth was already dashing back to the house and barely heard Dusie say, "You didn't see me tonight. You got that?"

And then she got behind the wheel of Dr. Crews's yellow Karmann Ghia and drove off.

Elizabeth came bounding back into the room.

"Pip? Open your eyes, Pip, please, look at me. Pip? Come on, baby, let me see your eyes. What happened tonight? You've got to talk to me. Did he hurt you, Pip? . . . look at me . . . please . . . " Pip would not, so Elizabeth put both hands ever so gently but firmly on her face, turning to look at her squarely."

"I'm tired, Bree . . . just wanna go to sleep . . ."

"Where were you tonight, Pip? Try to remember. Why are you so groggy, baby? Were you drinking? Did you get stoned? Where were you before I got here?" but then she realized she did not smell even the slightest trace of alcohol.

"I dunno," Pip mumbled, "really . . . don't remember . . . why does everybody keep asking me questions. I just wanna . . . sleep . . . please . . ."

Dr. Crews stepped away from the window long after watching Dusie drive off in her car. "I hope she kills him," she said, with a conviction Elizabeth would never forget.

And then she picked up her coat and walked toward the door.

"Where are you going? You're leaving? You can't leave. We've got to get her to the hospital, for God's sake."

"Elizabeth, you have to understand. I have to leave. I can't be seen here. That's for *her* protection. And *yours*."

"Protection? From what? It's a little late for that, don't you think?"

"I'm sorry, but I must go."

"I don't fucking *believe* this. What's the matter with you? Look at her. She's in some kind of state of shock or something, I dunno . . . but something's terribly wrong. I think maybe she hit her head. I think she has a concussion or something."

"Look. She doesn't want to go to the hospital. And you can't force her. She has also asked me to leave, and reassures me that she can handle this. I have to respect her wishes."

"You can't possibly believe this. I thought you knew her better than anybody in the whole fucking world, man."

"Oh? And *you* do?"

"Just look at her. She's barely conscious. She wasn't drinking. She isn't stoned. Her skin is cold and clammy, she was puking her guts out when I got here. All she wanted was aspirin because her head hurt."

"I'm not a medical doctor."

"Well I'm not either, but I know a fucking concussion when I see one."

"You know nothing. Do not lecture me, girl. I made some mistakes and, God knows, I'm sorry. I'm not infallible. I've lost her respect and that's my own fault. But I don't owe you any explanations."

"Why is this about *you?* What the hell does this have to do with *you?*"

And then Dr. Crews just left, without another word, walking across campus to her office where she intended to hole up until the inevitable phone call that would herald the downfall of her reign at Willard College for Women.

"Pip? Pip, listen to me . . . where are the keys to your car?"

"No, nobody drives my car . . ."

"Oh, yeah, I heard that . . . What's making you so dopey, baby?"

"Hurts . . ."

Or Hertz? Elizabeth wondered.

"Where does it hurt?"

"It was stupid . . . I fell . . . the locker room . . . the stairs . . ."

"Pip, did you hit your head?'"

"I dunno, maybe . . ."

Elizabeth ran her fingers through Pip's hair feeling for a bump or laceration.

"Gotta do me a favor, Bree . . ."

"What is it?"

"Tell Coach . . . I can't fence . . ."

"What?"

"Never gonna . . . fence again . . ."

"Baby, what are you talking about?"

"I think I . . . I kinda . . . hurt my hand . . . oh man . . . it really hurts . . ."

"Let me see, baby, let me see . . ."

Pip simply didn't have the strength to resist anymore. She seemed, moreover, to be sinking deeper into some soporific state. Carefully, Elizabeth pulled the hand from its sweatshirt pouch, as Pip gasped and winced and then cried out just to be touched, and Elizabeth's jaw dropped, and the tears welled up in her own eyes, empathetically.

"Oh my God . . . oh Pip . . ."

Elizabeth unzipped Pip's sweatshirt then and pushed it gently off her shoulders, horrified by what she saw.

"Look at me, come on, baby, let me see your eyes, OK? Just for a second."

"Don't . . ."

"How many fingers am I holding up?"

When Pip pushed her hand away, she just put it right back. "How many fingers?"

"Three . . ."

"How about now?"

"You're relentless."

"That's right, baby, I am relentless. I will not stop. You will not outlast me, Pip, I'm telling you right now just give it up. Give me the keys."

"Nobody drives my car."

Where could the keys be? She must have had them when she came into the room, so Elizabeth tried to retrace Pip's steps. Finally she realized Pip had come into the room and dropped her stuff, but she was still clutching the keys as she dashed to the bathroom to throw up. And there they were, lying on the floor behind the toilet obscured by a rug and a wastebasket. She also found a prescription bottle nearly emptied of Percodan.

"Oh shit . . ."

She had left Pip alone for only thirty seconds, no more, to retrieve them, but when she returned she was asleep.

"Pip? Baby? Wake up. How many pills did you take? Try to remember."

But Pip just moaned.

"Pip, if you don't wake up right now, I am going to call an ambulance . . . do you hear me? I'm calling an ambulance . . ." she stood up.

"No . . . no please don't please . . ."

"Then you have to get up right now and walk. Come on, baby, get up, wake up . . ." she pulled Pip upright, "we're going to take a little walk."

"No, Bree . . . I don't want to."

"Get some fresh air. You'll feel better . . . come on, put your arm over my shoulder, that's good, I gotcha . . ."

"You can't drive my car."

"Yes I can. And I will. What's your father's name again?"

"Huh?"

"Your dad's name. I forgot."

"It's . . . um . . ."

And there it was, that hesitation, the confusion. Elizabeth knew all too well. Had been there herself.

"That's what I thought."

"Just wanna sleep . . . let me go to sleep, Bree, please . . . gotta put my head down . . ."

"If you fall asleep on me, baby, I have to call an ambulance. I have to get you to the hospital now."

"Fine. I'll be fine . . ."

"Did I ever tell you about the car crash I was in when I was a kid? I had a concussion."

She knew that would get her attention.

"Out cold. Totally black. Don't know how long. I was pinned under. Trapped."

"You hate it . . . being trapped. I know this . . ."

"First thing I remember . . . I heard somebody say: it's gonna blow up. And I was just lying there in the dark."

As she was telling her tale, she was riffling around until she found Pip's wallet and put it in her breast pocket.

"I heard my dad's voice as he was trying to pull this stuff off me, and I was wondering, hmm, am I going to blow up? Not fear, just like, matter of fact, you know? But, my dad said I was going to be all right, so I had absolute, total trust and faith in that. I never even vaguely perceived any fear in him. So there was no fear in me."

"How did you get out, kitten? How?"

"That thing must have weighed a million pounds and he lifted it up, by himself, like Superman."

Pip mumbled something very distant about how she couldn't bear the thought of seeing Elizabeth hurt.

"That's right, baby, you couldn't stand it, could you? If I was trapped, and I was hurt like that . . ."

"No, it feels terrible . . ."

"That's right it feels terrible, you hate it, don't you?"

"I hate it . . . please don't hurt . . ."

"But I do. So what would you do?"

"Um . . . pick you up . . . carry you . . ."

"Yes, you would. I know you would. And what if you couldn't pick me up? I mean, just think of how awful that would be."

"Awful . . . I'm sorry . . ."

"So you've got to help me. Help me, Pip, please . . . Carry me . . ."

# CHAPTER 27
# Foiled Again

Dusie drove Dr. Crews's car across the bridge and through the mountain tunnel that linked Weston to its southern suburbs, headed for her parents' home with the radio blaring her favorite song "Don't Fear the Reaper," by Blue Oyster Cult. Her plan was to get the loaded handgun that her father kept in the top drawer of the nightstand on his side of the bed, but she hadn't considered the possibility that her parents would be home fast asleep in that bed when she arrived. And Bram wasn't home, either. Assuming he was hanging out at his favorite tavern a couple of miles down the road, she decided to drive there, armed with Pip's precious foil.

Dr. Crews's car was almost out of gas, so she grabbed a ring of keys from a peg board in the kitchen and went into the four car garage, disarming the security alarm before pressing the button that opened the door shielding her daddy's prized Duesenberg from the modern world. She had just pulled out of the long driveway and turned into the cul-de-sac when she recognized the headlights of her stepbrother's Porsche approaching.

Bram's inebriation was past the legal limit. Confused by the sudden vision of his father's car blocking the way like a big fat creamy cow idling in the road, he stepped on the brake, stopping about forty feet short of "The Duesie." Wondering why the old man would be going out at this hour, Bram got out of his car and attempted to walk a straight line toward the vehicle, shielding his eyes from the high beams. When he heard Dusie's piercing shriek, an accusation followed by eternal damnation, it was already too late. The cow became a charging bull. And Dusie rammed Bram hard, throwing him backward against the hood of his Porsche, pinning him. By the time she stopped accelerating, Dusie had bulldozed her stepbrother and his car into a heap. Then she jumped out wielding the Italian grip, proudly.

By the time the police arrived, they found Dusie dueling with the neighbors, whose pajamas were showing beneath whatever old mink or cashmere overcoats they had thrown on. A couple of them were doctors and they were trying to get to Bram, but Dusie was like a mythic force to contend with, turning men to stone. She had smashed out the windows of the Duesenberg and pounded its fine, shiny finish beyond repair, unleashing a lifetime of righteous outrage that could no longer be dismissed or trivialized or overmedicated. At long last, Dusie had cried rape and no one could stop her *rape!* not even after she lost her voice and was tackled to the ground by three police officers. *Rape! Rape! Rape!*

Yes, well, and so there.

She was handcuffed, shoved and locked into the backseat of a police cruiser for safekeeping until the cops could discern the meaning of this bizarre scene.

Mr. and Mrs. Hertz, who were roused when some neighbors rang their doorbell, came running to find a squad of paramedics in the painstaking process of trying to free Bram from the wreckage, a task made more difficult because of the possibility of a spinal cord injury. A special effort was made when they found out that he was a lieutenant, sir, in the marines. While the strongest guys huffed and puffed against the unbelievably heavy old car, just to push it back a couple of inches off Bram, some rescuers deftly shoehorned a cervical board between his back and the hood of the Porsche. He had to be completely immobilized, strapped to the board and padded for support, before he could be moved a fraction of an inch.

Bram was conscious the entire time, although he was in shock and could not recall or articulate what, exactly, had happened. He was feeling no pain, so he assumed he was just drunk and got stuck somehow between some very expensive wheels. He even joked and laughed weirdly about his predicament and couldn't understand why all these people were standing around in their slippers looking so stone cold sober, when he was accustomed to "seeing them with cocktails, drunk off their asses."

On the advice of the neighborhood doctors, the Hertzes insisted that Bram be rushed to a certain suburban hospital with a state-of-the-art trauma unit and a superior neurology department. The police car followed at a slower pace, headed for the same hospital but without the urgency since they were escorting Dusie, whom they presumed would be crazy regardless of the speed. The officers had been informed by the Hertzes that the disheveled, raving beauty they had in custody was their daughter and an escapee from Weston Psych. The Hertzes made it clear that they did not want Dusie returned to *that* hospital.

Dusie was delivered to the ER for a rape screen and psychiatric consult only moments after Bram was rolled into surgery to have steel rods implanted that would stabilize his spine, preventing further movement and injury. The Hertzes were informed that his spinal column had been severely damaged in the thoracic area at the T4 level, meaning that his legs and trunk were paralyzed, that he had no feeling below the nipples. They would not know for some time whether or not his paralysis was permanent.

With their son in the hands of the best available neurosurgeon, the devastated Hertzes returned to the ER to check on their daughter. They heard her whimpering, "No, no, not *me*," from behind a curtain barrier they had no inclination to breach. Dusie was emotionally spent, but still empowered by surging adrenaline and her own very personal sense of triumph, which is why they had her in restraints and dosed with Valium. She resisted them regardless, squirming and clenching when she felt the initial pressure of the icy speculum, crying, "Stop it! Stop it please. *I* wasn't raped! How many times do I have to tell you? Get that thing out of me!"

They paid no attention to her whatsoever. By the conclusion of the examination she was woozy Dusie and subdued as they wheeled her upstairs to the psych ward.

With both of their children lying unconscious in the hospital, the Hertzes summoned Dr. Valentine, who made an unprecedented house call. When he arrived at the Hertz home just before dawn, the police were finishing up their inquiry, having little or nothing to go on, except for that yellow Karmann Ghia parked in the Hertzes' driveway.

Just as the Hertzes said they had never seen it before, Dr. Valentine strode toward them asking, "What is Dr. Crews doing here?"

"Dr. Crews isn't here."

"I saw the car in the driveway, and I just assumed . . ."

"Excuse me, sir, do you know the owner of the vehicle?"

"Yes, I do, officer, it belongs to Jo Crews."

"And who are you, sir?"

"Linton Valentine. I'm a friend of the family, and Miss Hertz's doctor at Weston Psych. At least, until late last night when I received a
highly irregular phone call from Dr. Crews informing me that Miss
Hertz, my patient, was firing me."

The Hertzes were astounded.

"Miss Hertz was discharged from the hospital tonight in the care
of Dr. Crews. That's all I'm at liberty to say. If you want to get to the
bottom of this, I strongly urge you to contact Jo Crews. Now, if you
don't mind, officers, I need to speak with the Hertzes in private.
Both of their children are in the hospital tonight."

Once he was alone with the Hertzes, Dr. Valentine apologized for
not calling them the night before, but he had assumed, however er-
roneously, that the matter could wait until morning. As much as he
disliked Dr. Crews, he had no reason to believe that any harm would
come to Dusie in her care, or certainly not that quickly. Trusting Dr.
Crews, a *psychologist*, was the big mistake he had made and he
would never forgive himself.

That being said, Dr. Valentine switched into an advisory mode that
would have impressed Iago, making it clear that he was sharing his
opinions and theories with them as a friend, first and foremost.
Everything they discussed that morning behind closed doors, he
said, was privileged and confidential. He had suspected for some
time and, given the events of last night, now was reasonably certain
that the relationship between Dr. Crews and Dusie was *unnatural*.

Mrs. Hertz went pale. Fortunately, Dr. Valentine was packing his
pocket-sized Valium samples, anticipating this sort of thing.

It was Dr. Valentine's belief that Dr. Crews had violated the ethics
of her profession in more ways than one. Perhaps, he speculated,
Bram had somehow found out about this ungodly affair and threatened to expose the *lesbian lovers*.

Had Mrs. Hertz not been so downed out at the time, she would
have been wailing. As it was, she said, "Oh."

Valentine speculated that since it was Dr. Crews's precious career
on the line, she may have exercised her hypnotic powers over the

mentally disturbed and extremely vulnerable Dusie, as much a victim in her own right, and had *inspired* Dusie to run down her own beloved stepbrother.

As the Hertzes sat there on the chintz-covered divan with their mouths agape, Dr. Valentine strongly urged them to call their lawyer to consider bringing a lawsuit against Dr. Crews. He also said he could not impress upon them enough the importance of sending Dusie immediately to any one of a number of fine private mental hospitals away from Weston to shield her from intrusive inquiries, not to mention the influence of Dr. Crews and all of her deviate friends. He also thought it likely that the police would want to question Dusie as soon as she was conscious. So unless the Hertzes were prepared to face the prospect of seeing their daughter charged with assault, possibly with intent to kill, they should get her out of town, *stat*. They could then tell the police that she was far too ill to speak to anyone about anything, and for an indefinite amount of time. With Dusie hospitalized in another city, he said, they would be able to protect her from a police interrogation for months.

He was happy to recommend some of the finest facilities, suggesting they choose between Chestnut Lodge outside Washington, D.C., McClean Hospital in Massachusetts, or the esteemed Institute of Pennsylvania Hospital in Philadelphia, where Dr. Valentine had been trained himself, and still counted so many of the psychoanalysts there among his friends. Mrs. Hertz listened to this as if she were consulting a travel agent, being most taken with the idea of having her daughter in Philadelphia, where she might be introduced around the Main Line by the Hertzes' friends, the Stiwtin family. That being settled, Dr. Valentine was dispatched to make the arrangements to send Dusie off like a package to Philadelphia.

In the meantime, the suburban police, Officers Votiff and Nivarina, juiced at the prospect of investigating a case weirder than anything going down in the city, were talking *hinky*. This Hertz incident certainly didn't look like your average cul-de-sac fender-bender foil attack swordslashing to them, no sir. And they were very anxious to get "this Joe Crews guy" on the horn to ask him if he knew where his cute little car was. They also wanted to talk to those Hertz kids as soon as they were conscious. Being told that both Bram and Dusie were likely to be asleep or be otherwise incoherent for another twenty-four hours, at least, they waited politely, priding themselves on their more genteel, suburban approach to crime. When Officers Votiff and Nivarina did return to the hospital, Bram was there, but Dusie was gone. And no one could say where she was.

As for Bram, it would be weeks before he could be interviewed, as his injury was severe and he was heavily medicated on morphine, lapsing intermittently into states of incoherence, despondence, and lucidity. When Officers Votiff and Nivarina finally got to speak with him, the strange things he said and the even stranger way he said them only added to their confusion. He told them he was surprised to hear that he had been conscious at the scene because he could not remember anything about it.

"What was the last thing you remember?"

Blink, blank, blink went his eyelids, fluttering, like he might be having a little seizure, and they were not certain of the procedure. Call the staff; lose the interview. They decided to stick it out for a minute, and Bram did come back around. Sort of.

When asked if he could think of any reason why his stepsister would "run him down with a, um, Roadster . . . er . . ."

"Duesenberg."

"Duesenberg. Right.German made . . ." Votiff caught the rolling of Nivarina's eyes askance, which meant his partner was calling him a dork, because Duesenbergs were made in America, man.

"So anyways Lieutenant Hertz, er, ah, sir . . . we got a witness, a neighbor, he says your stepsister tried to kill you with your father's car."

"Did she?" he scoffed. "Far out . . . feisty little chick, isn't she? Ya gotta love her."

Here, Nivarina, interjected: "So you're fond of your stepsister."

"Are you kidding, man? Have you ever *seen* my little sister? She's a *model*."

"Hey, we hear ya. She sure is a pretty girl."

"So, getting back to the incident, Lieutenant . . . Can you think of any reason your stepsister would run you down with a big old car, and stab you right through the arm, and open your friggin face with some fancy friggin' sword?"

"She hates men. Crews brainwashed her. It all started with Crews."

"Josephine Crews?"

"Yeah."

"Lieutenant, sir? Were you aware that this lady doctor, Crews, is a practicing homosexual lesbian?"

A practicing homosexual lesbian? He had to think about that for a moment. With stern, studious aspects, the police officers looked to the lieutenant for his expertise in these matters, and they actually copied everything down word for word when Bram shed some light on the character of Dr. Crews.

"The biggest carpet-munchin', pussy-lovin', ball-bustin' bulldyke on the planet is what she is. That is one scary bitch, man. She is dangerous."

"Whaddaya mean 'dangerous'? Lieutenant?"

"Feminism, gentlemen. She fills their heads with that crap. If those bitches get their way, they'll be going into combat." The men shuddered knowingly—perish the thought.

"Do you know if Crews and your stepsister were ever involved in a homosexual lesbian affair?"

"Wouldn't be surprised. Where else would my little sister get this fucked up idea she's a dyke? Like anybody would believe that. Oww . . ."

His eyes clamped shut, and he appeared to be having trouble swallowing. His throat was parched and he needed more painkillers.

"If you could just answer one more question please, Lieutenant . . . sir? Lieutenant Hertz?"

"Huh?"

"Can you recall what you and your stepsister were fighting about?"

"That dyke . . . tough chick . . . fights like a tiger, man . . . She had her chance. Blade was in her hand. She could've killed me."

The interview came to an end then, leaving both officers feeling "freaked out" as they watched the lieutenant fall into a paroxysm of weeping.

"I wish she would've . . . killed me . . . damn . . . why didn't she just kill me? One stab . . . one lousy little stab through my neck . . . I'd be dead. I wanna be dead . . . Why can't I be dead?"

And then he started begging them please to lend him one of their guns so he could shoot himself. "Please, man, I can't live like this. They think I don't know but I know. I'm never gonna walk again. I can't feel my own dick."

The officers glanced at each other, horrified at the prospect of what Lieutenant Hertz faced.

"I've got buddies from 'Nam laid up like this from fighting the VC, man . . ." he cried, "What the fuck am I supposed to tell them, huh? I got beat up by my little sister?"

Suburban stories of a domestic nature that did not involve a homicide, regardless of their weirdness, were not covered by the Weston media. The only reason the Hertz story got a couple of inches in the "Region" section of *The Weston Gazette* was because it involved the trashing of an extraordinary antique car by the former underwear model for the newspaper's own Sunday Supplement. The incident was deemed a tragic accident.

WCW had its share of scandals over the past hundred years, but never one so seemingly motiveless as The Dusie Debacle. There were hardly enough facts to even piece together a minor ludicrous rumor. The best anyone could fabricate and circulate was that Dusie had a "nervous breakdown" because Pip broke up with her, and then she tried to kill herself by crashing her daddy's car. In this version, her stepbrother just happened to step into her self-destructive path. He may have been trying to save her—a hero!—but she had been too crazed, hopped up on drugs no doubt, and had mistaken the accelerator for the brake. In an old car like that, who knew? Since nobody seemed to know where Dusie was, the gossips just assumed she had been sent away to Zurich for a complete mental overhaul. The only thing the WCW community could agree on was that this must have been a freak accident because Dusie Hertz was surely incapable of deliberately hurting anybody.

Officers Votiff and Nivarina had finished up at the Hertzes' house and returned to the precinct, where they finally got a call through to Dr. Crews at the college. Sitting at adjacent desks, Nivarina did all the talking, while Votiff listened in on another phone.

They noted that Dr. Crews reacted with fear and dread. She didn't know yet what had happened, and they wouldn't tell her outright either, saying only that there had been "an accident, possibly an incident." Because Dr. Crews was clearly distraught about Dusie, Nivarina reassured her that Miss Hertz had not been injured. Dr. Crews admitted to having taken Dusie out of Weston Psych, believing it was in the patient's best interest, for complex reasons she was not at liberty to disclose because of doctor–patient privilege. She said that she brought Dusie to her apartment because it was late and her patient had nowhere else to go. After getting Dusie settled on the couch, she said goodnight and that was the last she saw of her. She claimed she hadn't discovered until morning that Dusie and her car were gone. She assumed that Dusie had slept through the night, then got up and went to the college.

"She stole your car?"

"No. She borrowed it."

"Do you know where your car is now?"

"No."

"Do you know where Miss Hertz is now?"

"You *know* I don't, and I really wish you would tell me, because I'm extremely concerned. I'm her doctor. I have a right to know where she is."

"Did you call the Hertzes, I mean, on account of the fact you're so worried?"

"No, but I was just about to do that. I didn't want to alarm them unnecessarily, and frankly, officer, the last place I would expect Ms. Hertz to go is to her parents."

"Well that's where she went. And that's where your car is."

"What can I say? I'm shocked."

"Do you know Miss Hertz has a brother?"

"A stepbrother actually. I can't recall his name. We've never met."

"Did she ever talk to you about her stepbrother?"

"If she did—and I'm not saying she did—I wouldn't be able to divulge that."

They asked her numerous questions about Dusie and Bram, but Dr. Crews continued citing doctor–patient privilege.

"Does Miss Hertz have a boyfriend?"

"Not that I know of."

"Does she have some kind of psychological problem with men?"

"I'm sorry, officer, I don't understand the question."

"I'll put it another way. She says she's a lesbian. Is she?"

"If that's what she told you, why are you asking me?"

"Well, being psycho and all . . . she could say anything."

When Votiff and Nivarina got off the phone with her, they looked at each other knowingly across their desks.

Hinky.

# CHAPTER 28
# Slapfight

Contrary's abortion was scheduled to take place at the Women's Health Center on the third Wednesday in May before the WCW graduation weekend ceremony and festivities. WHC was the antithesis of the Free Clinic, a sterile, high-tech suite on the seventeenth floor of a contemporary skyscraper in the midst of downtown Weston. Protesters were pretty much encamped on the sidewalk outside the main lobby, harassing everyone who entered or exited—even though thousands of people worked in the thirty-story building, and the WHC suite occupied only one-third of a floor.

Elizabeth went with Contrary to WHC by bus, jumping off a couple of blocks short of their destination. As they approached the building they saw the "anti-women protesters," as Elizabeth called them, noting they were "mostly men who you just *know* by looking at them have never had sex in their lives, and probably never will." She was trying to be chipper for Contrary's sake. Poor Contrary. She felt dreadful as it was, her characteristic verve all but obliterated by her sense of guilt and pending loss, not to mention her fear of pain and medical procedure.

Elizabeth threw her arm around her friend, announcing like a soldier, "We're goin' in," and then pushed past the oppressive ravers who shoved glossy photos of grotesqueries into their faces, shouting incoherent scripture, something about whores and fornicators.

The first stage of the abortion procedure was payment in full and by money order only. The patient was then ushered through a labyrinth of waiting rooms and cubicles, all separated from the main waiting room by the second of two buzz-locked and bomb-proofed doors.

Elizabeth stood out among the harried mothers, sisters and friends, mostly teenagers, and a few hang-dog, would-be dads who weren't legally old enough to drink yet in this state. You had to feel sorry for the guys, too. They looked genuinely miserable, subjected as they were to the collective female glare just because they had penises.

Anyone could tell why a woman was there because of her outfit. Skirts meant abortions. As if the procedure itself weren't traumatic enough, the clinic required outpatients to wear skirts, presumably because it was easier. But the geniuses who came up with the dress code were obviously unaware of the invention of pantyhose, which women generally wore with skirts. And pantyhose were about as convenient, efficient and comfortable in a bloodbath as a bikini. Besides, college women did not wear skirts if they could help it. Skirts were for rare occasions, usually nerve-wracking ones such as job interviews, internships and anything involving their mothers.

As Elizabeth waited for Contrary, reading *Beowulf*, she felt relieved to be wearing her uniform Levi's and boots. She figured she looked like an I.U.D. appointment.

By the time Contrary was released, the anti-womanists were pepped up from hot cocoa and cookies, so leaving the building was even more traumatic than entering it had been. Like coitus and its consequences.

Seeing that Contrary was peaked and pained as they walked toward the bus stop, Elizabeth hailed a cab. Contrary protested because the cab ride from downtown to WCW was expensive, but Elizabeth insisted, saying that she would pay for it herself. As the cab headed up the hill, Contrary peeked into a little sack of complimentary contraceptive paraphernalia that the clinic staffers handed out like goodie bags at a Margaret Sanger theme party.

"Foam and condoms," Contrary grumbled. "Yeah, right, like I'm ever gonna have sex again."

"It's over now," Elizabeth said, not knowing what else to say. She patted the back of Contrary's hand, gave it a reassuring double squeeze and then pulled away. She was uncertain anymore of the appropriate touch rules for female friends.

"It's so strange," Contrary said softly. "I feel so . . . relieved. I'll be damned, but I'm so relieved."

She was bleeding clots, sure, but she felt she had control once more of her life and was resolved never again to lose it. As they approached a Catholic cathedral near the college, Contrary asked the cabbie to pull over. Elizabeth followed her into the church, but stopped short of the dipping font of Holy Water, preferring to wait in the vestibule. Contrary put a Kleenex on her head, respectfully, and went into the sanctuary to light a candle among the rows of red and blue votives flickering beneath the statue of the Blessed Virgin. Then she knelt there for a while praying and sobbing demurely. Eventually she removed the tissue from her head to dry her eyes and blow her nose, tugging irritably at the hem of her wool skirt, causing sparks from static electricity like some would-be miracle. She was careful to use euphemisms when profaning the makers of *energized* pantyhose.

While Contrary was doing an extra Act of Contrition for any and all prior irreverence, a nun in full habit approached Elizabeth. Naturally, Elizabeth greeted her politely with a smile, as was the custom on her planet, and got a face full of scorn. Sister Sourpuss then said something to the effect that she was horrified to see a woman idling in the church vestibule "dressed like a man, in dungarees."

Elizabeth thought it best to bid her farewell with too much politeness and otherwise bite her tongue as she stepped outside to wait, congratulating herself once more for rejecting Catholicism at the age of five.

"What's the matter, sister? Crucifix get to ya?" Contrary asked when she joined Elizabeth outside on the steps. She flicked what was left of the Holy Water on her fingertips into Elizabeth's face.

"Just testing."

When Elizabeth did not recoil like something supernatural, Contrary smirked. "That should put an end to the ugly rumors."

Having grown up with sisters, Elizabeth realized that Contrary intended to alleviate her upheaval by abusing the female in closest proximity. Elizabeth was determined not to let her.

"Whore."

"Fornicator."

Their walk to the college was uphill all the way, and they added to the invigorating challenge by taking the shortcut: an inconspicuous set of concrete steps—there must have been a million of them—up to the campus. And Contrary was bitching the whole way about her pantyhose binding in all the wrong places because, in her tremulous distraction following the vacuum aspiration, she had put them on backward.

She attempted to take her mind off the climb by sharing with Elizabeth her Five-Year Plan for self-improvement. Among her objectives was to graduate from WCW with departmental honors and the Hortense Masterson Memorial Book Award for Excellence in English Literature, which was referred to as The HMMBAFEEL (prounouced with unwavering reverence: "HUMba feel.")

She knew full well this would rankle Elizabeth, who planned to win The HMMBAFEEL herself but was too cool to admit it. Contrary's five-year objective was law school. Her immediate objective was to earn money. She announced to Elizabeth that she would be spending her summer waiting tables at Abe's Tavern. Like everyone else at WCW she was also going to quit smoking, lose twenty pounds, and get a new hairdo.

"There's nothing like a new hairdo to make you feel better about your life. But what about you, Your Highness? What's your Five-Year Plan? A Ph.D. in Punctuation During The Age of Reason, and marriage—oh pardon me, how bourgeois!—*cohabitation* in a garret with your beloved Bohemian, Dr. Maddocks?"

"I don't make Five-Year Plans."

"Ooh, you're such an existentialist. What about this summer? Can you think that far ahead or is it just too much *future* for you?"

Elizabeth told Contrary that she intended to stay in Weston for the summer.

"Really? Oh goody!" Contrary expressed a giddy pleasure at the prospect of carousing with Elizabeth on her nights off, "That is *such* good news. Have you found a place yet?"

"Ah . . . yes . . . actually . . . and, jeez, you know, it's such a coincidence, too, because I'll be living upstairs from Abe's. The Penthouse."

"The Penthouse?"

"Uh-huh."

"You mean the *penthouse* Penthouse?"

"Yeah. Isn't it amazing? Gracie and Decker will be living there, too."

They were referring to a sprawling four-bedroom apartment on the entire top floor of the three-story building owned by Abe whose namesake tavern occupied the ground floor. Deep in the cleavage of mid-to-lower Upper Alban Hill, The Penthouse had been rented or occupied by Willard women since the Dawning of the Age of Aquarius. Prospective roommates had to be approved by renters with seniority, based on certain criteria. Most salient among the requirements was a ban against men, and straight women were allowed only under special circumstances. Very special circumstances.

Contrary had paused momentarily to catch her breath, clutching the iron railing and looking at Elizabeth in bafflement: "I don't understand. I thought The Penthouse was an *exclusive* club, you know? Like for old bearded ladies and their nubile initiates?"

"No, actually, that would be the D.A.R."

While Contrary was fond of Decker, she included Gracie Fisk on her list of daddy's little wawas. Her nose was a bit out of joint because Elizabeth and Gracie were becoming friendlier. Contrary blamed this on their similar socioeconomic backgrounds, of course, as well as their curious predilection for "good-looking Jewish geniuses." Gracie also appeared to enjoy the company of lesbians, although she was unequivocally straight.

"What is it with you and Gracie and Decker?" Contrary asked. "You're like kai-kai by proxy."

Elizabeth laughed.

"I just don't get it. Next thing you know, you'll be telling me that Pip Collier is living there, too."

Elizabeth stopped laughing.

"Oh, Lord."

She crossed herself with sincere piety this time and they climbed in silence for a while. Nothing but the sound of sparking pantyhose and then Contrary turned to her and said, "Okay, look, I've been holding my tongue about this for a while now, thinking maybe this whole situation of yours would resolve itself but, obviously, it hasn't, so I just have to say something, OK?"

Elizabeth would have held her breath if she had not expended it all on the ascent.

"I like Pip. You know I do. And Lord knows I didn't want to, but she just won me over in about two seconds that night we played poker. She's a *pip*—she truly is. And it's just awful what happened to her hand—my God!—I don't think there's a person on this campus who doesn't feel for her. You, more than most, it seems, since you've been helping her out so much. She certainly does seem to rely on you, doesn't she? You're a good person, Elizabeth, to give her a hand. But sometimes, you know, being a good little helper bee can be, well, misleading. It can get you into trouble."

"What kind of trouble is that?"

"I believe she sees your friendship differently than you do."

Elizabeth had to pinch herself on the bridge of her nose to staunch any confessional outburst in the same way she would treat a nosebleed. After all of these months, putting off this high risk conversation for lack of the right opportunity, here it was, and all she could do was bite her tongue. She had reached the point of no return where speaking the whole truth would only make her friend feel like a fool. And that was the last thing she wanted to do right now.

"Hey, you scoff, but I've seen the way she looks at you. I think she's madly in love with you. I think she's trying to seduce you."

"Contrary, I don't . . ."

"Just wait, please, hear me out. She's very clever, that girl. She takes you a little farther each time. One step at a time: first, it was the tutorial experiment, then the fencing, then the poker. And now she's convinced you that you can be roommates, using Gracie and Decker to make it all seem perfectly innocent. But get real. Seriously. How far do you think you can go in this curious friendship of yours before the inevitable?"

"What's the inevitable?"

"Oh, come on . . . she's going to make a play for you—bigtime—once you're roomies and she's got you right where she wants you. And then, there's no graceful way out. You're gonna be in one hell of an awkward situation, and she is going to get hurt. She might even think you've been leading her on. Just like that lesbian movie with—who was it? um . . . Audrey Hepburn—don't ya just love her?—and, ah . . . oh yeah, Shirley MaClaine, I think."

"Do you mean *The Children's Hour?*"

"Yeah, that's the one. You know, I think they're teachers or something at a girl's school? And some ee-vil little bitch girl from hell starts a rumor that they're lesbian lovers—of course they never actually say the word. They're not lovers, but then, we find out that Shirley secretly *does* love Audrey—and really, who doesn't—and . . ."

"As I recall," Elizabeth interjected, "she *hangs* herself."

"Yes, it's so tragic, isn't it?"

"So, you're afraid Pip will hang herself if I reject her?"

" 'If' you reject her? Hmph. Actually, I was hoping that she would hang *you*—you little dink." Contrary whapped Elizabeth with her contraceptive goodie bag. "Yeah, you laugh . . . you'll see."

They plodded onward and upward for a while not so much lost in their thoughts as hiding out. Elizabeth hoped the subject would be dropped, but no such luck, as Contrary started in again, "Do your mommy and daddy know you're gonna be making lesbian lanyards at *Camp Dyke-Amok* this summer?"

It was a mother of a staredown.

"This discussion is not about my relationship with my parents, Mary Constance."

"Then, what the hell *is* this discussion about, Elizabeth?"

"I dunno. You tell me. You started it. You keep harping on it."

"Hey, I'm just trying to talk you out of committing social suicide, that's all."

"Let me get this *straight:* you're saying that if I rent a room in an apartment this summer—six people total, three dykes and three straight—then I won't be invited to tea with the Queen Mum? Well, then pass me the hemlock, sister, because that's *it* for me. I am socially suicided."

"That depends . . ."

"On what?"

"How many bedrooms there are. And, by the way, didn't you jump down my throat not too long ago for using the word 'dyke'? You said only dykes have the right to call themselves dykes."

Contrary paused to study Elizabeth's profile, hoping to find some fracture in her design to explain this, because she was not responding. So Contrary continued:

"I'm guessing there must be some rule that says if you hang out with lesbians as much as you do, then you can use the 'd' word because you're a . . . what? A dyke-by-proxy?"

A couple of half-smiles met halfway and so marked the place they would forever remember where they put an end to what little remained of their pretense to froshy naiveté.

Something about Elizabeth's reticence then caused Contrary suddenly to back off, but she probably went too far with the gag order. "Forget it, OK? I retract that question. Don't tell me. My hormones are making me *homo*cidal. We shouldn't be talking about this. Not now . . . maybe never."

"Am I being dismissed now?" said Elizabeth, bristling, "Are you dismissing me, Mother Superior? After I spent the whole day trying to be there for you?"

"*Be* there for me? That's presumptuous. I would've been perfectly fine without you hanging around all day feeling sorry for me in this stupid skirt, like this never would've happened to you, Little Miss Puss-in-Boots."

"I would love to know what I ever said or did to make you think that. I've never seen your situation as anything other than bad luck that could happen to me, to anyone."

"Yeah, but right now it's happening to me."

"So why the hell are you taking it out on me? What did I do? I wasn't the one who got you pregnant for chrissakes. Why don't you unleash your damn . . . *Doberman* hormones on that jerk Brian? Jeezus, Mary, Contrary and Joseph. I'm just trying to be your friend, and all you can do is rip into me."

"Fuckin' A. You deserve it. You think you're so goddamned superior. You're just so—so cool, aren't you?"

"I don't think that."

"Sure you do."

"No, I don't."

"Yes, you do."

"Do not."

"Do too."

"Don't."

"Do."

"I would really love to know where you get off accusing me of being self-superior," Elizabeth protested, "when I'm just trying to fend off your cheap shots, for crying out loud."

Contrary started crying. Out loud.

"Oh man," Elizabeth groaned, offering Contrary a helping hand as they arrived at the landing that marked the halfway point up the seemingly endless steps and acted as a rest stop with its built-in bench.

"Let's just chill out here for a second, OK? You really shouldn't be exerting yourself like this. You're white as a ghost. We should have taken the damn cab all the way back. I should have insisted."

"I'm fine."

Though they were both practically choking for air, they fired up a couple of refreshing cigarettes. They sat on the bench beneath a lamppost equipped with an automatic light-sensor that was flickering indecisively between day and night. Twilight on the hill offered a spooky reprieve. There was the sense that everything had already been irreversibly transformed and nightfall was just an afterthought. Same as words. Even what Elizabeth said next, with a plaintive aspect, had an underlying quality of finality in seeming transition.

"You're right about Pip . . . she *is* in love with me. Quite seriously."

"Holy shit. Did she actually say that? You've talked about this?"

"Contrary, I . . ."

"Did she make a play for you? Did she touch you?" and indeed she seemed exceedingly titillated by the prospect. "Did she, like, try to kiss you or something? What's so funny?"

"Contrary, I'm trying to tell you that I . . . *I* kissed *her*."

"Wha?"

"I kissed her. Full on the mouth."

"No . . ."

"Yes, and everywhere else, too, every inch of her, I have kissed. Because I love her. I have *never* loved anyone but Pip."

Contrary was dumbstruck, to say the least. She even sputtered: "Since when, ah, has this, how long has this, for chrissakes, I'm just . . ."

"Interim."

"Interim? You've been . . . all this time? This has been going on since January?"

"Yes."

"I think I'm gonna be sick."

Elizabeth looked away.

"This is unbelievable. How could I not know this? How could you not tell me about this? I thought we were so close. I felt so close to you. And you've just been lying to me? All this time?"

"Contrary, I . . ."

"Well, you've certainly made a fool out of me, haven't you? I mean, how stupid can I be, huh? Wow. You really showed me, huh? You really are the master bluffer, aren't you? The most shameless, deceitful, poker-faced fraud. I really feel like I'm gonna be sick."

"Now, wait just a second here. I just told you how much I love someone, for once in my life. And that makes you sick?"

"You just told me you're a dyke and you've been lying to me all along, pretending to be my friend. Yeah, that makes me sick."

"Well, do you know what makes me sick? I'll tell you what makes me sick. What you went through today. All of that pain and sadness you'll remember forever. And for what? For some empty, unseemly screw . . . with an insensitive, unlikable, stupid, asshole frat boy, who you never even gave a *damn* about in the first place. You liked his ass, as I recall. *That* is what makes *me* sick."

She ground out her cigarette butt in cement, as a parting gesture, and said: "I don't need this bullshit. I don't deserve it. I am out of here."

Elizabeth let herself into Pip's room with her own key, assuming, or rather, hoping that Pip would be at dinner, because she had not been eating much lately. Elizabeth guessed that she had lost ten to fifteen pounds in the past two-and-a-half weeks, and she didn't have that kind of fat to burn. The only thing that helped her appetite, and lifted her spirits somewhat, was marijuana. Unfortunately, it did not also act as a painkiller. It seemed only Percodan worked for that. She had gotten a script from one of the doctors who took care of her that night in the E.R., which astounded Elizabeth considering they had come very close to pumping her stomach for fear she might have taken a potentially lethal overdose of that very same drug.

It required an incredible effort on Elizabeth's part to convince them that this was not a suicide attempt, but rather an accident. When some smart-ass neurology resident suggested that such over-doses don't just happen by accident, Elizabeth practically slapped him upside the head trying to get him to listen and take seriously her description of Pip's condition before she started popping the Percs.

"Who are you again?" Dr. Ari Ganz asked.

"I'm her friend."

"Willard girls?"

"Willard *women*, yes."

"Figures."

He had an accent that she guessed correctly was Israeli, based mostly on the fact that she found him so damned attractive. And it was only because the attraction was mutual (and it was a slow night in the E.R.) that he listened to her at all.

"Pre-med?"

"No. My dad's a doctor."

"Figures."

Still, it got results.

"As a matter of fact, her *mother* is a doctor," which was still some-thing of a curiosity in those days, "a pediatric oncologist, no less, Dr. Collier at Children's Hospital of Philadelphia."

Quite a few nurses and doctors, who could not help but eavesdrop in such close proximity, especially on a slow night, now took a keen interest in Elizabeth. One doctor poked his head out from between the curtains of a nearby cubicle and asked:

"Did someone here just mention a Dr. Collier?"

"I did," Elizabeth replied.

"Hannah Collier? From CHOP in Philly?"

"Yes."

He came right over and plucked Pip's chart from Dr. Ganz, who followed him to Pip's side, relaying the information that Elizabeth had given him about a possible head injury. Elizabeth could hear the authoritative older doctor speaking gently to Pip as if she were his own daughter. He introduced himself as Dr. Levine. Emerging from the cubicle sometime later, he asked Elizabeth if Pip's parents had been called yet. To which she replied no, because Pip would not permit it. He was so incredulous that he asked Pip to confirm this, which she did with an unexpected clarity considering she did not know what day it was.

Elizabeth overheard Dr. Levine telling Dr. Ganz that he was going to call a Dr. So-and-So, who Elizabeth learned was the chief of neurology.

"In the meantime, let's get some head shots . . . and the hand. I'll be back."

Elizabeth heard Dr. Ganz ask Pip if she knew who had brought her here. She couldn't understand Pip's mumbling response, but after Dr. Ganz told Elizabeth that they were admitting Pip for observation, he said not to worry. "Your friend is going to be fine, Ms. Kitten."

Pip was curled up on the bed facing the wall, which was pretty much the position she had been in since the "accident."

"Hey, baby," Elizabeth said, dropping her stuff in a chair and climbing in bed to spoon her.

"My parents are coming this weekend. And my brothers. What am I going to do? They can't see me this way. I can't do this, Bree . . . I can't deal with this . . ."

"I know, baby, but we'll get you through this. Everything's going to be OK."

"Just hold me, please, don't leave me alone . . ."

"I gotcha, don't worry, I'm not going anywhere. I won't leave you alone."

# CHAPTER 29
# Perjury

When word got out to competitors in the fencing world that the indomitable Pip Collier had broken her fencing hand in a freakish fall, even those opponents she had pissed off the *piste* were extremely sorry to hear it, and highly empathetic. Everyone from Buffy, the President of Willard, to Hans, the Baron of Beef, was upset about it. And then there was Poins—poor devil—who took it harder than most. Pip was his pride and joy. Only two weeks before she had won the highest level collegiate competition of her career, and penetrated the ranks of the elite: "A" classification, world cup, and, if she wanted it enough, she had a very good chance of qualifying for the Olympics.

Poins was in the gymnasium that Saturday morning of the May Day revels, along with quite a few others, mostly members of the festival committee, including a lot of Dicks from the brother school, in a joint effort (and on so many levels), coordinating the day's athletic contests and fun-filled activities for the whole family.

When Pip walked into the gym, accompanied by Elizabeth, conversations didn't cease outright at first, but were gradually reduced to an incredulous undercurrent and then to near silence, as they realized what they were seeing. Then you could have heard a foil drop. For their champion was dressed, not in whites, but in white dressings. Her fencing hand and wrist were in a cast, supported by a sling. There were splints on all four of her fractured fingers, taped together in pairs.

When he saw his injured minion, Poins was so overwrought that even his French failed him. He made a speedy retreat to his office until he could collect himself.

*Damn those tile steps* that had been responsible for so many wipeouts over the years. Handymen had been dispatched "to put down safety treads or runners or whatever the hell those things are called," as the order came down from the President herself, in defiance of some campus historic preservation law that had prevented them from fixing the steps all these years. The president and her administration were fretting about the possibility of a lawsuit. Pip's father was, after all, a lawyer, *and* from Philadelphia.

But Pip had grossly misrepresented her injury to her parents, and without accurate information, they could only be as upset as she directed them to be. As far as they knew, their stoical daughter had simply broken her wrist.

When Dr. Collier saw her daughter the weekend of graduation, she was shocked. Her face was so gaunt and pallid and her eyes doleful. She didn't *have* an expression, she *wore* one, impassively, like the mesh on a fencing mask. Pip's mother simply could not believe all of this damage, palpable or disguised, had been done in a tumble down some stairs—especially since that was the most common lie told in the E.R. by abused women and children. A classic. Her mother insisted that Pip come home to Philadelphia immediately after graduation to be examined by her colleagues who were hand specialists.

Unfortunately, what they had to say was not particularly encouraging. Hands were "complicated." The doctors all made the same face when asked if she would ever fence competitively again. The best they could offer was a little riff on how the human body is an amazing thing (yeah yeah yeah), and hands are especially good compensators. She could always fence with her right hand, right? Right, she could do that. Well, then, she was lucky to be ambidextrous. Not necessarily, she replied, explaining that there is, in fact, a left-handed advantage in fencing, which is why she had trained the left from the start.

Pip called Elizabeth one night from Philadelphia, where she was getting her third second opinion, to tell her how "lucky" she was.

"Well, I certainly hope you explained to your doctors, in pornographic detail, why *I'm* really the lucky one."

Getting Pip to laugh had become Elizabeth's objective. And this attempt proved successful.

Pip had been terribly upset that Elizabeth would not accompany her to Philadelphia. It wasn't just that she would have enjoyed having some company during the six-hour drive, it was her fear that if left to her own devices—or lack thereof—Elizabeth would become involved with one of those fools of hers at court. After all, Elizabeth could only go so far into Pip's exclusive world of women. Her ego demanded and devoured the attention of men. But to what end? This was more than a mystery to Pip: it was agony. And they were running out of time. If she could not feel secure in Elizabeth's love when they were apart for two days, there was no hope for maintaining a long distance *affaire de coeur.* It was unrealistic and probably unfair to both of them, Pip concluded. It would only make Elizabeth even better at bluffing than she was now, which was a disturbing thought.

"I really wish you would come home with me sometime. You would be very welcome here. My parents know how I feel about you."

"I know, Pip, and that's just it. I think it's the fact that your parents *know* so much that makes it hard for me."

"Why?"

"I dunno."

"Yes, you do."

"I guess I'm just . . . I think it has something to do with my identity . . . I don't want to be defined as just being one way . . . I guess it makes me feel confined or something . . . too much in that world."

*That* world?

Had to pull back from that one for quite some time.

"Pip?"

"If that's the only reason you're not here in this bed with me right now, then why can't I go with you to visit *your* family?"

It was a good question.

"Do you have any idea how strange it was for me to see your dad that day at Fey House when he came to pick you up? To actually speak with him—and stand there pretending like you're just some little dink who lives on the third floor and that I don't know him from Adam?"

"I'm sorry you had to go through that, Pip, but . . ."

"But what? I think your family could handle it . . . us being together, I mean . . ."

"Probably . . . it's just . . . I dunno, Pip. Maybe I just can't handle it. I'm sorry."

"When worlds collide," Pip said, which struck Elizabeth as some newfound resignation. "No chance of that happening, is there, Bree? If we got in the car one day and headed north to South."

"I'm sorry, baby, truly I am."

"Maybe *that's* why you're so hopelessly confused about your worlds. What else could you be growing up north in South?"

During another phone conversation, Pip speculated, "Maybe if I didn't look like such a dyke . . ."

"That's ridiculous."

"Is it? Hey, I can do femme. I can dress like a girl. I've done it before. I grew up wearing Villager dresses and skirts and sweater sets, too, you know. I've got the fucking pearls."

This made Elizabeth laugh.

"I can even walk in heels."

"No."

"High heels."

"No way."

"Spikes . . . yes . . ."

"I don't believe it."

"I can. I'm telling you. It's just like any other sport to me. If I can ski, ice skate, and surf, I sure as hell can walk in a pair of high heels."

"Prove it."

"Oh, I'll prove it."

"Baby," she purred, "I am living for that day . . ."

Elizabeth and Contrary saw each other frequently that summer, but only because Contrary was waiting tables at Abe's and Elizabeth hung out there a lot. They had not spoken to each other since their slapfight in May. The consistency with which Contrary and Elizabeth avoided each other without calling attention to it in such a small world was impressive, especially as Elizabeth had been braced for an all-out offensive—behind her back, of course. But that did not happen. They expressed mutual respect for each other's privacy. There was also Contrary's depressed state following the hormonal upheaval of her abortion, which didn't start to lift until midsummer.

They certainly continued to take a keen interest in each other's love lives from afar. Elizabeth espied some of the looks Contrary and Vaclav exchanged, knowing that Contrary would be breaking that vow of celibacy, after all. Soon. And how.

Contrary, in turn, could only marvel at the number of guys Elizabeth attracted by just sitting there minding her own business. Whenever she was in the bar, it was like watching one miniature Elizabethan drama after another, with lines and scenes and acts played out by self-appointed rivals for her affections when none had been offered. Contrary never once saw Elizabeth initiate a conversation with a guy she did not know. She never made the first move. In fact, her every action in that environment was merely a response to something done or said to her by some guy. Her answers were invariably polite and remarkably patient, considering she was more likely to be subjected to a barrage of assinine questions than not. On busy nights, there was no keeping up with the drinks Vaclav would deliver from this or that gentleman over there. And it was hardly necessary to point the guy out, because they were always easy to spot, anxiously awaiting her gratitude, according to the drill. She was perfectly happy to follow through. It was necessary for her to do at least one of three things: nod, smile, or laugh. If she liked who she saw, she might do all three.

But that was the extent of the exchange, usually, unless, of course, Her Majesty bid the subject to come forth from the crowd and be heard. It always struck Elizabeth as significant that the guys who bought her drinks from afar were the least likely to make pests of themselves, or to expect anything more in return than her polite regard.

So the drinks lined up like opposing pawns in chess all hopelessly blocked—she couldn't possibly drink that much—eventually to be taken discreetly from the game board by Vaclav.

Pip did not seem to understand Elizabeth's true detachment from them, the men. Contrary had caught that flash of fury in Pip's eyes on several occasions when she walked in unexpected and found Elizabeth surrounded. It happened because their schedules were a bit out of sync.

Pip was working longer hours as a research assistant for a prominent psychologist at Weston Psych and Elizabeth's own summer job couldn't have been cushier. Dr. Maddocks had gotten her a gig as a private tutor in "literature appreciation" to a gaggle of high school kids from affluent Upper Alban Hill families. The kiddos, as she called them, expected to be accepted into Ivy League colleges, but they hated to read books. Elizabeth had been surprised when Dr.

Maddocks called her into his office back in May to ask if she was interested in the tutoring job, because she hardly felt qualified. But he contended that what she lacked in certification, she made up for with pure enthusiasm. These kids didn't need any more stuffy, boring prep school scholars to alienate them from literature forever, they needed to be exposed to Elizabeth's infectious excitement.

"Like a cheerleader?" she asked.

"Exactly," he answered. "A literary cheerleader."

As it went, the tutoring paid well, was great fun, and allowed her to make her own hours.

Contrary was working at Abe's one midsummer night during a particularly invigorating electrical storm when Pip walked in—surprise.

"Pip?" said Elizabeth, "What are you doing here? What's wrong?" As Elizabeth turned her back on her fools, one of them refused to go quietly.

"We have to talk," Pip said to Elizabeth.

"Who's she?"

Pip intervened, "She asked you nicely to go away, so go away." Still, he stuck.

So Pip told him to "Fuck off."

He seemed momentarily stunned by her fearsome command, so she lacerated him, "What part of *fuck off* don't you understand?" which made him back off, but not without the predictable parting shot:

"Dyke."

"Dick."

"Pip, don't. Just ignore him," said Elizabeth. "He's an idiot. He's just drunk."

"That's supposed to appease me? Finding you here with some drunk idiot?"

"I wasn't *with* him, for chrissakes. Don't be ridiculous. What's going on? I thought you were working late tonight . . ."

"Yeah, obviously . . ."

"Oh, come on."

Pip led Elizabeth to a booth in the back so they could talk privately. Elizabeth usually sat at the bar in order to avoid being served by Contrary, but Pip wasn't bothered in the least. In fact, she and Contrary had become rather cute and playful with each other.

Tonight, Contrary stepped up to the booth and spoke to Pip as if Elizabeth wasn't there, in her teasing patois, snapping her gum.

"What can I getcha, hon?"

Pip ordered a Dewar's on the rocks with a splash.

"Somethin' for the missus?"

Pip looked at Elizabeth, who shook her head, then back at Contrary. "Nothing for the missus, thanks."

After Contrary left, Pip said, "Dusie's in town for a week."

"You talked to her?"

"Jo's lawyer called me."

"So, what's going on?"

"The police have already interviewed her. Something's up because they want Jo to come in for more questioning."

"What does this mean?"

"It means the police aren't buying the *single bullet theory*."

That is, the theory that a crazed Dusie acted alone and was solely responsible for her stepbrother's injury, but could not also be held accountable because she was legally insane at the time.

"It's possible that the police are conducting a criminal investigation . . ."

"Criminal?"

"It's possible. And, if so, they can question anybody and everybody who saw Jo or Dusie that day she went into the hospital."

When Contrary returned with Pip's drink, Elizabeth dropped the nonsense and just asked her outright to bring another one.

"They can't find out about you and Dusie."

"What if they ask me point blank?"

"Lie."

"I should perjure myself?"

"Lying to the police isn't perjury."

"What if I'm deposed? That would be perjury," Pip seemed to ask the ice cubes she was rattling in her glass. She had been learning how to drink that summer.

"Pip, I know this upsets you and I'm sorry, but what if you, or we . . . what if we all just told the truth?"

"The truth?" she snapped. "What's the truth?"

Elizabeth looked away, thinking, oh God, here we go, and counted to herself slowly to three.

Pip followed Elizabeth's eye suspiciously, assuming she was looking at some guy.

Four, five, six . . .

Pip lowered her voice so much it was as if she were mouthing the
words, though Elizabeth had no trouble understanding: "Jo told
Dusie to *kill* him."

She would never say Bram's name.

"And we all know this. So unless we all agree to perjure ourselves
Jo's fucked."

Seven, eight, nine . . .

"That's the truth, Breedlove." She rose then as if from a jolt, and
stood looking down upon Elizabeth, who looked even downer at the
worn red Formica tabletop. Pip leaned way over the booth in order
to put her lips right to Elizabeth's ear—she had taken to taunting her
with their intimacy in public—and said, hotly, as if really disgusted,
"You're a dyke. How about *that* truth. You can't even admit it to
yourself, or anybody close to you, and you're telling me now that you
would announce this to the whole world?"

"I don't know, Pip, I just . . ."

"No, you don't know, do you? About telling the truth? To what
end? We all get screwed by the truth."

Then she straightened, tossed back the drink, put the glass
down—clack—and walked.

Elizabeth was still sitting by herself in the back booth staring at
the wall after last call when Vaclav locked the door behind the strag-
glers and Contrary cleared the tables.

Having completed her various tasks, Contrary approached Elizabeth carrying a couple of drinks.

"Scotch rocks splash," she said, "on the house."

Elizabeth looked surprised, but grateful.

"Trouble in vampire paradise?"

Elizabeth snuffed out her cigarette butt in the ashtray, answering
with her eyes.

"Mind if I sit? My pups are killing me." Being on her feet every
night was brutal, but she had lost some freshman fat because of it, so
she looked terrific. Her heart-shaped face and her perfect complexion were radiant at the cheekbones from the exertion of waitressing
and Vaclav.

"May I bum one of those?"

Elizabeth put her finger on her cigarette pack and pushed it slowly across the table toward her.

"Thanks. You're in a chatty mood."

Elizabeth shrugged.

"You know, I've been watching you for weeks, sister, trying to get a read on this . . . *thing* you're into, up there, whatever it is, and I've come to the realization that it's not you being a queer that really bothers me." She exhaled a long stream of smoke in Elizabeth's direction, "What's troubling is what's in between."

"Yeah, well . . ."

"What's that about?"

Again, Elizabeth shrugged.

"Boy, girl, boy, girl . . . you're like a demonic Alban Hill hostess with a seating chart."

"It may seem that way, but that's not how it is."

"I can't pretend to know much about it, but from where I'm sitting this can't have a happy ending."

"And you and The Lion of Prague are assured eternal bliss?"

"Hey, at least *our* hopeless romance has a chance."

They talked a while longer, finishing their drinks, and walked to the door. Elizabeth told Contrary that they played poker a lot in "vampire paradise," especially Wednesdays, late into the night, and invited her to come upstairs sometime.

Upstairs, Elizabeth found Pip walking down the hallway after her bath, wrapped in her robe of thirsty white terrycloth. Elizabeth followed her into their bedroom, stopping short to lean on the doorjamb and watch as Pip sat down on the edge of the bed and began to rub lotion on her smoothly shaved legs. As another side effect of her "accident," there was the compulsive showering and bathing, sometimes twice a day, and the meticulous exfoliation of her legs and underarms—the bikini line was looking like an art class demonstration of the vanishing point.

"What?" Pip asked.

Elizabeth stepped into the room, shut and locked the door, and said, "I would."

"You would what?"

"I would perjure myself for you."

"I would never ask you to do that."

"I know. But I would. I would do anything for you, Pip."

"Really? Well, then stop fucking around with those guys."

"I'm not fucking around with any guys, baby. I swear to God."

"What do you think? I'm an idiot? I hit my head, so now I'm an idiot?"

"No, for chrissakes, Pip, what are you talking about?"

It scared Elizabeth when she got like this: so volatile, with each breath she took on a new mood. Who? Elizabeth wanted to shout: Who are you?

"I can't take it, seeing you with those guys. Why are you doing this to me? Dammit? Why?"

She hurled the lotion bottle, which was plastic, fortunately, at the closet door. No harm done. Elizabeth retrieved it. God knows, she had done it before.

And just as abruptly, she turned contrite. "I'm sorry . . ."

"It's OK, Pip. I just wish you had a little faith in me—that's all. I've never done anything to justify your suspicion. It's not based on any reality."

"I know. I'm sorry. I just get scared."

"Scared of what?"

"I dunno, like, some guy—one of those guys . . . I mean, you don't really know them, Bree. I'm afraid some guy's going to hurt you like . . ."

"Like what, Pip?"

But Pip would not respond.

"Don't be scared. There's no reason to be scared for me."

Elizabeth filled her palm with the balm and dropped to her knees before Pip, who was pouting—at first. But then she smiled as Elizabeth rubbed the stuff, like liquid silk, up her legs slowly toward the vanishing point, determined to defy its seeming infinity.

# CHAPTER 30
# Dusie Ex Machina

Dusie had returned to Weston from Philadelphia after the 4th of July, which she had spent with her parents' Main Line friends, the Stiwtin family, at their beach house on the Jersey shore. The Stiwtins, Lillian and Sterling, and their three children, Sterling III, Kelly, and Vern, had turned out to be not half bad people after all, however full of themselves. As Dusie's condition improved at The Institute, the Stiwtins had insisted she visit them almost every weekend at their lovely home in the suburbs of Philadelphia.

Sterling, who attended nearby Haverford College, was infatuated with Dusie, and because she was nice to him, everyone assumed that they were an item. The reality, of course, was that Dusie was more interested in Kelly, the daughter, a sophomore at another nearby college, Bryn Mawr, one of the Seven Sister schools. Every time Dusie heard a reference to those Seven Sister Ivy League women's colleges, she would roll her eyes and announce quite proudly that she was a student at the "eighth sister school, Willard College for Women," and note that WCW had the distinction of still being exclusively *for women*.

Dusie returned to Weston with a healthy glow from a week in the Jersey sun, so emotionally stabilized that she seemed positively thoughtful. Having undergone psychoanalysis five days a week for nearly six months, she was much more accomplished at articulating her feelings and ideas. She told her parents calmly that she was extremely angry at them for suing Dr. Crews and asked them please to drop the suit because it would only make her crazy and sick again. And after some consideration, her parents agreed. The nightmare of having both of their children seriously hurt and hospitalized all this time had been sobering. They had enough to deal with tending to Bram, and they did not want to agitate Dusie again. So the civil suit against Dr. Crews was dropped.

Dusie also surprised her parents by asking rather sweetly if she could visit her stepbrother. Bram had been in residence at a special rehabilitation facility out in Tumbling Rock Valley for people paralyzed from spinal cord injuries, where they learned how to make the best of the worst. It took a lot of time, of course. Bram, in particular, was a tough case because he was despondent, barely speaking to family and friends who came to visit. The third day Dusie was home, her parents took her to see him. She insisted on visiting with him alone. When she saw him, she burst into tears, but she did not apologize.

"You did this to yourself," she said, sniffling.

He still claimed not to have any memory of that night she ran him down. So, she pulled her chair closer and leaned in to ask him a single question:

"Did you hurt my girlfriend, Pip?"

Nothing.

She touched the scar across his face. "Did she cut you? Did she stab you?"

"Who?"

"Pip? My girlfriend. Pip. You hurt her, you fucking . . . I hate you, I hate you. I hope you die. I hope you die a *million* deaths. I'm gonna keep *killin' you and killin' you* over and over again, because of what you did, what you did to Pip. I'm your hell! D'ya hear me? Brother, dear? *I am your hell*. You are never ever *ever* getting out of my hell. Never. Ever."

"Dyke," he said.

And she spit in his face and left.

The next day, Officers Votiff and Nivarina dropped by to see how Dusie was doing and to ask her some questions. It was slow going at first because they had not realized what a stunning young woman she was, having first made her acquaintance when she was a raving lunatic with unwashed hair and no makeup, trying to stab them with a foil. As she sat with them on the patio by the pool wearing a demure yellow gingham sundress and espadrilles with laces crisscrossed above her shapely ankles, they found her beauty unnerving.

She looked so breezy, while they were dripping from the midsummer sun in their three-piece polyester suits.

For a while, Dusie did a stand-up job answering their questions. But she didn't have the stamina to maintain her equilibrium for the hours they stayed, and inevitably she made several statements that would prevent quite a few people from choosing their own destinations.

"Why was Dr. Crews's car here at your parents' house that morning?"

"I drove it here."

"You just took it?"

"I borrowed it."

"Did you ask her if you could borrow it?"

"No. I just took it. I knew she wouldn't mind."

"How did you know that?"

"Because she told me."

"You said you didn't ask her."

"I didn't. Not that night. I mean, she told me I could borrow her car whenever I wanted."

"That's very generous of her."

"Yeah. She's like that."

"You must be good friends."

"She's my doctor. That's different from friends."

"Does she let her other patients borrow her car whenever they want?"

"How should I know what she does with her other patients?"

"Did you ever borrow Dr. Crews's car before that night?"

"Um, lemme think . . . no."

"That was the only time?"

"Yep."

"Where was Dr. Crews when you borrowed her car?"

"Same place as me. At her apartment. She was in her room. Asleep."

"How do you know she was asleep?"

"I dunno, her door was closed. It was late. What else would she be doing?"

"Why did you borrow Dr. Crews's car, Miss Hertz?"

"Ms."

"Sorry. Ms. Hertz."

"I wanted to kill my stepbrother."

"Why did you want to kill him?"

"He abused me."

"When did he abuse you?"

"All of my life . . . most of it, anyway."

"When you say 'abuse' what do you mean exactly?"

"Sex. Sexually. He sexually abused me. He raped me."

"Did he rape you that night?"

"No."

"And yet you were screaming 'rape.' Do you remember that?"

"Not really. I was sorta out of it."

"Did Dr. Crews know that your stepbrother sexually abused or raped you?"

"Why do you keep asking me about Dr. Crews? This doesn't have anything to do with her. This is about me and him."

"We know this is difficult for you, Miss, er, Ms. Hertz, but if you don't mind, please just try to answer the questions to the best of your ability. Did Dr. Crews know about this sexual abuse?"

"Of course. She's my doctor. She knows everything about me. She saved my life in high school because I was puking up my food. I got anorexia because of Bram abusing me. My parents hate her, can you believe? She saved my life and they hate her. I mean, what kind of message does that send to me, you know?"

Votiff and Nivarina didn't have a clue as to how they should respond, but it didn't matter because Dusie went on without them.

"I could not believe they were suing her."

"Your parents are suing Dr. Crews?"

"Not anymore. I made them stop it. It wasn't right. She was just trying to save me from that dickhead, Dr. Valentine. He abused me, too. Make sure you write that down and underline it: V-A-L-E-N-T-I-N-E."

Votiff and Nivarina could barely contain their excitement.

They questioned her about that for a quarter of an hour, during which time she began to squirm, losing her concentration. Her mother brought out a fresh pitcher of iced tea, refilled their glasses and handed Dusie her medication. After Mrs. Hertz left, the officers continued.

"Did Dr. Crews tell you to confront your stepbrother?"

"Yeah. She's been telling me to do that for years. She said I couldn't really heal until I did."

"Telling you to do what exactly?"

"Confront him. Like you said."

"Did Dr. Crews tell you to *confront* him with a car?"

"Huh?"

"Did she tell you to run down your stepbrother with your father's car?"

"That's stupid. Why would she tell me that? She told me to shoot him with Daddy's gun."

# CHAPTER 31
## Camp Understanding

Late in the summer, after another fight with Vaclav, Contrary ventured upstairs to the Wednesday poker game. It was early evening and she arrived at The Penthouse door carrying a six-pack and a little brass peace pipe. Before she knocked, she checked to make sure her shirt collar was unbuttoned low enough to prominently display her gold cross, just in case. She took further reassurance in the fact that she had downed a garlicky hoagie for dinner.

Marsha answered the front door, which was actually in the back, and escorted Contrary down a long hallway of hardwood floors and big oak doors. She counted four bedrooms and did the math. Yes, she thought, they were definitely sleeping in the same bed. That put to rest any possible doubt. The hallway ended where the large adjoining living room, dining room and kitchen began. There were three enormous windows overlooking an unlikely little cobblestone street with buildings squeezed together like houses on the pricier properties in Monopoly. But no hotels, just homelets, little stores with awnings, eensy boutiques, tiny restaurants and taverns, like a miniature village at the heart of a residential neighborhood of Upper Alban Hill, always teeming with nicely dressed folk out for a stroll or, rather, *perambulating*.

Most notable was Weston's oldest and most esteemed jazz club, Happy Frank's the favored haunt of Dr. Crews and her many musician friends, in their various evolving permutations as bands over the decades. It was, in fact, where Jo had first made her romantic feelings toward Pip known so many years ago. This had been the only downside Pip had considered in her decision to live here and it was fairly minor, the dread prospect of bumping into Jo, coming or going from the club. But Jo had no intention of coming anywhere near Pip.

Somehow Contrary stepped into the Penthouse living room scene without blanching and offered a boisterous greeting all around. From where she stood she could see into the partially open kitchen where Gracie was at the gas range filling orders for her positively sublime omelets. Decker was cross-legged on the other counter strumming an unplugged electric guitar, looking even more like their cute boy mascot in one of Gracie's oversized WCW T-shirts. The others were flopped about the living room. There was Gretchen hunkered on the floor at one end of a large coffee table that was the center of their cozy universe. She was employing the law of gravity to clean an ounce of pot, separating the seeds from the leaves placed on a slight incline created from a double record album held open like a book, so they would roll down to the inside fold.

"A bit twiggy," was the general consensus, but the seeds were "nice and white."

All told, it was a pretty typical collegiate scene of the '70s: seeds rolled, omelets bubbled, guitars unplugged and everybody inhaled. But then came the hard part as Contrary was invited to take a seat in the only available chair, which was opposite the big shabby sofa where Elizabeth was spooned into Pip, and they made not the slightest adjustment in their languid repose to spare Contrary the embarrassment and intrigue of trying to make sense of all those lovely, bare, entwined legs.

There was no air conditioning up there, just fans, so everyone was stripped down to their skivvies, literally men's underwear, the one exception being, of course, the only actual man there. Decker wore jeans regardless of the season or climate, and yet he was the only one who was not sweltering. Otherwise, the whole lot of them were flip-flopping around in rubber thongs and featherweight cotton boxers with undershirts that could have been ripped from Stanley Kowalski.

"Oh dear," said Contrary to Elizabeth so everyone could hear, "you didn't tell me Wednesdays were 'strip poker' night." It got a big laugh, especially when she warned:

"Well, *gentlemen*, put on your birthday suits because I've got enough layers of polyester here to work with fucking plutonium."

Pip's mushroom omelet was ready, so she and Elizabeth had to bestir themselves, an effort that brought to mind the slippery reluctance of a raw egg separating yolk from white. Contrary couldn't help but notice Pip's sinewy figure in slinky dishabille. She had been betting on gross body hair, *au naturel,* and was surprised to find her so exquisitely groomed. Sensitive to Contrary's discomfort, Pip stopped short on her way to the kitchen, and caught her staring. "You look hot, McNaught . . ."

Contrary's bisque doll complexion appeared unusually glazed and doubly flushed under Pip's gaze, being so distracted that she had no snappy comeback, and blamed it on heat stroke. Pip suggested to Elizabeth that she scare up some cooler, comfy clothes for Contrary from Pip's own wardrobe, since they were closer in height. She recommended Contrary choose from the collection of matching green surgical scrubs she had accumulated from her mother. Contrary followed Elizabeth down the hall to the bedroom, and slipped into a fresh set of scrubs Elizabeth pulled from Pip's drawer in the dresser they shared.

Admiring herself in comfy surgical guise before the mirror, she couldn't help but notice the solitary photograph, a Polaroid instant, wedged between the glass and wood frame. She leaned in for a closer look, squinting one eye against a lick of smoke.

"I'll be damned," she muttered, "you really *do* make a cute couple."

Elizabeth who was sitting on the bed sidesaddle, with her back cushioned by pillows against the antique ebony headboard, met Contrary's eye in the mirror and flicked her the kiss-off just as Contrary had taught her.

"What about you and The Lion of Prague? What was the fight about?"

"What makes you think we had a fight?"

"Didn't you?"

"Well . . . yeah, but . . ."

It never took much to get Contrary to spill her craw.

"Remember when I said I would never have sex again?" Contrary scoffed, rolling her eyes, "Yeah, right. To hell with that. We made love last weekend and I swear to God it was like . . . I dunno . . . It wasn't like any other time. I'm so in love. Seriously. I never felt this way before. I would marry him in a heartbeat just to keep him here."

"Hm," said Elizabeth, taking care not to express any more apprehension than that, determined to avoid another slapfight.

She also made it very clear that she would never allow her relationship with Vaclav to interfere with her going to law school.

"So what were you fighting about?"

"Well it wasn't a fight exactly . . . he just sort of surprised me, that's all . . . I wasn't prepared . . ."

"For what?"

"He's Jewish."

There was always the same tempo for Elizabeth's outburst of laughter, a couple of eighth note chuckles followed by the quarter note leading to cacophony.

Contrary felt she deserved this, had expected this and so sat still and endured this.

"I can't believe it. There is justice in the world. Your Lion of Prague is Jewish. Well, well, well. Welcome to *Camp Understanding*, Mary Constance."

"Thanks," she mumbled, "and, um, . . . *shalom.*"

"It's a start."

That night they played one of their more wayward I-dare-you little games where the winner had to do a shot of tequila along with her profits. Contrary was on a winning streak so, needless to say, she missed the last bus out of Babylon. She had no idea how she managed to pass herself off as merely sleepy when she called her mother to tell her she would be staying at the apartment of friends. As long as they were Willard girls. She passed out on the lumpy couch for the night.

Upon waking the next morning, she didn't know, at first, where the hell she was, but had to find out really fast because she was going to throw up. Mercifully she found the bathroom before she hurled. The retching was finally over and she felt much relief as Elizabeth appeared at the door with a warm, soapy washcloth and a fresh towel.

"Avaunt spirit!" Contrary cried, but quickly inserted a polite little "thank you," and resumed: "Quit me! Quit me now. Go back to Hell where you belong, you blood-sucking creature of the night! Or . . ." looking around, "What time is it?"

Elizabeth's reply got lost in her sleepyhead yawn, so she had to try again, quite hoarse, but audible, "Egads. So, it wasn't just a bad dream. We really are on speaking terms again."

"Aw, shit, I know, what have we done?"

Contrary wanted a shower, so Elizabeth fetched her the necessary toiletries, as well as that first refreshing cigarette of the day, already smoking.

"Ahhhhhhhh . . ."

Elizabeth apologized for the rather uneven room service there at The Penthouse Country Inn, being so remiss a hostess.

"And you call yourself a Willard girl."

Elizabeth affected contrition.

"It was bad enough I had to sleep on that disgusting, grody couch—Jesus, Mary 'n' Joseph, it was like sleeping in a fucking petri dish of God knows *what* kind of mutant venereal vampire festering in there . . . all those decades of unholy debauchery."

"Next time I'll have it sanitized for your protection."

"Next time? Oh you poor dear ignorant girl, if you were truly gracious, you would gladly take the sofa, and I would sleep with Pip."

Elizabeth's grin was the one where she bit her lower lip, eyes brightening: "Don't even say that in jest."

"Yeah, right, like I could say it any other way."

The phone started ringing, so loudly amplified by the barren hall that Contrary covered her ears in hangover hell, doing Munch's silent scream. Elizabeth left her to her toilette and headed toward the phone. But Pip got there first, stepping from the kitchen holding a steaming coffee mug, dressed and ready for work.

And no matter how many times she saw Pip in a dress, Elizabeth was still stupefied with appreciation. When it was hot and humid like this, she wore one of her light cotton summer frocks. Sleeveless with a modest neckline not too low in the back or too clingy, just pinched enough at the waist to insinuate a curve. The stylish length for summer dresses was to the shin. And Pip's dress buttoned in front all the way up or all the way down, depending on the optimism or pessimism of the moment.

Elizabeth heard Pip say: "This is Ms. Collier."

It was Officers Votiff and Nivarina asking her if she could come to their station house to answer a few questions about her former roommate, Dusie Hertz, and her former teacher, Dr. Josephine Crews. Pip told them apologetically that her heavy work schedule over the next couple of days made it impossible to drive all the way out to their suburban location. So they offered to come into town. As a matter of fact, they would be coming into Weston Psych tomorrow to talk to several people there, a Dr. Madison, a Dr. Valentine and a Nurse Macadoo. Perhaps they could arrange to talk to Ms. Collier there, too? They promised it wouldn't take more than an hour or so.

Pip, white-faced and shaking, hung up by throwing the phone receiver. She would have flung anything else within reach had Elizabeth not been there at the ready, with one grip on the telephone cord to reel in the receiver before it could hit anything, and the other grip on her lover's uninjured wrist to reel her in before she could hit anything. Trashing things had become Pip's method of stress management since she quit fencing. It was almost as if she had never fenced at all, as if the whole body of her ability and accumulated experience had simply *quit* her. She would even lose her balance sometimes like a normal person, which was almost frightening to anyone who knew her before.

*Knew her before.* That was the phrase Elizabeth always said to herself these days, as she marked the alarming transformation in Pip's face. There were various ways that Elizabeth phrased it, but one word remained the same and it was always required: *before.* Before the rape: B.R. This had become the B.C. of Pip's personal history.

Elizabeth took great care not to touch her hand, which was tricky since she would reel blindly when enraged, conditioned automatically to lead with her fencing hand. Elizabeth came to the rescue quickly, catching Pip in a hug from behind for the purpose of pulling her backward, stumbling off balance, which sent her tumbling into Elizabeth's lap, as they both dropped into the arms of a lumpy old comfy chair. It went perfectly according to her plan. With strength and confidence, Elizabeth secured and comforted Pip, whose entire being seemed easily to conform within reach of Elizabeth's arms.

It was something to see.

And Contrary was the one who saw it that morning as she came shuffling down the hall after her shower, following the compelling aroma of freshly brewed coffee, looking for her hostess with the mostess. She was just about to enter the living room when she was stopped in her tracks by a most unlikely sight, sidestepping quickly to avoid detection, not because she was spying, but rather, respecting their privacy. The profound intimacy of the scene demanded it. This completely unexpected vision of Pip tucked kidlike in Elizabeth's lap was breathtaking.

Contrary tiptoed back down the hall and ducked into the bathroom, leaving the door ajar while she deftly created some sound effects, coughing, cranking the noisy old faucet, flushing the toilet, knocking over a box of tampons and a stack of Dixie cups—"oops," hadn't meant to do that.

She pulled the door shut quietly when she heard them start walking together to the back front door. Kissing on the steps.

In a moment, Elizabeth knocked on the door:

"You can come out now Contrary, the lesbian has left the building."

Contrary and Elizabeth brought their coffee mugs into the living room where it was much cooler to sit and sip before they went their own separate workaday ways.

Elizabeth was uncharacteristically subdued. Even by dread morning standards.

"May I ask you a question? Seriously."

"If such a thing is possible," Elizabeth replied, with a feeble smile.

"What are you going to do when she leaves?"

For a while she just shook her head, downcast.

"Sometimes, I think, I dunno, she's already gone."

Contrary wasn't about to touch that one.

"So . . . without Pip . . ."

Without Pip? She couldn't bear the sound of it.

"So, are you gonna be a dyke now? Or what?"

"You mean, am I just a dyke with Pip, or . . ."

"Yeah, that's what I mean."

"Who wants to know?"

"I believe I speak for the entire tristate area."

"I really don't know how to answer that . . . honestly, at the moment. I can't get past this . . . loss . . . I dunno . . . summer's almost gone. . . ."

On another part of Alban Hill, about a half-dozen blocks from the WCW campus, Dr. Maddocks was in the kitchen of his own house pouring boiling water from a tea kettle into the paper funnel filter of the Chemex carafe on his stove. He had a Cannonball Adderley record playing on the stereo because that worthy jazz musician had died the week before. Not surprisingly, it was Dr. Crews who had called him with the news about Cannonball, and she had seemed so much weepier than he deemed appropriate. But then, no weeping ever would have been the ideal in his own personal Platonic Republic.

The phone started ringing and he turned the music down before answering it. It was Officers Votiff and Nivarina. Dr. Maddocks fired up a cigarette as he listened to their request. In his gruffest, pre-caffeinated voice, intimidating even to his scruffy sheepdog, Boswell, he told the officers that he would not answer any questions, personal or professional, involving a colleague or a student. And he was careful to make it perfectly clear to them that this was his policy regarding all of his colleagues and students equally. When they pressed, he pressed back.

"Has a crime been committed?"

"That's what we're trying to determine, sir."

"I can't imagine what I could possibly tell you that would help you to determine that."

"Please, if you could just answer a couple of questions."

"Such as?"

"We would really prefer to talk to you in person."

"Since that's unlikely to happen, Officer Votiff, I suggest you take advantage of this opportunity, while I'm in a *good* mood."

He explained in the most terse, superficial terms possible how he knew Dr. Crews and Dusie. Then they asked him how he would describe the relationship between Dr. Crews and Dusie. Again, he answered with the plain facts. When they asked him if, to the best of his knowledge, the relationship between Dr. Crews and Ms. Hertz went beyond doctor–patient or teacher–student, he bristled.

"Dr. Crews expressed nothing but concern for Ms. Hertz appropriate to their professional relationship."

"So, you spoke with Dr. Crews about Ms. Hertz?"

"On one occasion. Yes," he replied, though he was chiding himself privately for giving them even that much, reminding himself to be more chary. They asked him to describe the occasion, and he obliged them. He was greatly relieved when they told him that was all they wanted to know, for now, and thanked him for his time.

He didn't like the sound of *for now*.

After they hung up, he quickly dialed Dr. Crews's home number. He told her about the call and asked her flat out, "Jo, what the hell is going on?"

Meanwhile, back at the station house, Officer Votiff picked up his phone and told Nivarina to do the same, reading out a number for his partner to dial, while he dialed a different number. After a second, he looked at Nivarina, who said, "Busy."

Votiff also said, "Busy," and hung up his phone, ruminating, "Looks like Maddocks and Crews are having themselves a little kaffeeklatsch."

# CHAPTER 32
## Come

"Come . . . ," she said. "Come with me . . ."

"I can't . . ."

"Please . . ."

Pip had been beseeching Elizabeth for weeks to accompany her to Philadelphia for the wedding of her cousin, Kelly. And Elizabeth had been resisting, with profuse apologies, saying she could not endure an entire weekend of high church, high jinx, and high delectation in the suburbs of Philadelphia appearing exclusively as the "And Guest" of the family's official lesbian. Surely it would be, a fate worse than the dread dining hall weight check: having to promenade right up the center aisle of some Main Line Protestant church with the Collier entourage. All those beamish boys. She could just imagine the round robin.

"*Who* is she?"

"One of the girlfriends . . ."

"She's lovely."

"Which brother?"

"Penelope."

"Oh dear."

"Her poor mother . . ."

"My heart goes out to her . . ."

"Well, Hannah had to have her career . . ."

"A woman can't have both."

"There's your proof."

"It's tragic really."

"Honestly, I think all of you are making way too much of this. I'm sure it's just a phase. These crushes are short-lived. Not like boys."

"I agree. It's fairly common . . . perfectly harmless."

"It's not as if they actually, well, *do* anything."

"Frankly, I can't imagine what there is for girls to do."

"A little hand-holding, cuddling . . . perfectly harmless."

"Shush! All of you. Here comes the bride . . ."

The Lesbian Girlfriend. Elizabeth shuddered to think.

"But you *are* my girlfriend . . ." said Pip, softening more intimately: "Aren't you my girl?"

And yes, of course, she was. Then why wasn't she responding?

"Bree?"

"Did you ever bring a girlfriend to a wedding before?"

"No."

"Why not?"

"Lots of reasons . . ."

"Name one . . ."

"All right, um . . . well, there's always the classic, and one of my personal favorites: I didn't want to make a 'spectacle' of myself, assuming, of course, that's the only reason anyone who's gay would have for wanting to bring a date to a wedding."

"That's pathetic."

"Welcome to the heterosexual world, Breedlove."

It dawned on Elizabeth that her aversion to being The Lesbian Girlfriend might not be about sexual orientation at all. Maybe it was about commitment. What really bothered her was the constraint implied by the term "girlfriend." She did not express this to Pip just then because she needed some time to think about the implications. But Pip figured it out soon enough.

In bed one night in a record-breaking heat wave they rode at its height, they were pitched into their own brackish drink, making a surf of white sheets as the lovers devolved from having been upright to going downright. And then it was a long slow crawl all the way back into the swell of some unfathomable sea.

Or they were just fucking. Who the hell knew?

Just can't imagine what it is that girls do.

Pip dropped back, pulling Elizabeth on top, slick and soft and sweet—my god—wanting only to be engulfed before the tidal return of her memory ruined everything. Until then, she could still make love entreating the deities of ecstasy.

"Oh God . . ."

"Come . . ." she whispered. "Come with me . . ."

And it was a cinch to oblige her, or at least to follow close at hand. Elizabeth was thrown clear in a paroxysm with her hands clamped between her own legs, and her mouth agape, screaming in total silence until sensational waves smoothed her out to an easy float. At which, she opened her eyes to find Pip already looking back at her from "way over there."

"Gives new meaning to the expression *getting off,* doesn't it?"

And they burst out laughing.

"I love to see you laugh . . ."

"That's because you crack me up," she reached for Elizabeth, "come here . . ." Back into her arms, she was murmuring, "What am I going to do without you?"

"Same thing I'm going to do without you."

"Date Dick?"

"Ha ha . . ."

"Come . . ." she said. "Come with me . . ."

This time to a different end.

"You know I can't, baby."

"I know," she sighed. "I know . . ." They were both introspective for a long time, and Pip was not sure if Elizabeth had fallen asleep or not when she said, "I'm having second thoughts . . ."

She was awake, but just barely, mumbling soporifically: "What about?"

"Tulane."

That got her up. She flicked on the bedside lamp so she could see Pip's face.

"What do you mean?"

"I don't know, I'm not so sure Tulane is the right place for me anymore . . ."

"Because of Dr. Crews?"

"Partly."

It was perfectly understandable that Pip would have serious reservations about following in her mentor's footsteps, given where Dr. Crews was standing at the moment, "in deep shit," as it were. There were also academic and career reasons. Her summer job at Weston Psych had been exposing her to the theories and research of some of the most progressive thinkers in the mental health field, the neuropsychiatrists.

"A year ago these plans were written in stone . . . And now," she shook her head, "nothing is as it was before."

Elizabeth used this rare opportunity to ask her, carefully:
"Before what?"

Pip shifted somewhat. "Before you, love."

"Hm jeez . . . That may be a dubious distinction, Pip, considering . . ."

"I didn't mean it that way."

"Well . . . what would you do instead?"

"I could stay here . . . go to the U of W."

Elizabeth was thrilled. "We could stay together."

Better still Pip said, "We could live together."

Elizabeth's silence bespoke a resounding *uh-oh*.

"Or . . . maybe not . . ."

"Pip, I didn't say that I . . ."

But Pip shushed her by putting her finger gently to her lips:
"Shh . . . it's OK kitten, I misspoke. I'm sorry, I get too anxious sometimes. There's no way I would want us to live together now, I mean,
beyond this. You're way too young."

"Oh, and you're so old?"

"I've sowed some wild oats."

"Yeah, and you've reaped some wild women, too, haven't you,
baby? Double digits in the dark? And that was just on school nights."

"I wouldn't go that far."

"Sure you would."

"I don't need that anymore."

"Yeah, but, what about when you're down there in Louisiana and
you've been alone for, like, a whole five minutes?"

As they were drifting off, Elizabeth teased, "I bet the backrooms
are fucking infernos in New Orleans." She licked the tip of her finger
and touched it to Pip's lip, providing a sizzling sound effect.

Pip went home alone to Bryn Mawr. On the day of the wedding,
she came downstairs at the Collier residence dressed in a navy,
double-breasted, linen and silk suit, and a white, crepe de Chine
shirt with a plunging neckline and French cuffs. The original plaster
cast on her forearm had been removed so that a parade of hand specialists could palpate her palpus, and in its place was an aluminum
splint wrapped with a bandage. Consequently, she needed assistance
putting on her pearls, a long strand, and a pair of round gold cufflinks, engraved with the WCW insignia.

"These are lovely," said Dr. Collier, as they enjoyed a private moment over coffee at the kitchen counter. Assuming the cufflinks were a gift, Dr. Collier gave pause, hoping Pip would offer even a modicum of back story. But Pip held her tongue because they had been given to her by Dr. Crews.

Her daughter's love life was pretty much a mystery to Dr. Collier, though she had always encouraged all her children to speak freely. She meant "love life" in the conventional sense of dating or being in an exclusive relationship. It did not occur to her that there might be other options. As a doctor, she had to be heavily insulated "against the thousand natural shocks that flesh is heir to," but as a mother it would be difficult to process her daughter's reputation as a lesbian Lothario whose kiss was just not a kiss—ask anybody—but a potential force of levitation.

"How's Elizabeth?" Dr. Collier asked.

"Fine."

The Collier family had been introduced to an extremely self-conscious Elizabeth at graduation and it was clear to them that their Pip was smitten with this kitten. But Elizabeth just seemed too young and, perhaps, ambivalent for such a serious relationship.

"What do Elizabeth's parents think about the two of you *cohabitating?*"

"I wouldn't know," was Pip's bitter reply. "They don't even know I exist . . . let alone *cohabitate.*"

"I'm sorry, sweetheart. That's a shame."

She swept a wavy forelock away from Pip's downcast eyes.

"But it's the Breedloves' loss. Every parent should be so lucky to have their daughter introduce them to someone as dazzling as you."

"Thanks, Mom."

"Well, it's too bad Elizabeth couldn't come with you."

Pip shrugged.

"I take it you two had a fight?"

Pip nodded, reaching for her cigarettes.

"I *do* wish you would quit smoking, Pippen. It's such a deadly habit."

Pip regarded her mother with a kindred forbearance as she handed her the pack.

"You're a bad influence on me, daughter dear." Dr. Collier glanced toward the door, as if on the look-out for hall monitors, before enjoying a "once in a blue moon" smoke herself.

"So, who is your mystery date for the wedding? Do I know her? Oh, and by the way, before I forget, your great Auntie Hattie, has warned us all that if you show up at the wedding with a) your 'lady-friend' or b) wearing trousers . . ." and here Dr. Collier gestured broadly, "she will stand up. And drop dead."

Pip affected introspection for a moment and then she asked, "Doesn't that pose some sort of paradox in physics?"

"I hope not," said Dr. Collier, reaching for the ashtray, with a most gracious smile, "because your father and I are counting on you, my dear."

Pip's "mystery date" was none other than Miss Dusie Hertz. On several occasions earlier in the summer when Pip was in Philadelphia seeing the hand docs, she had called Dusie at The Institute of Pennsylvania Hospital just to ask how she was doing. After spending nearly two months in the rarefied air at the Institute as a guest (in-patient) receiving the appropriate psychiatric care, as well as the proper doses of the right medications, Dusie had actually gotten well. Pip could hear such a difference in her voice and tone on the phone, it was almost difficult to visualize her face as they spoke. Having never known Dusie in any state other than labile, at times vi-olently so, it was all the more striking for Pip to perceive some stabil-ity taking hold, a self-control. She had been making a conscious effort to modulate her voice following invaluable instruction she re-ceived in a drama workshop at the Institute, which turned out to be quite extraordinary for the simple fact that the group included pro-fessionals, some distinguished, some celebrated, most down from New York for treatment. Dusie represented the sort of raw material New Yorkers in general and theatre people in particular appreciated.

Dusie had been seriously contemplating the WCW motto that en-couraged her to choose her own destination. Making the women of the world safe from Bram, had been empowering, to say the least. But it wasn't just valour she needed, it was poise. She decided she had what it takes to become a supermodel and eventually, perhaps a movie star. But as she was "getting old," she figured that image and illusion were the keys to developing the Dusie Mystique, by which she was certain to succeed.

After her rather elucidating hospital experience, she accepted the kind and generous invitation to spend the rest of her summer with

The Family Stiwtin, at their stately pre-fab Tudor mansion in the
Buckingham Mews sub-development of Devon.

Pip drove over to Devon on that Saturday afternoon in August to
pick up Dusie and stood in the flagstone entranceway of the Stiwtins'
home like the world's most self-assured prom date minus the cor-
sage, charming the world's most clueless parents, Sterling and
Lillian. They were impressed, which means the same thing as "relieved" on the Main Line, to be informed that Pip was *somebody's*
daughter.

When Dusie appeared at the top of the staircase, Pip just stopped
talking in the middle of a sentence. For two years, Dusie had only
ever *dreamed* of seeing that expression on Pip's face—as if it weren't
already enough of a thrill to be seeing her at all, given the nightmare
of their last encounter—and she felt her heart swell. Still, she remembered her training in the crucial timing of the beauty pageant
pause before descending gracefully in a peachy halter dress with a
full skirt lapping at her knees.

Timing.

"Hello, Pip."

"Hello, Dusie."

With a breathy voice and a playful wink beyond the Stiwtins'
range, Dusie said, "You look very handsome."

"Thank you. You look . . ." and Pip just shook her head, which was
spinning, because Dusie's appearance struck her as being defini-
tively:

"Stunning."

Dusie's glossy lips said, "Thank you," but her eyes said, "I know!"

With smooth precision she performed a *pirouette,* showing off
the engineering marvel of her dress: "Isn't it fabulous? Very Marilyn—don't you think?"

Think? Had the Stiwtins not been standing there agog themselves,
Pip would have revealed the sentient extent to which Dusie's dress
completely *impaired* her ability to think.

Dusie paused in the midst of twirling to showcase the backless aspect of her outfit, sweeping her cascading curls upwards with both
hands, into a topknot while she glanced over her shoulder at Pip,
and *vogued* just long enough to get a reading on her ex-lover's telltale pupils. Dusie knew that the pupils never lied. She was thrilled to

observe that the subject's pupils were transfixed and dilated "to the max" as Pip stared at Dusie's bare back.

Sterling, a harmless pompous ass, told Dusie she looked "positively pulchritudinous, my dear."

Like her husband (and so many of the good people living in the suburbs of Philadelphia), Lillian had a congenital irony deficiency. Fortunately, Pip, being from the area, was quite familiar with and sensitive to the special needs of the irony-impaired. Which was the only way she could have kept a straight-face when she was, in fact, quite shocked by a remark Lillian made regarding Dusie's pulchritude:

"Don't you just want to eat her with a spoon?"

"Is a spoon required?" Pip asked. "Because I have been told it is perfectly proper to pick up Dusie and eat her with your fingers."

She let them ponder that piquant remark for a moment and then mercifully got their derailed train of thought back on the Main Line track.

"But then, you know we're all savages over there in Bryn Mawr."

Indeed, the Stiwtins of Devon got such a self-superior kick out of Pip's remark that they completely forgot their uncertainty regarding the proper place setting for dining on Dusie.

At the wedding of Pip's cousin, Kelly, the round robin that ensued in the pews was sparked by the vision of the Collier family's official lesbian making history—and a spectacle of herself—with her usual sultry insouciance, flaunting her ladyfriend, she of with the pulsing runway prance right up the center aisle, defying the proper pew procedure for girls: traditionally, a limp-armed delivery by ushers more given to blushing than brides.

There was actually murmuring as Pip passed and even some jaw-dropping, head-turning, neck-craning activity—obviously out-of-towners—but then, Pip was also wearing a pantsuit.

"Dear God."

Another historic first.

Pip had promised her mother, after all, to make a proper spectacle of herself. Espying her great, great Aunt Hattie with mouth agape—though decidedly seated—Pip gave her the official *secret lesbian club* wink. Oh, yes, and one for her ladyfriend. When the homophobic octogenarian did not stand up and drop dead as promised, Pip caught her mother's eye and shrugged apologetically.

There was no time for Collier family introductions in the pew beyond some quick whispers, smiles and nods, which Dusie returned with her little semi-circular waves. Pip's favorite moment occurred when she leaned slightly forward to look down the Collier row, and saw her brothers' heads all cocked at the same angle and turned in her direction, intent on getting another glimpse of this Dusie. Her father had been looking as well, but quickly remembered himself, sat back and faced forward, wondering if the Phillies were in town that day or on the road and whom they might be playing. Focus on the Phils, he coached himself, just focus on the Phils.

Her seemingly apoplectic brothers, Thomas, Wills, Kevin and Dennis felt no such need to disguise their never-ending astonishment regarding their little sister's way with women. A couple of months ago she had introduced them to Elizabeth, and now this Dusie, who was making them woozy.

Pip affected her sweetest little sister smile, batting her eyelashes, as she had only one thing to say to the lot of them: *Eat your hearts out, boys.*

Pip had the closest relationship with Dennis, who was only two years older and so like her in appearance, mannerism, intellect and temperament that they were assumed to be twins unless proven otherwise. Inevitably, they had clashed at times when they found themselves attracted to, or *attractive* to, the same person. Neither Pip nor Dennis was willing to admit the extent to which their romantic and erotic exploits had overlapped throughout their lives—tracing all the way back to grammer school and a girl named Eve—for fear of courting perversity and rivalry and God knows what other kind of disaster of biblical import. It was enough to say that both of them had inadvertently acquired more in the way of carnal information about the other through common lovers. Mostly, this had happened by accident, which was bad enough, but a couple of specific incidents had led to some dreadful albeit, discreet scenes following the discovery that both Pip and Dennis had been seduced and deceived by the same girl simultaneously.

The reception was held at the home of the bride's parents, who were Pip's Aunt Bunny and Uncle Kent. Their families had grown up together. Kelly, the bride, was as close to having a sister as Pip got.

Kelly's little brother, Trent, was still in high school, going into his senior year at The Stoner School, which was aptly named considering the party going down in Trent's attic room spanning the third floor. While the official reception festivities were taking place outdoors on the sprawling grounds staked with green and white tents, there were impromptu gatherings at various private venues throughout the house.

Pip was upstairs looking for a quiet unoccupied room with a phone so she could call Elizabeth when she bumped into the bride, who was exceedingly pleased to see her and pulled her along, insisting that she use the princess phone in her room, talking a little too fast for her lips maybe. As she put her hand on the doorknob, she said to Pip, "Come on in, coz. You are going to *love* this."

"Here comes the bride . . ."

Kelly gave Pip a little push into a big girlie bedroom with eight bridesmaids changing from their gowns into their play clothes, mostly kicky little frocks or short shorts, but some bathing suits with matching cover-ups or sarongs anticipating a dip in the pool or hot tub under the stars later on.

"Have you all met my favorite kissin' cousin, Pip?"

They had, and greeted her accordingly with kissing sounds and moans and groans and all manner of teasing, pretty typical of otherwise highly repressed straight women when they are exceedingly intoxicated, flashing tits and offering tongues. So Pip just kicked back on the bed with its elaborate canopy and frilly, lacey, fussy stuff— even her pillows had little pillows things. Positioned perfectly to enjoy the rest of the show, she picked up the pink princess phone and put in a call to Elizabeth, watching the bridesmaids taking turns snorting lines of cocaine off the glass top of the vanity, which made them want to dance even more than usual. Lou Reed's "Rock n Roll Animal" was playing on the turntable, and it made them bounce listening to "White Light/White Heat," the perfect music to snort coke by.

Elizabeth was not home.

Trent's party upstairs was the peak of '70s decadence, which meant it was the most fun. The atmosphere was getting thicker by the hour and no doubt would end up being sickening from the constant passing of joints, bongs, pipes and roach clips. Trent was overseeing a veritable apothecary of the very best these Stoner preppies could acquire and offer, set out in dishes like mixed nuts, including reds, yellow jackets, black beauties, white cross, orange sunshine, purple haze, blue microdot, green mescaline, little panels of brown windowpane, Quaaludes aplenty and a bottomless bowl of Valium. This being the crystal methamphetamine capital of the world, there were white rocks the size of marbles on glass blocks or mirrors, with single-edged razor blades for help yourself slicing like a cheese ball, and freshly cut plastic straws for one's snorting convenience. Of course, the trendy drug, at the time, was cocaine.

Dusie would have none of it, though she certainly enjoyed the fun being generated up here in this gathering of *heads,* as they referred to themselves. And there was air conditioning. Surrounded by prepster groupies in continuous rotation playing for her attention, Dusie felt comfortable enough to rest the poise for a while and just blather. She was surprised to find it easier than expected to turn down selections from drug samplers being served around the room along with the fine munchables. She was finally feeling the benefit of being on the right medications with the proper doses.

"I feel, like, totally centered, man, seriously, y'know, it's that cosmic balance yin-yang and yen . . . um . . . thing," she was saying to her pets, kicked back in some nooked cranny, a short distance from Pip in this otherwise expansive, multi-faceted cathedral of an attic playroom. She kept an eye on Pip, who appeared to be the focal point of an extended group of Collier cousins occupying a suede conversation pit in one corner with an equally oversized glass-topped coffee table strewn with the implements of marijuana and cocaine. Dusie watched Dennis, who was sitting to Pip's right, lean forward over the table to snort a couple of lines, followed by Pip.

"Wow," said Dusie, and since it was not unusual for someone in a scene like that to simply say "Wow" at any given moment, there was no need for her to explain that the reason she said it was because she could not get over the resemblance between Pip and her brother Dennis. Their hair was the exact same color except Pip's was cut shorter. Both had removed their suit jackets and were in white shirt sleeves.

Pip dropped back into the deepest darkest modular divide with her forearm resting languidly over her head and her shirt half untucked, looking pre-ravished.

Dusie wisely decided to don her mantle of poise once more in order to approach the clubby Collier cousins without showing fear, and then penetrate the conversation pit perimeter. Destination: Pip.

Someone handed her a joint and she took it, but only as a means to an end. Looking over at Pip in the corner she smiled like the dickens, becoming more and more aware of her power to hold an audience in thrall.

"Shotgun?"

This elicited oohs and ahhs and catcalls and growls as Dusie lowered herself so smoothly into Pip's lap, slipping one arm around her neck in order to play more privately with her hair.

Putting the lit side of the joint in her mouth between her teeth, she leaned even closer to her ex-lover, delivering a steady stream of smoke precisely through the slightest parting of Pip's lips. All the while, Pip's eyes never left Dusie's, which afforded Dusie the perfect opportunity to check her vitals. While she was not pleased to find pin pricks for pupils, particularly as their cozy corner was fairly dark, there was no mistaking the thrill of Pip's pulse.

When Pip had a headful and could not take anymore, Dusie passed the joint for anyone to take because she didn't want to look away, and that was when their lips kind of drifted together briefly, lightly touched. Was it a kiss? Who started it? What were they doing? As the tips of their tongues touched, then both mutually backed off because the only other option was to go forward.

Only Dennis was in a position to see this and he got an eyeful. None of Pip's brothers or cousins were accustomed to seeing Pip being demonstrative with a girlfriend, and it was quite titillating but also intimidating. Clearly, Dusie had Pip in the palm of her hand.

Feeling Dennis's eyes most keenly, Dusie got the next joint coming around and turned to him:

"Shotgun?"

Certainly, Dennis was game, but he looked to his little sister for the go-ahead anyway. She shrugged, which he took to mean exactly what he wanted it to mean. The next thing Pip knew, Dusie was sitting on Dennis's lap and Pip now had the best seat in the house to watch Dusie tantalizing her brother with her luscious lips almost touching his. And suddenly Pip didn't feel so well. Too much sibling *overlappage*. She was having jumpy flashbacks of Bram Hertz, seeing something in Dusie's face or manner—or God knows what—that made her remember. Pip turned pale, and made her way as briskly and inconspicuously as possible down to Kelly's room once more, relieved to find it unoccupied. She lay down on the bed and called Elizabeth again.

Three-thirty in the morning. No Elizabeth. Decker, their nocturnal roommate, had just gotten in from some vacation place with Gracie and really had no idea where Elizabeth could be, except that she was not at the apartment. As they hung up, she wrenched against the impulse to throw the Princess phone out the window. The rage was especially difficult to control under the influence of cocaine, so she punched out a bunch of Kelly's frilly pillows, without doing any harm.

As she left the room shortly after, she saw Dusie walking down the hall toward her. Dusie had been looking for her all over, and was concerned that she had fled the party room because she was feeling sickish or pissed about the Dusie Shotgun Show, or both.

Without speaking or even thinking, Pip pulled Dusie back into the darkened room and shut the door, kissing her in a rapture up against it.

"Oh, Pip . . ."

This make-out moment went on way too long with too much abandon to justify saying that "nothing happened"—"not really," as minor cheaters tend to say—because Dusie was approaching levitation being launched off of Pip's legs. And Pip? She was out of control, being unaccustomed to this extreme level of intoxication from a "cocktail mix" of agents.

Ultimately, she said, "I'm just gone."

Dusie had pushed off suddenly, gasping, "Wait wait wait," because she needed to think. She was not exactly keen on the notion of having Pip—at long last, love—if, by her own admission, she was not even there.

"What are we doing here, Pip?"

The voice of reason.

"I don't know what's going on with you and Elizabeth, but I still think you really love her, and maybe you're really pissed at her, and you know, Pip? I don't wanna be, like, you know, the thing you use to punish Elizabeth. I don't want us to be together like this, if this is just something you're going to regret. I've already been something you regret, Pip. I'm not going back there. No way, man. Uh-uh."

The room wasn't totally dark because the windows overlooking the back lawn were lit up and flickering like a carnival, as the party hearty diehards were still going strong beneath the stars: disco dancing and poolside dousing, and bridesmaids chased across the lawn by dipsy satyrs and fumbling fauns all trampling the sod. And yet the flick of a switch on a fussy little lamp that Dusie turned on, glowing soft as a pink-gold ring she wore, rid the room of all that garish light and sound. There was just Dusie standing before an enchanting oval mirror, smoothing her hair, attempting to retrain all that remained of her poise at this wee hour. Just Pip still over there where Dusie had left her, braced against the door, panting for more.

Pip turned the key in the lock and made her approach, stepping up behind Dusie but not quite touching.

"Look at you," said Dusie, looking straight-ahead at Pip's reflection in the mirror, "you are, like, totally wasted, man. I've never seen you so fucked up as this. Doing all that blow. It's not like you, Pip."

Even less like Pip was the fact that she did not respond. Did she purposely ignore Dusie's questions and observations or was she somehow oblivious to the loaded implications of everything Dusie had said?

"You're a vision," Pip said, lifting her hair up in order to kiss her nape, loosening the knot of Dusie's halter top with her teeth, no less, until the suspension went slack and collapsed. Dusie stood watching as Pip worked her over, feeling her mouth at her back, spine-tingling her to distraction, single-handedly stroking her breasts, while her injured left hand relied, as Dusie herself did, on the strength of Pip's entire arm for support. She would have dropped otherwise, limpsy to the carpet.

Surely, Dusie had never looked or felt so naked. Something about the fullness of her skirt, gathered at the waist like a Degas ballerina's made her seem so utterly exposed, shocking even, to herself.

Pip led her to the fluffy canopy bed and gently tossed her so she landed prone. As she tried to turn in retroflex arching hoping to embrace her, Pip rendered her helpless again by stripping off her skirt, exposing her spine all the way down. And then it was all a blur to her, having all she ever wanted, it seemed, to feel wanted like this by Pip, who had never afforded her more than a fraction of passion and was now transporting her so wholely that she seemed to outreach her grasp.

"Oh Pip . . ."

And yet. It didn't make sense. It wasn't like Pip to *do* her without being done herself. Even as Dusie cried out and clawed and begged and finally just caved under fucking pressure unbearable, insensible, ineffable this pleasure, something was sorely amiss. It just wasn't like Pip. It felt to Dusie like stolen pleasure. Like those fools in Ali Baba and Sinbad movies who discover a cave filled with treasure and roll around in heaps of gold coins, which always ends up belonging to some really testy monster who then has the hapless idiots for lunch.

Being too wasted to get behind the wheel, Pip insisted that Dusie stay at the Collier house, which was just a couple of blocks away, so they could walk. The sun was coming up when they tiptoed into the house. There were no guest rooms available—honestly—since the whole Collier family was in town, so Dusie slept with Pip. When Pip woke up around noon, she could not believe what she had done. She found a note from Dusie, who had left earlier and when she found out it was Dennis who had so generously offered to drive her back to Devon, she called Dusie, who was on her way to the shore with the Stiwtins and could only give her a couple of minutes of phone time, which ended in anger, starting with Pip's accusatory bent:

"It's Dennis, isn't it?"

"What?"

"My brother. You're going to date my brother, aren't you? I'll bet he already asked you out and you said yes and you've picked out the dress."

"Listen to you! Pip! For God's sake, you've really gotta see somebody about this."

"You want to fuck my brother."

"Oh, come on, Pip, because I feel like I know him I guess. OK? I mean, jeez, he is so much like you . . ."

"He's like me with a dick, you mean."

"Well, yeah, I guess, if you *must* be vulgar."

"Vulgar? Oh, pardon me, Miss Mildmanners."

"Don't be silly."

"You sure seemed to be enjoying yourself in his lap last night."

"We were just kidding around, Pip."

"Kidding? Looked more like lap-dancing from where I was sitting. But, hey, you know, it's perfectly fine with me because you're free to do as you please."

"I am? Oh, thank you, master." It was an excellent dreamy Jeanie imitation.

Pip made it clear she wasn't taking any personal questions about her relationship with Elizabeth at this time. But obviously, something had gone seriously wrong.

And what of Pip and her brother?

"What's going on with you and Dennis, Pip? You've always been so close."

"Don't," Pip started, "do not talk to me about brothers, Dusie. You are *not* one to comment on anyone's relationship with her brother."

"What's that supposed to mean?"

"I just don't appreciate you and my brother going behind my back."

"Whoa, man, you are *so* paranoid. Maybe you should cut back on the dope."

"I'm not paranoid if what I suspect is going on between you two is, in fact, true. I know you. I know my brother even better."

"Then why don't you ask him?"

"I will."

"Good. You do that, Pip."

Again, the embittered laughter was so unfamiliar.

"You're going to go out with him, aren't you? You've already decided. Admit it. Just tell me the truth."

"Please don't be angry, Pip."

"I won't be angry if you just tell me the fucking truth."

"OK, well, um, yeah, he did kinda . . ."

*"Kinda* what?"

"He kinda, like, kissed me."

"Really? Ah, well, hm, when did he do that?"

"What difference does it make?"

"I just want to know. Just tell me when?"

"Last night—if you *must* know. When I went downstairs looking for you, Dennis followed me." And they found themselves in a guest room looking out the window over the backyard revelry.

"Is that it?"

"Yeah. We just kissed a little bit."

"So, that was right before I saw you in the hall."

"Yeah."

At that, Pip just hung up on her.

She found Dennis in the basement game room playing pool with Kevin. She walked up to him, got right in his face to deliver the most vociferous speech. "You fucking back-stabbing bastard. Fuck you, Dennis." Followed by a shove that knocked him off balance enough to stumble backwards into a table, toppling a chess game in progress—though not at that exact moment—between Wills and their dad.

"Uh-oh," said Kevin.

"Oh shit," said Dennis.

And Pip just glared at him once more looking really pained, unwittingly eliciting both his, as well as Kevin's sincere concern.

"What the hell was that?"

Dennis just shook his head as a warning not to ask him again even though Kevin and everybody else in the family already knew that rule. Dennis and Pip never shared any particulars of their conflicts, whether large or small. Even when they were little kids, their belief in privacy always took precedence over any actual issue or upset. This was primarily due to the fact that, for a long time, Dennis was the only person privy to the truth about his little sister's sexual nature. He was admirably self-disciplined for her sake at a very early age and fiercely protective.

"Let's just say I tripped and knocked the table over, OK, Kev? Let it go at that."

"That's cool," Kevin shrugged, "but, if I were you, brother, I wouldn't be playing with this particular pack of matches."

"Yes, you would—*if* you could."

"I said: if I were *you.*"

When Dennis was looking for Pip sometime later, their mother told him that his sister had gone over to see their cousin Trent.

"Oh, you know, dear," said Dr. Collier, "something to do with The Car."

Trent was a gifted mechanic and he and Pip had spent many hours working together on her car. But Dennis knew Pip's excuse for visiting Trent was "totally bogus," although he would not have let on in front of anybody, least of all, their perspicacious mother.

Pip felt as if she had crawled all the way back to Weston on Sunday afternoon, she was so down, despite the Dexedrine she had taken to offset the Percodan in order to stay alert for the drive. Trent had filled the "prescriptions" for her that morning. When she found out that Elizabeth had been away for the weekend visiting her family up north in South, the gravity of her guilt made it all pretty much downhill from there for the rest of the summer.

The first of the last big fights began when Elizabeth came home from an afternoon of tutoring with a copy of the new *Mugs & Plugs* in hand.

"Fresh frosh from the field."

The look on Pip's face as Elizabeth announced she had volunteered to be a Big Sister was an entirely new one for Elizabeth to contemplate and recreate in her sketchbook.

"A Big Sister? You?"

"Yeah, me." Elizabeth was fussing with god-knows-what in some drawer, as she was wont to do when agitated.

"Everytime I turn around you're downstairs with some college boy trying to dog your leg, and now I have to deal with you on the prowl for lap cats and *pussy?*"

They both scotched the impulse to laugh.

"Hey, you're the one who keeps telling me I'm in some kind of *dyke denial,* and that I ought to get out there and—do what? I dunno. And now you're telling me I'm just a dyke for you? Your own private dyke."

"So you *are* checking out the girls?"

"That's what you got from what I just said? For chrissakes, Pip, are you tripping?"

"Just tell me who. Show me which one you want."

"Yeah sure, Pip. I'm placing an order right now for a little dink to be my '*virgin*' love slave. Wanna frisk me for her picture? I don't know about you, baby, but I'm in the mood to be strip searched."

Not amused. Pip was too intent on studying the mug shots: Exhibit A. It did not take long for her to conclude: "This one." The mug shot she pointed out belonged to a—she glanced at the name—"Cleo Darcy."

Elizabeth snatched the pamphlet out of Pip's hands and pitched it hard at the open window, a symbolic gesture, since there was a screen, and it bounced off it. "Stop it. Just stop it, Pip. You"ve got to stop this now. This is madness. You're sick and you need help and I can't do it. It's beyond me. I'm sorry, baby. I tried."

"Where are you going?"

"I dunno, just gotta go, gotta get out of here."

"No, wait . . ."

"Hey!"

Pip had grabbed her by the forearm, roughly. Elizabeth considered the vision of Pip's uninjured hand clasping her wrist so tightly pulsating that it hurt.

"Oh, now, see, there," Elizabeth's sarcasm was fluent, "you have no idea how *nostalgic* this is for me, yes, indeed. Your grip takes me right back to high school. Just like my boyfriend."

So much so, in fact, that Pip even cut her off with a yank, and a menacing growl: "I am *not* one of your fucking boyfriends."

"Oh, yeah, you are. Right now you are."

She had rapid-fire reflexes and flinched, anticipating a slap across the face whenever she saw a hand raised like this, in the instant. But Pip smacked the wall beside her head instead.

While they were grappling, Pip picked Elizabeth up and tossed her onto the bed where they made love furiously, struggling for dominance, up and over and down and under and . . . until they wore themselves out and fell cleaved together into some sleeping peace.

\*   \*   \*

Pip felt most threatened by women, believing that every dyke in Weston would be making a play for Elizabeth the second Pip drove out of town. One woman, in particular, was worthy of Pip's dread, the tall, dark and handsome, Jada Katz, Willard's own student photographer-at-large. Jada had been one of Pip's dining hall tablemates, but more like an alternate really since she lived off campus and ate so few of her meals at the college, or, at least, so few of them in the dining hall.

Pip and Jada had a fleeting flirtation the first semester of Pip's junior year when Jada, who was a sophomore, was casually invited to join Pip and her pals for one of their spontaneous subterranean pool parties at Willard Hall in the wee hours following a night of terpsichorean revelry at The Titan. They would all go skinny-dipping supposedly to cool off, but would invariably become overheated again with the lights dimmed for a most romantic effect, pairing off in the water along the sides for a more intimate synchronized swim, whether in shallow or deep.

Jada had brought her camera, preferring to be fully dressed and taking photographs if they didn't mind, for art's sake. (She was going through her Deborah Turbeville phase at the time.) Pip, she found, was a wonderful model because she was so comfortable in her own skin and unblinking. She never felt the need to mug for the camera. And the camera loved Pip. One of Jada's finest photographs, a standout in her portfolio, was a photograph of Pip lying on the diving board very solitary that night. While women were coupling and impassioned all around her, she seemed to doze above it all, unaware that Jada was photographing her. When she did eventually turn her face and open her eyes, the camera was right there. And then, so was Jada, and this culminated in a make-out moment that never connected with any other aspect of their lives. In fact, they were laughably incompatible.

And now Pip could not bear the thought of Elizabeth becoming the one thing that she and Jada had in common.

Jada lived in a huge old house that had been rented, in its entirety, by a group of Willard women, mostly Pip's classmates, as well as tablemates. There had been a lot of parties at the house, and occasionally Pip and Elizabeth would attend. Recently Pip's suspicions were confirmed when she caught Jada eyeballing Elizabeth, in rapacious anticipation. Or so it seemed to Pip. Jada, in turn, having that photographer's eye—for an eye—could always sense when she was the focus of any focus. Oscillating slowly around the crowded room, she found herself snagged by Pip's eyes.

Jada smiled easily.

Pip smiled back.

Jada was sipping champagne from a plastic cup.

Pip was leaning back against a wall, with her arms folded loosely across her ribs, turning an innocent stick of chewing gum into a lascivious lingual workout between her front teeth, slowly enfolding it with the tip of her tongue. All the while conveying the message:

*Breedlove is mine.*

# CHAPTER 33
## Go

The day before Pip was to leave, she got a call from Eustacia "Stacy" Maxwell-Peters, Dr. Crews's lawyer, informing her that Officers Votiff and Nivarina had arrested Dr. Crews.

"On what charge?"

And then she barely heard the answer, something about conspiracy to commit assault with a deadly weapon and attempted murder. She was staggered.

"Attempted murder? But how? How can it be? She wasn't even there."

"That's why they're saying 'conspiracy,'" said Stacy, in her peremptory manner. She told Pip not to worry, the charge was incomprehensible and totally ludicrous. Not a chance in hell, she added, that there would be a trial. She couldn't explain anything more than that because she was on her way to the station house to bail out her client. There was one more thing, however.

"Jojo wants me to give you a bit of advice that she prays you will take to heart and follow. Go."

"Go?"

"Yes," said Stacy, spelling it out for her. "G, as in girl, O, as in other. *Go!*"

Sometime later, having smoked all their cigarettes and killed half a bottle of scotch, Pip volunteered to make a cigarette run, somewhat ironically, since what she needed was fresh air. While Pip was out, Elizabeth checked around to make sure all of Pip's stuff had been packed and was surprised to discover the equipment bag containing

Pip's fencing gear stashed under the bed. She pulled it out and un-zipped it, removing a bundle of workout clothes, which she tossed on the bed in an offhand manner like any other sullied laundry. But as it fell into the light and unfurled somewhat she realized what it was.

"Oh my God."

Pip's workout uniform, her white T-shirt and sweatpants, were splattered stiff with rusty brown blood. And then her shoes and socks and almost everything she removed and tossed onto the bed was ensanguinated.

There were strips, ripped crudely from a white terrycloth towel, and spotting one at the bottom of the case, she reached for it, realizing it was wrapped around something. Immediately, she recognized the distinctive shape and feel of the Italian grip of Pip's steam blade. But Pip never carried her precious foils like this; each had its own case.

"What the hell?"

It was broken. The strongest blade made had snapped, not at the flex point in the *foible*, which is the most likely place, but two-thirds of the way down, at the *forte*, the strongest section closest to the grip. It left the most menacing looking shard. The guard was badly dented, and as she handled it, dried blood flaked off. She found the rest of the blade at the very bottom of the case. It occurred to her, at last, why Dusie had taken one of the electronically rigged foils Pip used exclusively in formal competition, and ripped the wiring out. It was the same kind of foil, the only difference being the groove into which the wire was glued, and it was doubtful anyone but a made-for-TV forensic pathologist would notice, and only if the circumstance was homicide.

As she held both pieces of the foil up to the light over the dresser, her eyes fell upon the only photograph exhibited in the entire frame. A Polaroid snapshot of the two of them together taken back in April, about two weeks before the rape. It had been taken as a test shot, somewhat fortuitously, perhaps, by Jada Katz, down at the Weston University Field House when Pip was the last one standing in the highest level collegiate fencing competition for women in the Northeastern U.S. Pip had eliminated each and every one of her op-ponents—pissed them all off the *piste*—dozens of them, in an excru-ciating daylong endurance test unlike any other Pip had fenced.

That day was the best, as dazzling as she was in her whites and shiny gold metallic vest. Her face beamish, dimpled—in the swarm of well-wishers wanting to hug and especially to kiss her. Through the clusters Pip extended her hand for Elizabeth to take and pulled her in, building up momentum like a jitterbug spin, enough to sweep her up off her feet on high and catch her on the way down for a deep, soulful kiss full on the mouth in front of everybody—scandalizing the provinces, and thrilling just about everybody else. And, for once, Elizabeth had not been mortified that her true heart was bleeding out for anyone to see. She actually felt the same emotion that she expressed, in real time, in the here and now, which was new to her.

Elizabeth had slid smoothly down over Pip's hip, keeping their arms interlocked behind each other's back. And Jada photographed them abreast like this.

In the white border at the bottom of the picture, Elizabeth had written:

*Captain Blood.*

Oh my God, she thought, as she looked at it now, horrified: I did this. This is all my fault.

As she raised her washy, bloodshot eyes, she got another fright, caught her breath, and drew up straight, because there was Pip's face, now pallid and gaunt, reflected in the mirror from where she stood in the doorway, with her hands in her pockets, and her voice *doloroso:*

"The first time I saw you," said Pip, "you were looking at me in a mirror. Like this. Except . . . you were standing in the doorway and I was in front of the mirror . . . holding my steam blade . . . in salute. But look . . . now it's the opposite, isn't it? The blade is in your hands . . . and it's . . . broken. How did it break? And you're crying. What does this mean?"

"Pip, I . . ."

"Is this the *last* time I'm ever going to see you? This is the last time I'm going to see you, isn't it?"

Elizabeth was too overcome at that moment to answer, so Pip pressed:

"Please don't cry. It kills me when you cry. Kills me . . ."

"I'm sorry, I can't help it, baby, it breaks my heart seeing this stuff. And now you're saying this is the last time we're ever going to see each other? Why?"

Pip stepped into the room and then up to the bed, looking down at the bloodied stuff spread out on display, shaking her head so slowly.

"I'm sorry, Pip," Elizabeth sniffed, still holding the broken blade in one hand, with the grip in the other, "I'm so sorry . . ."

"Why are you sorry? What have you done?"

"I wasn't there. You were alone. I let you down."

And Elizabeth was even more beside herself to see Pip still looking over her own things, appearing not just confused, but frightened by that confusion, like a person with Alzheimer's.

Looking to the broken foil at hand Elizabeth asked: "How did this happen, Pip?"

She dropped the pieces on the bed.

"I don't know," Pip mumbled. "I don't remember."

Elizabeth plucked up the tattered, bloody T-shirt, and tossed it at her. "How did this happen, Pip?"

She caught it automatically. "I told you. How many times do I have to tell you? I fell down the goddam steps . . . I fell back . . . backward . . ."

That was the first time Elizabeth heard her say she fell backward. "Why would you fall backward, Pip? Why would you be standing on the steps backward? You said you were done practicing, that you were going down to the locker room."

"I don't know . . . Please stop asking me these questions, please . . ."

"All this blood, Pip? Where did all this blood come from?"

"It's my stuff, right? Must be my blood."

"You didn't have any cuts, baby. You weren't bleeding."

"Why are you doing this? Why are you doing this to me? Please just . . . it's our last night, Bree . . . please . . . let me just leave . . . without this . . . please. I can't deal with this . . . let me go . . . let me go without . . . this . . . please . . . please don't hate me . . ."

"Pip, I love you more than anything. I just . . . I just want you back . . . I just want you to be yourself again . . ."

What a sad face Pip had then—the saddest face Elizabeth ever saw.

"You do hate me then. You do. I can see it in your eyes."

"No, you're wrong. I could never hate any part of you—as long as you still love me. I just need for you to help me to understand. I couldn't be there for you then, Pip, and that kills me. So please let me be there with you now. Please . . . please, Pip, let me be there with you . . . I don't care if it hurts me. It can't hurt worse than this . . ."

*You think you're gonna hurt me, Penelope? Get real.*

Pip went for the scotch bottle and poured herself a glass. She said something so quietly, hanging her head so low that Elizabeth could not hear: "What? I'm sorry, I couldn't hear . . ."

"I hate myself."

"Why?"

"If I hate myself you can't possibly love me, so you're lying . . . You hate me. You do. Just say it."

"Why do you hate yourself, baby?"

"I'm so stupid. I make stupid mistakes."

"What mistakes?"

"So many . . . so many . . ."

"Tell me one."

Again, Pip mumbled.

"What? I'm sorry."

"I should . . . I should have . . . . killed him . . ."

"What did he do to you, baby. You can tell me. It's OK. You can tell me anything . . . anything."

"I had the chance. Couldn't do it. Couldn't just kill somebody like that. I just didn't believe he could hurt me."

*Oh shit, he cried, when he saw her lying at the bottom of the stairs. Her eyes were closed. She wasn't moving. Oh shit, oh shit, don't be dead, please don't be dead. Fuck, man. He ran down the steps, dropped to his knees beside her, and felt for a pulse in her neck. He opened her eyes. Her pupils were even, but they were fixed and dilated. Oh fuck. Wake up, come on . . . Wake up, you fucking dyke . . .*

*He picked her up and carried her to the showers, laid her down under a showerhead and turned it on full blast, until she came around. When she sat up, she started vomiting.*

*She did not know what was happening, or how long she had been unconscious. Her head hurt so badly. She kept trying to get away from the water, but he kept holding her head back under. He said she couldn't get out until she stopped throwing up, making a mess. Rinse it all down the drain, clean it up, soldier.*

*Seeing that she was shivering violently and her teeth were chattering, he adjusted the water to make it warm. The vomiting sub-*

*sided. She stopped shaking. She started to realize what was going on. He told her to stand up. Dizzy, she staggered, stumbled back against the wall. Threw up again, but so painfully dry now, retching. Her vision was blurred. And really this could not be happening. He could not be serious about hurting her.*

*Drop these, soldier. He used the foil as a pointer, and when she hesitated to unknot her sweatpants, he put the tip beneath her navel, and gave her a jab, nearly broke skin.*

"He had my blade. He threatened me with my own blade. He stuck the tip to my neck . . ."

Pip went to the stash of Percodans she had purchased from her cousin Trent that night of the wedding, as Elizabeth stood by horrified.

"Pip wait, you're taking too many of those. No you can't, baby, you've been drinking . . ."

"It hurts. It hurts so . . ."

"Don't take those, Pip, I'm telling you, you'll be sick, I can't let you . . ."

"Fuck you. What do you know?"

Elizabeth just rushed her then and knocked the vial out of her hands. The Percs went flying, mostly on the bed. There must have been fifty of them.

"I'm not going through this again, Pip."

"It hurts."

"I'm sorry for that, but . . ."

"You don't know what hurts. You don't know hurt."

"Look what he did to you, Pip. Look at this bed . . ."

Their voices were considerably raised.

"Look what that fucking monster did to you, look at . . ."

Pip cold-cocked her. Backhand. Full force across her right cheek, sent her flying stunned into an end table, toppling a lamp. It took her a moment to recover but they were making progress in her mind, so this was necessary perhaps.

"This is what he did to you, baby."

"No," Pip cried, "you did this, you did this to me. This is all your fault."

Another attack, closing the distance with her accelerating lunge knocked them both to the floor.

"It's *your* fault. I was strong before you. I was strong."

Elizabeth cried out. Pip pinned her to the floor with her knees.

*Aw that hurts, doesn't it? Lieutenant Hertz. Excruciating pain. His weight and strength, pinning her down immobilized her out-stretched arms by kneeling on her humerus and shoulder bones. "See my little trick? It's a good one, isn't it a good one? I call this the crucifix. See? Isn't it clever? I could make you do anything this way. See I can break your little fingers one by one and you can't stop me. So if you bite me that's what I'm gonna do.*

*"Now . . . Let's see . . . which one is your fencing hand? Come on, tell me, which one is it, huh? Eeenie meenie mine mo . . .*

*"This is your fencing hand . . . you do everything with this hand . . . don't you huh? Come on, tough girl . . . fight back . . ."*

"You don't know pain . . . you don't know fucking pain . . . you cause pain . . . you inflict it. Where were you that night?

"What night?"

"Who were you with?"

"When? Dammit, Pip, let go of me. Ow. Hey . . ."

Pip grabbed her hand, got her third finger in her fist, and pulled it back, putting Elizabeth in a paroxysm of agonizing pain, and helpless to move, though she tried.

"You stood me up. You fucked me up. Tell me . . . say it . . ."

Elizabeth was writhing with all of her might now, she could not bear the pain anymore. So she said what Pip wanted her to say.

"It's true. You're right. I stood you up. I fucked you up. It's all my fault."

A slap across the mouth knocked the words right out of her, and split her lip.

"I knew it. I knew you would cheat on me. Well, I cheated on you, too. How's that feel?"

"What?"

"It hurts, doesn't it? There's some pain. Now you're getting close . . . closer to what I feel, but still nowhere near."

"With who? When? Where? Why? Stop please . . . it hurts . . . it really hurts . . . I don't understand . . ."

"Dusie. I took Dusie to Kelly's wedding."

"Like your girlfriend?"

"Why not? She isn't ashamed to be with me."

"No, Pip, please, stop . . . hurts, it hurts . . ."

"Yes, it does."

"No, don't, please you're . . ."

"You want to be with me? Huh? You want to be there?"

"No, don't, please," she cried, an outcry, the sound of agony.

Pip released Elizabeth's broken finger and stood up quickly as Elizabeth curled with her hands clamped between her knees to staunch the pain, screaming in complete silence. A vacuum.

"That's how it feels," Pip mumbled, watching Elizabeth curled at her feet. "That's how it feels . . . that's how it . . ." voice going hoarse, "feels," stooping to scoop her up off the floor. She laid her on the bed like the finishing touch to an avant garde work of installation art depicting her own shocking Season in Hell. And then she shocked herself, unfolding Elizabeth gently, opening her arms, her legs. She laid her bare, made love to her. While Elizabeth loved and hurt and burned and sobbed throughout, holding on for dear life.

Pip stumbled into the hallway, down the stairs, out into the night and walked it off, ending up on campus sitting by the pond consulting with the koi fish. When she let herself back into the apartment it was that darkest time before dawn because she could not bear to face Elizabeth in the light of day. She need not have worried since Elizabeth had popped a couple of the Percodans and was not likely to wake up anytime soon. She had fallen asleep on her side amid all of that bloody stuff of nightmares, half-clad, with her injured hand extended like she was dreaming about panhandling.

Then she gathered up her gear, putting everything back in the equipment bag, realizing it would be the most incriminating evidence against Dr. Crews. Since no one knew of its existence and could not have deduced it, Pip was not sure it even qualified as missing evidence, but she was taking it with her regardless. She and Dusie had discussed it and decided that Dusie would lay claim to anything belonging to Pip that might possibly turn up, most likely among Dr. Crews's possessions. She would, in effect, act as a surrogate victim for Pip.

In the short time it took for Pip to pack up, it was daybreak. Cold kind of russet, regardless of the season, the only steely thing still produced here in the steel city.

Nothing in Pip's life, thus far, had been as difficult as taking a seat on the edge of the bed then to gaze upon Elizabeth's sleeping face elucidated without artifice and see what she had done to her love without knowing why she had been powerless to stop it. What kind of monster had compelled her to brutalize her beloved? Her True Heart? She had pinioned and pounded her into the floor. She shuddered, she was so ashamed. Her own hand was throbbing from the retortion of the passion bash. She tossed down another Percodan, chasing it with Dexedrine.

She took the snapshot from the mirror frame, and used King Solomon's method of settling the matter of which one of them got to keep their one and only picture of themselves by cutting it in half. She stashed the slice of herself in the left breast pocket of her jean jacket and slipped the jacket off, placing the seeming doeskin, so balmy with body heat and fragrance of Blue Grass, over Elizabeth. Pushing her hair gently back from her cheek to expose her ear, she was just aghast to see the florid contusion from her cheekbone to her jawline, starting to turn black and blue. "Oh God," she whispered, abject to a degree beyond anything she could ever have imagined. She put her lips to Elizabeth's ear to kiss her, so choked up she could barely whisper: "I'm so sorry . . . forgive me, please. I love you . . ."

And then she was gone.

Elizabeth opened her eyes and stared at the cracks in the plaster wall feeling Pip's tears evaporating on her face as a pain stinging worse than any other.

Dr. Collier did not go into Children's Hospital or see patients at her satellite Bryn Mawr office on Fridays. So she was in the backyard tending her garden when she thought she heard a car in the driveway and walked around the side of the house to investigate.

"Pip? Pippen? What are you doing here? What's wrong?"

Pip had gotten out of her car and staggered as she turned in the direction of her mother's voice.

"Mom."

Her mother caught her in a bracing embrace, walking her into the house, at the entranceway calling out for Mrs. Young, their housekeeper. She could smell the Scotch.

"Dear God, have you been drinking and driving? It's not even noon."

"No, it's from last night. I've been up all night."

"Why, Pip? What happened?"

"I'm sick, Mom," she said, unable to catch her breath. "I'm so sick. I can't go on like this. I'd rather be dead."

Pip collapsed on the leather chesterfield in the den in her mother's arms.

Mrs. Young appeared in the doorway looking puzzled and then concerned. She knew from the pediatrician's most soothing manner that something was seriously wrong even before she was kindly asked to bring Dr. Collier her medical kit bag.

"I lied to you, Mom, I'm sorry. My hand."

"I know, baby," said Dr. Collier, attempting to take Pip's pulse, "and we can talk about that later. Right now I just need for you to lie still for a second, OK?"

Mrs. Young hurried back into the room with the doctor's case. Dr. Collier put on her stethoscope and wrapped a blood pressure cuff around Pip's upper arm. After gauging the pressure, she listened to her daughter's lungs.

"Can you take a deep breath for me?"

No, not really.

"Honey, what did you take? I have to know."

Pip told her, watching her face, trying to gauge the extent of her own shame in her mother's eyes. But all she saw was her own pain, excruciatingly self-contained. She tried to say, "Mom I'm so ashamed. I'm so sorry," but it was so hard to breathe and her mother shushed her ever-so-gently, calmed her down.

"Don't talk, baby. Just lie still."

Dr. Collier reached into her case for a prefilled syringe of Narcan, and told Mrs. Young, simply, firmly, to go to the phone and listen carefully as she gave her instructions on what to say exactly to the operator who answered her call to 911.

Elizabeth reported for Big Sister duty the first day of frosh orientation at Willard Hall, where the freshbabies had assembled for refreshments while waiting to meet their Big Sisters. She stepped up to the overdressed utility table with official sister nametags and various and assorted sundry sisterly items, to see the junior who was in charge: Harriet "Harley" Dibble Standish.

She and Harley had become friendly because, as fellow English majors, they had so many classes together. They also knew each other from The Titan, but that was not something they discussed within earshot of civilians. Elizabeth liked her because she played against English major type. She didn't get that nickname for being bookish, after all, given instead to an excess of tacky leather apparel, Harley looked more likely to graduate with a double major in dominance and submission.

But Harley was a daddy's little wawa deluxe who hailed from the Valley that was the bane of Contrary's existence: The Tumbling Rock Valley. Harley did most of the biker dyke posturing, in general, and her uncouth behavior specifically, at any given highfalutin' affair involving Republicans and/or her mother. She was famous for having once used the edge of a tablecloth as a napkin at a formal dinner party, which, according to legend, was the reason she was sentenced to four years of hard time at WCW.

"Hi, Harley."

"Hey, Elizabeth, how are you—ooh, ouch what happened there?"

"Tragic Shuffleboard accident."

Harley couldn't help but laugh, though she apologized at the same time.

"Forgive me if I appear to be surly or something, but I can't smile, you see."

"Must be weird, you being such a smiley person."

"Smiley?"

"Yep. Cheerleader type. I'll betcha you were a cheerleader, weren'tcha? Come on, 'fess up."

If she was, she was not giving it up in this lifetime.

"So. Are we cool?"

"Cool is not the word." Harley leaned forward to speak more privately. "I believe the word is *hot*. Check it out." She was using her chin as a pointer, for discretion's sake, in the direction of the big piano parlor where one of many clusters of frosh were socializing.

"Red shirt, jeans, clogs . . ."

Elizabeth would have smiled if it were possible. A little bruising along the cheekbone, was healing rapidly and no longer swollen, and was easily covered with makeup and by letting her hair fall forward. Thank God class didn't start for another week.

"Whaddaya think?"

Elizabeth let her eyes do the smiling and nodded her approval. "OK Harley, how may I be of assistance?"

"We've got Renaissance Survey, and the Hardy Seminar. Take

home midterms and finals and class notes and the occasional private lecture or review." She winked cutely. Just kidding, of course.

Elizabeth promised her assistance.

The deal being done, Elizabeth approached her assigned sister, who was already exhibiting early signs of becoming Miss Popularity.

"Cleo Darcy?"

"Yes?"

"I'm Elizabeth Breedlove, your Big Sister."

Cleo beamed. "Far out."

"And I am not the dour spinster I appear to be, I assure you."

It was an awkward handshake since Elizabeth had the third finger on her right hand wrapped and taped in a splint.

"What happened there?" Cleo asked innocently.

"Freak lawn bowling accident."

As she led the bright-eyed towhead out the front door of Willard Hall. Elizabeth noticed that her little sister wore her straight-legged Levi's extra slim and on the short side, showing off both her boyish ass and her girlish heels.

Cleo noticed Elizabeth noticing and smiled to herself.

Once inside Cleo's single, no-nonsense kind of room on Whitman 2, Elizabeth said, "Welcome to Willard," pulling a joint from her pocket and handing it to the wide-eyed dink, who gushed: "Far-fucking-out. This is college?!"

"Pretty much."

Elizabeth had gotten more dexterous with her left hand over the past couple days. After firing up the joint, she handed it to Cleo, who accepted it eagerly and with no uncertain experience. She impressed her Big Sister even more when she said, "That must hurt . . . here let me give you a shotgun . . ."

"Well, that's very gracious of you. You'll make a fine, fine Willard girl."

Marveling at her little sister's nonchalance, Elizabeth watched as Cleo put the smoldering ember end of the joint into her own mouth, clamped between her pretty teeth, and then leaned in as close to Elizabeth's mouth as she could get without qualifying as a kiss, to blow smoke directly from her own mouth into Elizabeth's receptive lips, which were slightly parted, as she inhaled deeply. Elizabeth picked up the scent of Dr. Bonner's peppermint soap.

\* \* \*

Jada, like everyone else Elizabeth encountered, could not help but notice the split lip, and winced.

"Miniature golf mishap."

Jada's laugh was big enough for both of them. She was clearly smitten. Elizabeth was awed by her long straight hair with the sheen like Black Beauty. Jada started talking about the filmmaker, Lina Wertmuller, and it took a moment for Elizabeth to realize that she was being asked out.

"You mean, like, a date?"

"Yes. Like a date, but if you're not comfortable with that . . . I didn't mean to be presumptuous."

"I'm sorry, I'm just a little . . . not myself right now."

"I understand." And she did. Jada knew this one would not be easy. Pip was a hard act to follow. "You miss her."

Elizabeth looked up into Jada's eyes for the first time.

"What's the name of the film again?"

*Swept Away.*

The Trial of Dr. Crews took place almost a year to the day of the incident. And it had become a tabloidian travesty. And it ended with a jury, who were clearly not her peers, deliberating for an hour and forty-five minutes—which included lunch—before returning a guilty verdict. There were seven women and five men, and it was the seven sisters who sold her down the river, claiming to be horrified by what the prosecuting attorney herself referred to in court as unnatural relations between women. Dr. Crews was successfully cast as the evil, man-hating puppeteer who had planted false memories of incest and rape in Dusie's susceptible brain, thus inspiring her to assault her own stepbrother with a deadly weapon, in this case, a classic car, with intent to kill. As far as Elizabeth was concerned, the trial of Dr. Crews had been Theatre of the Absurd. And she was glad she had been home on summer break and not in Weston at the time.

# CHAPTER 34
# Ghost

One of the unique privileges enjoyed by seniors was the opportunity to select any dorm room on campus, based on a lottery. So at the end of junior year, they gathered in the music parlor of the Willard Hall student union to draw lots. Like the draft or the deli, lowest numbers went first. Classmates who intended to be roommates could use the lowest number between them to choose a suite for two or three. The lottery lasted all afternoon until dinnertime, after which everyone returned to stake their claims.

Elizabeth and Contrary went to the room draw together. Contrary was thinking "ace low," for good luck as she stepped up to the bowl of lots and took the deep plunge, rattling around in there for a moment, and emerging with a plastic chip on which was written:

"Ah . . . um . . . oh . . . aw shit . . . a fifty-two."

Elizabeth followed with a more delicate dip and withdrew:

"Ah . . . um . . . oh . . . hm . . . well . . . OK . . . a twelve."

"Twelve?"

"Twelve."

They surrendered their lots to the proper authorities for verification and entry into the sacred lottery log. Dinner was in an hour and there was one more decision that needed to be made and registered before then, but they were not quite ready to make it, so Elizabeth suggested they "shoot some stick."

"Excellent idea."

So they ambled from the music parlor and through the stone Gothic cathedral-style hall to see if the billiard room was available. They found it there for the taking and pulled the huge sliding doors

of golden oak smoothly along their tracks until they met in the middle, closed to within a hairsbreadth.

"Rack 'em up."

"Twelve. I can't believe it."

"I can. It is *so* like you to pull a twelve."

"Yeah, well, I studied really hard for this one."

"Aw, save it for your lit *clit* seminar, sister, where you can 'aw
shucks' the chinos off your *manservant* Maddocks, who actually be-
lieves he's your tutor—poor devil."

"Better than being beholden to Beatrice, your medieval maiden-
head."

"Yeah, yeah, jealous—just name your game."

"Slop."

"Oh, man," Contrary whined, "not slop again."

"Or," Elizabeth said, brightening, "we could play slop."

This bandying across the baize was a ritual in which they made
fun of themselves because they knew only one pool game and they
were such shameless bitches they didn't even care to learn any others.

"OK, slop it is, if you insist. But only one game. OK?"

"OK."

Three games later, Elizabeth said: "You know it's not too late if
you want to back out."

"Yeah, it is. What am I again? Stripes or solids?"

"Solids."

"Aw shit."

"Then why are you stalling?"

"I'm not stalling. *Au contraire,*" Contrary replied, affecting the
snootie-tude of daddy's little wawa with an academic bent: "I am
merely engaged in cerebration."

"Uh-huh. Well, then . . . cerebrate *this.*" One whack and a clackity-
clack sank two of her balls.

"Ooh. Prince Spamlet means business."

"So what are *you* cerebrating, Good Friend, Fellatio?"

"I've been trying to figure out why you've been pretending not to
be really upset about something these past couple days."

"I don't understand. What makes you think I'm upset?"

"Hm. I wonder. Might it be the three years I've known you? Give
me some credit, would you? You might fool the others, but I can *al-*

*ways* tell when you're faking that orgasm, sister. Come on, 'fess up. What are you so upset about?"

"I'm not upset, all right? I am not upset. I don't know what the hell you're talking about."

"Uh-huh. Let's see, how does that line go again? *'Methinks thou doth protest too much.'*"

"Methinks thou doth stall . . ."

"Oh, OK, then. My mistake. But just to be on the safe side, you might have an eyelash or something out of place—so you better check into that right away."

Contrary leaned over the table to take her shot, which she missed, *curses,* straightened, and, continued: "It all started with that letter. Ever since you got that letter. And *don't* tell me you don't know which letter I'm talking about. Because you practically broke my arm to get it back when you dropped your books, and I got to it before you did. Just trying to help, Your Majesty."

Elizabeth used her turn at the table to avoid even a chance glance meeting of their eyes, for as long as possible, while she was in emergency emotional lockdown: all imprisoned feelings please return to your cells immediately for further internalization.

Contrary could only stand by quietly watching as Elizabeth proceeded to sink her three remaining balls, circling the table once before she called it: "Eight ball in the corner pocket," and smacked it there successfully.

"Ooh, that was lovely."

"Thank you."

"Best out of seven?"

"You know we can't. We've got to go."

"Relax already. There's plenty of time."

"Not really. You're scared, aren't you?"

"Scared? Bah!"

"You are, I can tell. What will the neighbors and the nuns think?"

"I repeat: Bah!"

Elizabeth muttered something under her breath that Contrary didn't quite hear clearly.

"Did you just call me a pussy?"

"No, actually, you just did that."

"You did. You called me a pussy."

Elizabeth just gave her the old eyeball of forbearance while lighting a cigarette, striking the match and giving suck.

"Oh, and you are just so cool," said Contrary.

"If you say so."

"Why don't *you* do it then?"

"Hey, I told you I'd be glad to."

"No. No, wait. We stick to the plan. I'm doing it. I'll do it."

"Pussy."

"Do you know how much I hate you?"

"I do."

"Always remember that."

"I will."

*I do. I will.* Indeed. The Shakespearean significance of that was not lost on Contrary.

As they put the table back in order and emptied the ashtrays, Contrary draped her arm over Elizabeth's shoulder affectionately to pull her close. "Ha!" Fake out!" It was just a ruse to get the "little pint pot" in a headlock long enough to give her scalp a good knuckle scrubbing.

Elizabeth's laughing indignation was muffled as her bosom buddy all but smothered her in those cushiony bazooms of hers, but somehow she got her mumbling message through.

"Don't make me hurt you."

"Bah!"

"I'll bite you. I will."

"I bet you would, you little bloodsucking vamp . . . Yeow!"

Quick release.

"I warned you," said Elizabeth, collecting herself, smoothing the ruff. "And don't *ever* touch the hair again or you're going *down*."

"You wish," Contrary scoffed. "Dream *on* . . ."

"And stop chewing up the scenery, for chrissakes. We have to be convincing without making spectacles of ourselves."

"Yes, Mr. DeMille."

"Your antics are for naught, McNaught."

"Don't you be McNaughting me, you Bre . . ."

*Screeeeee . . . ch!* Contrary slammed on her vocal brakes to avoid hitting that second "e." Phew. That was a close call. No one who knew her well would address her as Breedlove, let alone the sacred "Bree." Especially not Contrary.

It was the Breedlove that dare not speak its name.

Luckily, Elizabeth had been turned away from Contrary at the time, preoccupied with her bookbag-cum-purse looking for a brush and mirror to repair her noogied crown. Otherwise, she would have seen the big cartoon word "Whoa!" pop right out of Contrary's eyeballs on springs.

The dynamic duo made their entrance once more into the lottery scene. Elizabeth found her favorite place to lean on the Steinway in the corner, chatting affably with classmates and friends, both major and minor, while watching Contrary. When she spotted most of the poker gang hanging out there before dinner, Contrary turned pale or, rather, paler.

"Holy shit, man, look at this."

"You can do this."

"We've got to tell them."

"No, we can't. Not yet. Not until it's settled."

"But right after . . ."

"No. You know you can't."

"I'm vampire feed."

"It'll be fine. Just follow the plan."

"The plan . . ."

"Remember what I told you. Just act it out . . . *the play's the thing*, eh? Drama. *Screw your courage to the sticking place . . .*"

"If you make one more Shakespeare reference, so help me God, I'm going to punch your bright little lights out."

The murmuring throughout the room could not obscure Contrary's larger-than-life personality as she approached the lottery official's table, attracting attention despite her intention to be low-key. She stood before the tribunal for the purpose of forfeiting her lousy lot, she said, which she would not be needing because she and "Little Miss Number Twelve over there," would be choosing a double together as roommates.

All eyes were directed to Elizabeth, who smiled serenely, blew a kiss and waved. Contrary's response was to mouth the words, "Kiss my ass."

"Roommates?"

"Uh-huh."

"You? And Elizabeth? Breedlove?"

"Yeah. The one and only. Isn't she a peach?"

The poker gang were all within earshot of Contrary, but it was Helen who overheard it first.

"Did I just hear Mary Constance say she was rooming with Elizabeth?"

There was a collective pause, during which everyone seemed to be not so much outraged as running the numbers quickly through their brains, handicapping the odds before putting in a call to the campus bookie. Let's see now, how much were they in for *this* time in the schoolwide pool inspired by the mysterious love life of Elizabeth Breedlove? Hmm. What would her sexual preference be this semester?

Elizabeth maintained her usual cheeky reserve. She was entertained by the entertainment her peers derived from the mythos surrounding her sex life. They were so clueless they didn't even know how clueless they were. Contrary qualified as her closest friend, in part, because she *knew* the extent of her own cluelessness.

So few of her close friends had even the faintest idea of where her heart was at any given moment, or her mind or her mouth. She was such a dissembler. And many felt threatened by her sex life. Why? Were they worried that if *she* could do it—whatever *it* was—that they could do it too? It got to Elizabeth sometimes, the sense of being chased by a very peeved gang of Willard girls with big butterfly nets hoping to catch her so they could pin her wings back on a board to be labeled once and for all. Gay? Straight? Bi? Kai? Lez? Dyke? Fem? Het? Saph? Or what? Some new hybrid not yet named? A singular aberration: a one and only?

And what of Mary Constance McNaught? Had she been seduced or infected or bitten or bewitched? She did seem rather enchanted after all was said and done, surprised, herself, to discover how secure and comfortable she felt resuming her stance at Elizabeth's side. Not at all mortified as she had expected. Not even embarrassed enough to die. Was it possible, she wondered, that the act had empowered her in this totally unexpected way? Was that the charge Elizabeth got from it?

"Amazing, isn't it?" she heard Elizabeth say.

"What's that?"

"The H bomb, Dr. Fermi," with a sweeping gesture over the crowd now dispersing and departing—because *nobody's* sex life was more compelling than the dinner bell—"the atmosphere didn't burst into flames as you feared it might."

"Does that mean we can have sex now?"

"Only if you beg."

"Yeah, you always did strike me as the dominatrix type."

"Ah. So that's your little fantasy of me."

"Hey, the only fantasy I have of you, sister, is the one in which you can kiss *my* ass."

Elizabeth kissed the air instead.

"Do we have to push the beds together?"

"Of course."

"Well, you better not do it before I move in, OK? So help me, God, if those beds are pushed together when I pull up with my dear mother and the twins, I will drive a stake through your heart."

"Fine."

"And, furthermore, missy, I better not see any *Playboy*s or *Gay News* or dildos or—God forbid—any of your little bimbos lounging around in their edible cotton candy underpants."

"I don't have any dildos."

"Really?"

"Really."

"Huh. That's funny."

"How so?"

"All the straight ladies I know have at least one."

"Yeah, well, I don't."

"I said 'straight' ladies."

"Oh, and I'm what?"

"Hey, you tell me. I've been trying to figure it out for three years now, on behalf of the tristate area, and the only thing I know for sure is that *you* are a horse's patoot."

"Uh-huh."

"Maybe if you had a vibrator like a normal, healthy, heterosexual woman, you wouldn't need to . . . well . . . do whatever it is you do with your little bimbos."

"You think? Well, you straight ladies certainly don't need me to tell you where you can put those dildos. But I would *love* to know where I can get some of those edible cotton candy underpants."

"Well, you know you've got a birthday coming up . . ."

"My birthday was last month."

"Exactly. So what's it gonna be? Huh? Tell me tell me please please . . . Can we please live in . . ." and Contrary offered up her litany of favorite room choices, all in the fancy-schmancy dorms. While Elizabeth listened thoughtfully, pretending as if Contrary actually *did* have a say in it, which she didn't.

"Well?"

"The master bedroom at Fey House," was Elizabeth's plaintive reply, which wrested guffaws from Contrary, assuming the joke was payback for the wicked noogie. But then, Contrary's face fell.

"Oh no. No. You can't be serious."

"I'm serious. Dead serious."

Contrary surveyed the room swiftly then, searching for an emergency exit. The French doors to the terrace were ajar. "Come on." She got a fist on Elizabeth's lapel, which she didn't release until they reached the farthest corner of the terrace, overlooking the slope of the yard leading down to the pond.

"Sit," she commanded, indicating the low stone wall at the edge, which was broad and flat like a bench. So Elizabeth sat.

"So that's it. I knew it. I knew something was up with you. You're a sneaky little shit. You couldn't tell me what you wanted, could you? Not before I gave up my number. And you call *me* a pussy? Did you think that I'd back out just because you're a lunatic? So what else is new?"

Elizabeth was strangely slow on the draw considering her hyperwit all day, or maybe because of it. "I don't expect you to understand and I can't possibly explain, so please just . . . I dunno . . . Save your breath, OK? Because nothing you say is going to change my mind."

"Oh no? Maybe I can't change your mind, but I can keep you from getting that room. Without a roommate you won't have that room."

Elizabeth barely turned her face enough to regard Contrary from the acute corner of her eye: "You would do that to me?"

"Maybe. If I knew it would save you from your sorry self."

"You gave up your number."

"Well, you certainly made sure of that, didn't you? But that doesn't matter. I'd just go to the back of the line and get a single in Whitman or something. Wouldn't make much difference to me now, would it?"

"You couldn't pull it off, not in a single. You need me."

"Oh? Like you're my only best friend?"

"Fine. Fuck me over then. I'll just pick Fey Five, get my old room back."

Contrary muttered "Saints Preserve Us," in extremis, and put her hand on Elizabeth's shoulder.

"I'm not going to fuck you over. Far be it for me to keep you from living with your ghost. I can see you're haunted either way."

Elizabeth's gaze followed the incline of the yard all the way down.

"Where is this coming from, man? I thought this was over."

"Over? Yeah, well . . . so did I," Elizabeth said scornfully. "It will never be over."

"Who are you? Fucking Heathcliff?"

"Maybe. Maybe I am."

"*Oh Nellie, I am Heathcliff!*"

"So what if I am?"

"Then you're pathetic. You're telling me that you're going to let that selfish bitch Cathy, who snubbed you for that limp-ass Linton, and then died on you halfway through the book—you're going to let her haunt you to death? Where is your head?"

Yes, well . . .

When Elizabeth sighed like that, Contrary knew better than to underestimate its depth or mistake it for harmless resignation. To Contrary's trained ear, it was like a blaring dispatch from H.Q. warning her that the suspect was armed and dangerous: approach with extreme caution.

"Why are you doing this to yourself? Huh? I thought we got past this a long time ago."

"We?"

"Yeah. We. *Not* The Royal. Nothing royal about it. Nosiree. This 'we' is personal, my friend, very personal indeed."

"How so?"

"I just can't go through this again. Just tell me what that damn letter was about . . . who sent you that letter that's making you so upset?"

"I'm not laying this on you. I never did that to you. I never would."

"No, you never would, would you? You would never trouble me or anyone else with your troubles, now would you?"

Elizabeth's agitation was apparent in her increased antsy-ness. "I don't understand what you want me to say here? What am I supposed to say?"

Contrary's frustration was also escalating, but unlike Elizabeth, she had a very short fuse and no qualms about laying her troubles on anybody.

"How can you be so fucking brilliant and dense at the same time? You're impenetrable. That's why you have no use for a dildo—let alone a man."

Elizabeth turned to stone, while Contrary quickly apologized.

"Aw shit. I'm sorry. Really. That was harsh. I shouldn't have said that. I didn't mean that. Look. All I'm saying is that I don't want you to say what you *think* I want to hear, for chrissakes."

"I am not impenetrable."

They knew from the slapfights of yesteryear when to shut up for a while.

"You really have no idea, do you—of how much work it is to be your friend. You won't let anything out and you won't let anyone in."

"I talk way too much."

"Oh yeah, sure. You talk. But what do you talk about?"

"Everything."

"Everything, but yourself."

"I have nothing to say about myself that hasn't already been said more eloquently behind my back."

"Where did you ever get this totally warped notion that you can spare the people who care about you, the ones who love you, the intensity of your true feelings, just because you won't say it out loud?"

"I dunno. Honestly. I wish I did."

When Contrary was searching for something in her oversized, overstuffed purse she would get in up to her elbows. She found her Lady Buxton cigarette case, fired up a Benson & Hedges, and said, "You know, I was thinking . . . If only you could be the kind of friend to yourself that you've always been to me."

In one breath, Contrary had paid Elizabeth one of the greatest compliments of her life and also offered her the best advice. She was extremely touched.

"Why don't you just try something totally radical and give it up? All of that classified information. Get some catharsis, for chrissakes. You need it bad. I mean, what are you, like . . . Satan? Are you from a galaxy far, far away? Are you K.G.B., Natasha?"

"Please don't make me do the accent. You know I can't do accents."

"That's for sure," Contrary replied, "but you could do Lassie. What is it, Lassie? What is it, girl? What's that you say? A big mountain just fell over on Elizabeth? And you need some sticks of dynamite? Oh and a pack of matches? No problem. Come on, girl, let's go blast Elizabeth out of that mountain."

Noticing the twitchy makings of a full-blown laugh on Elizabeth's lips, Contrary dared to tousle her hair a bit, too, taking a short break for a little levity to offset the increasing gravity. More high seriousness followed, as Contrary shared a memory with Elizabeth.

"Sorry, but I have to violate the gag order you placed on any and all references to a certain person . . . " she said, "Remember that summer when we were playing poker for shots of tequila, and I passed out on that grody couch . . . next morning I'm puking, remember? Praying to the porcelain god . . . ugh . . ."

"As if I would ever forget such a tender moment, darling."

"Well hell . . . you never forget anything, do you?"

"Not yet, but check back with me when I'm forty-five."

"Funny though, that you should say 'tender moment,' because that's what it was: a tender moment . . . when I saw the two of you in that big ugly chair . . . you were holding her on your lap like a child . . . It didn't seem possible . . . this complete reversal of everything I believed about your relationship with her. Oh, Jesus . . . I'm sorry . . ." Contrary had made herself cry, and needed a moment to buck up, digging through her purse for the little pocket pack of tissues she always kept in stock, being, as she described herself: "an easy cry." She blew her nose, then continued:

"I have no idea what that was about, um . . . Obviously something bad had happened, I dunno, but the way you were comforting her. It was so . . . profound. I mean, here you are, this little dink, cradling the great, all-powerful Pip in your arms. It just blew me away. It made me wonder if Vaclav would ever hold me like that . . . I'm still wondering."

Contrary had never seen Elizabeth cry, or rather, try so hard *not* to cry, and this proved a Herculean challenge beyond her ability.

"So your 'vow of silence,' this twisted belief that you're sparing people from some emotional reality or something, I dunno, but it doesn't work. I wasn't spared, Elizabeth, your devastation when she abandoned you. You never said a word, but I *knew,* and I *felt,* and I *saw* . . . your heart . . . break."

That did it. Contrary passed the pack of tissues.

"This woman, whose secrets you still hold with such loyalty and vigilance, this woman who once needed your strength and love so much, does she have any fucking idea of the burden she left with you? Do you think she knows? Does she care?"

"Please . . . don't . . ."

"I'm sorry, but I am begging you, please, for the sake of your own sanity, don't go back there. Pick any room, any house, anywhere but Fey House."

"I'm sorry, but I have to . . ." she mumbled, " . . . gotta go . . . I just . . . I dunno . . . I'm sorry, truly . . . can't take anymore . . ."

At that, she made a spectacular exit. Instead of using the steps, Elizabeth just jumped off the wall right there, which was about a ten foot drop. And, quite remarkably, she landed on her feet, even on a grassy slope, in perfect equipoise. Most observers would have called her action cat-like, but, in fact, it was more like a fencer.

"Jesus, Mary and Joseph. What are you doing?" Contrary called out after her, but Elizabeth did not turn back. Zigzagging her way down the hill through the Japanese maples all Elizabeth heard was: *Que faites-vous?*

What are you doing?

Remembering this was the question Dr. Crews had asked Pip in the note from Paris that was stashed beneath a bottle of Blue Grass still intoxicating her brain, as sure as if she had just squeezed the blue atomizer.

*Que faites-vous?*

What are you doing?

Over and over.

The letter that Contrary believed was responsible for reopening this deep wound was from Dr. Crews. Elizabeth had not had any contact with her in two years since a jury found her guilty of God-knows-what. Dr. Crews was still incarcerated downstate and had another full year to serve out her sentence. Having waited that first year, like a widow in mourning, she felt maybe she might begin the process of reestablishing, in some small way, communication with Pip. She wanted only to begin the process of making amends, hoping eventually to be forgiven, possibly even one day to be redeemed.

And she wanted Elizabeth's forgiveness as well. Her letter was neatly typed, half a page, courteous, cautious, contrite and concerned. But it really only served one purpose, of course, and that was to ask Elizabeth if she knew the whereabouts of Pip. And, if so, would she be willing and at liberty to provide this information to Dr. Crews?

Because Dr. Crews was hardly in a position to make any inquiries at the WCW alumnae office, she was wondering if Elizabeth "would be so kind" as to do this for her: to find out if there was anything more current on Pip than her parent's address. But, of course, Elizabeth had already done that.

Had that been all she wrote, Elizabeth would have gone on breathing like normal. As it went, she got the wind kicked out of her instead when Dr. Crews confessed that the only thing she knew about Pip was that she had withdrawn from Tulane without ever having set foot in New Orleans. Elizabeth wrote back just to say that she was sorry, but she had even less information than Dr. Crews.

She came to a standstill at the edge of the pond in a staredown with some plump koi fish, as if she were pissed off and blamed them for the shallowness of this little reflecting pool, wishing for an abyss into which she could simply step, drop and drown.

# CHAPTER 35
# A New Hairdo

Every senior knew exactly what to expect in her room assignment because of the lottery, and some had given up a fair amount of their summer vacation to the contemplation of their dormitory décor, as if in training to become their mothers. These were typically the first arrivals who invaded the peaceful perimeter in cars so over-packed they ascended on a slow roll heavy as armored tanks winding up Deerborn Way, like the entourage of this year's dictator all anxious to be installed at the palace of an itsy-bitsy military state.

Some dragged trailer hitches and joined the veritable convoy of rental vans and trucks commandeered by myopic novices driving up and down and—uh-oh!—sideways, hither and thither and—oh-no! oh no *no!*—backwards. Such was the stuff Chief Pierson's screaming post-traumatic nightmares were made on.

Willard women were generally adept at directing daddies, brothers, boyfriends, maintenance crews—the actual relationship was immaterial—they were all the same sorry guy on moving day. They were hernias, ruptured discs and heart attacks walking. But just barely. And they had only one face between them, which they shared, in passing, on the stairs, the endless stairs, humping and bumping boxes and steamer trunks and TVs and "Dear *God* Almighty, what did she put in this box that could possibly weigh this much?" Theirs was the abject expression of man-pride at last gasp, which each and everyone of them would consider well-spent just to call the *other* guy a pussy.

Whipped.

Both Elizabeth and Contrary returned to school that September with nary a fuss or a floor plan. Elizabeth was already settled in at Fey House, being the mistress of the master bedroom, by the time Contrary arrived with her mother and "the twins," Peter and Patrick, her little brothers. Just as Elizabeth predicted, Mrs. McNaught was more than sufficiently impressed with the stately Fey House accommodations, and really had no idea it was the lair of blood-sucking lesbian vampires. The twins were in junior high school, so Contrary found it necessary to deliver the occasional smack upside the head, affectionately, as they were tripping over their own feet in disbelief to find themselves in "a real live girls school." They were stupefied in Elizabeth's presence.

"Hoo boy," Contrary teased, "Wouldja put some clothes on, please."

There was really nothing immodest or titillating about Elizabeth's outfit, it was just that Contrary's brothers were at that age when boys start to develop their x-ray vision.

"You could be wearing a pup tent, sister, and they'd still be agog."

Even though Contrary had precious few boxes, she would not allow her mother to unpack any of them, insisting that her mother already worked hard enough slaving over everybody but herself. And Mrs. McNaught "got the hint," she said, with a rare and guileless grin, revealing the extent to which she was prematurely wrinkled. She was delighted to observe that her daughter was "jumping out of her skin," obviously, because she was so anxious to be alone with her roommate and best friend, so they could catch up on a whole summer's worth of girl talk.

After kissing her mother and the twins goodbye at the door downstairs, Contrary went bustling back to the master bedroom to make a phone call, wondering where Elizabeth had gone. It certainly was odd to see a telephone in Elizabeth's room. As much as she loathed the intrusive contraption, it had become necessary for her to have a private phone line installed, in order to maintain the pretense that she and Contrary were roommates. Contrary was, in fact, moving in with Vaclav. Elizabeth would never be comfortable with this ruse, some would say "fraud," but Contrary had asked for her help or complicity, so Elizabeth had agreed, rationalizing that a friend in need took precedence.

While Contrary was on the phone with Vaclav, Elizabeth was upstairs. She had gone to see if her old room was inhabited yet, and found the door wide open and the room quite empty; its inhabitant had not yet arrived. The place had a fresh coat of off-white paint and the casement window had been left open for ventilation. ELizabeth climbed over the window sill onto the fire escape. Contrary to Contrary's contention that Elizabeth had made a melancholy room choice, standing here once more had the opposite effect on Elizabeth's mood. She felt quite light-hearted and optimistic.

On her descent to her new window below, she retrieved a bottle of champagne she had chilling in an ice chest stashed discreetly against the red brick wall thick with ivy. And she really gave Contrary a fright, kind of intentionally, though she would never admit it. When she came gliding so quietly through the window it could only be disquieting.

Contrary turned and gasped, "Oh my," clasping her hand to her bosom as if she would swoon outright. Seeing the champagne bottle held aloft by Elizabeth, fortunately, kept Contrary upright as effectively as if a vial of "spirits" passed under her nose.

"So that's how it's done, eh?" she said, finding herself hard-pressed *not* to imagine how it was done (or undone).

"Ground Control to Mary Contrary . . ."

"Huh? Oh . . . sorry. How long was I gone?"

"Just a few hours."

"You know, sister, I hate to admit it, but there really is something entrancing about this place, not at all spooky like I expected, more like, um . . . I dunno . . ."

"Sexy . . ."

"Yeah. Definitely sexy. That bathtub—Good Lord!—it's decadent."

"Ah, yes . . . if that tub could talk . . ."

"'The Tale of the Tub.' Uh-huh. Spare me. Let's pop that cork."

"Good idea. The tiny bubbles will clear our heads."

Contrary told Elizabeth that Vaclav and a couple of his "Eastern Bloc buddies," all doctoral candidates at Weston University—and soon to be her roommates—would be over in an hour or so to move her belongings to a house a couple blocks down the hill toward the WAFA campus. There she would share a room with Vaclav in a house with his buddies and their girlfriends, six of them altogether.

When the phone rang Elizabeth jumped. "What the hell? Jeez-us, you're telling me that human beings are capable of getting used to that?"

"Yes, Miss Havisham, and they also know when you hear that ringing sound? You're supposed to do this. Watch carefully and learn."

Contrary answered the phone like a persnickety personal assistant.

"Whom should I say is calling, please?" Pause. "Christian? Seriously?" Pause. Contrary smothered the receiver with her palm, whispering, "Chip Christian? Is he serious?"

Elizabeth took the phone. "Hello, Chip. Yes, that was Contrary."

Contrary didn't like seeming familiar to someone she had never met, and so she disliked this guy before meeting him. She sat impatiently waiting and rolling her eyes to hear ELizabeth doing some cutesy stock character:

"Tonight? Ah, to tell you the truth, Chip, I'm going to hang out with the girls tonight and catch up. What's that? Oh, the usual 'girl school' stuff, you know, do each other's hair and nails, *Cosmo* sex test, séance, panty raid and pillow fight . . . uh-huh, oh yes, absolutely, we always wear our baby doll pajamas around the dorm . . . What's that? Sorry, this is the girl's treehouse. No icky boys allowed."

The second Elizabeth hung up, Contrary pounced.

"Chip?"

"Charles H. Christian."

"You mean like: Judas S. Priest?"

"Yes. Exactly. But he answers to the name of Chip, can you believe?"

"Wow, that is so strange, sister, really strange." She was referring to the coincidence of Chip and Pip. "I know I've made a few offensive remarks—all in good taste and good fun, of course, over the years—about your attraction to men of the Jewish faith, but, really, I didn't expect you to go completely in the opposite direction."

She had met Chip at the country club in South. He had grown up in a neighboring town and attended a rival school, so she did not know him before that summer. He lived in Weston, where he was finishing his residency in dermatology at Weston University Hospital, but he visited his hometown frequently in order to golf. The scenic lakeside links of the South Shore Country Club were considered among the best in the state. And Chip Christian could have been a pro. He was what they called a *scratch* golfer, meaning he had no handicap. That is, until he met Elizabeth and was smitten to his own detriment, because he happened to be in the market for a bride— and that's exactly how he phrased it, too—and Elizabeth fit the bill.

Elizabeth, on the other hand, had only climbed him because he was there. Since everyone in her hometown considered them a swell couple and showered them with encouragement, it made her life a lot easier. Being romantically linked with him meant that she didn't have to answer any questions about her real life, specifically her love life. Their relationship was such a nonrelationship from her perspective that she didn't even consider it necessary to stop seeing him after she returned to Weston for school.

Contrary listened politely to Elizabeth's Intro to Chip 101 without revealing her intuitive apprehension about him. There was no time for further discussion anyway as Vaclav and his buddies arrived to move her stuff to her real residence.

Before she went downstairs to join Vaclav, Contrary looked around the room and said:

"OK, sister. Let's do it."

"Do what?"

"Push the beds together, of course."

It felt like something rich and strange when Elizabeth finally found herself alone and locked her door.

She had the champagne bottle by the neck, as there was a fair amount of the bubbly left, and carried it around the room taking moderate swigs. It was dinner time, but she wasn't hungry and she didn't feel like visiting with the incoming just yet. So she wandered, instead, into the legendary closet in search of the legendary jean jacket. It had softened to the consistency of chamois cloth. She took it from the closet and stood before the mirror on her dresser, stripping to the waist before slipping into the jacket. It was a nice fit surprisingly, except for the long sleeves, but they rolled up comfortably. Pip had always turned the collar up to hug the neck like a fencing jacket, and if Elizabeth turtled her head down a bit, she could still pick up the faint fragrance of Blue Grass. The self-indulgent jacket ritual never failed to arouse and was invariably resolved by an orgasm or a weepfest. Sometimes both.

*Do not* unsnap that breast pocket, she warned herself referring, of course, to the one on the left. Her true heart. Don't. Don't do this. Do not. But resistance proved futile. Okay, fine, then just do it and get it over with already, knowing for damn sure the demons had to be exorcised at some point anyway, now that she was back here.

She opened the pocket and pulled out her half of the snapshot Pip had tucked in there after cutting it in half that nightmarish darkest-before-the-dawn day when she left Elizabeth far behind. Elizabeth never failed to shudder when she saw her old nickname for Pip, in her own hand, written in the white border of the photo, because it read only as: *Blood.* She flopped down on her newly configured would-be double bed and fell asleep sans weepfest, sans orgasm, sans everything.

She fell into a febrile state dreaming of love-making with Pip, or rather, agonizing because she felt herself coming slowly to consciousness when she wanted to stay asleep in the sweet place, but, naturally, the effort to dream can only have the opposite effect.

But then again, it felt so real: the warm hands opening the jacket she had fallen asleep wearing, feeling a certain tug as the jacket was being unsnapped, and then the heartwarming sensation of fingers and palms passing over her bare skin, stroking her breasts, and the touch of teeth that wrested a moan taking hold, suckling. Increasing heat and writhing, pressed against her lover's body, murmuring:

"Please, baby . . ."

"Yes?"

"Feels so . . . oh . . ."

"Miss me?"

"So much . . . so . . ."

"I'm here . . ."

"Not real . . ."

"No? Feel . . . how real . . ."

"Oh, God, baby . . ."

She cried out and clutched. In being satiated, became conscious, and opened her eyes, to find the reality confirmed.

"Cleo," said Elizabeth, with a wistful welcoming smile.

"You were expecting someone else?"

"Just confused . . . I guess, dreaming strange dreams."

"I always get suspicious when you call me 'baby.'"

"Got in late?"

"Yeah, traffic on the turnpike."

In all their room draw discussions, Elizabeth had never mentioned, nor had Contrary ever surmised, that part of her reason for wanting this room was so that Cleo could have the one above. They were not in love, but over the past couple of years they had become close enough to be friends and lovers without any power struggle or conflict with other lovers, that is, as long as other lovers did not find out. And this arrangement would certainly help.

On the following morning, Elizabeth decided to drop in on Dr. Maddocks, and ambled through the main classroom building toward the cozy wing of the English department. As she approached the open door of Dr. Brock's office, she heard raucous laughter, which she recognized immediately as Contrary. Tutor and tutee were in a *tête-à-tête*, puffing elongated, ultra thin cigarettes like old club ladies with cancerous wit, and sipping the ghastly vending machine coffee from paper cups.

Elizabeth paused in Dr. Brock's doorway to jump into the badinage like double-dutch. And then she jumped out to visit Dr. Maddock's larger, chairman of the department type office, to get an authentic mug of joe from his own automatic percolator, a privilege allotted to a precious few.

When Elizabeth appeared in his doorway, Dr. Maddocks rose from his desk and approached her gregariously, nearly tripping over his snoozing dog, Boswell, and clasped her hand in both of his, practically hollering, "Welcome back, friend! How the hell are you?" because he was so boyishly happy to see her. "Boy!"

"Tolerably well, thank you," she replied, mimicking him.

With a jolly laugh he fetched her a fresh cup of coffee, remembering that she took it black, and invited her to have a seat in the comfy chair.

Her admiration for him had become immense. Over the summer he had sent her amusing postcards with clever literary references, nothing too personal, but she read them over and over as if she were trying to crack The Maddocks Codex. He was always decorous, even when he teased her. "I hope that your extended exposure to freshwater lakes and sunlight didn't cause you to shrink. It never occurred to me to ask as a prerequisite of tutorship that the tutee be *Sanforized.*"

The temperature was still in the eighties, so Elizabeth was wearing her trusty old denim mini-skirt, and when she crossed her tan gams, she caught his fleeting glance, marveling at his restraint, as ever.

As they got caught up, Elizabeth continued to unnerve him with her caginess regarding her personal life. He had become captivated over the years by the tight net she cast over all her friendships, which made people feel exclusive with her even though she was exclusive with no one. He had done her the rare honor of taking her into his confidence somewhat on matters of faculty politics, which was unprecedented, but he trusted her. He had even revealed some details regarding his personal life, though within the bounds of good taste, hoping to dispel any stuffy old professor image she might have of him.

It became more important to him than he would ever admit that she perceive him as an attractive male person. To this end, he let it slip last semester that he had been asked out on a date by a younger woman (zounds!) and former student. He had never volunteered a follow-up report (the date had been a disaster), but he had been disappointed that Elizabeth had not shown enough interest to ask. As close as he felt toward her academically, she remained personally aloof. But then, she would have said the same thing of him. They were very much alike that way.

He did allow himself, however, to consider her physical fitness, on the whole, in light of his own. Did she find him physically attractive or, at least, suitable? He was twenty years older, sure, but he was no slouch. Tennis kept him in shape, but maybe he should take up jogging. It was the latest craze. But, oh hell, he hated jogging.

"Dr. Maddocks?"

"Yes?"

"Did you just ask me if I like to jog?"

"Ah, oh? Hm? Oh yes or no, er . . . your summer *job*. How was your summer *job?*"

The better the teacher, the quicker, and more convincing the recovery from daydreaming such as this. Perked him right up.

Senior year brought family upheaval for so many of Elizabeth's classmates that it was hard not to imagine that some curse had been placed on the whole graduating class. Many of daddy's little wawas were suddenly loosing their daddies if not to divorce, then to the dread cancer. Contrary's father lingered with emphysema, and finally lung cancer. She was called home a couple of times, along with her brother, the priest, and her other siblings to deliberate over whether or not to perform Extreme Unction. Yet he lived on. In misery, making misery.

Contrary had been in the work-study program since junior year, bussing tables in the dining hall, wearing a blue food services smock over her school clothes and that loathsome hairnet. She was certain that her classmates made fun of her behind her back, but she was entirely wrong. With so many of their own country club mothers unexpectedly facing financial and/or emotional ruin, as their husbands abandoned them for younger wives, any one of them could have found herself in a hairnet.

One night when Chip dropped by Elizabeth's room unexpectedly, as he was wont to do with the hope of walking in on one of those panty-raid-pillow-fights, he finally achieved his other big goal, which was to have sex with Elizabeth in her room, and maybe even spend the night. Somehow, she had been able to avoid this situation for most of the Fall semester, but then came the inevitable.

As Chip lapsed into a post-coital coma, Elizabeth managed to crawl out from under him and fled to the bubble bath. He knocked on the door sometime later, fully dressed and jangling his car keys, looking exceedingly pleased with himself. He perceived nothing of her resignation as he leaned against the sink looking down at her, fixated by her breasts among the bubbles. He said he had something important to tell her. The other women he had been dating, some of them for years, no longer interested him, and he intended to break up with all of them.

"Don't do that," she said.

"I'm not asking you to do the same."

"Yes, you are. Maybe not this minute, but that's the next step."

"Well, steps have to be taken, Elizabeth, and I'm very serious about this relationship."

"We've only known each other for what? Five or six months? You barely know me, Chip."

"What's to know?"

Not a wise question to raise when wooing an enigmatic egomaniac. Elizabeth could only roll her eyes and giggle at his utter cluelessness.

"I'm serious," he said, "I think I love you," with all the emotional resonance of the Partridge Family song.

"I know you think you do, Chip, but . . ."

"I know how I feel, thank you very much."

"What about the way I feel?"

"I know you're falling for me, too. You can't fool me."

"You are so arrogant."

"So are you," he replied with a toothsome grin, "that's why we belong together."

He gave her a dispassionate buss goodnight and left.

He proposed to her on Christmas Eve. She said no, thank you, nicely. He wouldn't take no for an answer, so she finally agreed to think about it, at least. She was still thinking about it through Interim and then into the spring. Several days before the spring break in mid March the Ides brought her something to beware:

It happened early one evening after dinner. She had been in bed with Cleo. Afterwards, in the glow, she had slipped on her kimono and gone to the window for no particular reason, but to breathe in the fresh air. Looking out over the dark backyard, she had just noticed someone standing in the distance beyond the spotlight, further obscured by a cluster of evergreens, topiary and shrubbery, when Cleo stepped up behind her, slipping her arms around her waist and nuzzling her neck.

"What's the matter?" Cleo asked, noticing that Elizabeth had gone pale and appeared to be holding her breath. Following Elizabeth's curious gaze, Cleo asked:

"Who's your Romeo?"

It was at that moment that a car came up and around the bend behind Fey House and pulled into the parking lot, illuminating the seeming apparition briefly, as it seemed then to vanish back into the darkness and distance following the road away from the house. But not fast enough before a flaxen flash of hair was gleaned. Either Elizabeth had nothing to say or was unable to speak, but she was shaking so that Cleo pulled her back into the room and shut the window.

"Jesus, El, you look like you saw a ghost."

Elizabeth just shook her head oddly and got to work on a paper that was due in a few days. About half an hour later, Elizabeth was in the midst of an animated discussion about Tristram Shandy with Cleo who was sprawled across the bed treating the compound cravings of the munchies and PMS with a bag of chips whose crunchiness so disturbed the peace it should have had a curfew.

The phone rang and Elizabeth shushed Cleo and her chips before answering: "Hello?"

There was a lot of noise in the background that sounded like a party in progress or a bar maybe.

"Hello?" she said, once more.

Eliciting no immediate response, she was about to hang up when she heard:

"Hello, Breedlove."

What ensued was an awkward semi-conversation blurred by emotionality. It had been Pip posing as Romeo, and she had run off in a panic when she realized that Elizabeth was living in her old room. She had not known this when she went up there just to see the place again.

"But jeez, Pip, you know, you could have identified yourself. You could've come in, for crying out loud."

"You weren't alone," she said plainly, "I didn't want to intrude."

She was staying at a hotel downtown. She would be leaving early in the morning.

Elizabeth's attempt to resume her inquiry into the who, what, where, when and how of it all came to a halt as Pip told her: "I'm not alone."

Silence.

"Oh."

She was calling from Abe's Tavern where she was supposed to be meeting someone for a drink and asked Elizabeth if she would join them.

"We have to talk," Pip said.

"Not necessarily, Pip."

Abe's was fairly crowded when Elizabeth arrived, a little late. She found Pip sitting alone in their old booth in the back reading the newspaper. When their eyes met, they both forgot what it was they had been reminding themselves not to forget: to be cool, to buck up.

Elizabeth greeted her with a lop-sided grin, leaking curly smoke, exhibiting what was known around campus as traditional tutorial posturing. It was clear Elizabeth was relishing that brief, but emphatic time in a young woman's life when nobody amazes her so much as herself. She slipped into the booth opposite Pip without a word, until the wait-person came and went with their orders. Campari and soda on the rocks for Elizabeth, and a cup of coffee for Pip, who looked tired, even a bit puffy. Or maybe it was just her new hairdo. She was wearing her hair a bit longer, chin length and very straight, a conservative, blunt cut page-boy. Classic preppy. None of the old edginess or style.

"You look," Pip started to say, but found herself mute with emotion and could only smile and nod, which prompted Elizabeth to respond:

"I know. So do you."

The person she wanted Elizabeth to meet, "Jan," was also running late but would join them shortly.

"Does Jan know about us? I mean, our torrid history?"

"Basically."

"Basically?"

"Without violating anyone's privacy. I know how private you are."

"Yeah, well . . . So. Jan, huh?" envisioning some stone butch babe with a post-doctoral attitude. "What does Jan do?"

"Computer software programming."

"What's that?"

"The future, Breedlove, the future."

Like a guy so desperate for something to say that he brings up the local football team, Elizabeth said, sardonically, "So how about that Dusie, huh?"

Pip laughed, albeit nervously. "I know. Isn't it amazing?"

Dusie had changed representation again, signing up with the upstart von Lobenthal Agency, and by doing so getting caught up in the New York model wars. But, to the victor went the best jobs, and she was doing top-priced advertising, runway and fashion magazine work in New York, Paris and Milano, appearing in cosmetics commercials on TV and auditioning for movies. At the moment, she was living with a German model named Britt, when she wasn't off to exotic locations on magazine assignments.

"Have you seen her?"

"Not recently. We talk on the phone occasionally. She's doing very well. She's up for a part in the sequel to *Cyber Coeds.*"

"Little Dusie: Happy at Last."

Pip could offer only an ennervated smile, like a person who is chronically depressed. But Elizabeth still got a charge from seeing even a glimpse of her dimples. When Pip told Elizabeth that she was finishing up her final year in med school at Johns Hopkins, then her weariness made perfect sense. And Elizabeth was quite delighted to hear it and greatly impressed.

Elizabeth told Pip that she had been taking Fine Arts courses over the years, some down at WAFA with the real artists, who were extremely intimidating. Her drawings and paintings had been exhibited in WCW student and faculty art shows.

"I'm very glad to hear that you're pursuing your art."

"I don't pursue my art," Elizabeth replied, "my art pursues me."

"I should have called ahead of time. I didn't really know whether or not I should call. I mean, not knowing how you would feel about, I don't know, about . . . seeing me, I guess. I'm sorry. I was afraid."

"Afraid of what?"

Pip couldn't bear the intensity of Elizabeth's eyebeams a second longer and turned away.

"I thought this would be easier."

Elizabeth scoffed: "Why would you think that? I mean, I would have guessed it would be hard as hell. But not to worry, I'm not looking to elicit any catharsis here. I'm a senior, you know. I live for my tutorial."

"Why is it so hard for you to look me in the eye, Pip?"

That comment had the desired effect of ensuring that Pip would look Elizabeth in the eye.

"I'm a little nervous, I guess, seeing you again. And, Jan, well, it's really important to me that you accept my commitment to Jan."

"Relax, Pip. You know I'll never make a public scene."

"I'm sorry you're so bitter."

"It's not bitterness, Pip. It's memory. Everyone else forgets. I don't forget. It's a blessing. It's a curse." She toasted herself with her glass mug. "It's a floor wax and a dessert topping!"

Her antic disposition ceased, however, as Jan approached the table and took a seat, sliding into the booth beside Pip, and extending a hand to Elizabeth.

"Elizabeth," Pip said, and this may have been the only time Pip had ever referred to Elizabeth by her first name: "this is Jan."

"Nice to meet you, Elizabeth," said Jan.

"Jan," Elizabeth echoed, as if from across an abyss, "Jan."

Because Jan was a man.

Jan released Elizabeth's boneless hand and slipped his arm possessively around Pip, who was staring so hard at Elizabeth her eyes were teetering somewhere on that thin line between manipulation and surprise, surprise!

"Whoa," said Elizabeth, and there was a second of uncertainty as to whether or not she would recover, but she did. She was, after all, a Willard woman. She rallied in disaster.

It was Pip who spoke next, as if she had been rehearsing it.

"Jan is my husband."

Elizabeth exhibited all the warning signs of a serious head injury as she mumbled oddly, "Husband? As in, married?"

"Yes."

"You and . . . Jan here . . . are married?"

"Yes, I am her husband," Jan interjected. A bland man. A man so bland, in fact, he couldn't even qualify as *very* bland.

Elizabeth's expression burst forth somewhere between mirth and torture. "Well. Then. Best Wishes!" she said to Pip. "And, ah, congratulations to you, Jan," remembering the proper salutations before going overboard. "Congratulations! Felicitations! Mazeltov! Peace, love and jeez-us Christ, I've gotta get out of here. Sorry. Gotta go. Gotta date. Gotta dance! Sorry, really nicetameetcha . . ."

Out in the street Elizabeth reeled maniacally as she tried to hail a cab and nearly got hit by a car. Pip had followed her out and pulled her back to the curb.

"I can't believe what you just did to me," Elizabeth cried, "I can't fucking believe it. How could you? How could you, Pip? Do you hate me? You must hate me."

"No, no, I don't hate you, please just . . ."

"Please what? What Pip?"

"Please try to understand."

"Understand? Oh, I understand. You're fucking married. You fucking married a fucking man."

"You have a right to be angry. It was wrong what happened between us."

"Wrong? Now you're saying it was wrong? My God, Pip," she said with a gut-wrenching gasp, telling herself *don't cry:* "Being with you was the only thing that ever felt right to me."

*Don't cry, do not cry, no crying, no.*

"I still feel so terrible for hurting you like that: for hitting you. My God. I was out of my mind. I was so sick . . ."

"Don't," Elizabeth interrupted her sharply, raising her palm like a crossing guard with a little stop sign on a paddle, "I swear to God, Pip, I would gladly take the heartache and the, and the, ah, *thousand* natural shocks that flesh is fucking heir to than this. Anything but this. Why did you call me? Why didn't you leave me the fuck alone?"

A cab pulled up.

"Please . . ." Pip got hold of Elizabeth's wrist as she was reaching for the door handle.

"Please what?"

"I'm so sorry. I had no idea you would be upset. I didn't think you could possibly care—didn't even expect you to speak to me at all, let alone see me, after what happened. Breedlove, please . . ."

Elizabeth looked at Pip's grip on her wrist, as if to the count of three, before twisting her hand free to open the cab door.

"Forgive me," Pip whispered, tearfully, "forgive me."

Elizabeth looked up once more so closely into her face, eyes pierced and welling, ever-so-slightly, lightly touched her lips to her lips.

Just a kiss.

And then she jerked back, shook her head, and said, "No."

She would never forgive her for this.

"Ey, ladies?" the cabbie butted in, in a thick Weston accent, "Are you in or are you out?"

Elizabeth slid into the back seat, yanking the cranky door shut behind her and told the cabbie to go, leaving Pip in the street startling traffic.

"Willard College, please."

"You want the girl's school?"

"The women's college, yes."

"Women. Right," he replied, glancing in the rearview mirror as he pulled the car into traffic.

"Can't live with 'em. Can't live without 'em."

Elizabeth would have found his seeming empathy entertaining had she not been sitting in the darkness with her knuckles jammed between her teeth.

Back at school after spring break, Elizabeth, absolutely emotionless, announced her engagement to Chip. The announcement came as a shock to most and for so many reasons. The innocents who had not a clue showered her with girlie glee, jumping up and down in their baby doll pajamas, with mouse voices of glee: "Whee!"

It was Contrary who offered the most vituperative response when she heard of the pending nuptials.

"Are you out of your fucking mind?" but was quick to add, "Oh, and *best wishes.*"

Contrary was far too preoccupied with the stress of her own life to indulge what she considered to be Elizabeth's perverse attitude regarding sacred institutions. As far as Contrary was concerned, Elizabeth was the luckiest bitch on campus to have such a healthy, happy family back home in her little picture-postcard town, and she could easily afford her emotional detachment about marriage.

And then there was that pesky competitive thing between them regarding honors and The HMMBAFEEL. Contrary was thoroughly aggravated by Elizabeth's ability to unswervingly maintain a lead over her that she was simply unable to close. Moreover, it drove Contrary mad that Elizabeth seemed to do this effortlessly. During essay exams in class, Contrary would look over to see Elizabeth composing paragraphs including illustrative quotes off the top of her head to support her critical assertions. While Contrary was studying diligently, Elizabeth seemed always to be off on a date or going to still another party or club. How the hell did she do it? In addition to her tutorial, Elizabeth wrote three papers a week, read at least one of the classics, and pored over dense essays in literary criticism from Aristotle to her contemporary hero, Northrop Frye.

If Contrary couldn't match Elizabeth academically, then she derided her motivations and objectives. Because Contrary was intent on going to law school and needed honors and awards to distinguish herself on applications, she deemed herself the worthier candidate for The HMMBAFEEL. Contrary became increasingly preoccupied with this subject.

One day in the dining hall as the regulars had asembled for lunch, and Elizabeth was just arriving with her tray, she heard the set up. And rolled her eyes in advance.

"Elizabeth is just too cool for grad school."

"What's that, Mary Constance?"

"I was just saying to the girls here that it's hard to believe you give a damn about The HMMBAFEEL when you're not applying to graduate school or law school or anything. You're marrying a doctor. All you'll need is a Cuisinart and a tennis racket. But, of course, you'll always have your *Art.*"

Nervous snickers all around. Checking the exits.

"Maybe I don't give a *damn* about The HMMBAFEEL. But thank you anyway for respecting my right to choose my own destination."

"Marrying Dr. Christian? That's your destination is it? Well, I certainly do respect your right to choose. What you choose . . . well . . . as the saying goes: you make your own bed, you lie in it, right?"

Very clever, Mary Constance, said Elizabeth's eyes.

"And I wish you and Dr. Christian the very best. May you be blessed with two point two perfect children of opposite but equal genders, and an open prescription for Valium."

"Mother Superior?"

"Yes, Your Majesty?"

"How do you say 'fuck you' in Czechoslovakian?"

Furtive eyeballs made their rounds and maneuvered for emergency escape when Contrary replied:

"Fuck you."

"Ah, but then, something's always lost in the translation, don't you all agree?"

That was when their tablemates made a run for it. When just the two of them remained, they studied each other for a moment and then shared a grin of forbearance.

Elizabeth checked her watch and announced: "Table cleared in . . . oh, excellent! Just under half a minute. Two whole seconds faster than last Wednesday."

"Bunch of scalawags," Contrary growled.

"Yeah. Philistines . . ." Elizabeth added.

"Fornicators . . . speaking of which, here comes your little bimbo now," Contrary smirked, referring to Cleo.

And they would go on like that.

Except one fine day in late Spring when the lot of them seemed even more deranged than usual, facing their uncertain futures, the badinage had a vicious bite. No one could even figure out what exactly had set her off, but Contrary became so infuriated with Elizabeth, that she rose up from the table like the nine-headed Hydra and shrieked, "Everything is just one big fucking *joke* to you, isn't it?" The dining hall din ceased momentarily as everyone turned toward the back table, notorious for four years worth of unladylike behavior. As Contrary's voice dropped from a screech to a viperous hiss, those out of earshot lost interest.

"Well I am sick of it! Sick of it! Do you know what the biggest joke is? The biggest joke is that travesty of a wedding your dear, unsuspecting mommy is planning. That's the biggest joke of all. And everybody but that *schmuck* you're marrying knows it."

Not exactly true, considering that several of the others seated at the table appeared to be surprised and confused to hear it.

"And you expect us to come to your wedding? With presents? Like we're so happy for you? You're making a mockery of a sacrament, and I refuse to be a party to it."

Elizabeth had just asked her the week before if she would do her the honor of being one of her bridesmaids, and Contrary had accepted, saying she would be delighted.

Scooping up her books haphazardly, Contrary rushed off, red-faced, seething with tears.

Elizabeth was the only one who dared to break the smoke ring of silence encircling the table then, because none of them had escaped. There had been no warning shots fired.

"She's having a hard time," said Elizabeth, heavy-hearted, "family stuff, you know, and Vaclav . . . oh man . . . I feel so terrible . . . but how could I have prevented that?"

"Oh, now," said Helen, always the peace-maker, talking like an Eisenhower mom to Elizabeth, "I'm sure she didn't mean anything by it. You two kids just get carried away sometimes."

Much to everyone's relief, Cleo Darcy entered the dining hall then and ambled down the center aisle—weight check!—because she loved the attention her ass demanded. And was oh maybe one of the two or three women who ever felt this confident about it. She slid her tray beside Elizabeth's and peeled off her tawny suede jacket, which matched her complexion and shoulder-length angel hair. No sooner did she start to eat her lunch than everyone at the table, except Elizabeth, skipped out.

"What'd I miss?" Cleo asked, chomping through a couple of fingers of french fries with one hand while reaching under the table with the other to give Elizabeth's thigh a more intimate squeeze. Finding Elizabeth crestfallen, she asked, "What's up? What the hell, El?"

"*Que faites-vous?* What are you doing? What am I doing? Why am I doing this to myself?"

Cleo was quite familiar with this portion of Elizabeth's periodic head-banging and browbeating.

"Do me a favor, Cle . . . Tell me to call off the wedding."

"Call off the wedding."

"Why should I call off the wedding?"

"Well, let's see now, hm . . . What could it possibly be?" She made a cute professional face. "Oh! *Light bulb!* I know. Could it be you don't love him?"

"How do you know I don't love him?"

"Because you tell me that every other day."

"I'm sorry I've become so tiresome."

Cleo's face bespoke forbearance. "My opinion? I don't even think you *like* him."

"But how do I know really? Maybe this is just how it is. He thinks he loves me and he's so sure about getting married. Maybe he knows something I don't, and I will learn it eventually."

"It's not a class you have to ace, El."

"Maybe it is."

Elizabeth's tutorial board, which took place in the coziest parlor of Fey House, went so well it lasted six hours, which was some kind of departmental record. Dr. Maddocks, the two faculty readers, and Elizabeth proved to be a fun, bookish bunch, and they all got tight on the scotch and sherry she provided, along with a lovely cheese and cracker sampler to absorb the shock. By evening's end, they were yelling strange academic things in high delectation.

The day before graduation, Elizabeth stopped by Dr. Maddocks's office to pick up her graded tutorial. As he handed back her seventy-five page essay, which she had bound in the traditional, no-nonsense black, he said of her two readers, "My word, they had no criticisms of your work. They just wanted to talk with you about books for six hours, which reaffirmed my absolute confidence in you."

"Thank you, Dr. Maddocks."

"You know, of course, that we forgot something that evening."

Elizabeth looked puzzled, but soon realized that he was referring to the traditional tutorial hug. Their combined self-consciousness turned a simple gesture into a tragicomic spectacle. He stepped left, she stepped right, he reached this-a-way, she reached that-a-way. By the time they engaged in the actual hug they were both so blustery and blushed, they just wanted to get the hell out of it.

That being done, Dr. Maddocks asked Elizabeth about her plans for the summer, nay, for the rest of her life. And she had no way of knowing that he had been trying to get up the nerve to appear this casual with her for years. When she told him that she was getting married in a couple of weeks, he got the strangest look on his face, one she had never seen before. He appeared dumbfounded. Was it possible?

Somehow he managed to recover enough to sputter the obligatory best wishes or some such—trying to sound sort of happy for her, but wondering why the hell she had not told him until now.

She was wondering the same thing herself. And in that split-second, she felt it, some kind of tinge or tightening in the vicinity of her heart. But it was too late. She felt like she was in a Browning poem, "The Statue and The Bust", about a lady of Florence and a duke who fall in love at first sight as he is passing by her house on her wedding day, and after what seems to be a million stanzas, nothing ever comes of it because they are both too ornate or something to act. And so they end up as a couple of statues commissioned in tribute to a love that never was.

After the graduation ceremony, Dr. Maddocks approached Elizabeth in his gown, flying his Ivy League colors, and gave her an avuncular hug and a buss on the cheek that went rather smoothly because they were not alone. She introduced him to her family, who were, naturally, charmed. He was even a good sport about Chip, offering the strapping fellow a hearty "Congratulations!" as he shook his hand, really hard. When he said to Dr. and Mrs. Breedlove how proud they must be of their daughter because she had gotten departmental honors and The HMMBAFEEL, he was surprised by their nonchalance. They smiled and shrugged but, yes, of course, what else? She's Elizabeth. A Breedlove. They would expect nothing less.

Elizabeth was standing arm-in-arm with Gracie and Helen on the quad being photographed when she saw Contrary walk by and tried to catch her eye. But Contrary persisted in treating Elizabeth as if she were invisible.

Yes, well.

Upon entering WCW, Elizabeth had been forced to confront the menace that was Freud, but she left the place knowing that from now on, she would be her own worst enemy.

# CHAPTER 36
## Scratch

Elizabeth remembered what her old pal, Reuben Shockor, had predicted about the future of Willard girls: that they would all end up married to guys who golf. And sure enough, Elizabeth was the first among her WCW classmates to make Reuben's prophesy come true. It was of little consequence to Elizabeth that her marriage was loveless. As far as she could see, marriage was like organized religion: you had to have one before you could dismiss it. She figured she might as well get it over with. Divorce would set her free.

Until then, her living situation would prove tolerable enough as long as her husband didn't ask too many questions about her personal life. Conveniently, his curiosity about her *never* took precedence over his fascination for golf. Like the perfect roommate, he was rarely home, preferring to spend his weekends golfing with his buddies on day trips or sleepovers, driving, chipping, putting, steering themselves through suburban clubs at dawn looking for the perfect links. Salient among her memories as a newlywed were those afternoons spent at the club (where else?) getting glassy-eyed in the grill room with the golf widows all performing their wifely duty as a rapt audience to whatever conversation took place between their husbands pertaining to golf and medicine, or another installment in their series of "what if . . ." round-robins involving sensitive hypotheticals such as:

"If you *had* to blow a guy—any guy in the whole world—who would it be?"

Without the slightest hesitation or equivocation, Chip said, in all sincerity of drollery, that he would be honored to service his hero,

golf legend, Jack Nicklaus. He hoped that Elizabeth would understand and respect this.

"I do," she said.

Thus went the wedding vows of the blowaways.

But they got along well enough in bed as long as she was careful
not to make any sudden movements. That first year after college,
they lived in a dreary first floor apartment of a Victorian house that
pretended to be renovated when it was really only maimed, on the
fringe of a stately neighborhood that pretended to be safe, when it
was really only over-priced.

Elizabeth and Contrary had bumped into each other on the bus
one day chugging up Alban Hill from downtown. During that hair-
raising, cliff-hanging ride, they bonded as a matter of survival, and
found themselves on speaking terms again, which, according to his-
torical pattern, meant that they were between slapfights. They would
hang out occasionally at their old haunts, usually with several other
WCW familiars. A few of them were engaged or married, but the vast
majority were cohabitating. They were all straight (although the jury
was still out on Vivian). But getting together as couples proved trying. Contrary, for one, had never warmed to Chip (but then, neither
had Elizabeth).

And Elizabeth never got much past the smiling, head-bobbing
stage with Contrary's Lion of Prague, and could never understand a
word he said. When thrown together at couples affairs, Vaclav and
Chip, being like matter and antimatter, were automatically annihi-
lated in each other's presence. Elizabeth found all couples gatherings excruciating, for the most part, because of the way women acted
so differently around their men, Willard women especially. That was
one disadvantage to attending a women's college, Elizabeth soon realized. Reentering the so-called "man's world" proved to be regres-
sive, something of a letdown, probably analogous to the post-World
War II experience of Rosie the Riveter and the women who played
major league baseball when Johnny came marching home again, hurrah hurrah.

It was the economy more than anything that instigated the next
slapfight. It happened in the fall following graduation when everyone was desperate to find a tolerable starter job in the pit of a most
abysmal economy and a glut of college graduates with liberal arts de-

grees. Contrary had been working hard at a couple of jobs bucking up for law school.

One afternoon early in November, she called Elizabeth to tell her that some highfalutin' D.C. law firm—Bogaty & Fandray, representing one of Weston's most successful, reputable and beloved old family companies in an antitrust suit against another one of Weston's most successful, reputable and beloved old family companies—was hiring more "legal assistants" (meaning: cheaper than paralegals) to search documents at their client's corporate HQ. The lawsuit had been going on for years, having expanded ludicrously from the original suit to a countersuit to a counter-countersuit, and was now on the verge of becoming a counter-counter-countersuit, the convoluted process of which reminded Elizabeth too much of fencing.

For some reason Elizabeth never quite grasped, Contrary thought they should both apply for the job—there were thirty openings, after all—but Elizabeth said she was not interested. She had been looking for something at least vaguely related to the arts community. But Contrary was so insistent that Elizabeth finally agreed to apply.

When Contrary found out that Elizabeth had gotten the job and she had not, she snarled: what further proof did they need that the HMMBAFEEL was the most important award in the world? Of course, Elizabeth knew that the only reason she got the job over Contrary was because she did not give a damn about the job, and that was exactly the attitude Bogaty & Fandray were looking for in a legal assistant.

Even worse, it turned out to be plummy, a good-time job, which Elizabeth downplayed to the point of referring to it as a sweatshop, giving Contrary much to relish for having been spared. She got suspicious when Elizabeth mentioned in passing that she was going to San Francisco. It was impossible to disguise that level of fun. Not only could she and her co-workers stay in nice hotels, dine at trendy restaurants and go out on the town, they were actually expected to do so. *Being* fun was a job requirement, though that objective did not appear anywhere in print. They were sent, in part, to psych out their peers from the Weston firm representing their adversary, Donton & Yinzer, who weren't allowed to spend any money or have any fun.

When they sent Elizabeth back a month later Contrary just wanted to bitch-slap her.

It was a temporary position, slated to last a year or so, and her greenhorn co-workers were either studying for the LSATs or waiting to hear from law schools, so the job was basically a way to kill transition time. When the Federal Trade Commission stepped in, ordering a temporary document freeze in the case they were actually paid *not* to work.

One afternoon, Elizabeth got a call from Cleo, who desperately needed help on her Shakespeare midterm. Zounds! A Shakespeare emergency! Sound the alarum. Elizabeth dropped everything and rushed right up there for an intensive tutoring session. Cleo lived in the third floor wing of Fey House with a former girlfriend, Vicki, who was out of town at the time.

She had not seen Cleo since her wedding because Cleo refused to see her alone now that she was an unhappily married woman. Cleo claimed to respect the "sanctity of marriage," to which Elizabeth replied:

"Whatever the hell that's supposed to mean to a dyke. Cleo, how can you respect the sanctity of a ceremony that you are prohibited from participating in? As if your love for someone doesn't count?"

"Hey don't look at me, El, you're the one who got married."

"There's no sanctity in my marriage."

"So you got married under false pretenses."

"No, actually, I think I got married under *true* pretenses."

She would have to contemplate that one at another time.

"Why did you do this? I don't understand. Why?"

"I didn't care enough to do otherwise."

"What the fuck does that mean?"

"I'm not really sure, but I think it's a kind of suicide."

*Poof.*

"Everything just went *poof* in your mind, didn't it? It does not compute."

It had, indeed, gone *poof* in Cleo's mind, but not just for the reason Elizabeth would describe. Cleo had been startled by the role she had been assigned in Elizabeth's scenario. She had experienced a little thrill at the prospect of being more seriously involved with Elizabeth, and this was highly irregular, because theirs had always been a friendly, light-hearted affair. It had never interfered with any other relationships either of them had or sought to have. Cleo was forever developing crushes on women she would meet, always coming to Elizabeth with the news like a giggly girl in junior high school, and Elizabeth would be delighted for her sake. Seeking Elizabeth's approval, she would invite her up to meet her latest This-is-The-One, and Elizabeth would do her best to accentuate the positive.

At the moment, Elizabeth was still ranting, but fortunately decided to come to some conclusion in their lifetime only to discover that Cleo had been daydreaming.

"I'm sorry," Cleo said, a trifle embarrassed, "but you lost me on *poof.*"

Elizabeth reached for the nearest pillow and womped Cleo upside the head with it. Cleo retaliated, which led to a Global Thermonuclear Pillow Fight. Suddenly, a dozen buxom bookworms in baby doll pajamas, armed to the teeth with one hundred percent goosedown, came bouncing into the room squealing and pelting each other until feathers were flying and ponytails were askew and everybody collapsed into one big tittering heap of girl's school phantasmagoria.

Elizabeth had Cleo pinned on her back by holding down her wrists and straddling her hips. They were panting from exertion and laughing like kids.

"You are down for the count, Darcy."

"Damn," she replied, "how do you do that? I'm bigger than you."

"You forget I was trained in the ancient pillow wrestling arts by the master, Matt Manfred.

"And now," Elizabeth said, seductively, "it is time for your lesson."

"Yes, mistress."

She leaned forward until the tips of their noses almost touched, about to kiss her it seemed, but shifted, putting her lips to Cleo's ear instead, whispering so that Cleo shivered and squirmed, knowing that Elizabeth was just teasing, but feeling teased just the same.

For the next couple of hours, Elizabeth tutored Cleo in the quirky testing methods of Dr. Beatrice Brock, which was more invaluable information, and certainly more difficult to grasp, than Shakespeare. (Dr. Brock had gotten tenure, by the way, after which she had told Dr. Maddocks that she now felt free to "loosen up a tad" and show a little of her "eccentric side." To which Dr. Maddocks had replied that he now felt free to take that sabbatical.)

When the lesson was over, they agreed it was a perfect night for star-gazing on "the beach," referring to the rooftop. The weather was unusually mild and there was a fullish moon, so Cleo got out her sleeping bag and they climbed up onto the roof from the fire escape just outside her window. And it certainly felt cozy up there, lying side by side, passing a joint, getting into space.

Cleo seemed intent on discussing their relationship. While Elizabeth seemed intent on getting laid.

"As I recall, our relationship is based on the concept that we *have* no relationship, right?"

"Affirmative," was Elizabeth's reply: "It just happens when it happens."

"Spontaneous . . ."

"Like combustion . . ."

"Serendipitous . . ."

"Indeed, even, at times, *transplendent* . . ."

Their laughter was masked by the swishing leaves, being surrounded by the tops of tremendous trees.

"Just a couple of chicks hanging out," said Elizabeth, rolling over on her side toward Cleo, and in a familiar, cuddlesome manner, to rest her head on Cleo's shoulder and her leg on Cleo's leg, a position that became increasingly erotic, as her method of linking legs.

After a long comfortable silence, Cleo said, "Hey . . . El?"

"Hm?"

Elizabeth's hand had worked its way up under Cleo's flannel shirt and was relishing the smooth bare skin over her ribs and then her sternum and then . . .

"Whatcha doin?"

Cleo had the most compelling breasts.

"I really miss you, Cle . . ."

"I miss you, too, but . . ."

Since Cleo did not order an immediate cease-fondle, Elizabeth continued to indulge the compulsion, while Cleo returned to the subject of their relationship. She was saying that she felt as if Elizabeth had never really taken her seriously.

"Oh, come on . . . you can't be serious . . ."

"What was it Contrary used to say? Hmm . . ." Cleo ruminated sarcastically, "Oh, yeah. I remember. She called me 'your bimbo.'"

"Oh, come on, Cleo, you know that was just her way of expressing affection. She always liked you. Besides, *I* never called you my bimbo. How long have we known each other? Almost four years now? You know . . . when I say I miss you, Cle, it's not just about sex."

Elizabeth knew the risks of entering into this uncharted relationship territory, but Cleo had never gone there either and deserved whatever light Elizabeth could shine on it. She was surprised, furthermore, to be feeling, well, *anything*.

"Cleo, you are one of the only friends I've ever had in my entire life, who never made me feel like I had to tell them only what they wanted to hear or risk losing them."

"Really?"

"Really."

"Wow."

"Is that serious enough for you?"

Hoo boy, was it ever. Went right to her head. Four years of telling herself that she could not get seriously involved with Elizabeth, because Elizabeth was never going to get seriously involved with her, and now this.

When Cleo asked Elizabeth about her "curfew," Elizabeth told her that The Chipper was out-of-town, as usual, somewhere in North Carolina with his buddies chasing a little white ball around.

Elizabeth became more amorous: "I am just dying to kiss you . . ."

She had, by this time, secured her position leg-wise, and crawled half-way on top with her uppermost thigh on the inside of Cleo's, who was feeling the persuasive effect of this steady, ramifying pressure, the throb, and caused her naturally to hook her other leg over Elizabeth's, thus doubling the arousing effect of the frottement for both of them.

"You're not betraying any trust, Cle," Elizabeth reassured her, with her lips touched down lightly on her lips waiting for clearance to pull up to the gate. "You're free and clear of any guilt here."

"Maybe I don't want to be free and clear," Cleo replied.

This time Cleo gave Elizabeth her mouth. And the Fey beach party turned into a sleepover.

The marriage was not even a year old when Chip got an offer to join a big dermatology practice in Hilton Head, South Carolina, that was too good to resist. Not only could he play golf all year round, but it was a wise career move, as there was a real future in mole removal, what with skin cancer so rapidly on the rise. Elizabeth could not recall Chip ever looking happier than when he told her that the South was the place to be for golf and melanomas. He decided they were moving come May and went about making the arrangements.

Elizabeth, on the other hand, could not recall having ever felt so panicked. Even if she had loved her husband, she seriously doubted she could have moved to South Carolina with him. It did not help that she was also unemployed. Her clock-radio had sounded the alarm one morning with a news report that the lawsuit had been settled suddenly out of court. The party was over. In more ways than one. The whole decade was over. What to do?

And then, a miracle. One that would go down in her personal history as The Miracle of Dr. Maddocks. For lo, he called her the first week of March, out of the blue, announcing that he was on sabbatical, and was wondering if she would be interested in being his assistant on a special project for Weston's most prestigious museum. He needed a Gal Friday, "A Ms. Gal Friday, I should say." The job started on April Fool's Day (how apt!) and ended in November. The project office was in the Weston Museum of Natural History, on the third floor, he told her, just past the mummies. The office had no windows or air conditioning, he said, but the cafeteria served tolerable coffee and excellent banana cream pie. Was she up for it?

"Absolutely," she replied, as if she had completely forgotten that she was moving to South Carolina in two months. When she told Chip about the project, he was incredulous that she would even consider it (without knowing that she had already accepted it) and told her he would not allow it. After days of quarreling, she contended that eight months apart would strengthen their marriage, and much to her surprise, he believed it.

Elizabeth had not seen Dr. Maddocks in a couple of years when she reported for her first day of work. She found him strikingly changed in appearance, although he was the same Dr. Maddocks in essence.

"Well, hello, friend! How the hell are you!"

She did a double take when she saw Dr. Maddocks because he seemed to˙ have had a makeover. His grizzled beard was smartly snipped, his khakis had a permanent, professional crease, he wore a navy blazer over a crisp white polo shirt, and Italian leather loafers. Even his scruffy sheep dog, Boswell, had been to the salon and looked adorably buffed and fluffed.

"Wow," she cried, when she saw him, "I didn't know Bosie had eyes."

She thought the big bow for a collar was a bit much though.

Elizabeth had heard about his recent marriage to a Weston socialite and widow, Phoebe Winters, a true dynamo. She had her own local television show. She had mothered a gaggle of children, now grown and scattered around the globe, from previous marriages too mind-boggling to list. Elizabeth imagined the new Mrs. Dr. Maddocks burning his old beatnik turtlenecks, mothy cardigans, and Hush Puppies, and mixing the ashes with various herbs and spices to make a lovely potpourri for the powder room of her enchanting Victorian home on Upper Alban Hill.

As for her own spouse, Elizabeth tried not to wince when Dr. Maddocks asked about Chip. She knew how odd it must have sounded as she explained that her husband was moving to Hilton Head in May. Dr. Maddocks listened to her somewhat flustered explanation with a polite but discerning grin fixed on his face, which she recognized as the same grin he got in class when some dim bulb spoke nonsense and he didn't want her to feel put down. Dr. Maddocks would never humiliate a student, or anybody, that way. It was one of his noblest qualities.

Elizabeth maintained the pretense that she would be moving to, well, wherever it was her husband had gone. Did she even bother to jot down his forwarding address? Dr. Maddocks humored her, talking cheerfully about South Carolina, as if he had written the travel guide for the state, regarding her with increasing wryness and concern as he told her the state flower or the state bird just to make her laugh.

When she started showing up at museum receptions and other highfalutin' social events with a variety of bachelors, a few of them notorious party-boy heirs-apparent to Weston's royal families, Dr. Maddocks began to feel extremely uneasy. And his supremely perceptive and clever wife became "particularly concerned for Elizabeth," as she so tactfully put it. Not only was her husband's little married sidekick dating, she was also spending seven days a week working with him in a precious little makeshift office in the positively Darwinian surroundings of a grand old building filled with dinosaurs and mummies. Pretty sexy stuff. Elizabeth also accompanied Dr. Maddocks to countless dinners and luncheons for the project. It was Phoebe's brainstorm to invite her to live in the guest apartment of the charming carriage house behind her home, to keep an eye on her.

Elizabeth's new and luxe little nest had a Pullman kitchen and a comfortable sitting room off the bedroom, all furnished with rustic antiques and house gifts from Phoebe's famous guests. Periodically the housekeeper would come over from the main house while Elizabeth was at work and tidy up, replacing the towels and sheets. It would have been easy, under these cushy conditions, to fall into the princess and the pea routine, but Elizabeth was all too aware of the seductiveness of such surroundings. Come Fall, she would be out of a job, a place to live, and a husband.

What will you do? Where will you go? and all of those questions that caring family members and friends asked were met with a shrug.

Shortly before the project ended, Dr. Maddocks was driving Elizabeth to work, pretending not to know that she had gotten only three hours of sleep from her seemingly insatiable partying. In addition to his feigned distraction, was his real distraction. While he kept his left hand on the wheel at all times, his right hand was in constant motion as he worked a stick shift on roller coaster roads, sipped a hot cup of mocha java (his wife had even upgraded the quality of his caffeine), smoked a cigarette, and went through a stack of office work and newspapers, which he had secured between his seat and the console, to give him something to do in his spare time at red lights. Then he whipped out his pen (a chubby Mont Blanc that Phoebe had given him, which he secretly despised) and worked on the museum budget report.

Whoever said scholars don't work with their hands should have seen Dr. Maddocks in action.

"I got a call from your former adviser last night," he said.

She had to think about that for a second longer than he could bear, evidently, as he prompted himself for her: "Dr. Crews?"

"Oh?" was all she could bring herself to say at the particular hour—not a morning person, she.

Dr. Crews had been out of the slammer for a year-and-a-half, he told her, among other tidbits. She had just written a book—whoops: green light.

Later at lunch in the museum cafe, he mentioned Dr. Crews again.

"I'll let you in on a secret."

"What's that?"

"Jo fell in love with one of her students."

"Shocking," she said dryly, "What are the odds?"

Sometimes she made him chuckle for no reason he could discern except that he found himself too easily delighted by her, in general, as the summer had burned through the old stone walls of the museum office, and maybe scorched their brainy brains somehow, making them fonder than they would have been in a more temperate climate. The rising heat produced hallucinations and a peculiar elation at times. Strange things happened. Sometimes Elizabeth would imagine the mummies inching closer when her back was turned.

"I've often wondered how that student felt about her. It's amazing their affair was never exposed during the trial. I was interviewed, you know, by the police. A truly dreadful experience. And then, Jo's lawyers, who were even worse. They wanted me to be a character witness, but I regretted to inform them that if they put me on the stand, I might do Jo more harm than good. Not intentionally, of course, but I wasn't about to perjure myself."

He glanced at her curiously as he took a bite of his Turkey Devonshire, but he found her expression, as ever, unreadable. After a well-tempered silence, he said:

"I trust you in a lot of ways, Elizabeth . . . ways in which I would not trust a wife."

She glanced up. What on earth did he mean by that?

"I wish you trusted *me* that way."

It was difficult to look into Dr. Maddocks's eyes because his glasses were so thick, but at a certain angle and in a certain light, it was possible.

She was so dumbstruck by the deeply personal implications of his statement that all she could do was redirect.

"Did you trust Dr. Crews that way?"

Loaded question. He took a moment.

"At one time, I did . . . yes."

Of the trial he said only this:

"I didn't lie to the police, but I didn't tell them everything I knew either. Frankly, I didn't think Jo's love life was relevant to the case. I believed then, as I do now, that Jo was wrong to get involved with her student. It's a sacred trust that should never be violated, but I wouldn't throw her to the wolves for it either."

She could've kissed him for that.

"These things happen," he said tentatively. "Who has the right to judge?"

They both reached for their coffee cups at the same time.

"I confess I'm still troubled by the particulars of that case. I found it so confounding. I always felt as if something was missing, something really crucial."

They didn't call him professor for nothing.

That night, after still another museum event Dr. Maddocks and his indefatigable sidekick had pulled off with their usual aplomb, they found themselves alone, sitting out on the back deck of Phoebe's house. Elizabeth had noticed that Dr. Maddocks invariably referred to it as "Phoebe's house." Sometimes, she got the impression that he felt more like a guest there than she did.

It was late August and a companionable balminess had persisted in their atmosphere all evening. There just happened to be a marvelous full moon, too. Phoebe was out of town, but her youngest child, a teenaged son, was staying at the house on vacation from prep school. A rather dubious chaperone, Junior had his own plans, and Dr. Maddocks knew better as the new stepdad not to question him when he went out for the evening wearing a Sid Vicious T-shirt and his hair stiffly spiked with Dippity-Do. The best part was when Dr. Maddocks asked Elizabeth if she could elucidate for him the poetry of "this Vicious fellow and the band, ah . . ."

"The Sex Pistols?"

"Ah, yes, that's it," he chuckled.

"What do you want to know?"

"Do you, er, like them? Do you listen to them?"

"Why? Would you like to borrow a tape?"

Elizabeth found herself enchanted by the boyish side of her mentor in the moonlight. She felt cool in a green silk dress, but her heels were killing her. She kicked them off as inconspicuously as possible, sitting on the edge of a cushy lounge chair, because to lean back in such an oversized piece of furniture at that point would have appeared wanton. A couple of citron candles flickered between them.

"I'm not going to Hilton Head," she said.

"No," he replied, leaning with one elbow propped on the railing, "I didn't suppose you would."

"I talked to a divorce lawyer this afternoon."

"Have you told Dr. Christian yet?"

"Not yet, ah . . . is there any wine left?"

Dr. Maddocks lifted the bottle up to the moonlight to gauge its depth, and decided in his insufferable optimism that it was half full. As he rose gallantly to refill her glass, reserving a fair amount for himself, he said, "Do you need reminding that the Maddocks treatment for divorce is exhausting work, not introspection or contemplation?"

Since he had been divorced several times, she wasn't sure whether his advice was sagacious or delusional. Mostly, she didn't like it that he had switched into his paternal mode. She wasn't looking for paternal at the moment. She wanted the boyish side back. She stood up and went to another section of the railing, resting her arms on it as she looked out over the darkened back yard.

"My son, Angus, felt much better after his divorce when he took an entry—and exit—level position at a canning factory while he was working on his doctorate."

"So what you're telling me is, 'Get thee to a cannery'?"

He laughed as the breeze through the trees sent the hem of her dress billowing about her knees.

"You can tell me it's none of my business, friend," he said softly, "but what *are* you going to do?"

"Quite honestly, I have no idea what I'm going to do, or how I'm going to do it, but that doesn't scare me as much as trying to come up with some tidy plan." And at that, she laughed that devil-may-care laugh of hers which scared him sometimes—like now, for instance. Her diffidence gave him goosebumps.

"Are you really that existential, friend?"

"It's possible . . . but more likely, I'm just foolish."

"There's always graduate school . . ."

She scooped up her shoes and skipped off, barefoot and spritelike, down the steps and out across the lush lawn. As she negotiated the narrow paths through Phoebe's garden, he held his breath anticipating her Jack-be-Nimble jump over his wife's beloved bed of perennials. He got such a kick out of her irreverence and derringdo. As she bounded up the staircase of the carriage house, he worried she would get splinters in her dainty ducks. Of tantamount importance was whether or not she glanced back at him before letting herself into the apartment, even if it was to see him still standing there at the deck railing, like a fool captain whose ship has run aground.

He could sense her every movement over there much later as he lay in bed reading a John Updike novel, *Couples*, of all things. Since Phoebe would have nothing but the most tasteful window treatments, white sheers or lace curtains in every window, the ones in the guesthouse seem dappled by the shadows Elizabeth cast as she moved about the apartment. Restless. She seemed forever restless. Sometimes, on overheated nights, she stood talking on the phone by the window barely draped, herself, in a luxurious kimono, as if she did not know he could have seen her—if he had ever mustered the nerve to look out his own window.

He tried really hard not to notice her coming and going at all hours, wild and enigmatic as she was. That creaky old carriage house staircase provided the host with far more knowledge in the way of a guest's private life than he wanted or could bear to know. He certainly knew when she wasn't alone, and she was rarely alone. She had more suitors than Penelope with Odysseus out of town, but none of that mythic wife's fidelity. My God, he sometimes wondered, was she a nymphomaniac? He referred to her men as her baseball team. He worried especially about the drugs. Sometimes he caught a whiff of dope if he happened to rise in the middle of the night to step outside with his wife's cranky old Lhasa apso, Boris, who couldn't piddle without an audience. He worried about the drugs because of rumors he heard regarding the use of cocaine by the spoiled rich Upper Alban Hill boys Elizabeth had been running around with. Dr. Maddocks doubted that Elizabeth was fully aware of how fully aware he was, thanks to Phoebe and her countless informers, and quite frankly, he didn't welcome the intrusion into her privacy any more than she did.

The evening before Elizabeth was to leave for South Carolina, her sole purpose being to ask her husband, in person, for a divorce, she was invited to the main house for one of Phoebe's legendary soirees. Despite the mercifully dimmed chandeliers and candlelight, it was clear Elizabeth had been crying. Phoebe gave her the most understanding woman-to-woman glances and reassuring pats on the hand there, there, poor dear being confident that Elizabeth was too infernally cool to express the full extent of her marital disaster publicly, and also secretly glad to be rid of her. Gad, she was glad to be rid of her. But there was no point in rubbing the poor dear's nose in her disgrace.

At one point during a highly animated discussion led by the terminally clever and riveting hostess, Elizabeth looked up from being momentarily withdrawn, and caught Dr. Maddocks gazing at her so intently from where he sat at the head of the table that she got stuck. The light and angle being perfect, she was thrust through the lenses and zoomed right smack dab into the kindred core; and for the six second eternity that they looked at each other as they never had before, she knew that they never would again. And her prescience could only promise regret.

As it went, she left early enough the next morning to avoid saying goodbye, leaving nothing behind but a proper thank-you note for Phoebe, and a promise to call Dr. Maddocks as soon as she had done the deed down South.

But she never called.

For months afterward her friends and acquaintances and even members of her immediate family would telephone the residence looking for her, but Dr. Maddocks never knew what to tell them. It was embarrassing, nay, even humiliating. They were supposed to be friends, but he had neither her forwarding telephone number nor her address. He had to hear from someone up at the college many months later that Elizabeth was back in Weston and happily divorced.

He was disappointed she had no interest in going to graduate school, but far more astounded that she would shrug off the valuable connections she had made working with him, not to mention Phoebe's fabulous social network. How could she be so cavalier about opportunities that were hers for the taking? At the very least, she could have remarried well. But mostly he just felt hurt that she had never called.

Not long after, he had to give his own marriage a failing grade. He couldn't say why exactly, but he found himself driving home from the college, day after day, gripping the steering wheel harder to stop the trembling from increasing dread at the prospect of facing Phoebe. In a remarkably short period of time, she had become as nerve-wracking to him as the Sphinx. Each night she asked him a more critical question, a more puzzling riddle, whose insufficient answer would put her in a snit, sometimes a rage, and bring him that much closer to pulling out his own beard. A man may walk on four legs in the morning, on two at midday, and on three in the evening, but the Sphinx could not see into the future and take into account the multi-divorced and remarried man who walks on his knees in timeless Romance.

# CHAPTER 37
## Cruise Control

Contrary to popular assumption, prison had softened Dr. Crews. But not in any way that compromised her essential strength of character. She certainly could have done without the public humiliation, but she had the private consolation of knowing, at least, that she had protected Pip from being subjected to any further ugliness.

Despite the fact she lost her license to treat patients, she was able to keep up her good works in her field thanks to a network of loyal supporters in the gay community. After two years in prison, she had secured an administrative position at the Elysian Center, an extraordinarily progressive clinic in Weston that addressed the special needs of sexual minorities in such a comprehensive and unique way that it was becoming a national model. Her actual job title was Supervisor of Consultation and Education. But she also "volunteered" her services as a lay "counselor." Her colleagues and co-workers all exercised extreme discretion in regard to this work. Words like "therapy," "patient" and "fee" were never used.

No more Jungian caves for her. Being in jail had made her crave sunshine and open space. The Elysian Center occupied an entire townhouse that had been gutted and stylishly renovated, and her third floor office had a soaring ceiling with skylights, in addition to front windows overlooking a charming street. The walls were white and there was just enough thriving plant life to provide a becalming background allure instead of an encroaching rain forest.

Dr. Crews looked as cheerful as her office on that afternoon in the spring of 1982 when Elizabeth set foot, albeit tentatively, on this brave new psychological frontier of her former adviser, teacher, rival, and for one rancid moment they would both just as soon forget, her enemy. They made peace. Elizabeth had been summoned for reasons as yet unknown. The first thing Dr. Crews asked of her, nay, insisted upon, was to please stop calling her Dr. Crews. She preferred Jojo or Jo, having dropped her professional title years ago, though she was not required to do so. She would always be a professor and did not mind if former students, colleagues, associates and friends referred to her as such.

Elizabeth took a moment to mull over the options. Hm. She decided on Jo, since that extra "jo" in there just seemed too cutesy, given the tragic aspect of their strangely entangled personal histories.

She had not seen Jo in about seven years, aside from the photographs local newspapers had run with their unabashedly yellow reportage. The photos had reappeared in the paper during the happier circumstance of the publication of her provocative first book, *Felonious Females*. It was well received, and even had its moment, brief but exhilarating nonetheless, on the bestseller lists. She had a good laugh anytime it was implied that the book had made her fabulously wealthy. The only reason she made any profit at all was because her advance for the book had been so pitiful, and she was grateful her royalties allowed her to finish paying off the massive legal fees generated by her ordeal. Because of the book's success, she got a substantially higher advance for her second, putting her, as she liked to phrase it, "in the black once again," with her mischievous grin and a little wink.

She asked Elizabeth, as tactfully as possible, how she supported herself.

"You know," she said, "now that you mention it, Jo . . . I'm wondering that myself."

She was joking, of course. Primarily, she did freelance work as a graphic artist, and took on unique projects occasionally, which she referred to as "odd jobs" while studying graphic design and fine arts part-time at WAFA. Weston was a small town with a tiny arts community, and she had great connections for getting engaging project work at Weston's Museum of Art, its public television station, its glossy city magazine and various other publications. One alternative weekly ran an irreverent little cartoon strip she had been developing. Her favorite projects involved magazine illustration, but when she needed "real money," she harvested the freelance jobs farmed out by advertising and public relations departments of major corporations—more than a few of which had their world headquarters in Weston.

"I live hand to mouth," she said with an easy grin and no uncertain pride, "but it's both hands." Elizabeth got work when she needed it, and lacked for nothing, as far as she was concerned. Her biggest expense, aside from taking classes, was art supplies. And the only thing she coveted was space, more space, specifically studio space.

But the true luxury she enjoyed, which most people she observed felt that they lacked, was freedom. She did not owe anybody anything, carried no credit card debt, and worked her own hours, for the most part. She never got bored, and best of all, she found time to do art for art's sake.

"I live a charmed life," she said. There were lots of perks. She got invited to most of the fun stuff, *comped,* as they said, doors opened for her, tickets to concerts, plays, exhibits, openings: "Events aplenty, galas galore. And now," she added, wryly, "you're offering me free psychotherapy. Wow. What can I say?" Jo made the offer quite seriously, as something she felt she owed her, but she encouraged Elizabeth to think of it not so much as therapy but as "just talk, like friends." Elizabeth said she would think about it.

Which brought them to the main reason Jo wanted to see her. She was about to begin the research for her third book, and she asked Elizabeth if she would participate in the project—anonymously, of course, as one of a dozen or so women she would be interviewing.

"Gosh," said Elizabeth. "*Déjà vu.* I feel like you're asking me to volunteer for your tutorial experiment."

Jo chuckled cautiously, considering the outcome of the last experiment.

"What's the subject?"

Jo was sitting with her elbows on the armrests of her futuristic ergonomically superior desk chair, fingers forming the peak of a pyramid at her chin.

"The subject of *this* book . . . is rape."

Elizabeth was taken aback, waiting for Jo to elaborate. The project involved something called "posttraumatic stress," which was a syndrome, she said, the symptoms being psychological as well as biochemical. During her lengthy explanation, Jo walked Elizabeth though the basic workings of the autonomic nervous system. And while this was elucidating—to be sure—all Elizabeth really wanted to know was, "Why me?"

"A lot of what I'm writing about concerns the trauma not only of the rape victim, but of the other people in that person's life."

Elizabeth blew a smoke ring in the direction of Jo's gimlet gaze, imagining some spiraling disk of Mesmer. Jo still had the power. But she did not make the rules.

"So. I'm the other person in . . . *that* . . . person's life?"

Jo nodded from behind the pyramid, with one eye framed in the tip, which brought to mind legal tender.

"All right," said Elizabeth, "I'll bite," remembering a bazillion good reasons not to trust this woman, but trusting her just the same, with a warning:

"No *manigance*. Promise me. Swear to me."

Their reacquaintance proved to be agreeable, and as the dinner hour had arrived, Jo asked Elizabeth if she would like to continue their conversation at a Lebanese restaurant across the street.

"Are you seeing anyone special?" Elizabeth could not help but ask, now that they were friends and all.

"Mm . . ." Jo hummed. "Special doesn't begin to describe this woman." She told Elizabeth about her paramour, Claudine, who was—surprise!—French. As soon as Jo finished her book, she said, she was moving to Paris with Claudine.

"Forever?"

"Maybe," she smiled, "if I live that long."

By the time the Turkish coffee came, they were comparing notes on mutual acquaintances. When Dr. Maddocks's name came up, Jo declared, "Geoff had a thing for you."

"He *told* you that?"

"Let's just say I could *feel* his admiration."

"We never had a chance."

"Did you ever take a chance?"

"Of course not."

"Well, there you are."

The statue and the bust.

"I have to say it really blew me away when I heard he got divorced," Elizabeth confessed, pushing back a long strand of haphazard hair that kept falling over her right eye, "especially when I heard that *he* left *her*. Gosh, I just assumed he was a happy newlywed. He sure seemed happy to me anyway."

"Maybe that had something to do with you."

"Flattering, but doubtful. Although I do remember him joking around one time. He had this little typewriter, an Olivetti, that was so old, he said it had a key for *I Love My Wife, But Oh You Kid!*"

It did not escape Jo's notice that Elizabeth laughed, at times, like a person whose only other option is to weep.

"So how is your love life these days? Anybody special?"

"They're all special, Jo. I'm not *going steady* if that's what you mean."

"So tell me about your special men."

"Why do you assume they're men?"

Jo scoffed. "For you, Elizabeth, there will always be men."

The way Elizabeth shrugged and looked away made Jo realize something. "You're not kidding, are you? You see women? Seriously?"

"I don't always see them, Jo. Sometimes it's too dark."

"Cruising? You? I'm surprised."

"Well, then," she smirked, "my life is complete. That *has* been my objective after all . . . to surprise you. You just assumed you could bully me into doing some kind of femme fadeout, I dunno . . . And I failed to see the irony at the time."

"What irony is that?"

"We were fighting over a *girl*, Jo."

After dinner, Jo insisted on driving Elizabeth home in her snazzy blue Peugeot.

"Will you come and talk to me, Elizabeth?"

Elizabeth occulted her own discomfort with a scoff and a joke, as usual. "Jeez, I dunno, Jo. I barely have time to talk to myself, let alone to a therapist."

"A friend, not a therapist. Remember: we don't use the T-word."

Elizabeth gave Jo directions to her studio apartment on the North Side, a wannabe neighborhood in the process of gentrification. There were riverfront lofts mostly, inhabited by a wide range of artists and some street kid squatters. They called this stretch of converted old factories and warehouses Terminal Way because it was chiseled into the stone portal of a former distribution center for a food processing plant. As they drove through the city toward the main bridge connecting downtown Weston to the North Side, Jo tuned her radio to her favorite jazz station, and was ecstatic to hear Les McCann and Eddie Harris playing "Compared to What?" "A classic!" she cried, cranking up the volume and stepping on the gas.

Clearly, prison had not put a damper on Jo's verve at the curve.

As they pulled up in front of Elizabeth's building, Jo noticed several streetwalkers loitering around a neighboring stoop, and sighed.

"My heart bleeds for the sisters."

"Yeah, well. Save your bleeding heart for pissing off Republicans, professor. These sisters are fraternal, by which, I do not mean to say men."

"Lady cops?" Jo asked, facetiously.

"Weston's finest."

Indeed.

"It's Bust-the-Johns Month on my block, you see. It gets *very* entertaining in the wee hours."

"I can imagine."

They sat in the idling car a moment longer, conversing while also fixating on the vision of undercover cops in five-inch heels.

"Check out the one in the sparkling hot pants."

Jo smiled. "She looks like a nice girl."

"Officer Novak."

"Hm."

"She gives good arrest."

"Girl," Jo laughed, "are you for real?"

"Compared to what?"

Naturally, this cracked Jo up. Elizabeth was reaching for the door handle, about to say good night, when she felt Jo's hand on her shoulder and paused. The faux hookers, being bored and snoopy, were all watching.

"Thanks, Elizabeth," was all she wanted to say.

Jo waited until Elizabeth was safely inside her building before driving away, wondering if the intense scrutiny she had received from the cops was about racism, homophobia, jealousy, or all of the above. Or maybe they just recognized her mug from the local news as the *succès de scandale*.

It was after two in the morning when Elizabeth quit painting for the night, washed her brushes and gazed out her fourth story window, drawn by strobe lights from police cars as still another ho-hum bust went down. The suspects were the same old rubes, out-of-towners mostly, businessmen who partied hearty on expense accounts and went out shopping for blowjobs in rental cars. Officer Novak was handcuffing a pudgy john she had shoved face down on the hood of a car for insulting her femininity. After she put him in the paddy wagon, she joined her partner, who was holding out a trench coat for her to slip into. As she pulled off her wig and raked her fingers through her real hair, she glanced up and saw Elizabeth standing in the bay window, a long-stemmed wineglass in hand.

Some time later, all the cops and johns were gone, except for Officer Novak, who was leaning on her undercover car smoking a cigarette, still looking up at Elizabeth. A stainless steel ring holding two keys dropped four stories and hit the pavement with a dull metallic clink near Novak's throbbing high-heeled feet. She did a quick lateral scan of the vicinity before scooping up the keys and letting herself into Elizabeth's building.

When Elizabeth showed up at the Elysian Center the following week to be interviewed for the book, it actually seemed more like psychotherapy. Jo was pleased, but also more formal.

"That sexy cop you pointed out to me last week . . ."

"Officer Novak?"

"Are you really involved or were you just kidding around?"

"Involved."

"Seriously?"

"Sexually."

"Hm."

"What?"

"I can't help wondering if you're attracted to women who are armed."

"You say that as if there have been so many."

"You told me that the first time you saw Pip she was holding a foil."

"Don't go Freudian on me, Jo."

"Tell me about the cruising."

Elizabeth recounted a couple of recent experiences, which left her feeling "Just plain drained from the wretched excess."

"Is that a good thing or a bad thing?"

"I'm just curious, in light of these adventures . . . it sounds a bit sadomasochistic."

"You think I'm sadomasochistic?"

"You told me that you prefer the rough-and-tough-girl stuff to the touchy-feely stuff."

"That's true. But it doesn't make me the Marquis de Sade."

"How rough does it get?"

"Come on, Jo. It's just playful. Nobody really gets hurt."

"Are you sure?"

"Of course I'm sure. Why are you looking at me like that? Hey, I'm just living my life, you know. I'm not breaking any commandments. I don't think so anyway." She stopped for a moment to consider if that was entirely true and got confused on a couple of technicalities.

After weeks of visits, the book interviews were indistinguishable from the psychotherapy. Jo asked her why she preferred the company of men to women, when she seemed most attracted to women sexually.

"I know this must sound absurd, but women terrify me." Elizabeth laughed, but she wasn't kidding. "I have never related to women as easily as I relate to men, as friends or lovers. Men are so easy to understand compared to women. And men never crucify me for being with women, But women, jeezus. My policy with straight women, is, *never ever tell them the truth*, even if they ask a million times. God knows I've learned this the hard way. If I'm honest, they run screaming. If I'm evasive, then it's not much of a friendship, is it? And dykes? Yikes."

She was staring at one of the many framed photographs on Jo's credenza. The photo depicted a group of women in prison togs, all holding up copies of her first book. She couldn't help noticing how utterly happy these women appeared to be behind bars.

"It has occurred to me that I've sought sanctuary with men mostly to protect myself from the *feminine animus*. I've never been devastated in love by a man. Only a woman."

"Pip, I presume," said Jo.

"She crushed me."

"Sorry to hear that. I know how it feels."

"She was the love of my life. And she crushed me."

"You're a bit young to be so sure. There will be others, Elizabeth. Besides, you and Pip may someday make amends, as friends."

Elizabeth shook her head. "I don't think so."

"You have no faith in friendship?" Jo asked.

"Do you?"

"This isn't about me."

"No, please, I really would like to know how you feel about this, considering what you've been through. Can you truly say that you have faith in friendship?"

Come to think of it, thought Jo, no, she really didn't. But she was reluctant to admit that.

"I mean, with everything that happened to you, all of the people you thought were your friends abandoning you, like Dr. Maddocks."

"Geoff didn't abandon me."

"No? Then you're still in touch?"

Jo appeared pained. She and Dr. Maddocks hadn't spoken in seven years. On those rare occasions when their paths crossed, they both pretended to be blind.

"I didn't expect him to stick by me as long as he did, to tell you the truth," Jo said. "He certainly was loyal. At least he never told the police about my relationship with Pip. And he was appalled by it."

"I know. He told me."

Jo adjusted the lovely silk scarf at her neck, collecting herself before proceeding with a litany of apologies and confessions.

"I brought it on myself. Mea culpa. I made one arrogant mistake after another. I take full responsibility. I *did* tell Dusie to get her father's gun and shoot Bram. And I showed total disregard for her health and welfare by doing so. I thought that there was less chance of her getting hurt, herself, if she confronted him with a gun." Jo was shaking her head, looking off in a reverie for a moment. "When I think of what might have happened—dear Lord—she could've been hurt so much worse or even killed. And Pip, my God, how I failed that girl. And you, because of her. My judgment back then was . . . so impaired."

Jo diffused the tension by reaching into her purse for a pack of sugarless chewing gum, offering Elizabeth a piece.

"What flavor?"

"Blue."

Elizabeth accepted and they both sat ruminating for a while.

The next time Elizabeth went to the Elysian Center for a friend-talk-interview session, she sat with her sketchbook in her lap drawing what appeared to be a severed head of unspecified gender. Jo had decided it was time to have that talk Elizabeth dreaded.

"Why can't you talk about Pip?" Jo wanted to know.

She looked up.

"Is it because of me? To spare my feelings? Do you think I can't bear to hear the details of your relationship?"

Elizabeth stopped drawing and sat back, drum-rolling all ten fingers on the arms of her chair for a moment before she said: "Maybe *I* can't bear to hear the details of my relationship."

She allowed herself a moment to get lost in contemplation of Jo's eminently sketchable visage. Inspired, she flipped to a fresh page. Without looking up from the work at hand, Elizabeth said, "You would wait forever for me to ask you. Wouldn't you?"

"Ask me what?"

"Where she is." Hers was a rapid-onset agitation. "Where is she, Jo?"

Finally, thought Jo, who had been waiting all these months for Elizabeth to exhibit something . . . anything in the way of common curiosity. Half a year had passed without a single question regarding Pip and now such urgency.

"Where the hell is she?"

Jo leaned way back in her ergonomic swivel chair, interlocking her fingers behind her head, and crossing her shapely gams before she said placidly:

"Philadelphia."

Elizabeth inhaled slowly through her nose and exhaled abruptly through her mouth drawing more intensely as she asked, "You speak with her frequently?"

"Once a week."

"For the book?"

"For the book. We don't discuss anything personal, unless it's directly relevant to post-traumatic stress."

"Ah, but surely all roads lead there."

"Do you mean I can rationalize anything?" she laughed. "Of course, I can. But I don't do that anymore. And if I did, Pip would cut me off. She established very precise boundaries for our reacquaintance, Elizabeth. And I honor them."

"Have you . . . have you seen her?"

"No. I haven't seen her since"—she swallowed hard, her throat was dry—"graduation." Even though it was over, really over, she still felt the loss and incredulity when she thought of how long it had been.

"Does she know I'm involved?"

"Yes, of course."

"That must make her laugh."

"She wouldn't laugh about that, Elizabeth."

"That's because she's from Philadelphia. People from Philadelphia can't laugh. Especially not at themselves. Pip couldn't even laugh at me and I am *truly* ridiculous."

Jo regarded her quite seriously.

"Do you tell her what I tell you?"

"Of course not."

"I wish I could believe you, Jo."

"I understand why you can't, Elizabeth."

The calmness of Elizabeth's voice belied her true feelings, which were evident in the way she held the pencil to the page.

"Does she ever ask about me?"

Heavy pressure.

"No."

The bold black lines scored the paper, she lost her temper and scribbled all over the page. Having defaced the drawing, she ripped it carelessly from the sketchbook, balled it up, and made a three-pointer from half-court to the wastebasket. And then she stood up.

"Elizabeth . . ."

"I'm sorry, Jo, but I don't think I can bear to hear this right now. I have to go. I'm really sorry."

It was clear to Jo that Elizabeth wanted to bolt because she was on the verge.

But Jo stopped her with a single gesture, demonstrating she had not lost her superpowers as a "puppeteer." Extending her hand, she asked Elizabeth to take it, please. Elizabeth regarded her skeptically, rolling her eyes because she lived in dread of these sorts of encounters—still, she took it grudgingly, finding it smooth and warm, her nails neatly trimmed and buffed. A tasteful gold WCW class ring graced her pinky and Elizabeth could not resist the tactile impulse to run her thumb over it. Elizabeth had one just like it.

"Look at me," Jo said quietly, and when Elizabeth did, she added emphatically, "I said that Pip doesn't *ask* me about you. She does, however talk about you."

Elizabeth tried to pull away, but Jo tightened her grip.

"A lot."

She was determined that Elizabeth was not going to walk.

"What happened between you two?"

"Why don't you ask her?"

"I did. I want to hear your version."

"Just . . . don't even go there, Jo . . . please . . ."

"Why not?"

"What's the point?"

"Insight."

"To what end?"

"Peace. Peace of mind."

Elizabeth sighed again and closed her eyes momentarily as if she were trying to remember something when she was, in fact, smarting. When she opened them again, she tried to shrug it all off, as usual, saying, "It doesn't matter anymore. It was a million years ago."

"It matters tremendously."

"Look, Jo, I know what you're doing here, but I really don't need this."

"You still blame yourself."

"Of course I blame myself. Hey, as you say: mea culpa. It was my fault. She couldn't forgive me."

"I think it's you who can't forgive yourself."

"Well, how the hell can I? It never would have happened if I had been there like I said I would. She was only there because she was waiting for me."

"That doesn't make it your fault."

"But she blamed me. Don't shake your head. She did, Jo. That night before she left for Tulane, or wherever the hell she went, we had such a terrible scene because I found her bloody clothes and, my God, that broken blade. It was horrifying. Until then, I could tell myself that if she couldn't remember, then maybe, I dunno, maybe it wasn't as brutal, or she fought him off and he ran . . . but when I saw that stuff, I just knew . . . And I knew she knew . . . maybe not much but enough . . . enough . . ."

She paused to catch her breath.

"I realized omigod, it doesn't matter about blame or fault or what's true or what's false. All that matters is that I let her down, I disappointed her."

Jo was positively ferocious as she strong-armed Elizabeth with a tug, "Look at yourself, girl. You won't even let yourself cry."

"Let go of me, Jo, please . . ."

"No."

"Let go. Seriously."

"She wants to talk to you."

"Oh, is that so?" spitting out the words. "Well, I don't want to talk to her. You tell her that."

"I think it's high time the two of you talked about all of this unresolved anger and guilt, my God. You both need so desperately to forgive each other. You need closure."

"Closure? I haven't seen Pip in what is it? Seven, eight years? I can't say four years, because that wasn't Pip I saw at Abe's with her *husband,* Jan the man. Seven, eight years? I'd say that qualifies as closure."

"Maybe *she* needs closure."

"Oh, now you're guilting me? Hey. I refuse to make it easier for her to feel better about what she did to me. And I will never pretend I'm happy for her in that goddam sham marriage."

"Elizabeth," Jo said cautiously, "there are some things you need to know."

She looked toward the ceiling, in mock beatification, groaning, "Oh Lord. Now what? Let's see. No wait. Let me guess, Hm. I know. She had a sex change operation so she could crush me this time—as a Dick. Better still: she could crush me *with* a dick."

Jo did not like the sound of that laugh. That was not a good laugh.

"Honey, Pip is divorced. I'm sorry, I thought you knew that."

"How would I know that? How the hell would I know that?"

"I don't think her marriage lasted much longer than a year."

"But . . . But why?"

"I guess she came to her senses after her daughter was born."

Since Elizabeth's hand went limp, Jo released it.

"Pip has a daughter . . ." Elizabeth seemed mostly to be talking to herself and rather distractedly. "Jeez-us . . . ah, whoa . . . didn't see that one coming . . ." Shaking her head as she gathered her belongings she said, "I guess that would make her . . . what? About three or four?"

"She just had her fourth birthday in July sometime."

Elizabeth paused to do the math in her head, still mumbling.

"That means she was . . . wow . . . this is so strange . . . Pip must have been pregnant when I saw her last . . . jeez-us . . ."

That laugh again. Absently, she took the handle of her black portfolio, didn't even look at Jo, really just kind of waved, going somnambulantly toward the door, reaching for the handle.

"Elizabeth . . ."

She glanced back over her shoulder, just enough to lend Jo her ear.

"Elizabeth."

"Yes?"

"Pip named her daughter Elizabeth."

"What?"

Elizabeth turned her face to the door again, but this time she put her hand and head against it,

"*Oh . . . no . . . not again . . . please . . . not again . . . God I hate her . . . I hate her . . . I hate her . . .*"

Jo came over with open arms and for once Elizabeth allowed herself to be comforted with a therapeutic hug. It was the first time, in her entire life, that she cried on someone's shoulder.

# CHAPTER 38
## Backroom

Elizabeth did not return to the Elysian Center for weeks. When returning Jo's calls, she always phoned when she knew she would get her machine, just to reassure her that she was fine. Because Jo was worried.

Since their last conversation had ended with a catharsis the likes of which Elizabeth had never experienced before, she should have been cured. But contrary to psychoanalytic belief, speaking the unspeakable doesn't always set you free. Sometimes it just sets you off. And the real reason Elizabeth was avoiding Jo was that she was on a binge and did not feel like owning up to it. Along with promoting better mental health, Jo had triggered Elizabeth's most rebellious response. And that, of course, led to Bacchanalia. Elizabeth had been cruising.

Outskirts on the South Side was the place, of late. There was live music and the *grrrls* would dance. A pool table dominated the lounge downstairs, which was referred to as the "rec room" because it brought to mind those adolescent make-out parties in the basement recreation rooms of friends. Elizabeth could never quite get past her apprehension that at any given moment, the overhead lights might glare on and somebody's mother would come down the stairs carrying a clothes basket under the pretense of doing the laundry at eleven o'clock on a Saturday night. Downstairs at Outskirts a low-hanging light with a green glass shade hovering above the pool table was the only illumination, so there was major action in the periphery, though thankfully a continuous loop of loud music drowned out all but the most incredible orgasms. And some nights were rougher around the edges than others.

As much as Elizabeth liked to play pool, she only went downstairs at Outskirts when she was looking for certain mayhem. She found it one night when she was on a winning streak, holding the table as one challenger after another put their quarters down and stepped up to play her. One sore loser accused Elizabeth of having an attitude problem because she was wearing an old concert T-shirt from the Violent Femmes, who were, in fact, three guys. When Elizabeth won, the woman yanked her by the T-shirt into the shadows, seemingly intent on rending the offending garment off her, and ended up losing her own shirt, instead, whimpering gratefully to be so unencumbered.

Several nights later, Elizabeth was sitting at her drafting table before the picture window looking into the twinkling city just across the river. The vista was uplifting despite her sorry mood. She was in the midst of separate but unequal quarrels with two girlfriends and two boyfriends who were all demanding something of her that she felt unable to give, and the symmetry was killing her.

Mostly she was thinking about Pip. She had donned her ritual jean jacket, planning to go out and about shortly, and was thinking The Titan ambience best suited to her strange mood. She was flying solo. Having a glass of wine before she left she felt very much like trashing it. She reached for the phone, but lost her nerve and hung up after the first ring. Fifteen seconds later her own telephone rang, startling her so that she sloshed red wine all over her hand to a bloodied effect and dropped the X-acto. The answering machine screened the call. After a whir and a beep came Jo's soothing voice, "What's up?" because she had a feature on her phone for identifying callers. Feeling embarrassed and defeated by technology, Elizabeth picked up.

"Jesus, Jo, did I get you out of bed?" Considering it was only 10 P.M., it was doubtful she was froggy and groggy from sleep. "I'm so sorry."

"It's all right, really," Jo sniffed, and cleared her throat, "What's up?"

"You must be so pissed . . ."

"You bet I'm pissed. Where have you been, girl? I've been worried about you."

"I'm sorry. I've been sort of . . . out there."

"Hm."

"Yeah. Wild woman."

"How's the wine?"

"Red."

"Spilled any blood?"

"No, but I've sucked a lot of jugulars. Does that count?"

"Cruising?"

"Like there's no tomorrow."

"*Is* there no tomorrow?"

Jo recognized the glub-glub sound of wine being poured and said, "Why don't you just throw that down the drain now, honey, and be a homebody tonight? Curl up with a good book. Get some sleep. Come see me tomorrow; we'll talk."

To which Elizabeth responded with a sigh followed by a swallow and the admission, "I can't," evidently meant to cover all three suggestions. She picked up a little brass hash pipe, cleaned the teensy screen, packed the mini bowl, applied some fire and took a tremendously long, deep drag.

"What are you doing to yourself, Elizabeth?"

"Flirting with disaster obviously."

"Why?" Jo yawned.

"I don't know."

"I think you do."

"I can't stop thinking about her . . . can't get her out of my mind . . . I have dozens of drawings here just piling up . . . Why can't I get past this Jo? Why can't I let her go?"

"Maybe that's the wrong question."

Pause.

Lately I've been getting into fights."

"What do you mean by 'fights?'"

"I've been hanging at Outskirts, sometimes Dawn's. The best kept secret about Dawn's is that it's really much tamer than Outskirts on certain nights. At Outskirts, I'm black and blue from playing pool downstairs at Outskirts. Or slam dancing with the ladies upstairs to some grrl band, which always gets me into trouble—pissing off somebody's girlfriend. Last week some raging bullbitch tried to run me down in the parking lot for dancing with her underaged protege. And just the other night some woman came into the bathroom at Dawn's just in time to catch her girlfriend trying to drag me into a stall, and got so turned on fighting about it, they both worked me over."

"Why are you doing this?"

"Isn't it obvious?"

"What's obvious, Elizabeth, is that you're playing a dangerous game . . ."

"Yeah, but it works."

"Because I . . . just want someone or . . . something . . . somehow . . . a person, an experience, *anything* to be more powerful than my memory of loving her."

"You're going to get hurt, Elizabeth."

"C'est penible . . ."

"Pourquoi?"

"Mea culpa."

What compelled her to go to Jo's office on that particular day, when she knew Jo would not be there, so she would not have to face her after all these weeks of avoiding her? Tuesdays and Thursdays, she always said: she was never in her office on those days because she worked with underprivileged kids at a youth center. Elizabeth had something for her that she wanted to drop off. As she rounded the landing, ascending to the third floor, she could see that Jo's office door was open at the end of the hall, and she could see Jo partially sitting at her desk, swivelling slowly back and forth in her ergonomic chair with her fingers interlaced behind her skull against the headrest, elbows pointed and raised. She was talking to someone.

"Damn," ELizabeth said to herself, because just as she was about to retrace her steps swiftly and quickly, hoping to sneak out before she was spotted, but Jo swivelled back in her direction.

For the first time since Elizabeth set foot in Weston on the day she started college, she experienced a sense of the randomness of the universe beyond any manipulative human effort. And this was evidenced by the look on Jo's face, now speechless, maybe a little helpless even: a look of honest, unadulterated surprise. No manigance, no contrivance, no dingus. No way Jo could have puppetmastered this show. This was an event as random as turbulence.

Elizabeth was finally free to act instead of react.

With Jo's eyes upon her, she made her approach following a heady trail of woodnotes—floral, spicey, and stepped up to the door and saw *her* standing there at the window, her thick, flaxen hair in a long, loose French braid ending with a curly quiff between her shoulder blades. Dressed in an elegant charcoal power suit, white blouse, short skirt, heels.

Pip had just come from a job interview at the University of Weston Hospital. She had dropped in on Jo totally unexpected. And Jo had only been there for some unique reason involving a change of plans at the youth center.

"Interview?"

"University of Weston Hospital. Neurology resident."

Seeing that Elizabeth was staring, Pip asked, "What?"

Elizabeth had been taken with the vision as well as the notion of Pip in a mini-skirt. Not to mention the creamy silk blouse that drew even the casual observer's eye to the decolletage, and seemed to be moving constantly.

"Nice pearls," Elizabeth smiled sweetly.

"Jo's right," Pip said, "you're still a smartass."

"Well, what did you expect, doctor? That I'd end up chasing Valium with vodka at some ladies luncheon at the club?"

Pip shrugged noncommittally as any doctor.

"Of course, there's still time," Elizabeth added wryly.

"How about it, Breedlove? Will you have dinner with me?"

Elizabeth shrugged. "All right."

They went to a restaurant downtown and spent hours getting reaquainted. Pip talked most about her daughter, and Elizabeth enjoyed seeing each and every photograph.

Pip smiled and said, "It's really great to see you again, Breedlove. You don't know how many times I've thought about calling you."

"Hey, I'm in the book . . ."

"Yes, I know: E. Breedlove, 725-3990."

Elizabeth was visibly impressed.

"That's how many times I've thought about calling you."

"So what stopped you?"

After dinner, Pip drove Elizabeth to her apartment in Terminal Way, accepting her invitation to come upstairs and see the place. It was ridiculously small as Elizabeth had promised, but it was completely redeemed by the most remarkable picture window view of Weston across the river, and her fastidiousness was immediately evident as another antidote to claustrophobia. Clearly, there was a higher order in Elizabeth's chaos. Floor-to-ceiling bookshelves sagged with hundreds of tomes bearing titles so weighty the owner seemed suspiciously Faustian. There was a big iron easel, a desk with a computer and printer on top, a drafting table, and a tiny dinette set. A futon bed fit perfectly into a niche surrounded on three sides by windows. Her canvases were stacked against the walls. As Pip was enjoying the Weston vista, Elizabeth cued up some haunting music on the stereo, with a hard-driving beat, which gave the illusion of interacting with headlights flashing on a distant bridge.

Elizabeth stepped up to her kitchen counter, which looked like a play set for kids. "What can I get you to drink? Oh hell," she said, answering her own question, "Let's uncork the Remy."

"You've got expensive tastes for a starving artist."

"It's the company I keep," Elizabeth insisted, "I know a lot of diehard bachelors. Diehard bachelors bear generous gifts. But only if you don't expect anything of them. You'll appreciate this because it's from Decker."

"Decker? You're still in touch with Decker?"

"Dr. Decker. Yes, he drops by occasionally and we tear up the town."

"Doctor?"

"Physics."

"How's Gracie?"

"I wouldn't know," Elizabeth replied with no uncertain bitterness, "I lost her in the divorce."

Elizabeth uncorked the bottle, coated some bulbous snifters, and passed one to Pip. Since Pip seemed bemused by the extravagant glassware, Elizabeth explained that the snifters were part of her Divorce Crystal Collection. She was laughing as she opened her tiny closets to show Pip their delicate contents.

"I have all this precious crystal, but no pots and pans! Fine bone china place settings for twelve . . . in an apartment that barely seats two for cereal."

After Elizabeth's self-mocking riff subsided, Pip asked, "Who's this?" pointing to one of the many canvases stacked against the walls.

"Ah . . . That's Amanda . . . Amanda Glass. My muse of the moment."

"Is she your lover?"

"All muses are lovers, Pip, in one way or the other."

"So, that's a yes?"

ELizabeth shrugged and changed the subject, asking Pip about her marriage.

"I really believed that Jan and I could be together like friends, you know, with common goals. A cooperative effort to raise a child."

"What were you, communists?" Elizabeth joked, "I mean a cooperative effort Pip? Really?"

"We considered ourselves very sophisticated."

"Yeah," Elizabeth piped up, "I had one of those *concept* relationships. It always backfires."

"It was a perfectly predictable disaster."

"Did you cheat on him, Pip?"

"Cheat?" Pip couldn't help but laugh. "Spoken like a woman who doesn't have malpractice insurance, an au pair, day care, two cars, and a mortgage."

"Oh," Elizabeth bristled, "so, I don't have a life? And you do?"

"I'm sorry, Breedlove, that came out all wrong. It was offensive and I meant no offense."

"It's okay, Pip, it's just a touchy subject with me, because I hear women say things like that all the time, and I can't help thinking, hey, you know, that's your choice, girlfriend. You wanted all of these things. Your lifestyle wasn't forced upon you."

"You're right. I'm sure you have pressures I can't even imagine, and I don't hear you complaining. I admire you, Bree, for finding a way to do what you want to do without making excuses."

"Yeah, well," Elizabeth scoffed, "don't pin a medal on me yet."

Pip sat down on the industrial gray metal stool in front of the drafting table. Spotting an X-acto knife, she uncapped the blade and rolled the tool through her fingers with a certain dexterity. This rather peculiar gesture had the effect of drawing Elizabeth's attention to the dramatic scar on Pip's wrist that intersected the black leather band of her tasteful Cartier tank watch. And Pip didn't even need to look up to confirm that it commanded Elizabeth's attention.

"You can imagine the looks I get from patients." She snickered, "And then, of course, there are the ones who are afraid to ask, assuming a suicide attempt."

"Well, Pip," Elizabeth said, "It looks like a miracle of modern medicine to me." Because obviously Pip's hand had been restored. She had been so bold as to trace the scar with her fingertips. An action that seemed to have a mesmerizing effect on them both.

After a while Pip said:

"I was suicidal, Breedlove."

"I know."

"Hospitalized. For a long time."

This, she did not know.

Pip's self-ironic tone belied her struggle to overcome her sense of failure but certainly Elizabeth perceived it.

"Yes, Breedlove, I more or less spent my first semester of graduate school in a psych ward on suicide watch."

Elizabeth stopped tracing her scar to enclose her hand instead, and said very quietly, "I'm so sorry, baby." She had not intended for the term of endearment to come out, but it seemed for a moment, to cross a multitude of barriers that had built up between them. And Pip turned in her seat to rest her face on Elizabeth's breast as they embraced. Purely, it seemed for the purpose of comforting each other. Until the telephone compelled them to pull away.

While Elizabeth considered the phone she watched as Pip untangled her braid and shook her gorgeous hair free sending shiny waves lapping down her spine. And Elizabeth's, who was riveted by this vision of Pip playing with her stuff. She raised the snifter to her lips, inhaling the heady vapor before relishing the silky burn of cognac going down, and thought that anyone who says women age awfully is a blind idiot.

Elizabeth was mentally sketching Pip's classic profile line by line when the phone rang. She didn't pick up so the answering machine clicked on. The caller was, as she said, some guy. He left an amusing message and then the machine clicked off.

"What's so funny?" Elizabeth asked.

"You and your men. You'll never give them up, will you?"

"Why should I? I like my men. They've certainly turned out to be much better friends than women, in the long run."

"What about as lovers?" Pip asked, returning a certain degree of Elizabeth's snideness, "in the long run?"

"Women as lovers . . ."

"I can't rule out the Breedlove Effect on Men."

"Wasn't that the subject of your tutorial? And while we're on the subject," Elizabeth added, "What was your tutorial about anyway?"

Pip thought for a moment before she replied, "I don't know."

They were still chuckling as they said goodnight at Elizabeth's door somewhat formally, thanking each other for the company, and then scoffing at their own formality, even though they were helpless to avoid it. They gave each other those little chicken pecks on the cheeks, which can only leave a person at the end of an otherwise lovely evening feeling a vague sense of embarrassment.

After Pip left, Elizabeth sat at her drafting table, drawing in one of her sketchbooks while making a few phone calls and then she went to bed.

An hour or so later, she was jolted from REM sleep by the door buzzer, and crawled through a mound of pillows and bedding to open the window and look over the ledge. It was Officer Novak, m'am, answering her call for emergency assistance. Elizabeth pitched her keys out the window and fell back on the pillows, technically still asleep. In a moment, she was aroused by Novak, who appeared to be voguing in her increasingly inspired hooker garb, standing in the middle of the semi-dark room with the gleaming skyline as her backdrop and considerable illumination.

"Evening, m'am," Novak teased, mocking Dragnet, "What seems to be the problem?"

Elizabeth yawned, then said, "Um . . . I think I heard a prowler . . . or, um, ah, there's a cat up in the tree." She clicked on a little bedside reading light and watched as Novak disarmed herself. It was truly amazing all the stuff she had stashed in an outfit so skimpy you would have expected to see the telltale outline of a tampon. She produced her service revolver and checked the safety before setting it up on a bookshelf. And what's this? Handcuffs? Where did they come from? Did she have a utility belt like Batman under that micro miniskirt? She tossed the handcuffs at Elizabeth—private joke—followed by a well-endowed joint she claimed to have lifted off a hapless john during a bust, scoffing: "Ain't that America?"

"The world is a safer place because of you, Officer. Who knows the damage that might have been done had you not divested some paunchy accountant of his doobie while placing him under arrest for trying to buy a little blowjob?"

"Well, the world sure as hell isn't any safer because of you *artistes*," she teased only to find the teasing tables turned again, when Elizabeth rolled over prostrate, reaching for an ashtray that was sitting on a formidable stack of oversized hardcover art books that made a handy (and adjustable!) nightstand. As it was a stretch for her, the bedcovers slipped off her backside to reveal that all she wore for p.j.s this evening was a black thong.

Novak shared the common solipsistic world view: *I don't know art, but I know what I like.* Her aesthetic appreciation of the human figure was best expressed in a long-drawn, low-key "mmm . . ." sound from deep in her throat at the sight of "a bare-assed naked babe in a thong." Or "ai-yi-yi . . ."

She leaned back on the bench in front of Elizabeth's drafting table, as if it were her turn in a game of lingerie poker: "I see your buff ass in a thong, and raise you a long pair of legs in garter-less thigh highs . . ." as she was sporting the latest in leg fashion. Novak's gams made Elizabeth woozy without adornment, so this was certainly a tantalizing advancement in the stocking sciences, to be sure.

Having a job that sometimes required posturing like a prostitute did a number on her sexuality, which had always been the no-nonsense, no make-up, full-blown butch in the closet approach.

Novak noticed the telltale signs of an earlier visitor even before she turned on the architect's lamp that was clamped to the drafting table. She spotted the cognac and the two empty snifters.

"Company?" she asked, lifting the bottle to the light, "Ooh . . . a special guest." She uncorked the Remy and took an uncouth hit right off the top in mocking Elizabeth's seeming fetish for appropriate glassware and to hell with all of her Willard girl airs. She had pointed out to Elizabeth on more than one occasion that she had had a fairly steady diet of bitch burgers since the invention of go go boots and miniskirts. And she was pretty certain that Elizabeth's guest was a Willard girl.

"How do you know my guest wasn't a man?"

"Elementary," Novak said, holding up both of the cognac snifters to the picture window illumination of city lights bright enough to discern that the fingerprints on both glasses were too small to be a grown man and Elizabeth's familiar tinted lip gloss was obvious on this snifter while the other appeared to be clear at first glance, but closer examination revealed some colorless gloss along the rim.

"Some sort of lip balm," was her conclusion.

Only five minutes in the apartment and Novak had deduced that Elizabeth's guest was "a female, caucasian, approximately thirty years old with long blond hair—natural, no enhancement—in a single braid. And she had on a collarless white silk shirt, single strand of pearls, not a choker, probably twenty-four inches and two small gold hoops in her left earlobe—not sure about the right."

And Elizabeth looked spooked. "But how did you . . ."

Novak smirked and rolled her eyes as she reached over to the drafting table for the sketchbook Elizabeth had left open there earlier as she had been working from memory on a profile of Pip. So that's why Novak didn't know about the earring situation on the right side of her head.

Elizabeth was floored by the comic stylings of Officer Novak. When her laughter started settling to a flutter, she asked her: "Where the hell did you come from?"

Novak could only shrug.

"Old friend," Elizabeth mumbled, "haven't seen her in years."

"A girlfriend?"

"She was. She got married. Has a daughter."

"So what's that make you, kid? A homewrecker?"

"You know the only home I ever wreck is my own, Novak."

"You call this a home?"

"She's divorced."

"Oh, of course, divorced," Novak brightened, firing up a cigarette. "Aren't we all."

"You, too, eh? Jeez . . . Why did you do it?"

"It was easier than being a dyke."

She paused.

"Well, I know you didn't *do* her," Novak said.

"How do you know that?"

"Because you called me."

True.

"I also know that you *wanted* to *do* her so bad, didn't you?"

"Why do you say that?"

"Because you called me."

Officer Novak had her moments of brillance, thought Elizabeth, who would have been impressed even if she wasn't really stoned out of her mind.

"The question is," Novak continued, "What were you crying about?"

Really impressed. How could she have possibly ascertained that? Elizabeth snuffed out the joint in the ashtray on the nightstand, looking up at this seeming nocturnal apparition as if she realized for the first time that it was corporeal.

"What made you cry, kid?"

"Oh, just the usual stuff, you know: the destruction of the ozone layer, human rights violations, racial hatred, religious intolerance, sexism, censorship, those fucking Republicans, homophobia, AIDS, dioxin . . . you name it, I was crying about it. Did I mention those fucking Republicans?"

Novak absorbed that for a moment before saying: "That Willard bitch must've done a number on your head, huh?"

"Yeah, well . . . she's a professional."

"Occupation?"

"A neurologist . . ."

"Ooh, a brain doctor, is she? Well, well. So your doctor friend fucks with your brains. I'm the one you call to fuck your brains out."

"Have you always been this clever?"

"Sure."

"Why don't I know this?"

"Because this is the first time we ever had a conversation."

"You've been showing up at my doorstep every week like a Victoria's Secret catalogue, officer, and this is the first time you've ever mentioned conversation."

"Well, maybe I want something more normal here."

"Normal? Like you want to take me home for Thanksgiving to meet the family?"

"No, normal like maybe just once we could wake up together in the same friggin' bed in the morning. Do you know we've never even seen each other in the daylight? Always gotta split before the sunrise you know? We're like a couple of friggin' vampires."

"Hey, you're the one in the closet, officer."

"Well, you could come over to my place sometime, which sure as hell is more civilized than this. I could make you a real meal. I'm a pretty good cook. When was the last time you had a homecooked meal? All I ever see in this alleged kitchen of yours are the basic no-food groups, The Five 'C's: You've got your Cheerios, your cognac, your coffee and your cigarettes."

"What's the fifth?"

"The fifth is what I plead."

"Meaning?"

"Your *crank*, kid, which I'll just keep on pretending I know *nothing* about on the grounds that it *would* incriminate you and me both, O.K.?"

"I have no idea what you're talking about."

"Good. You stick to that."

Elizabeth sat up on the edge of the bed, putting herself within reach of Novak's seemly legs, looking up at her. "Are you gonna bust me?"

"I don't wanna bust you, kid, I wanna feed you."

"I never figured you for the nurturing type, Novak."

"I'm not. You're just so damn desperate to be nurtured."

"Like a suckling, you mean?"

Elizabeth got hold of Novak and pulled her in, slipping both palms up the smooth backs of her thighs, and then underneath her lycra micro mini to get a stabilizing grip on her very nice ass as she proceeded to kiss the bare skin at her midriff. But Novak stopped her arousing progress by putting her hands to her face and directing her gaze upward to meet her own.

"Are you in love with her? Is she the one?"

"Novak, I really don't think . . . ."

"Is she the reason you live like this? I need to know where this is going," Novak said, as Elizabeth pulled her down to take her there. But Novak was full of surprises and flipped her over so effortlessly, Elizabeth laughed to find herself suddenly prone, until she felt Novak behind her kneeling between her legs.

Sometime later, Elizabeth sat up in bed looking around, relieved to see that Novak had already left. But she kept going over that question Novak had asked: Is Pip the reason I live like this?

# CHAPTER 39
# A True Heart

On a Saturday evening, Pip found herself driving past Elizabeth's place and saw that the lights were on, however dimmed, which made her smile remembering. She had no business being in this neighborhood, of course, but she was restless. She had put her daughter, Beth, to bed, and was fortunate enough to employ an au pair, allowing herself a rare evening out with no particular destination in mind. She went out occasionally to cultural events or professional affairs, but she never did anything spontaneous like this.

When Pip pressed the door buzzer, Elizabeth appeared in one of a series of narrow windows high above.

"Romeo, Rom . . . Pip? What the hell are *you* doing here?"

"I was in the neighborhood?" Pip turned up her palms meekly, wondering whom she was expecting that she called Romeo.

"Sure. Right. You were out here looking for hookers, huh? Stand back, doctor."

Before Pip realized what was happening, a ring of keys fell from the window and landed on the pavement near her feet. So that was how it worked.

She let herself into the building feeling lighthearted as she made the ascent and somewhat winded after the exertion of four flights.

Elizabeth was waiting in the open door of her apartment.

"Damn," Pip gasped. "Hello, Breedlove . . . no wonder you're in such great shape."

"Come in, come in . . ." holding up her hands to apologize for not shaking her hand or giving her one of those social pecks, showing she was covered with pastels and polymers.

"Oh," Pip said, because Elizabeth wasn't alone. The pretty young woman who she recognized from Elizabeth's paintings was semi-lounging on the futon with her lips on a bottle of St. Pauli Girl. Her short, spiky hair was dyed platinum and she had a pierced ring in her belly button and one to match in her nipple. She was naked, obviously modeling, and Pip's entrance didn't faze her in the least, except insofar as she was wondering who the hell this woman was to Elizabeth.

"Amanda," Elizabeth said, "this is Pip."

Pip said it was a pleasure to meet her.

"Uh. Yeah. Sure. Hi," Amanda replied, without looking at Pip as she was glaring at Elizabeth.

"I'm sorry," Pip said, turning back to Elizabeth, "I should have called . . ."

"Nonsense," Elizabeth assured her graciously, "I'm so glad to see you."

"Are we done now?" Amanda interjected, irritably, noticing the palpable charge between Elizabeth and Pip.

"Ah, yeah . . . sorry, Mandy. We'll have to do this another night."

"What about The Titan? With Tyler and Pilar, remember?"

"Ah . . . yes, well, hm . . . why don't you go with them and I'll catch up later."

Amanda was fuming. She picked up her robe, but she did not put it on because she wanted Pip to see her in the round and get the full effect of her strut every step of the way to the dressing room adjoining the bathroom. And Pip certainly did appreciate her thoughtfulness.

Elizabeth, who had been watching Pip watching Amanda, recognized, at last, a familiar face from the past. And this one belonged to Pip, not her doppelgänger.

"A nipple ring." said Pip. "What's that like?—I wonder?"

But Elizabeth would not say, smiling coyly, dividing her attention between washing her brushes in the sink and keeping an eye on Pip and Amanda. Because Amanda had just had an epiphany of sorts, sexual as opposed to religious though. Here was a way to assert her claim in Elizabeth's territory, to piss on it, as it were. She would not go quietly into the night. Nosiree. She stopped in front of Pip, muse turned provocatrix, a veritable Erató.

"Do ya wanna feel what's it like?"

Pip's eyes brightened, darting from the offering at hand to Elizabeth, who answered her with a coy smile, remembering Pip in thralldom all too well, and never expecting to see her like this again, teased her:

"Hey, go for it, doc . . . you're a professional. You could say it's research and write it up for *JAMA.*"

"You're a doctor?"

Pip nodded, her eyes had narrowed considerably looking down at Amanda's ring, and when her fingertips brushed over barely touching, she played with it gently for a moment making Amanda shiver.

Elizabeth continued to swirl each of her brushes lovingly one by one in a special cleaner and preservative, with one eye cocked on the titillating action.

Pip thanked Amanda politely and Amanda did a little spin and strut to the dressing room to put her clothes on.

Elizabeth laughed and said, "So, Pip, you just happened to be in my neighborhood? Gosh, I hope you didn't bring your favorite car."

"Look, Breedlove, obviously you have plans for this evening and I'm sorry for intruding, I just . . ." she stopped talking because Elizabeth had silenced her by touching the tip of her finger lightly to her lower lip. For a moment she seemed entranced by pleasurable memories, but then she snapped back quickly, skittishly stepping away.

"May I get you a refreshing beverage? Wine perhaps?" And hearing a positive response, invited Pip to accompany her to the wine cellar. By this, she meant her oven. She opened the oven door to reveal a rack containing bottles lying on their sides. She had not bothered to have the gas turned on when she moved in. She had a toaster oven, a coffee machine and a tea kettle with a plug. What more did she need?

"If you're in a red mood, Dr. Collier, I have a lovely, full-bodied cabernet sauvignon, the perfect complement to a . . . sultry September night . . . such as this . . ." She straightened up, handing the bottle to Pip, who glanced at the label and shrugged sure why not?

"Let's retire to the drawing room, shall we?"

By this, she meant her drafting table.

Pip had forgotten what it was like to be in the company of someone so whimsical, who was not also a child. Elizabeth uncorked the wine and poured it into the appropriate long-stemmed crystal from her wedding gift collection.

"A toast," said Elizabeth.

"To what?"

"To toast."

"White or rye?"

"To all toasts, be they white or rye or pumpernickel or sourdough . . ."

They clinked glasses, and sipped.

Amanda emerged from the bathroom vacuum-packed in black lycra, micro-mini, black leggings and the requisite Doc Martens, which her petite frame and skinny legs did not look strong enough to lift. Similarly, she was chomping on a large wad of bubblegum her jaws did not look strong enough to contain, every bubble she blew seemed to drag her along. Without a word to Elizabeth, she clomped toward the door like the daughter of Frankenstein, turning back to Pip, flirtatiously blowing her a kiss which seemed more in scale with her physical capabilities.

"Ah, excuse me a moment," Elizabeth said, raising her finger, while Pip seemed supremely amused by her little muse predicament.

Elizabeth followed Amanda out into the hallway pulling the door after her nearly shut but not enough to prevent Pip from hearing Amanda's vociferous whisper and Elizabeth's mollifying mumble. But then, the telltale grappling and stumble step backward—thump—against the wall, which braced them through the ensuing make-out moment, however brief, until the grouty girl could be heard cooing with pleasure.

While this was going on, Elizabeth's phone rang and Pip was in the awkward position of not being able to avoid hearing the caller as he left a message on the answering machine. Evidently he was a close friend because he felt no need to reveal his identity and addressed her with keen familiarity. No sooner had the answering machine clicked off, then Elizabeth returned, apologizing sheepishly, wiping some smeary lip gloss from around her mouth. She was covered in acrylic paint and wanted a quick shower, ducking into her Lilliputian bathroom.

"Please, make yourself at home."

When she reappeared, she was wearing a fresh pair of black sweatpants knotted below the navel and a T-shirt ready for a workout. She found Pip sitting at her drafting table looking through one of her sketchbooks.

There was a loud buzz sound, which made them both jump. Elizabeth excused herself to lean out the window, which required that she crawl across her futon. At the sill on her knees leaning out, she giggled, and Pip heard a male voice, wondering was this the Romeo she had mistaken Pip for?

After some flirtation, she sent him away and leaned back inside, making a funny cartoon face of exasperation with an accompanying pratfall back onto the futon heaped with pillows in an alcove with windows on all three sides with micro-blinds, and the most unlikely lush fall foliage from a single enormous tree, the only one for a half-dozen blocks. Four stories high and it seemed to embrace that corner alcove of Elizabeth's to some giddy Swiss Family Robinson tree house effect. In fantastic contrast was that picture window featuring the diamond in a steely setting that was downtown Weston. Being here in this room cozy as a spider web, lights to limbo, as low as they could go, and that incomprehensibly frenetic hard-core music in the background, Pip felt like she might lose her head—or maybe get it back.

"What?"

"I feel like I'm back in your dorm room, Breedlove." She laughed outright. "You've still got them climbing the ivy, don't you? Amazing. The only difference I can see is that you're a lot younger now than the last time I saw you. And now you have girls on your baseball team."

"Hey, batter up."

"You really are a kai-kai, aren't you, Breedlove?"

"Honey," Elizabeth grinned, "I am the goddess of kai-kai. Feast your eyes . . . You may kowtow to me if you like."

Feast her eyes indeed, Pip was fixated. She had to struggle against the impulse to kowtow to her then and there, realizing that she had all but forgotten what it was like to feel this way. Her head was spinning at the vision of terminal sexiness her limbic brain remembered. Elizabeth was wearing those gravity-defying sweatpants just hanging on her curvy hips by a thread tied into a neat little bow that one tug would drop. And every day was laundry day in this paradise.

"Does that surprise you?"

"Yes."

"Why?"

Pip sincerely tried to find an answer, but she came up empty.

"I think it's because you had no faith in me, Pip. That was the mistake you made."

"That was one of many . . . mistakes I made."

Elizabeth went to the stereo and crouched down to peruse the shelves beneath it, which were packed with tapes, and now ancient record albums. "Ah, there you are," she said to an old album, standing up to put it on the turntable, also a relic. It was Van Morrison's "Moondance," which was "on the soundtrack" of her mind for that time Elizabeth associated most nostalgically with her first year at WCW. The second Pip heard it, she looked over at her wistfully.

Pip's expression of nostalgia conveyed that prevailing sense of loss that comes from a linear perception of personal history, whereas Elizabeth's expressions were, like her perception, synthesized, the sense of past, present and future in a continuous loop. A spiral wound so tight that everything happens, in the instant, at all times, and also unwinds forever. Point being: Elizabeth found "Moondance" as contemporary and relevant and uppermost in her mind, at this moment, as any other, as ever: *semper eadem.*

Elizabeth sidled up to her in order to see what she saw in the sketchbooks.

"These are . . . amazing," Pip observed.

When Pip flipped to the next page, she actually shuddered as she found herself in a staredown with an artful abstraction in black ink.

"Jo," she said, startled, as if Jo, herself, had just stepped into the room. Elizabeth had done the portrait months ago. It was just a cluster of triangles, essentially, but the way they were interlinked brought the subject to life in a complex way.

"So what's your diagnosis, Dr. Collier?" Elizabeth asked, referring to the drawings.

"Obviously," said Pip, "you're completely out of your mind."

"Yes, well, I have no doubt sketches like these are a dime a dozen at Weston Psych. *l'Art Brut,* and all. More wine?"

"Please."

"But it doesn't necessarily help to know the diagnosis, does it, *Herr Doktor?*"

"Not much. It's still a long, slow crawl . . ."

She was referring to psychotherapy.

"But a long, slow crawl to what?"

Pip thought about this for a moment before she replied. "To some memory of yourself intact, whole . . . in love . . ."

Pip flipped to the next page, and was even more astounded to find her own profile depicted there, large as life. Seeing the date at the bottom corner, she realized Elizabeth had done the drawing after her visit Thursday night.

"You did this from memory," Pip realized. "It's beautiful. I'm so . . . moved." In fact, she felt as if she were going to cry. She turned to the next page, but it was blank. The timing and the symbolism of it all made them both dizzy. And so they just stood there staring down at the clean white sheet of paper as if it engrossed them a million times more.

"I can barely remember myself in love," Pip said.

"I can remember," Elizabeth sighed, "too well sometimes. The sight, the sound, the taste, the smell, the touch. All present and accounted for. All too much. It overwhelms me. A blessing and a curse."

At that, she stepped away from Pip to reposition herself in the far corner of the picture window, looking out. She could feel Pip's eyes on her at an acute angle, and in a moment, heard her ask, "Why are you alone?"

An odd question perhaps given the evidence of an overactive social life, but, in fact, that's what she was getting at.

"I like it. I like being on stage solus."

"What would change that?"

"Who wants to know?"

What was the meaning of this silence? It was so much harder to answer than the question.

"I'm waiting, Pip."

"For what?"

"My True Heart."

More puzzling silence as Pip turned away.

"To tell you the truth, the only time I ever felt lonely in my life was when I was married to someone I didn't love."

"I know that feeling."

"Why did you marry him?"

"I hated myself."

"When you introduced me to him that night, was it because you hated me, too?"

"God, no . . . no . . ."

"Why then?"

"I thought you hated me . . . Given the way I felt about myself, how could you possibly love me?"

"You had no faith in me. Are you lonely, Pip?"

"I still get lonely though in the sense that I'm not as secure, in my identity, as you are."

Elizabeth could not stop laughing long enough to apologize for the outburst, and resumed listening.

"I know it strikes you as ridiculous, because when we met, I seemed so sure of myself, but I had never been put to the test. I thought you were ambivalent. But you weren't ambivalent, Breedlove. You always knew exactly who you were."

"Actually, Pip, I think it was more like I knew exactly who I wasn't."

"Still, you know who you are. I thought I knew who I was back then," Pip said, stepping up to the window beside Elizabeth. "But then I met you . . ."

Now she was standing right beside her, shoulders almost touching.

"But then, the rape, you know, it just . . . devastated me and everything I thought I knew about myself. I lost . . . I lost myself. And you . . . I lost you."

"You didn't lose me, Pip."

"Yes, I did. I took it out on you. You were just trying to help me and I really hurt you. I'll never stop being sorry for that."

Outside on the shiny black river, a barge was passing, slow as clock hands, imperceptible, under a bridge.

"It's like no time has passed."

"To me it's like a million years."

Elizabeth turned somewhat in order to set her glass on the table, inadvertently brushing Pip's arm with her own.

"You think I blame you."

Pip would not and then could not answer as she felt Elizabeth's fingertips lightly on the side of her neck and shivered, turning to face her. Elizabeth was tracing down the muscle whose name she had learned in an anatomy class for fine arts students, but could not recall for the life of her then.

"Sternocleidomastoid . . ." said Pip.

Pip shook her head slightly, slowly to steady herself, her tremulousness increasing as Elizabeth was touching her with both hands, all ten fingertips feathered at her neck, expressing something between a caress and a threat.

"I could have loved you forever, Pip, with all my heart."

Pip closed her eyes and swallowed hard as if in anticipation of an Elizabethan Beheading ax.

"I felt cheated."

"You were cheated. We were both cheated."

"Seven years . . . I still feel cheated."

Pip could barely muster a whisper, "So do I."

"Not once, but twice. And you didn't come back for me."

"But I did. I was still in love with you  . . ."

"You were married, Pip. You crushed me."

Elizabeth's thumbs were on Pip's choker stroking from pearl to pearl.

"And part of me just wants to crush you, too."

Pip looked at her with eyes pleading from some dreamy mist.

"The other part wants to . . ." Elizabeth's thumbs had ventured upward to trace along the shadow of Pip's lower lip, wanting her so badly, ". . . to remember us intact and in love."

With their lips so close, not kissing seemed so much more intimate and shocking, as Elizabeth suddenly released Pip and stepped away, leaving her feeling as if her skin had just been flayed from sole to crown. She couldn't even gasp.

Pip turned, she stepped away, she got to the door but Elizabeth caught her hand and pulled her back to stay. For a second they just looked at each other as if they were strangers, and then, passion, all too familiar. They collided with a kiss and dropped to the bed, grappling for dominance over the past instead of each other.

Somewhere in all of that twisting and turning, the long, slow crawl toward what they once were, intact and in love, things were said and understood. Stripped down to a single strand of words like pearls.

Nice pearls. Real pearls. Had that gritty-feel-against-the-teeth test familiar to Willard girls, genuine pearls.

"I did come back for you, Bree . . ."

Years of carrying around that precious cargo lifted with the pitch until one went down with the ship like sunken treasure and the other was set adrift.

# CHAPTER 40
# Bite Makes Right

Elizabeth was one of the eight women from her class who attended their five-year reunion. The Class of '29 had a better turnout and most of them were dead. At the Bloody Mary Brunch in the dining hall, Elizabeth joined the pitiful huddle of her classmates around their designated table as they sucked down Bloody Marys through straws and smoked cigarettes, even though every one of them had quit years ago. On that Saturday afternoon in October, they seemed determined to make up for lost smoking time.

There were several women there whom Elizabeth had never known except in passing. But she found them immensely likable the second time around. And it was good to see some of the old poker gang, Helen, Vivian and Gracie, even though Gracie gave Elizabeth the cold shoulder for no good reason Elizabeth could discern other than the fact that she and Gracie's ex-husband, Decker, had become friends *after* Gracie had left him for another man. It was especially unfair, thought Elizabeth, considering Gracie was now happily married to a great guy and pregnant with their first child.

And then, there was the strange case of Lonnie DeVane. She had arrived shortly after they were all seated for brunch with an effusive and open-faced familiarity, addressing each of them by name, including their more personal nicknames, and demonstrating an impressive recall of anecdotal particulars. Being Willard girls, they gave her the benefit of the doubt and tactfully went along until they had the opportunity to consult discreetly with the others. When Lonnie excused herself to use the ladies room, they discovered that not one of them had the slightest recollection of who she was. Quickly, they put their heads together and hatched a plan. Vivian was dispatched to the alumnae office to borrow a copy of their yearbook and by the time Lonnie returned to the table, she found them huddled around it.

"Oh, goody!" she bubbled, sidling right up to them. Immediately, she expressed her regret at having been out of town when the senior portraits were taken. "Yes, I did the semester in D.C., remember?" she asked of no one in particular, referring to a special program Willard offered to political science majors. "When I was working for Nader . . ."

"Ralph Nader?"

"Oh, you," Lonnie laughed, giving Elizabeth an affectionate little punch in the arm, "you always were such a kidder."

And as they pop-eyed each other behind her back, barely able to contain themselves, Lonnie turned the page and exclaimed, "Oh, there I am," referring to a candid shot taken at the annual Halloween Haunted House Tour at Fey, and they all leaned in for a closer look. She was pointing to a bowling pin with legs, claiming to have been part of the group costume depicting the freak accidental death of Perry "The Pinhead" Fey.

"Will you ever forget," she laughed, addressing Helen, Vivian and Elizabeth, "and Contrary was with you, I remember . . . you guys were so stoned, when Cleo came sliding down the banister dressed like Perry, without a head—oh my gosh what a riot—you all freaked out screaming and went tumbling backward on top of each other to the landing, rolling around in hysterics."

Elizabeth suppressed a gasp as Helen had a surreptitious grip on her forearm and was digging her fingernails in just to keep from freaking out then and there.

"You guys were laughing so hard, my gosh, they could hear you all the way up to Whitman . . ."

Helen let loose with a slap-happy shriek in the face of something even spookier than the ghost stories of Lonnie DeVane, and their attention was yanked to the center aisle.

"Weight check!"

"Well, I'll be damned . . ."

"Speak of the devil . . ."

"Oh my gosh . . ."

"Here comes Mary Constance . . ."

Bloody Mary herself had arrived just in time for brunch, and was bustling toward their table with a grin spanning five years, looking trim and elegant in a classic taupe suit and, of course, the requisite single strand of pearls. She was a corporate lawyer for a high-powered firm in Chicago and she was married to a guy named Bob Buckler, who owned a chain of sporting goods stores.

Contrary circled the table dispensing ill-timed air kisses and mis-directed hugs, as was the custom, saving Elizabeth for last, gushing with the old begosh and begorrah. "Look at you . . ." she bubbled, "you still have the *same hair* . . . And—good Lord—you've gotten so skinny. I heard you were in some kind of punk rock band with Reuben Shockor . . ."

"Ah, yeah, right," she snickered. "I'm the girl with the electric tambourine."

Elizabeth certainly did stand out at the brunch in her off-beat, art-student-style ensemble in that sea of suits in conservative neutral tones, with sensible pumps that matched the purse lest they dare disturb the universe. Hairdos had that metallic glint of pricey salon highlighting for the most part, blunt cut pageboys or bobbed, de-pending on the type of career, including motherhood. And everyone wore the uniform white pearls, except for Elizabeth, of course.

Elizabeth's pearls were black.

Now *that* was a statement.

"Ooh . . . I've never seen black pearls before," said Mary Constance. "They're really quite . . . strange . . ."

"Do you mean *strange* as in: '. . . those are pearls that were his eyes . . .' Do you think I've suffered 'a sea change, into something rich and strange'?"

"Oh, no, my dear, you haven't changed one bit," she beamed, sar-castically: "And see, I just knew you would put THE HMMBAFEEL to good use."

"Why, thank you, Mrs. Buckler."

Helen attempted to block, "Has anyone ever been to Hilton Head in April? We're planning a golf trip with our club and I don't know what to pack."

At some point later, Contrary made some reference to Elizabeth being a "dynamic individual," which sounded to Elizabeth like a per-sonnel assessment.

"How would you know, dear? Have you ever actually *had* a job? I mean, a *real* job?"

"Why, no," Elizabeth replied, in a seeming showdown of Brockian politeness, "do you mean I was supposed to? Oh jeepers, I completely misunderstood . . ."

"Oh just choose your own fucking destination already, like the rest of us, and get on with it."

"What makes you think I haven't?"

"Just a hunch. What really impresses me, is that you get away with it. How do you get away with it?"

"It's just a matter of priorities." was Elizabeth's reply. "I don't want the things that most people want."

"What about need?"

"I get what I need," Elizabeth said, as she sat back coolly blowing a smoke ring to create the illusion it was shaped by her smile.

It came time for the show and tell portion of the brunch when everyone passed around photographs of the following, presumably in the order of their importance and pride: children, dogs, cats, cars, shorehouses and sailboats. Husbands appeared incidentally, as in: "and this is our house at the shore . . . oh, that's my husband, Poindexter, back there catching seagull droppings with his bare hands before they sully the BMW."

Or some such.

Elizabeth looked at each and every picture, even the ones handed to her from some classmate she had never spoken with until that morning, paying attention and compliments to all, which was sometimes misread as facetiousness, but was, in fact, her true enthusiasm for any given moment.

"Hey Elizabeth, what about you?"

"Yeah, Ms. Breedlove . . ."

"Weren't you married or something?"

"Briefly. I've been happily divorced for about four years now, but I don't have a shapshot of that." From one of the breast pockets inside the man's crisply tailored blazer she wore, she withdrew a slim black leather billfold, which, according to the Law of Gender and Accessories, was a man's wallet. Elizabeth did not carry a purse, which was gender heresy, to be sure, and she claimed she did not need a purse, for the same reason men do not need purses.

"The need to carry a purse really has nothing to do with biological destiny, as we are taught in school," she theorized shamelessly. "It's all about pockets. The true definition of *purse* is the absence of pockets."

"Pockets," said Elizabeth. "Pockets will set you free."

A gaze was glinting between Elizabeth and Contrary as the former removed a snapshot from her (masculine) wallet, and said, matter-of-factly, and much to everyone's surprise, "This is my family," and passed it to Vivian, seated to her right. Vivian squinted her eyes, palpably puzzled, until she realized and smirked. The quaint lingo of their dainty college days, pronounced by Vivian, with husky petulance, transported them all instantly back.

"Far-fucking-out."

The next couple of girls, being the brand new old college chums, were not privy to the significance, and so nodded, politely confounded, and passed it on to Contrary, sitting directly across the table from Elizabeth. In a moment, Contrary's smug regard, as she looked at the picture more carefully, turned inside out and went slack-jawed. Helen, who had been peering over Contrary's arm to see, also, ahead of her turn, said, "Hey, wait a second . . . Isn't that . . ."

"Pip," Contrary answered. "Pip Collier." She looked up and across the table now at Elizabeth, reverting, involuntarily back to when they were friends, and became misty-eyed, she was so moved.

"And who is this darling child?"

"Pip's daughter—and my namesake—Elizabeth. We call her Beth."

Contrary was the only one truly to understand the significance. Reaching for a Kleenex to blot her nose and washy eyes, she smiled, without rancor or resentment, and said, "She takes after you."

At that, Lonnie DeVane snickered knowingly, and both Elizabeth and Contrary turned to her, with mouths agape, about to cry in unison, "Who the hell *are* you?"

But they held their tongues as the WCW chorus filed into the dining hall and got into position on a makeshift stage to sing the alma mater and several Willard ditties, which always sounded as if they had been written during The Roaring '20s. As for the alma mater, it was customary to stand and join together in song, warbling. Not surprisingly, the Class of '78, appeared to be the only alumnae who never knew the words.

"For shame . . ."

"We are a disgrace to our sisters . . ."

"Shut up and fake it, you bitches. No one has to know . . ."

During the previous year the campus had been a battlefield when President Buffy and her flying monkeys tried to carry out their ee-vil plan for WCW to go coed. Alumnae rallied and railed against it, demanding the resignation of President Buffy. The new president, Dr. Alice Hill, a single mom with a no-nonsense name, was introduced and delivered a welcoming address that was well received. When President Hill reassured them that there would be no more talk of WCW going coed—not on her watch, dammit!—she got a standing ovation, and then she brought the house down, as she unbuttoned her chic, tailored blazer to reveal that she was wearing one of the T-shirts students had printed and worn last year: BETTER DEAD THAN COED.

They were all choked up to their pearl chokers, except for Lonnie DeVane, who ululated like a widow about to hurl herself upon her husband's funeral pyre.

"Good God, woman!" Helen hissed. "Pull yourself together!"

That did it for Elizabeth and Contrary, who fled the hall under the pretense of going to the ladies room, claiming that they had both just gotten their periods (egads!). Instead, they skipped and dashed out the back door heading for cover through the topiary hedges to the pond, where they let loose with shrieks of incredulity and guffaws aplenty.

"Who . . . who . . ." Contrary cried, barely able to spew the words. "Who *is* she?"

"Did you see those teeth? She's a vampire."

"Maybe she's Fey Ray come back to haunt us . . ."

"Or maybe . . . hey, wait a second, I just thought of something . . ."

"What's that?"

"Didn't she say her husband's name was Doug Maples or something like that? It sounded so familiar . . ."

"Yes, now that you mention it. It did sound familiar . . . Doug, Douglas, Maples, or was it more like Marples . . ."

And then, in a simultaneous revelation, their eyes went wide as wide could be, and they blurted it out at the same time and with the same inflection:

"Dou-*glas Mar*-bles!"

They laughed until they gagged. Douglas Marbles was the tagalong Dick. Everyone had been too embarrassed to admit they had no idea who he was or where he came from.

"As I recall," Contrary said, when she was more composed, "he fell madly in love with Pip, didn't he? Gosh, poor little guy . . . he was so disappointed to find out she had no use for Dick."

"Hey . . . wait a second . . . something just occurred to me."

"What?"

"You don't suppose that Douglas Marbles loved Pip soooo much that he had a sex change operation . . ."

"Omigod, shaved his legs . . ."

"And now he is a she!?"

"And she is a dyke!"

"Lonnie DeVane!"

"Stop . . . please . . . stop . . ." Contrary had doubled over holding herself, begging Elizabeth for mercy.

Whoever Lonnie DeVane was, she certainly had done a couple of long-estranged *roomies* a great service. They took to the ornate stone bench pondside to collect themselves. Helen appeared not long emerging from the footpath through the Japanese maples, brimming fondly: "Hello, ladies, you're busted. I knew I would find you two bitches hiding out here in the bushes. The only thing missing is the weed."

"Yeah, that would be perfect right now."

"Have a seat."

"Gosh," said Contrary, "I haven't smoked since . . . I can't even remember when."

"Well, ladies, it's uncanny you should both mention it, because I just happen to have here in my . . . *pocket*," she said emphatically.

"You're packing?"

"Omigod. She's packing."

"I'm packing."

"Holy shit."

And this time, Helen couldn't help but ask, "So that's really a guy's blazer?"

"It is. In fact, this jacket was made in the early '60s for a guy named Romeo. I kid you not. See . . . his name is embroidered on the convenient *pocket* here."

They leaned forward for a closer look.

"That is so cool."

"Look at this lining . . . paisley, can you believe?"

"Must have been a wee Dick, this Romeo."

"Is that silk? Looks like silk . . ."

"Sharkskin . . ."

"So how come women don't have inside pockets like that?"

"Might distort the shape of the breast," was Elizabeth's theory. "And men would get all confused about what they were seeing, you know? Where's the breast? It would be like blotting the sun from the sky . . ."

The smoke was making its second pass when Gracie appeared on the garden path, spotted the trio, and cracked up, "Well, *there's* a picture I'd like to see in the alumnae journal. I had a hunch the bad girls would be hanging out here with the old koi fish . . ."

"Come . . . join us . . ." they said, in zombie voices.

"Yes . . . join us . . ."

There wasn't room for four so Gracie sat on Helen's lap.

After a while, Contrary looked at her watch and said: "We've got recess now until cocktails, right?"

"Yep," Helen replied, "cocktails at the president's house at six. Dinner at eight."

"Know what I'm thinking, gentlemen?"

"What?"

"Bedpost queens and one-eyed jacks."

Yippee!

"Where's Vivian?"

"She didn't make it out, I'm sorry to say. She was cornered by Lonnie DeVane."

"Poor devil."

"Do you think she's still alive?"

"Hard to say. She's been in there for what? A half hour?"

"Phew . . ."

"Hoo-boy . . ."

"Yeah, but we've got to try. We've got to . . ."

Somehow they managed to get a note to Vivian letting her know where they would be, suggesting that she ply her captor with beverages so that she would have to pee, and then make a run for it. No way Lonnie would know to come looking for them in the solarium. And they were right. The plan worked and they had the solarium all to themselves for the rest of the afternoon, playing for mixed nuts, until it came time for them to go their separate ways to their hotel rooms or homes to dress for dinner.

Elizabeth, Pip, Elizabeth Jr. and Rosalita, the au pair, all lived about four blocks away from the campus. When Elizabeth let herself into the house, she was greeted by Pip who was home for the evening, but on call. She put her finger to her lips to indicate that Beth was napping. They embraced and then Pip followed Elizabeth into the bedroom and lay back on the pillows watching Elizabeth as she went about the highly scientific process of undressing, showering, touching up the hair and makeup, selecting an outfit, accesssorizing and "*voilà*."

"You look beautiful."

She had decided on a black tuxedo-style suit definitely made for a woman and she wore it with a collarless, white silk blouse, unbuttoned to just above the cleavage.

"You need one more thing to complete the outfit," said Pip, and she went to her dresser drawer and withdrew a black velvet box. She stepped up behind Elizabeth who was standing before a full-length mirror affixed to the door.

"Lift your hair for a second."

Elizabeth felt the distinctive coolness and heft of pearls being slipped around her neck dropping to a length just above her cleavage.

"Perfect."

They both agreed.

The pearls warmed quickly against her flesh while her flesh actually melted in Pip's mouth at that place on her neck Pip could not resist sampling.

"Ah . . . um . . . Pip?"

"Hm?"

"Can you . . . um . . . oh . . . that feels so . . . um . . . baby?"

"Hm?"

"What was I saying?"

Pip looked up to see herself holding Elizabeth, who was smiling so sweetly she could have died.

Alumnae, some with spouses in tow, reconvened in toto for the evening events, a cocktail reception at the president's manse followed by a splendid catered dinner back in the dining hall. Afterward they dispersed to various other campus venues for their separate class parties. Elizabeth's class was assigned the parlor of the stately house dorm beside Fey House. Within hours, the husbands of the class of '78 were in the parking lot behind the house playing with each other's Porsches. One of the husbands, who was married to a classmate she didn't really know—thank God—was waiting to use the bathroom after Elizabeth, and was so tanked and anxious to pee he already had his penis hanging out when Elizabeth opened the door. She declined his incoherently lewd invitation to make use of it.

"No thank you," she said, ever so nicely, "I've already got one."

"Huh?" he said, circling . . . circling and then dropped, knocked insensible by the force of too much politeness.

"Oops."

Eventually, Elizabeth and Contrary found their way down to the pond, singing "Moondance," which was a really hard song to sing sober. The terrain was treacherous in heels, so Contrary was leaning heavily on Elizabeth, who was wearing a most confident pair of black Beatle boots—all Italian leather footwear being her one sybaritic indulgence.

But as they crossed a particularly dark patch of the lawn, they forgot how steeply it sloped.

"Whoa!"

"Yikes!"

"Oh no . . . ohhh no . . . oh no . . ."

"Whoops . . ."

"Wha?"

Contrary would have been food for koi fish had Elizabeth not held fast and used the downhill momentum to fling her to level ground near the big old tree, like a game they used to play as kids called "crack the whip." It was so mucky though that Contrary's pumps got stuck with a sucking sound.

"Oh fuck!" she cried. "Quicksand, Lassie! Go girl, go tell the stupid humans to give you a rescue chopper . . ."

Elizabeth was standing clear and offered her hand, but Contrary was flapping her wings to keep from being toppled out of her shoes, cursing everything and everybody from the koi fish to Elizabeth for laughing at her predicament, and doing shtick.

"Do you know what your problem is? You are such a child. You refuse to grow up. You just want to play forever. Well grow up—I say. Just grow up."

"Make me."

"See? See—ladies and gentlemen of the jury—a child. I rest my case."

"Yeah, well . . . Do you know what *your* problem is, Contrary?"

"What?"

"You're scared of me."

"You don't scare me. I've never been scared of you."

"You have *always* been scared of me."

"Oh, yeah?"

"Yeah."

"Why the hell would I be afraid of you?"

Elizabeth seized her then, deftly, pulling her from the muck right out of her shoes and backed her up against the tree.

"Because of this."

And before Contrary realized what was happening, Elizabeth kissed her.

*Full on the mouth.*

Oh my.

Having pulled her out of her shoes she now seemed intent on knocking her socks off.

She didn't put up a fight either. In fact, she found her hands just automatically encircling Elizabeth's tiny waist and then sliding up her back, pressing her in close, closer, without even thinking.

But just as that line was about to be crossed into the Zone of the Closest, Elizabeth's soft mouth detached, savoring in that split second what had been revealed to her by Contrary's palpable reluctance. Smiling triumphantly even though she knew this would mean Contrary would find it necessary to despise her for the rest of her life. But suddenly, Elizabeth laughed fiendishly—Ha! Fake out!—and in one fell swoop got that erotogenic piece of Contrary's neck between her teeth vampirically and sucked.

And sucked some more, until she felt her victim at a complete loss to think straight, feeling nonsensical: all swoony-eyed, quivery-handed, chesty-heaved, jelly-jointed, and chilly-spined—damn sensational, wasn't it? That kiss and this—she could never forget.

Poor Contrary had that kind of pale skin that blotches like hellfire if a fly lands on it, so this little suctorial tutorial made for a truly mortifying and unmistakable telltale blotch. When Elizabeth released her, Contrary sank somewhat down the tree trunk, as if she were prepared to genuflect just in case of the sudden appearance of some SWAT team of nuns who patrolled for this sort of thing.

"You . . . you . . . sister . . . are one of Hell's minions."

"Yeah, well . . . you look like Leda after The Swan dropped her off . . ."

"What the hell am I going to tell my husband? How the hell am I gonna explain this . . . this . . . *hickey?*"

Elizabeth shrugged and chuckled, in the process of lighting two cigarettes, handing one to Contrary. "Tell Bob you got bit by a lesbian vampire. I *guarantee* it will get you laid."

"Yeah, right."

"Are you kidding? Guys live for this shit." She mimicked all the guys in the world she had ever heard express this, in so many words: "Two chicks together? Ooh yeah wow man dig it . . . love to watch the ladies git down—you know, for the cameras . . ."

*As long as they're not dykes or anything.*

"Speaking of which . . ." said Contrary, "say hello to The Missus for me, will ya?"

"I will."

"Can I tell you something quite seriously . . ."

"What's that?"

"It really makes me happy to know that you found each other. You two really belong together. I mean, you'll always be a little dink, and Pip, well . . ."

"She's a pip."

Elizabeth's smile was positively beatific.

"Look at you," she slapped her affectionately upside the head, "you look so happy."

"I am. And, you know, I couldn't help noticing that you have a certain happy glow about you, too, . . . Mrs. Buckler . . ."

"I do?"

"Yes, you do."

"Seriously? You can tell? But I'm only five months."

"Hey, I'm Lassie, remember?"

This merited a genuine sibling hug, no fake-outs, no deeper significance: just sisters.

"Didn't Lassie deliver a baby in one episode?"

"Yes, and as I recall, she had to do an emergency C-section."

Contrary tousled her hair. Elizabeth ducked and dodged, smiling inwardly as she headed across the green. Ahead of her, all the winding roads and walkways were lined with luminaries. Countless white bags grounded by votive candles had been set out magically for this special occasion.

"Hey, sister?"

Elizabeth paused and turned, "Yes, Mary Constance?" still walking slowly backward.

"You kiss like a girl."

A pause to ponder that. Chuckle. Nod.

"Thanks."

Then off again across the lawn, until:

"Hey, sister?"

"Yes, Elizabeth?"

"So do you."